Dead Corpse

Nuzo Onoh

Canaan-Star Publishing

First published by Canaan-Star Publishing, United Kingdom.
www.canaan-star.co.uk

A Catalogue record for this book is available from the British Library.

ISBN: 978-1-909484-87-0

Horror

Book cover by Eugene Rijn R. Saratorio
Printed and bound in United Kingdom by Lightning Source, (UK) Ltd.

Dedication

To my brother, Dr Umunnakwe Josef Onoh, whose love and support has enabled me to pursue my passion and tell my stories with freedom and joy. I thank you, our "voodoo chicken". I love you to eternity.

Acknowledgements

My great friend, Ted Dunphy, who continues to support and encourage my writing, listens to my incessant moans and tells me to keep believing in myself despite everything. Irish, I thank you for being such an inspiration and a true friend. You're the best.

My cousin, Udodili (Jika) Igbokwe, who's had my back through so many ups, downs and tumbles. My wonderful "cousin of no regrets", you'll always hold a special place in my heart. Thank you.

Aeminder "Mindy" Sangha, whose unbelievable kindness when my mother slept re-affirmed my belief in the goodness of man. Thank you, Mindy. The Universe will always give you the very best it can offer.

Lucy Walton-Lange, whose amazing support has helped spread the word about African Horror. Thank you, Lucy for always being ready to help this very grateful writer. You rock.

To a very special person - Jennie Rigg! THANK YOU for believing in the story when very few did. Your support continues to inspire me to do better each time around, just so that I get the thrill of reading what you think about each story. And what you had to say about this one did not disappoint. Your awesome suggestions for improvement has given me a story I am happy to share with the world. Thank you!

Acep "Gorgeous" Hale!!! Where do I start? You saw greatness in my writing which I never saw and made me believe I had stories worth telling. Thank you, dear friend. My writing and I owe you more than you'll ever know and your brilliant input to this book has added that special something it lacked before you turned your thoughts to it.

A massive THANK YOU to ThatHorribleWoman (Rhys), whose constant support ensures my name is never far from the minds of my readers. Thank you sooo much!

4

To Sarah Carter - You took to my writing like a duck to water and proved that true horror indeed does transcend all boundaries. Thank you for your amazing input to this book, which has made it better than it would have been.

Very special shout out to Perry Lake, whose brilliant suggestions brought that extra something to this story. Thank you, Perry.

To Bob Morritt and Ian Smith. THANK YOU, GUYS! You are truly my awesome two! I thank the Universe for you, for your support and encouragement. THANK YOU!

More shouts out to Ashlee Blackwell, Becky Spratford, Melanie Marsh, Obi A Atuanya, Bonita Gutierrez, Montana Jordan, Donnalyn Washington, Jaqueline Stone, Obinna Emelike, Saumiko Saulson, Rafeeat Aliyu, Kerry E.B Black, Eric B. Thomasma and so many others too numerous to mention, for your amazing support of this emerging genre, African Horror. THANK YOU!!!

And of course, Prashant Parmar for that amazing story about the aborted court case and the supernatural river!!

Other books by Nuzo Onoh

The Reluctant Dead (2014)
Unhallowed Graves (2015)
The Sleepless (2016)

I

Walking-Grave and Corpse-Maker

Ω Ω Ω

There is a curse amongst our people, the *Igbo* tribe of Old Biafra, reserved for those we truly despise. We call them *"Ozu nwulu-awu"* meaning, *Dead Corpse.* This is because we believe that our dead never die when we return them to the grave-soil. The blessed dead will always reincarnate and return to their people for a second rebirth.

It is believed that a few unfortunate souls receive no second return for some inexplicable reason. They neither commune with the ancestors nor haunt the living. Their existence ends with their death. Their corpses become meat feast for the grave worms, dead corpses, lumps of rotten carcasses, without hope of a rebirth.

But in very rare circumstances, when a terrible injustice has been done, a dead corpse may refuse to lie still in the grave and walk once more amongst the living, leaving deadly devastation in its wake.

(From the Oracle of Ukari Village)

Ukari Village, 1980

The young woman on the mat let out a piercing shriek, her eyes bulging out in terror. She stared at a point just above the head of the stooped birth-aider, Efuru, who was gently manoeuvring a tiny blood-streaked head between the woman's spread thighs.

'*Ndo*... sorry,' Efuru consoled, her eyes still focused on the baby she was attempting to extricate from its mother's womb. 'It's almost over... look, I have the head already. Just a little more push and we'll see if you have given your husband a worthy heir or another dowry princess, ha ha,' Efuru's cackle was almost as desperate as the young woman's screams. An underlying panic shrouded her forced joviality. She cast furtive glances at both the blood-drenched straw mat and the sweat-drenched woman giving birth on it. Her own sweat dropped in an endless flow, staining her thin cotton top, occasionally merging with the blood-dampened floor of the hut.

Efuru tugged harder at the baby who should have exited the womb several hours ago, yet clung to its agonised mother with desperate tenacity. *There shouldn't be this much blood, not for a second birth*, Efuru thought, her brows furrowed, her rheumy eyes

9

glazed with ill-suppressed panic. She was so engrossed in the delivery that she failed to notice when the young woman ceased screaming. What drew her attention to the woman was a soft whimper, like the gentle sobs of a reluctant bride on her wedding night. Efuru looked up at the woman and froze.

The young mother was shielding her face with her right arm, as if hiding from a terrifying spectre. Her left hand was raised high, pushing away an invisible presence. Efuru stared at the raised hands of the woman, a cold chill gripping her heart. The pink palms that should have been mapped with the normal life-lines of humanity, were instead, stamped with the seal of death. Two black crosses, thick and raised, were imprinted on the palms of the young woman, right at the centre, the irrefutable brand of a reincarnate. It was just like Efuru's missing thumb, whose absence pointed to the ancestor who had reincarnated back in her, a great-aunt known as Efuru *Aka-ano*, Efuru four-fingers. The stark contrast between the young woman's pale albino skin and the dense black crosses made the scarring more startling.

Even as she watched, mouth wide in disbelief, Efuru saw the skin beneath the black crosses rip, as if slashed with a sharp blade. Thick blood gushed from the marked palms, drenching the yellow print blouse of the dying woman in seconds. Efuru knew the young mother was dying. She had seen the life-lines on her palms split, breaking the thread of her mortal existence. *Akala-aka* never lied.

10

A person's palm-lines held the truth of their destiny. A faded or split palm-line was the surest indication of early and sudden death.

'*Biko*... please... *biko*...' the young woman's hoarse voice pleaded, her terrified pupils focused at a point just behind Efuru's back. Her earlier screams were now reduced to desperate whimpers. Efuru shuddered, glancing quickly behind. She saw nothing, just the shut wooden door of the hut. Yet, her mind registered a malevolent presence in the room. The mud hut, which had been a burning inferno under the midday African sun but a few minutes gone, was now as cold as the chilled Guinness Stout she occasionally received from grateful husbands after she'd brought their new sons into the world. Her sweat-dampened skin broke out in goose pimples, sending frozen terror to her limbs. The hands tugging the baby went limp, weakened by the cold malignancy she sensed in the room. An unfamiliar rattle punished her tobacco-stained teeth as she strove to keep the flight from her feet.

'*Biko*... please, not now... let me see my daughter grow. *Ebele*... have mercy, just a little while longer... not for my sake but for my daughter. *Biko*...' The young mother's pale eyes were feverish, blood-streaked, coated with a mixture of terror and a strange defiance. They were still fixed at a point just by the shut door. They darted from left to right, not in the familiar dancing motion of the *Aghali*, albino, but rather, as if following the movements of some unseen presence. The thick mole on her nose seemed to grow larger, darker, like a black kennel-nut embedded in an over-ripe tomato.

Again, Efuru glanced behind, her breathing hard and fast, as if she were the one in labour. As before, she saw nothing, nobody, not man, woman, child or animal. *Amadioha! Duwe anyi! God of the gods, lead us to safety!* They were not alone in the hut. Efuru didn't need the cold skeletal fingers crawling up her spine to tell her there was another presence in the birth-room with them; two invisible guests, whose identities were as clear as their marks on the young woman's bleeding palms. *Walking-Grave and his sister, Corpse-Maker!* Efuru shuddered. She was in the presence of two of the most fearsome deities of the underworld, the death siblings, reviled and feared by the living, shunned and cursed by the ancestors. Efuru made a frenzied sign of the cross, staining her forehead and chest with the blood from the half-born infant. An uncontrollable shiver rattled her bony frame. Every human that drew breath knew the history of the terrible duo now lurking unseen in the room. They were the rebel offspring of the great deity, *Owu*, Death-Head, He whose name must never be spoken aloud by men for fear of an unexpected and calamitous visit.

The terrible siblings, seeking to usurp their mighty father, had used their inherited powers to commit the most heinous of crimes, resulting in their expulsion from the great deity's realm. The duo had fed on the souls of babies and the young, those who should have had scores of moon years to reach the end of their earthly journey but for their nefarious activities. With their crime, Walking-Grave and Corpse-Maker broke the long-established agreement that had existed amongst the deities of nature, the code that only the aged and wretchedly sick would be returned to the Earth Goddess' soil to join their ancestors for a rebirth. Their reputations as the thieves of the underworld and the scourge of mankind were well earned.

Efuru cast a pitying look at the bland face of the infant trapped between the open thighs of its doomed mother, half in and half out. It was a baby that would never cry, whose features would never animate, an innocent infant whose future had ended before it begun, doomed to follow its mother into the terrifying unknown of Walking-Grave and Corpse-Maker's cold realm, *Mbana-Oyi*. Efuru mumbled a low prayer for the dead baby, crossing herself as she spoke.

'Little one, innocent doomed soul, may the ancestors welcome you with loving arms, poor unfortunate child. May your journey be speedy, without fear, filled with light and laughter. May you be reborn to a better fate. *Ise,* so be it, in Jesus' name, Amen.'

The dying woman let out another shriek as a third black cross branded her forehead, scorching her pale skin and sealing her doom. With super-human effort, she pulled herself up from the mat, leaning forward to place her bleeding palms over her dead

13

infant's sleek head. Blood poured from the fresh cross on her forehead, mixing with her sweat, dripping down her face like bloated red worms, almost blinding her. Yet, Efuru saw a sudden resolve in the young mother's face, a steely strength that belied her earlier terror. She leaned into the uplifted face of her dead infant and began to mutter words, strange incantations chanted in a language which the birth-aider could not comprehend, ancient words known only to *Indi-ichie*, the old ones, the dead ancestors and the great gods. The woman's pale eyes danced a frenzied motion as she spoke, blazing with a fierce light.

Efuru felt an even colder terror grip her heart. Every grey hair on her head stood on end as she watched the macabre scene of a dying mother, who should have been keening for her dead infant, but was instead whispering some terrible words into its ear while her blood dripped on the dead baby's head. Efuru knew about the woman, about her powers and her ancient art. She had balked at the prospect of ministering to such a powerful medicine-woman when she was first summoned to the birth-hut but knew she dared not refuse. When Xikora summoned, everyone obeyed. Now she was witnessing that power, seeing and hearing things beyond any nightmares she'd ever dreamt.

The woman's words were rushed, like one that knew she was waging a losing battle with the invincible swords of time. Her breathing was harsh and fast as she fought to gasp precious oxygen to keep death at bay. Suddenly, the baby's eyes opened and Efuru gasped, scrambling away on hands and knees from the bloodied birth-mat. Her heart pounded a killing thud and her breath escaped her mouth in a raspy rush. *The baby was dead. She had seen it die, held its tiny dead head in her hands.* Yet, there it was, looking at the mother with an intelligent awareness that defied human development, a baby whose skin was as black as its mother's was fair, whose eyes were as knowing as a grown man's eyes. The woman, Xikora, took a deep breath, her pale skin starting to turn a dark purple hue as death drew ever closer. She smiled down into her baby's bright, black pupils and stroked its head with gentle hands.

'*O ga-adi mma!* It will be well with you, my child. All will be well with you, my son.' The baby blinked, once, twice. The dying mother covered her baby's eyes with her thumbs and this time, they stayed shut in eternal sleep. She took another deep breath and shut her eyes as if in silent prayers. Then she opened her eyes and a slow smile spread over her fast blackening face, a smile as cold as the deepest seas. Efuru's heart thudded with fresh terror at the sight of the dying woman's icy smile.

'Shameless cowards! Vile night-robbers! Gutless deities who would fight a mere woman at her weakest point!' The curses spilled from Xikora's mouth with venomous rage. 'Corpse-Maker, I see you, you disgusting apology of a deity, vile stealer of babies, shameless woman whose barren womb will never nurse a child's soul regardless of how many infants you consume. Hear me, vile creature! You will not have my son. I have sent him back to where he belongs, with my Earth Goddess, *Aná*. He is now in a safe place where your soiled hands will never reach him.' The young woman cackled, a wild laughter brimming with arrogance. She turned her gloating and pain-wracked face to the empty space to her left, her eyes still blazing pure hate. 'And you, Walking-Grave, cowardly stealer of youth. I see you. You think my young soul will fuel your powers and enable you to topple your revered father, *Owu*, the great Death-Head himself. Well, go ahead. Do your worst. My son is safe and my daughter will be protected by one more powerful by you and your disgusting sister, the great *Aná* herself, our omnipotent Earth Goddess. She will... destro...'

The young mother never finished her sentence. Efuru saw the woman's eyes bulge as her tongue drew from her mouth as if yanked out by invisible pincers. Xikora began to kick, choke, her arms flaying, her fists punching into thin air as if boxing some hated adversary. And yet, her tongue continued to protrude, dragged from her mouth by invisible tongs, growing to lengths that defied belief. Blood gushed afresh from her open thighs. The force of the gush finally pushed out the baby from its mother's womb, putting an end to the birth-aider's job. The infant clung to its mother by its umbilical cord. Efuru wanted to go to the woman's

16

aid, wanted to run till she was a hundred huts away from the birth-room of horror. But terror froze her limbs, kept her glued to the blood-stained floor. She shut her eyes, shutting out the horror unfolding before her. Her frail, old body shivered from the unnatural chill in the hut and her head expanded and constricted in dizzying waves.

A sudden still descended in the hut, the unmistakeable silence of death. Efuru opened her eyes and saw the young woman stretched out on the mat, her neck at an unnatural angle, her tongue, black as a mamba's tail, hanging all the way down to her chest. Again, she made another hurried sign of the cross as she gently covered the dead infant with its late mother's cotton wrapper. The cloth soaked up the blood from the wet mat in seconds. Efuru left the umbilical cord uncut. *Better to leave them joined together in death as they were in life,* she thought. Her job was done. She struggled slowly to her feet, feeling the arthritic joints of her knees ache and creak in protest.

'Walking-Grave, Corpse-Maker, *Onwu atu-egwu!'* Efuru's voice was a quivering whisper. 'Fearless Deaths! Great deities, this old woman salutes you,' she bowed deeply to the empty space to her right and left. 'Fearsome ones who harvest where they like, reaping seeds you never sowed, I pay my respects to you. I know your eyes have seen me and your shadows have hovered over mine. Yet, you tarry because I am not your meal. Your will is unfathomable to man. I leave you with your latest feast, two unripe fruits that should have been given the chance to ripen before you plucked them from the tree of life. But who am I after all, a feeble and foolish old woman, to question the will of mankind's doom?'

Efuru bowed again, took a final look at the ghastly black cross on the forehead of the blood-spattered dead woman and began to back out of the room. She shielded her eyes with her hands so that her gaze would not encounter the two death deities should they take it upon themselves to do mischief on her and reveal themselves in their terrible ghastliness. *Who can see death and live?*

***

Outside the birth-hut, Efuru took a deep breath, inhaling as if she had been devoid of oxygen for years. The heat of the afternoon sun was like a warm balm on her freezing bones. She noticed the group of people huddled underneath the mango tree, looking at her with silent appeal. Amongst them was the young daughter of the dead woman, a child of five moon years, whose pale skin and light blue eyes mirrored her late mother's own. A bright red scarf covered her kinky yellow hair while a woven straw hat shielded her face from the burning rays of the afternoon sun.

Her name was Ọwa, meaning Full Moon. Her mother had clearly expected glorious things from this unusual child, on whose behalf she had pleaded in vain with the two death-deities. The child's eyes danced with excitement as she waited with her father, her aunt and her grandmother under the shade of the mango tree. Several of the clansmen and women were with them, their faces terse, their bodies stiff as they waited for the birth-aider to give them the news of a safe delivery.

Ọwa broke free from her grandmother's clasp and dashed over to Efuru, her pale eyes dancing their habitual excitement.

'Where's the baby? Where's the baby?' Ọwa demanded, tugging the birth-aider's hand with unexpected strength. Efuru's heart skipped, an uncomfortable leap. The child's voice never ceased to startle her no matter how many times she heard it. It was the deep baritone of a full-fledged man on the lips of a five-year old girl. If ever there was proof of reincarnation, this was it. Except, no one had ever been able to pinpoint which ancestor had returned in the body of the little albino girl. The birth-aider pulled her hands from the child's grip and stepped away from her, her dark pupils coated with fear. She resisted the burning urge to cross her shoulders with the sign of the cross.

'Ọwa! Come back here, now. Let the woman be,' shouted the child's aunt, a tall dark-skinned young woman with thin, sharp features. Efuru stared at the speaker. She found it hard to believe that the dead albino woman was the twin sister of the tall woman who spoke so harshly to the child. Never had two sisters been so different, not just in skin tone, but in every aspect of their personalities. One lived with bitter resentment while the other had swaggered with dazzling pride.

'Let the child be. Come... come, child,' the grandmother's voice was gentle yet dead. Only her eyes burnt with a mixture of fury and despair which told Efuru that the truth was already known. The grandmother lifted her face to the skies, her eyes shutting out the blinding rays of the sun. She didn't need to look into the haggard face of the old birth-aider to know that all had not gone well with her daughter, Xikora. The absence of a new baby's healthy wail and the silence within the birth-hut told their own deadly tale. Her daughter and grandchild had not survived the birth ritual. *The child's dreams had come true after all, despite all the sacrifices they had made to the Earth Goddess, Aná.*

She heard the silent sniffles of her son-in-law beside her and turned a cold gaze at him. *Worthless weakling!* He had cost her her daughter's life! She had warned him not to get Xikora pregnant again after the birth of her granddaughter, Ọwa. She'd known what would happen, that no male birth survived for the *Nshi* women. But the foolish man was hung up on a son, an heir. Now he had his wish, a dead son, while leaving her with a dead daughter and a young granddaughter whom she was determined to raise alone as her destiny dictated. *Heaven forbid she left the child in the care of her useless father or worse, her aunt Chika. Chika would bury*

20

Owa alive within hours of getting custody. The old woman stared at her granddaughter where she stood beside the weary birth-aider, asking endless questions that remained unanswered. There was awe and pity in her eyes. She had known from the child's birth that Owa had inherited the gift of the *Nshi* women, passed from mother to daughter through countless moon-ages. She preferred to call it the curse. Occasionally, it skipped a generation as it had done in her case. She'd neither inherited the gift nor the pale albino skin that went with it. Nor had her other daughter, Chika. Hers was a black skin tone that kept her safe, free of personal fear and worry, unlike her late daughter. Xikora had been doomed to see what men would never see, hear voices and messages hidden from humankind, travel the dark realms of the ancestors and the deities as was her yoke to carry as a high priestess of the great Earth Goddess, *Aná.* And now she was gone, together with her son.

She had warned Xikora that the Earth Goddess was a jealous and unforgiving deity who demanded absolute loyalty from her priestesses. *Nshi* women neither married, charged a fee for their services nor hexed people with bad curses. But, the foolish girl wouldn't listen, thought she knew best, as always, egged on by the useless man she'd lost her heart and senses to. Xikora had flouted every rule of her calling and flaunted her powers with the pride of a peacock. And now, the Earth Mother had abandoned her to her fate when the two deaths came calling.

'There was nothing I could do,' Efuru's eyes were moist with unshed tears. 'They came for your daughter and her son and left their mark on her palms and forehead. *Ndo*… sorry… I failed you. But what can an old woman do against the might of the terrible death siblings? Your daughter died a brave death, a warrior's death, worthy of her great status. Your grandson went in peace. He was a beautiful boy. May the ancestors receive them and grant them a better return.'

'*Ise*… so be it,' echoed everyone gathered in the death-compound, young and old, save Chika, the late woman's twin sister, whose face remained stony.

The little girl, Ọwa, was also silent. Her eyes were fixed at the open doorway of the birth-hut where the bodies of her mother and baby brother grew cold on the blood-soaked mat. Her body was rigid with terror as she stared at the prone bodies, which should have been stretched out on the floor in death but were instead, rising, ever so slowly, hovering over the bloodied mat, as if borne by invisible hands. The blood-soaked cloth shrouding the baby fell off the little body and Ọwa gasped. The dead baby dangled in the air between their mother's thighs, swinging gently on its umbilical cord, as if rocking to a lullaby.

As Ọwa stared in wide-eyed terror, two dark shadows emerged from the mud walls of the hut, shadows that were as solid as flesh, shaped like gigantic humans, yet devoid of features. One of the

22

shadows resembled a pregnant giantess, a gelatinous black mass of hulking terror. The other looked like a colossal monster in the shape of a man, a faceless, hideous horror. Qwa shivered, a cold chill embalming her body. She began to tremble. *She had seen them before, in her dreams. She had seen the two exact dark shadows chasing after her and Mama in several recurrent nightmares!* In those night terrors, Mama always hid her in a dark place of safety. But they'd continue their deadly pursuit of Mama. And now, they had crossed the shadowy realms of her dreams into the real world and finally caught Mama.

Qwa saw them nod at each other over her mother's body. They crouched at each end of the corpse, their long arms bearing her up. Two wide holes opened up where their mouths should have been, holes that stretched into endless, cavernous depths. Then, they began to swallow her mother. As a python would swallow a living goat, they devoured Mama whole. Qwa shut her eyes, tight, very tight, shutting out the hallucination, the impossible nightmare, her wild imagination that was constantly showing her things that couldn't be; terrors like the talking trees and flying night-children, wingless children who perched from treetops to rooftops with the ease of birds, calling out to her, urging her to join them in their unholy flight.

She rubbed her eyes with her fists and opened them again. The oiled black shadows from her nightmare were still feeding on

Mama's corpse, one from her feet and the other from her head. It was a quick feed, concluded in a matter of minutes when the mouth-holes met at the point where the baby dangled underneath her mother's thighs. The pregnant shadow tried to grab the baby but the child repelled her arms. She opened her mouth-hole wider and leaned forward to swallow the infant. Yet, she could not devour the baby. A faint glow covered the tiny body of the baby, a glow that blazoned into a blinding light which lit up the dark interior of the hut. The dead child glowed with the light of the sun and burnt with the fire of the moon. Its fire chased away the feasting black shadows, scorching them and setting their dense charcoal to flames.

Qwa heard an unearthly howl, followed by a loud crack as the floor split in half inside the hut. The crack ran a zig-zag line all the way to the narrow door before stopping at a point just inside the hut. A low hum filled the air, a deafening buzz. A great form rose from the cracked floor, a swirling, undulating mammoth body that twinkled with a million black stars, cold hard stars born from the deadly eyes of a million bees. It was like nothing Qwa had ever witnessed in all the bizarre visions her eyes had seen. It was neither woman nor man, human or animal, earth or water. Yet, it was all of these and more. Its movement was fluid like a great turbulent river, yet it stood with the towering rigidity of a giant Iroko tree, twinkling with its million, black eye-stars.

24

On seeing it, the two black shadows shrank back into the red mud wall from where they'd emerged, their movements panicked, as if in great terror. They vanished in seconds, swallowed up by a denser darkness whose mammoth presence swallowed the tiny room of the birth-hut. Qwa stared with her mouth wide open, a tight knot rising from her chest to her throat, hurting, choking. She saw the swirling, twinkling colossēa raise the glowing baby from the floor, cradling it close to where its chest would have been had it been human. Its movements were gentle, loving, like the tender care of a mother. Qwa heard a soft whine, the first birth cry of a new-born baby, followed by a contented gurgle. Then, the baby vanished, its tiny black body merging into the blacker density of the twinkling apparition.

Qwa gasped, her cry as soft as the baby's own. The twinkling giant swirled around and their eyes met. For a brief tense minute, their gaze held, the burning red orbs of the unknown deity and the darting, blue eyes of the little girl. Qwa stumbled back, caught in a whirlpool of unfamiliar emotions, verging from confusion to pain, awe to terror.

'We shall meet again, child; when you are ready, you will seek me and find me waiting. Fear not. Q ga-adi mma, all will be well with you.' Qwa heard the voice inside her head, a voice that was both loving and terrifying, the voice of a goddess. The sound shocked her out of her stupor, sending her dashing back to her

grandmother, sun hat abandoned on the sandy ground of their compound. Tears streaked down her cheeks.

'*Nne-ochie*! Old mother!' Ọwa flung herself at her grandmother, wrapping her arms tightly round her legs.

'Child, what is the matter? What's chasing you? Who dares frighten my little moon in front of her dotting grandmother?' The old woman lifted her granddaughter into her arms, holding her close. She tilted her face up with a gentle hand. Ọwa's body trembled, just like the clan's cat whenever there was a thunderstorm. Her aunt, Chika, gave her a cold look, hissed loudly and walked away from the group.

'The bla… black sha… shadows swallowed Mama,' Ọwa finally stuttered, her eyes glazed with terror. 'The ones I saw in my dreams, *Nne-Ochie*. They swallowed Mama but they couldn't swallow the baby. The baby burnt them and the big, twinkling giant came from the ground and took away the baby and the bad shadows disappeared into the wall. *Nne-ochie*, they swallowed Mama… the bad, black shadows swallowed Mama.' The child began to howl as the impact of all she just witnessed finally hit her. Her cries were the haunting keen of a full-grown man and it sent a chill down the spines of everyone gathered underneath the mango tree.

***

People began to arrive at the mourning compound, alerted to the shocking news by the unseen village grapevine. Xikora was dead! The powerful high-priestess to the Earth Goddess was no more! Qwa was still cradled in her grandmother's arms, crying and coughing as the sobs caught in her throat. The villagers cast furtive glances at the child, whispering to themselves and shaking their heads in sympathy. Yet, none of them touched the child nor placed a comforting hand on her, not even her father who stood by silently, his eyes downcast. Qwa's pale colour and the deep masculine sounds that emerged from her voice froze all compassion in their hearts. They all knew who the child's mother was before she died, *what she was*. Xikora of the *Leloole* curse! Sure, she had healed a lot of them from various diseases and made their crops grow even when the neighbouring villages starved from drought.

But she had also cursed a lot of them.

They'd feared rather than loved Xikora. In her lifetime, she was also known by the nick-name *Q kwaku maa - She that restores or ruins a man as his creator made him.* It was not a nick-name given lightly, not when people came from around the country with their broken bones and wasted bodies, begging to be touched by the albino medicine-woman with the miracle hands. All it took were a few medicinal herbs, some strange incantations and payment in form of land or money, lots of money, together with a corn-cob for the Earth Goddess and every broken bone was straightened to its original strength, every ravaged body restored to full health. On the other hand, all it took was some sinister chants for strong bones to be shattered, healthy minds ruined and long lives cut short when the fearsome medicine-woman was offended. And it took very little to offend Xikora.

The villagers recalled that the dead woman was from the infamous *Nshi* clan, the clan of high-priestesses to the Earth Goddess, *Aná*. Theirs was the only bloodline that bred albinos in the village and they were the only albinos that were sacred from ostracism as was the norm with people considered marked with an unnatural hue. So, the mourners hugged the grandmother instead, offering their condolences to her, the poor woman cursed with the albino daughter and albino grand-daughter who was rumoured to have inherited her late mother's terrible powers. They made Qwa invisible and in her invisibility, Qwa mourned her mother with silent sobs. *Her beautiful Mama, who had shared the same skin colour as her, whose blue eyes danced as merrily as her own, whose yellow hair was thick and bright like dry corn straws, who could read her thoughts and tell her future delights before they happened, who showed her secret herbs and special places in the forests and bushes; her good Mama who would never come home again because she had been swallowed by the two bad shadows.*

Gradually, the rage grew in her, a dark rage that would stay with her through her childhood to her adult years. Ọwa made herself a silent oath. *She would find the two bad shadows and make them pay. She would make the brightest fire and just as the baby had done, burn them and kill them till they died. She didn't care if Nne-ochie told her off for playing with fire. Mama had taught her some secrets. She'll wait till she was a grown up and not afraid of anything like the grown-ups and find the two wicked shadows and kill them dead.* Ọwa's body shuddered with her rage and tears.

Her grandmother held her tight, looking helplessly at the birth-aider and the gathered crowd. Her mind reeled with what she had heard from her granddaughter. That a tiny child could see the death-feast of the two fearsome deities, Walking-Grave and Corpse-Maker, was a supernatural feat beyond comprehension. Not even her late daughter, Xikora, could lay claim to such powers. The myth of the two death deities was one every adult knew from numerous fables, tales of terror and mystery about the fearsome duo, handed down from generation to generation. Yet, this little granddaughter of hers, who had never heard the myth, had not only dreamt about the death deities but had seen them with morning clarity, describing what had so far been baseless fable in horrendous, gory details.

A sudden chill ran up the grandmother's spine, soon replaced by a deep gloom that stole the strength from her limbs. *What did the future hold for this poor child, this special child who was yoked with the cursed gift?* Instinctively, her arms pulled the child closer, tighter, fiercer.

***

In the dark interior of the mud hut, the body of the young mother began to decompose with the speed of rotten fish, bloating, peeling, festering. By the time the first villager ventured in several minutes after her death, her body was already crawling with grave worms, filling the tiny room with the unwholesome stench of an over-ripe corpse. It was as if Xikora had died from one of her own curses, the fearsome *Leloole* curse. Only her two hands remained fresh, firm and supple as if still oxygenated. The two black crosses had vanished from her palms, leaving them pink and soft, her lifelines clearly defined once again. Their albino pink hue was in stark contrast to the death-blackness of the rest of her body. The two fresh hands attached to the putrefied corpse brought the shudders to everyone that saw the body of the dead medicine-woman, together with the thick black cross on her forehead and the unnatural protrusion of her blackened tongue. People who knew her in life marvelled at the blackness of her skin, a skin which in life was as pale as ripe guava, just like her eerily preserved hands.

The greatest wonder lay in the sight of her dead son. Between her blood-drenched thighs, her tiny dead infant glowed a healthy dark sheen, warm with fresh innocence, sweet and peaceful. But it was the sight of the beautiful smile on his face that stunned the villagers. No one in living memory had seen a still-born baby smiling with the radiant and contented face of a living child!

***

The birth-aider, Efuru, would recount her story of the bedside visit of the two fearsome death deities to a thousand visitors. She would stress the fierceness with which she resisted when they tried to drag her with them into their cold realm. There were no witnesses to contradict her version of events. So, her imagination went into overdrive. Efuru's stories fuelled the fear the people already felt for the little albino offspring of the famous medicine-woman who fearlessly fought the two dreaded death deities and stopped them from taking her son with them into their cold realm.

Otherwise, how else could one explain the unnatural smile on the dead baby's face, the fact that the baby's body remained freshly intact, right to its burial, while the mother's corpse festered to rotten purification within minutes of death? And why did the hands remain untouched? What dark secrets were yet to unfold from the dead medicine-woman? Surely, the child, Qwa, was cursed with the same deadly powers of her mother. Why, even her own father had already abandoned her, leaving the family and the village as soon as his wife and dead son were buried.

And the villagers waved their arms over their heads to cast out the devil each time they came across the little albino child with the voice of a man, hiding their faces behind their hands to ward off the evil in her dancing, pale blue eyes.

Ω Ω Ω

2

The Fat-Man

Ukari Village, 2015

The Fat-Man was waiting for her by the dusty roadside, his dirty, white Peugeot parked right in the middle of the narrow untarred road, selfishly blocking other users. Not that he had any cause to worry about causing a traffic jam; there were no cars visible in either direction and Aku knew she wouldn't be seeing any vehicle for a long time. The dirt road led to a dead-end, right to her mother's white-washed bungalow, nestled in a deep grove, surrounded by a goat pen, a chicken coop, a herb garden and a small yam barn.

A small hut, a red-mud structure, served as their deity's shrine. It was in that shrine that her mother, Qwa, communed with their ancestors and their deity. She also received visitors in the shrine, nocturnal visitors, who only called at their house at midnight. Aku loathed their night visitors. They kept her awake and ruined her attendance record at college. She could hardly wait to graduate and escape their home for the freedom of the big city. Just a few more months of college and she was done – *free* – total liberty from her stupid so-called destiny.

Aku lifted her arm and glanced down. Her faux-leather wristwatch had the needles at 07.00hrs. Her aim had been to get into school before their daily mass assembly by 07.30hrs. But having overslept yet again, she doubted she would avoid the late-comers' detention, despite being a college student with just a few months to complete her studies. But Catholic schools had their own unique codes of conduct, especially when they had a principal called Father Ike, a fierce disciplinarian with a notorious fiery temper. To top it all, she also had to contend with the horrid fat man stalking her again, today of all days.

Aku sighed and quickened her steps as soon as she spied the white Peugeot. She adjusted her sunglasses and pulled her straw-hat lower, shielding her face from both the sun and The Fat-Man. The closer she got to the car, the louder its engine vibrated. There was a threat in the low hum of the car which dried the insides of her mouth and brought the sudden rapid thuds to her heart. She glanced behind her, peered into the lonely distance, seeking signs of human presence, anyone that wasn't The Fat-Man waiting for her in the white Peugeot. All she saw was the long stretch of dusty road and wild foliage blooming under the bright morning sun.

A small, dark shadow appeared at her feet. She looked up and saw a black kite flying low, seeking a grey lizard or a new-born chick for its breakfast. Through the dark lenses of her sunglasses, she spied a silver aeroplane breaking through the blue skies, leaving a trail of white smoke across the sky. She wanted to wave to the plane, alert the people inside of her plight. But she knew she would be just a speck to them from that distance, probably the size the black kite was to her.

'Sweet girl, come here,' she heard his oiled voice call out across the road. She swallowed, hard, dry. She kept her face straight, staring into the distance, feigning deafness. Her steps quickened, putting more distance between her and the voice. She heard a car door open and slam. Footsteps thundered behind her. She looked back, her heart racing as fast as the feet chasing her down. Two young men dressed in jeans and t-shirts bore down on her. One of them wore a pair of sunglasses which was as dark as his skin.

Aku started to run. Her book-laden satchel slammed against her side, hurting her ribs. She let it drop to the ground, feeling her body lighten, her feet quicken. She ran like an antelope, sure and swift. But she was no match for the two men. Her flight was brought to an abrupt end in minutes. She felt hands grab her arms, pull her long braids and halt her feet. She screamed, a cry of pain and fear. Her arms flayed as she struggled to free herself.

'Stupid girl!' One of the young men shouted into her ears, the one with the sunglasses as dark as her own. His hands were cruel on her arms. She knew her pale skin would bear the marks of his finger-prints for several days to come. 'You not hear our master call you, eh? Or you not know who our master is? Who you think

36

you are, eh? Stupid albino idiot. Other girls more beautiful than you go thank their lucky charm that someone as important as our master is interested in them. Instead you act as if you be something special, foolish girl.'

'Leave me alone,' Aku begged, hearing the wobble in her voice. She struggled, digging in her feet and twisting her arms to free herself. Her sunglasses fell to the ground, causing her pupils to dilate in a frantic dance of panic as the intense rays of the morning sun blinded her vision. She squeezed her eyes shut, feeling the tears of shame, fear and helplessness drench her cheeks. The men laughed, deriving pleasure from her terror. They sandwiched her between them, dragging her by the arms towards the white Peugeot. The pungent odour of stale sweat oozed from the men, coupled with the sour breath accompanying each word they spoke. One of them, the one in sunglasses, stooped to pick up her sunglasses and discarded satchel along the way, laughing mockingly at her as he carefully replaced her sunglasses on her face and hung the strap of her satchel over her neck. The book-laden bag weighed tight against her neck, hurting her windpipe. Aku wanted to adjust it, relieve the pressure on her neck, but their fingers were tight on her arms, cruel and merciless.

The Fat-Man was sprawled against the white leather of the driver's seat when her captors finally hauled her into his presence. Aku saw him through a painful glaze. He had one arm draped across the passenger seat while his podgy fingers held a cigarette to his lips, thin lips so at odds with the fleshiness of his face. He eyed her through the dense smoke swirling around his face, his eyes squinted, looking piggier than she recalled from her previous encounter with him. The knife marks scarring his face were stark and threatening in the morning blaze.

'Aku! Aku!' He shook his head, sighing deeply as he repeated her name. 'Why don't you want me to make you happy? *Chei!*' His voice was the voice of a head teacher admonishing a troublesome student. 'This girl! Why do you treat me like this? All I want is to give you a lift to school so you don't have to walk all that way in this heat. You know the sun is not good for your yellow skin, eh? Isn't it better to relax in an air-conditioned car rather than carrying that heavy schoolbag and sweating by the time you arrive for your lessons?'

He made a motion to his henchmen, an imperceptible nod. They dragged Aku to the passenger side of the car and forced her into the seat. The slam of the door had an ominous ring, like the metal clang of a prison gate, a prison that reeked of strong aftershave, stale sweat and cigarettes.

'*Oga,* master, please let me go,' Aku begged, fresh tears streaming down her cheeks. 'I want to walk to school. Please, just let me go.'

'Why are you crying?' He chuckled, tossing the half-smoked cigarette out of the window. His henchmen mimicked his mirth. 'Boys, what did you do to her? I hope you didn't frighten her?' His voice was a mixture of mockery and sternness. His face retained its patronising smile.

'*Oga*, we not do anything to her, I swear.' Sunglasses laughed.

'Sweet girl, you remember who I am, don't you? I told you my name when I first saw you last week. But in case you have forgotten, my name is chief Eze, son of the late Agu of Onori clan. As I told you, I'm the deputy local government chairman and very soon, I shall become the chairman,' he paused, looking her over as if she were a bowl of assorted meats. His tongue sneaked out, licking his lips. The sight made Aku's skin crawl. She turned her face away, staring out of the window, trying to reign in her terror, her wild imaginings. 'Sweet thing, I can give you anything you want, anything,' he continued. 'Just say the word. In fact, once you finish your final exams next month, I'll give you a job in my office and set your salary very high. Many girls in your situation will be dancing for joy at this opportunity.'

'*Oga*, that is what we tell her too,' chipped in Sunglasses from the back seat, leaning forward. She smelled the rankness of his breath. 'I swear, I don't know why you bother with this girl. She not be the only beautiful girl in the area even if she be the only albino in the village, apart from her witch mama. If you like, I can bring you ten girls whose beauty pass her own and they will be very grateful too, unlike this one.'

'Shut up,' The Fat-Man snapped, all humour gone from his voice. Aku wilted at the harshness in his voice, thankful it wasn't aimed at her. He sat still for several tense minutes, smoking a fresh stick of cigarette, deep in thought. The silence in the car was more terrifying than his earlier anger. Aku felt terror rise afresh in her heart. *What will The Fat-Man do to her? How will she ever escape his car and his henchmen?* The Fat-Man let out a deep sigh, tossed the cigarette stick to the ground and wound up the window. He leaned over to turn on the car radio. Aku shrank away, squeezing herself against the car door. He looked at her and smiled, a mocking smile, a knowing smile. His smile held something ugly that caused her heart to race faster. He upped the radio volume. A female gospel singer shrilled out some threats against Satan. Her voice grated on Aku's frayed nerves. It must have had the same effect on The Fat-Man because he quickly switched stations till he settled on one broadcasting the news. There was a news item about a gang of armed robbers being executed at the old prison grounds and a fatal inferno from a burst petrol pipe that claimed the lives of three hundred people in some unknown village.

'You see how poor people just like yourself are losing their lives just to make ends meet,' The Fat-Man said, his eyes leering at Aku's breasts before returning to the road. 'These people know the dangers of bursting a petrol pipe but they don't care. All they want is to steal petrol and sell it on the black market so they can feed their families. Now they're all dead,' he shook his head sadly, though she heard no compassion in his voice. He shoved his hand into his pocket. 'Here, take this for your hairdresser,' he pushed a wad of *Naira* notes in ₦200 denominations towards her. She turned her face away from the notes. *He could keep his horrid money. All she wanted was her freedom.* 'This is ₦10,000. Take it and there's more where that came from. After I finish sexing you today, if I'm happy with your performance, I shall give you much more than this. So, you have to make sure you pleasure me well today otherwise, I won't be happy with you.'

His words sent the chills of terror down Aku's spine. She heard the raucous laughter of Sunglasses behind her. *Holy Mary Mother of God, spare me!* This was what she had feared from the first time she laid eyes on The Fat-Man. She turned her head away and kept her trembling hands tight against the brown satchel resting on her thighs. Tears pooled in her eyes, curved a wet trail down her cheeks. She could hear the loud thudding of her heart in the claustrophobic interior of the car.

'Foolish girl! You be deaf or what? Take the money now before I knock your head,' Sunglasses shouted behind her. The menace in his voice sent Aku's hand to the notes, snatching them from The Fat-Man and pushing them into her satchel. *Oh God! Holy Mother!*

Save my soul from hellfire! The panic thuds hurt her chest beneath her cotton school uniform. She was now compromised. Wild thoughts raced through her mind. *What was she to do with the money? How could she prove The Fat-Man raped her and that the money wasn't payment for services rendered? Who will she tell? Who'll believe her word against those of an important man like him? Oh Holy Mother, save my soul, save me…*

'Good girl! You have done well. Make sure the hair-dresser makes your hair beautiful, okay?' The Fat-Man sounded pleased. 'I don't like those braids you have on. It's too bush, not at all sophisticated. Get your hair straightened and put nice Beyoncé hair extensions, okay? Next time, I'll take you to Enugu city to shop for fine clothes so that your beauty will shine.'

The Fat-Man pulled up behind a red car caught up in a cattle jam. He cursed at the cow herders and blasted his horn. Aku fumbled with the lock and jumped out of the car, almost falling on the pot-holed tarmac in her flight. She recognised the red car. It was her school principal's car, Father Ike's little Honda car. She ran towards it with a scream, hearing yet again the thundering feet of The Fat-Man's henchmen behind. She rapped on Father Ike's window, yanking the door handle. It opened and she fell into his passenger seat, slamming the door behind her. The door flew open just as quickly and hard hands began to pull her out of the car. Father Ike shouted and killed his engine. He leapt out of the car and rushed to her side where the thugs were already dragging her resisting body towards The Fat-Man's car.

'How dare you?' Father Ike's voice boomed with fury, his giant physique menacing even in his priest's garb. 'Let her go at once before I break your dunce heads,' Father Ike looked primed for a fight as he reached for Sunglasses. The thug ducked, avoiding the priest's fist. They looked at The Fat-Man for instructions. He waved them over to his car. With a curse, they shoved her towards the priest before running off to the white Peugeot. She stumbled to the ground, bumping her head against the car.

Aku scrambled to her feet, sobbing, shaking, her uniform covered in dust. Father Ike helped her into his car and shut the door behind her. He quickly got back into the driver's seat. 'You're safe, my child. It's ok,' he said, folding her hands in his large ones. His voice was a sweet song to her battered senses. It was the sound of security and goodness, just like her mother's voice. 'What happened? Who are those men?'

Aku tried to speak but the sobs kept choking her words. She was sweating despite the air-conditioning in Father Ike's car. It was the sweat of relief, coupled with shame. She felt like someone that had escaped a shit-deluged cassava farm.

'He…he said his name is Chief Eze… the son of Agu of Onori clan and… and the deputy local government chairman,' Aku stuttered, her voice low, guilt-ridden. To have the priest whom she held in the greatest esteem find her in such a compromising situation was a shame beyond anything she could bear. 'Father, I didn't ask him for anything. He has been following me in his car every day on my way to school. Then today, his men caught me and dragged me into his car,' Aku shuddered again. She turned to the priest, her eyes darting frantically behind her sunglasses. She pulled out the wads of *Naira* notes and handed them to the priest. 'Father forgive me because I have sinned. I did not confess to talking with a strange man the first time he spoke to me and I took the money from him. I didn't want it but he forced me, I swear in the name of our Holy Mother. I will do my penance but please don't tell my mother about this, please. I don't want her to stop me from coming to school. You know she doesn't like me attending our school and will use any excuse to stop my attendance and I'm almost at the end of my senior year and want to take my final exams. Please, Father, please, don't say anything to my mother about this.'

Father Ike kept hold of her hands, a gentle smile creasing his rugged features. 'It's okay, child. You need not worry about your mother hearing about this and I'll not make you do any penance because you have not committed any sin. Those men are evil men and you must promise me to always be on your guard. Try not to leave your house when the roads are deserted and always walk home with your friend, Ego, okay?'

44

Aku gave a fervent nod. Relief flooded her body. She had escaped certain molestation and would yet complete her sixth form with the help of the Blessed Virgin. The Fat-Man was a problem she needed to think through. There had to be a way to avoid him and attend college without running into him. For now, she had made it safely to school, thanks to the good Father and if she were lucky, she may yet make it to morning mass assembly on time.

***

Aku joined her class at the college sixth form section of the assembly hall, smiling at her best friend, Ego, as she squeezed into the space saved for her next to her friend.

'What happened?' Ego whispered. 'I was starting to think you might not come to school today.'

'I'll tell you about it later. It's that horrible fat man again. He caught me on my way to school. *Chei!* My sister, you don't know what I went through today.' Terror washed afresh over Aku, turning her skin a bright red hue.

'Blessed Mother!' Ego exclaimed, her eyes wide. 'What happened? What did he do?'

'Sshh! Later,' Aku's voice was hushed, her face coated with worry. She covered her mouth with her hand as she spoke. 'I can see Miss Obi looking at us. We don't want her to detain us after school and get us to do her filthy laundry and housework. After everything that's happened to me today, the last thing I need is Miss Obi's trouble.'

'Idiot woman,' Ego's voice was vicious. There was no love lost between her and Miss Obi, their biology teacher. 'That's why no man will ever marry her, not with her skinny meanness. She'll remain a wretched teacher forever, taking out her frustrations on students, while you and I'll make ourselves millions of *Naira* in Enugu city and drive around in posh cars, giving her the middle finger whenever we see her.'

'Ego! Sshh!' Aku tried to stifle her giggles but it was no use. Miss Obi's bespectacled eyes bore into them, her voice strident as she called out Ego's name for detention, even though the two girls were equally guilty of "assembly disruption". But, as was the case with the rest of the teachers, Miss Obi turned two blind eyes to Aku's behaviour. Father Ike had warned the entire school staff about Aku. She must never be exposed to the scorching sun nor bruised by a teacher's cane. Her mother was only waiting for the flimsiest excuse to pull her out of the detested Catholic school. The other teachers adhered to the principal's orders. But not Miss Obi. The biology teacher knew how close the two friends were, knew that Aku would never leave Ego to do detention alone. Punishing Ego was her indirect way of punishing Aku without incurring the principal's wrath. She would not be blamed if Aku insisted on exposing her skin to the blistering sun out of loyalty to her friend.

Aku allowed her thoughts to roam as the assembly dragged on. She could barely wait for the weeks to fly so she'd be free from Miss Obi forever. Ego had everything mapped out for them. They planned to go into business together in the big city, Enugu, set up their own dress-making shop and make lots of money. They'd been friends since their childhood, Ego and herself. Everyone in school called them sisters because they were never apart. Their tall slenderness mirrored each other and with only a few months between their birthdays, they were almost the same age. Ego had celebrated her eighteenth birthday a few weeks earlier while Aku needed to wait a couple more weeks for hers.

The two girls had something else in common. They were both fatherless, raised solely by their mothers. That fact alone made them unique in their small village, populated with parents who boasted of impressive broods. While Ego's father had died in her childhood, Aku had no idea who her father was, whether he was tall or short, hot tempered or calm, dead or living. It wasn't something that bothered her much, since it was the norm with the women of her clan to breed without husbands, save her late grandmother, Xikora, rumoured to be one of the greatest witchdoctors that ever lived. Aku figured her father must have been tall like herself, since her mother was tiny, barely reaching to Aku's shoulders. She gave an inward shrug. *Who knows, maybe one day, despite her skin colour, she might find a husband of her own just as her grandmother, Xikora, had done.* Aku allowed herself to imagine her perfect husband. She would like him to be tall and dark-skinned, very black. She didn't want to have anything to do with an albino man, didn't want children who would be cursed with the same skin that's made her life a misery. She might have three or even four children. She liked the names, Kanye or Dre, for her sons and Oprah and Jada for her daughters. She wasn't sure though if the Catholic church would allow her to give her children such unsanctified names. The church tended not to make a fuss if it was an *Igbo* name given a child. But once it came to the English names, they wanted something like Mary or Peter, Theresa or Paul.

Aku's nose wrinkled. She didn't want to give her children such boring names, church or no church. She'll have to wait and see. But, no way was she going to be yoked to the stupid so-called destiny of the *Nshi* women, eternal spinsters chained to their pagan deity.

'We fly to thy patronage oh Holy Mother of God...' Father Ike's deep voice cut through Aku's thoughts. Morning Mass assembly had begun, the start of another long school-day at *Our Mother of Immaculate Conception* Secondary School.

Ω Ω Ω

3

Night Diplomat

◆

The mud hut was lit up with wick-lamps when Aku finally arrived home for the divination ritual to the Earth Goddess, *Aná*. It had been a long day at school and Miss Obi had not only made them do her laundry and housework, but also cut the grass in her front garden. It was little wonder she was loathed by most of the students. While other teachers made the students do light housework for them as detention punishment, Miss Obi would heap everything on the girls, right down to painting her kitchen and climbing the mango trees to pluck her ripe mango fruits for her.

Even before Aku arrived at the entrance of the shrine, she could hear her mother, Ọwa, wailing the special divination songs to their goddess, her voice deep, melancholy. She sang in the mysterious tongue of soothsayers, the secret divination language, the oldest language in the universe, known to just a handful of mankind, the *Dibia* cult of medicine-men and medicine-women. Aku quickened her steps, aware she was running very late. Mama Ọwa was almost ready to shift into the *Áfá* consciousness to begin her mind-quest into the various spiritual realms. There, she would liaise with the forces beyond the realm of man, to seek answers and remedies to complex questions and problems on behalf of their community and village at large. Aku's main function was to assist in the *Áfá* process, keep watch on Ọwa's earthly body while her spirit journeyed into the various realms of the dead.

Ọwa was a Night Diplomat, the recognised high priestess of *Aná*, goddess of earth and fertility, wife of *Amadioha*, the omnipotent God of the skies, lightning and thunder. Ọwa's work was usually carried out at night, when the spirits and ancestors could be easily reached. Sometimes, Aku thought their lives were tied to the caprices of the moon. Her mother's journeys to the spiritual realms depended on the first and last appearances of the moon, as that was when the oracle was at its most potent and messages could be received easily from the various spirit realms. Aku never knew which spirit realm her mother would be visiting till they were inside the shrine. It could be to the realm of the ancestors or the realm of the benevolent spirits. Other times, it could be to *Ala Mmụọ,* the Land of the Dead and Devious Spirits or worse, to *Mbana-Oyi,* The Cold Realm, where Aku's dead grandmother, Xikora, was held captive by the fearsome death deities, Walking Grave and Corpse-Maker. That journey was the one that terrified Aku the most, the one she feared would be the end of her mother some day and the one that tested her apprentice skills the most.

Once a month, when the omens were right, Ọwa made that dreadful journey to *Mbana-Oyi.* Each trip left her drained and sick for several days afterwards. Yet she would go, put herself through the perils of the deadly realm to visit her dead mother, Xikora. Tonight, Aku knew that Ọwa's night diplomacy was taking her to *Mbana-Oyi* and Aku didn't feel confident about fulfilling her part of the divination ritual. She was weighted with miseries she wished she could pour into her mother's ears, miseries brought to her heart by the rich fat-man, chief Eze, the wicked man that had made her the focus of his unwanted lust. But she knew she would never share that trouble with her mother. Enrolling in the Catholic girls' school had been a hard-fought battle, one which was eventually won when Aku agreed to become a willing apprentice to the Earth Goddess, as was her destiny as an *Nshi* female. Any hint of trouble and her mother would drag her away from school. The Fat Man was a fish-bone in her throat which she must find a way to extricate without help.

Aku quickly removed her brown school sandals at the entrance of the shrine, stooping low to enter the dusky warmth of the mud hut that housed the clay statue of the Earth Goddess, *Aná*. The smell of smoke and fresh blood hit her nostrils. She could see the small wood fire burning before the statue of the goddess, as well as the numerous candles lit up in a circle around her. The white feathers of the sacrificial chicken lay scattered over the statue, sticking to the chicken blood that was splattered over the black effigy like red paint. The dead chicken, feather-naked and mangled, lay in a calabash bowl waiting for the goddess' blessings. It would serve as their supper later that night, imbuing them with more powers from the great deity.

With haste, Aku stripped off her cotton school uniform and knickers till she stood as naked as the day she was placed into her mother's womb. She gathered a handful of ash from the pile in the clay-pot to the corner of the hut and smeared her body with the dark soot. Soon, she was as black as the austere statue of their goddess atop her elevated mud throne. The same soot covered the naked body of her mother, even though Ọwa's pale albino skin broke through the ash in places like a painting in black and pink, just like Aku's skin. The soot would protect their lives and ensure they remained invisible to the malevolent spirits during Ọwa's soul-journey.

Soot was a vital ingredient for their ritual. Ọwa had told Aku the importance of soot when she narrated the history of *Igbo* creation. The legend went that when *Chukwu,* the highest God, created mankind, he had sent *Nkita*, Dog, to tell man to cover his dead with soot which would bring them back to life, ensuring mankind would remain immortal. The dog fell asleep on the way, so *Chukwu* sent the sheep instead. But the sheep, being of low intelligence, forgot the message and told man to bury his dead deep in the soil. By the time *Nkita* arrived with the correct message, it was too late and mankind had already buried their dead in the soil

53

and lost the gift of immortality. But a handful of powerful witchdoctors collected the mystic ash from *Nkita* and have since shared its powerful secrets amongst themselves, handing them down the generations to their successors. Qwa was one of them and one day, Aku would also join that exclusive secret cult who held the powers of life and death, if Qwa had her way. The soot Aku used tonight was only the symbolic one. The real Ash of Immortality lay in a secret place known only to Qwa. It would not come into Aku's possession till she passed her initiation and became a full-fledged Night Diplomat to their deity, *Aná.* Aku didn't believe in the rubbish story about the sacred ash. Only Jesus had the power to bring man back to life. But she humoured her mother by not questioning the truth of the legend.

After coating herself with the ash, Aku took some sacred *Nzu,* white chalks, and chewed them till they were soft mush. Then, she spat the mixture into her hand and smeared her eyes, her heart, and her private parts with the protective coat. *Nzu* would keep the core of her being safe from possession should an evil spirit slip through the portal created by Qwa's soul-journey. Finally, Aku picked up her beaded necklace of power, *Jigida*, draped it over her head and joined her mother at the foot of the towering black statue of the Earth Goddess. *Aná's* red eyes stared down at them with total detachment, her clay features austere and aloof. Dark power radiated from her, a power Aku found as terrifying as the red paint,

54

coating the cold pupils of the great deity. She shuddered and turned her eyes away from the statue. She didn't want to cause her eyes to sin by letting her gaze linger on the deity's statue for longer than was necessary.

Ọwa did not acknowledge her presence. Aku didn't expect her to. Ọwa's face did not reveal the black fury that was without doubt, seething within her heart. Aku knew her lateness was both a flagrant disrespect to the great goddess and a gross neglect of her duty of care to her mother's welfare. Once again, Aku cursed the wretched fat-man, whose actions had contributed to her school detention and subsequent lateness to the shrine. Ọwa's gaze was fixed at the blood-spattered statue of the Earth Goddess, her head flung back, her arms raised in invocation. Aku fell to her knees and joined her voice to her mother's in the sacred chant. As always, she stumbled over the divination words, unable to recall each complex word, the right inflection, the correct sequence of the mysterious tongue of divination. She sensed, rather than saw Ọwa's frown at her massacre of the secret tongue. Again, the familiar shame and guilt overwhelmed her, coupled with the constant resentment and rebellion against her inheritance, her unwanted fate, the heavy burden of following in the footsteps of a long lineage of priestesses to the Earth Goddess.

She considered herself a Christian, baptised by Father Ike. It was a baptism carried out behind closed doors and shrouded in total secrecy. As the only daughter of the high priestess of *Aná,* her recent conversion to Christianity was a coup for the Catholic priest. She dared not contemplate what Qwa would do should she discover Aku's betrayal of her calling and rejection of her ancestors. Each time Qwa entered into the *Áfá* consciousness to consult with the spirits, Aku awaited her return with a quaking heart, convinced the spirits would reveal her shameful secret to her mother. So far, they hadn't and her secret remained safe, while her anxiety grew as strong as her guilt. She was a daughter who had betrayed her two mothers, her earthly mother, Qwa, and her heavenly mother, Mary. She was resigned to her fate in purgatory. All she had to do was find a way to avoid hellfire.

Aku pushed away the image of the white-cassocked priest that had insinuated itself into her mind, feeling shame at her pagan nakedness and renewed resentment towards her mother. It wasn't fair that she wasn't allowed to be like all the other girls at school, care-free girls who would die before shaming themselves as she was forced to do most nights inside the secret shrine of the Earth Goddess. Worse, she would have to confess everything to Father Ike at the next confession and do more penance for her pagan ways. No matter how hard she tried to explain her situation to Father Ike, he refused to accept her excuses. As far as he was concerned, she was involved in demon worship each time she participated in the rituals with her mother. His harsh words rang in

Aku's ears for days afterwards till the next time she returned to confess her ancestral sins.

Qwa suddenly screamed and slumped to the floor, her head hitting the massive clay feet of the Earth Goddess. Her eyes rolled back, revealing only the whites. Aku quickly reached down and clasped her hands, feeling the spasms that wracked her body. Sweat poured down Qwa's face, dampened her body, making her hands moist and slippery within Aku's clasp. She dusted the ash on her head into her hands, firming her grip, ensuring Qwa's safety. To let go was unthinkable when Qwa's soul crossed over to the land of the spirits.

Aku began to chant the safety words, the powerful invocations to their ancestors which would awaken them from their dead sleep.

'Spirits!' she cried, 'I beg you to protect my mother, to fight the demons of the underworld that would seek to do her harm. Must I remind you that the safety of your descendants and the perpetuity of your names lie with Mother's night diplomacy? Without the secrets she steals from the spirits, untold disasters would befall our community and disease, sickness and death would be their yoke! I am still an apprentice, an infant witchdoctor, still suckling the breast of knowledge, unprepared to assume the mantle of leadership and take over the helm from my mother. So, I beg, our ancestors, awake! Intervene! You must use all your powers to protect my mother! You have no choice if you want your names preserved from obscurity!'

Then she began singing the lullabies to the spirits, the songs that would keep them enchanted and away from Ọwa while she traversed their realm. As Aku sang, the spasms left her mother's body. Ọwa's hands went limp, her body cold and stiff like a corpse. But for the loud, harsh breathing rasping from her nostrils, one would assume her dead. Aku's voice shrilled into the silent night as she tightened her grip on Ọwa's hands, swaying back and forth to the secret rhythm of *Áfá*.

Time ceased to exist. Aku was lost to the present and the realities of life in mankind's domain. A dense fog filled her mind, clouding her vision. Her voice grew hoarse from the chants and sweat poured from her face like rain water. Her aching knees grew numb and soon, her mind began to wander. *What if she failed her final exams because of maths? What if she asked her mother to give her a special charm to open her brain so that all the answers would be clear on exam day?* Ego had been asking Aku to make that request on both their behalf. Other students from wealthier homes were already paying bribes to some teachers to obtain the exam questions and gain an unfair advantage.

Aku heard a small whimper from the entrance of the shrine. She turned her head to look. A small child, a naked toddler, cowered in the dark corner, its small hands rubbing the tears from its eyes.

Next to the child was a ball of deadly bees, bound together by their sticky honeycomb. Their loud buzz filled the room, loud and deadly. The child reached out for the honey-ball, drawn by its strange music. The sight froze Aku's limbs. Terror gripped her heart. One touch and the child was finished. The bees would sting it to death, sting them both to death. She started to jump to her feet to get to the child and remove it from harm's way. She opened her mouth to shout out a warning.

At that moment, Owa's body jerked. Her grip on Aku's hands tightened. A violent convulsion seized her limbs and a low moan issued from her lips. Her features contorted and her eyes squeezed, tightly, bringing the furrows to her forehead. The child vanished in an instant, together with the bees. Aku's eyes cleared and the truth dawned on her. The child was a malevolent entity, a deceitful spirit who had taken advantage of her distracted thoughts to slip through the portal opened by Owa's night diplomacy. It meant one thing; her mother was in danger.

Aku had been warned about those risks but never believed such manifestations were possible. Now she knew better. Her aimless daydreaming had exposed Owa to the malevolent spirits of the underworld. It was time to bring her mother home. She prayed she would remember the right ritual, that she would be up to the task of saving her mother's life. She raised her head to the bloodied statue of their goddess and began to wail the prayer of deliverance to the deity. The hard soil of the mud hut bruised her knees as she struggled to maintain her grip on Ọwa's hands. The more Aku wailed, the more Ọwa fought... *the more they fought,* trying to keep Ọwa with them in their dark realm. Aku knew that her puny strength was no match to their supernatural powers. The longer the struggle dragged, the more she despaired. By herself, she could not bring her mother back. She realised that truth with mounting terror. She needed to awaken the Earth Goddess whom her mother served without reserve. Aku may not believe in the deity but she had to try something, *anything. Maybe she could call on the holy Virgin. But that'll be sacrilege. Father Ike would never forgive her. Her soul would rot in hell forever.* Aku intensified her prayers to the goddess, feeling the cold beads of sweat cover her naked body. Her breathing grew harsh, almost as loud as Ọwa's own. Her teeth bit down hard on her lower lip, bringing salty blood to her tongue. *Blood!* She had forgotten! To awaken the powers of the goddess, blood from the bloodline of her priestesses must be offered. That's what her mother had taught her. Ọwa was in no position to give blood. Her very existence now depended on Aku's actions.

Swift as a kite, she picked up the rusty blood-coated knife used in slaughtering the sacrificial chicken. She shut her eyes and stabbed her left arm, even as her hand held tight to her mother's hand. The pain was sharp, excruciating. She almost let go of Ọwa's hand. But she clung to it...just. She dropped the knife with a soft

60

moan. Her blood dripped slowly from the cut, *drip... drop... drip.* The dark clay of the Earth Goddess soaked up the gift, its dry surface greedy for more. But as Ọwa always said, *Aná* was a fair and just deity, who delivered what she promised. The quantity of blood was irrelevant. A single drop was sufficient to awaken her might.

Aku felt the ground heave beneath her. Her breath caught in her throat as she gave a startled cry. The earth cracked and the flies spewed out in their ferocious, deafening flight; the celestial flies, the forbearers of the great Earth Goddess. The swarm coalesced by the entrance of the shrine, whirling like a black tornado, sculpturing themselves in the smoky gloom till a dark figure emerged, a body formed from flies, a figure shaped like a woman, a towering, terrifying, night-black woman. The figure was so colossal it filled the shrine, seeming to extend beyond the dry, thatched roof. The fly-body swelled and rolled, whirled and surged as it undulated its terrible walk towards the black blood-coated statue. Aku's head expanded and contracted. Millions of hard glittering fly-eyes blinded her sight as the great goddess drew closer. Suddenly, the candles winked out, plunging the shrine in terrifying blackness. Aku's breath caught behind her throat; her limbs grew weak. A dark fog, denser than the towering figure of *Aná,* clouded her vision. Her hands let go of Ọwa's hands as her knees buckled beneath her. Aku fainted.

4

Mbana-Oyi – The Cold Realm

The blood sludge, the vast expanse of blood river, glistened in the eternal night of *Mbana-Oyi, The Cold Realm.* Alive with malignant intelligence, its stagnant mire stretched beyond what the human eyes could see. But the only human eyes that saw the blood sludge were dead eyes, young dead eyes, victims of the fearsome siblings that ruled *Mbana-Oyi,* the dominion of the untimely dead. The blood sludge, the collective blood of countless young souls now soured by corruption, pulsed with a silent power that brought shivers of unadulterated terror to each new soul that ended up in its sticky grip. Billions of cold, glassy eyes littered the red mire, staring with hopeless desperation into the black soil-sky of The Cold Realm.

Airless, odourless and soundless, *Mbana-Oyi* weaved its nightmares on its single visible victim, a young woman with skin of gold and hair of straw. Sunk to her waist in the farthest stretch of the blood sludge, Xikora lived out endless solitary days of eternal nights, absorbing the tragedies of mankind. Her dancing blue eyes held the wildness of madness, yet, glittered with defiant resolve. Each young soul that was stolen by the rogue siblings of death, told its own painful story; each pair of young eyes that dropped into the quagmire of the blood sludge, brought their own horrors with them, the violent, tragic horrors of their untimely deaths. Xikora saw them all, heard them all, absorbed them all inside each pore of her body, every tiny corner of her brain.

Hers was a prison without hope of escape, a curse without a cure. Her Earth Goddess was an unforgiving deity, a brutal mother who turned her back on the children that betrayed her. And for the love of a man, a mere mortal man, she, Xikora, the high priestess of *Aná,* had betrayed both her deity and her only child. For her punishment, she had been abandoned to her fate, the fate decided for her by her arch enemies, the rogue death deities, Walking Grave and his vile sister, Corpse Maker, she that devours the souls of infants in their mothers' wombs. They would seek to break her spirit, torment her soul to destruction. *Ha!*

Xikora's wild laughter rang out in the eternal silent expanse of The Cold Realm. *She'd shown them; in Aná's name, she'd shown them both! She had not been the most feared medicine-woman in her lifetime for nothing.* Even in death, even with the desertion of her deity, she had retained some of her powers. Her hands had not let her down in the end, hands she had sealed with the darkest charms and empowered with the strongest talisman in her lifetime. Her hands pulsed with a life of their own. They could transverse both the realms of man and spirit to gather the secret ingredients of her art.

And so, she had searched, probed, stretched her mind to its limit till she pierced through the black soil-sky of The Cold Realm and found her daughter's mind, made her very first contact with the child she had abandoned with death. Through countless nights, she had weaved her thoughts into her little girl's dreams. Except for her darkest spell, the *Leloole* curse, all the other secrets of her art, the greatest mysteries of the shrine which she had taken to her untimely grave, were now in her daughter's possession. In the end, she had trained her daughter in the ways of the cult of *Aná* as if she'd never left the realm of mankind for *Mbana-Oyi*. *Aná* must be satisfied with the priestess she had fashioned from the depths of hell, a priestess whose exploits in the underworld brought the rage of helplessness to even the two fearsome deities of death that were her jailors. Surely, it was only a matter of time before the Earth Goddess relented and set her free from the accursed trap of the terrible siblings; permit her to re-join her ancestors for a glorious rebirth.

***

Owa glided across the infinite vastness of the blood sludge, her eyes clear and bright in the shadow realm. Her movements were smooth, confident, fearless. She knew where she was going and what she would see – who she would see. She had made the journey countless times and each time, the rage in her heart never abated. Were the Earth Goddess human, Ọwa would have called her out, engaged her in a physical fight and forced her to free the pitiful creature trapped in the blood sludge of *Mbana-Oyi*, her poor mother, Xikora.

Ọwa spied her mother's exposed upper torso from a distance and sped up her flight. A thin, blue light seeping from her palms followed her trail, linking her to the black soil-sky of *Mbana-Oyi*.

'Precious daughter, my sun and moon, she that brings the tears of pride and regret to her mother's eyes! I welcome you, good daughter, with loving arms.'

The voice was the same as Ọwa remembered all those years of her childhood, lilting and strong.

'Mama! Peerless paragon! How my heart smiles with joy at the sight of you once again!' Ọwa hugged her mother, their phosphorous forms merging in a blazing combustion that lit up the shadow realm like fireworks. Mother and child giggled, laughed, their voices loud and joyful. There was no need for caution. A border war raged between rival villages in the land of the humans. Several widows and orphans would be created before the fighting was done. The fearsome guardians of *Mbana-Oyi* would not be back till their feasting was over and their bodies bloated with the souls of the untimely dead.

'Good daughter, how fare you? How is my granddaughter? Is she growing in our art? Will I ever get to see her? How long before she masters the art of night diplomacy and pays a long-overdue visit to her yearning grandmother?' The questions tumbled with excited frenzy from the full lips of the trapped woman.

'All is as well as it can be, Mama,' Qwa's smile was wry. 'Your granddaughter keeps resisting and I keep insisting. But, as surely as a new-born will seek its mother's breasts, she will follow her destiny in the end. As our people say, the termite can fly high and fly wide but in the end, it must fall into the long tongue of the wily frog,' Qwa laughed, stroking her mother's hand, rubbing the black mole on Xikora's nose, just as she did in her childhood. The blue light on her palms glowed even brighter, stronger. 'Look, Mama. See how bright the link-line is,' she raised her glowing palms to her mother's face. 'Yes, your granddaughter grows in our art with each passing day. I've had little need for the shrine-goat ever since she learnt how to guard my soul during my night-diplomacy. With Aku guarding over my mortal body, I have no fear of my spirit getting lost and becoming trapped in the realm of the dead. May *Aná* be praised for her goodness and protection.'

'*Ise!* So be it! You have done well, daughter. My pride in you is boundless. I hear the cruel ones, my vile captors, curse your name with frequent fury each time you visit. They pray for your fall just as I fell. They would do to you what they have done to me. But I laugh at them. I taunt them with your name, my daughter's name, Qwa, my full moon that lights up a beautiful world they can only visit but never inhabit. My daughter is no fool like her mother. She will not fall by the wayside as I did, never betray our Earth Goddess as her foolish mother did, not for the love of man or money.' Xikora's voice rang out with pride. 'Walking-Grave and Corpse-Maker are helpless where you're concerned. Their helplessness fills them with fury, and their fury fills my heart with glee. Good daughter, remain steadfast in your service to our Earth Mother and none can harm you till she calls you home. *Aná* is the oldest of all the deities, she who was before life and death were created. The favoured of *Aná* are the true blessed of the earth.'

Xikora lapsed into morose silence as was always the case when she recalled her glorious days as the powerful high-priestess of the Earth Goddess and the youthful folly that cost her that life and her eternal soul. Her thumb rubbed the mole on her nose with distracted frenzy. It was an action Qwa remembered from her childhood days, something Xikora did when she was deep in thought or plotting terrible damage to some unwary soul. Qwa remained quiet by her mother's side, stroking her hands gently, pink hands that pulsed with a vibrancy and warmth absent from the rest of her body. She willed the vibrant heat of her life-force into the cold heart of her mother, keeping her body afloat, avoiding contact with the blood sludge. She couldn't afford to contaminate her soul with the pain and fury of the countless young souls trapped underneath the gleaming sludge. She was aware of their cold eyes following her every move, watching, calling out to her with silent desperation. They would fill her mind with madness if she let their voices into her head. Unlike her mother, they did not possess the powers of the Earth Goddess, the secrets of spell casting. They could not rise from the dense mire that kept their souls submerged underneath the blood sludge. Yet, their countless, glassy eyes littered the thick red expanse, all seeing, all knowing, greedy and desperate for the heat of life.

Qwa placed her forehead against her mother's own and allowed the joyful thoughts to flow from her head into her mother's tortured mind. She felt Xikora's mind probe, reach out into her mind and take the pictures she freely gave. Images danced in vibrant colours. *Her daughter, Aku, sleeping peacefully on her bed, her sweet face calm and lovely in her deep slumber; a plump mother-hen digging the food dance in the sandy soil for worms to feed her little yellow chicks; the lush yam farms with mature tendrils climbing their wooden poles, forming a rich green sentinel over the yam tubers nestling in their raised mounds; Ebele, her white shrine-goat with the greedy mouth that chewed in the funniest manner; colourful masquerades dancing to the vibrant beats of the drums; happy marriage ceremonies and joyful libations to the great ancestors.* Qwa allowed all the good memories to flow from her mind into her mother's own, healing memories, soul-balm.

Gradually, the dark clouds lifted from Xikora's face, replaced by a radiant smile that almost brought some vestige of beauty back to the ravaged features. Ọwa's heart glowed. Her good memories had once again chased away the nightmares of *Mbana-Oyi* from her mother's head. It was a temporary relief. The horrors of the blood sludge would come back again to reclaim her mother's mind. But while the effects of her memory infusion lasted, Xikora would get some much-needed solace from her sad burden.

Ọwa's arm jerked. She looked down and gasped. The blue light had snapped from one palm, her right palm. A cold chill crawled into her spine. She had over-stayed her visit. She should have gone several minutes ago, before Aku's concentration waned. There was only so long the girl could guard her body and guide her soul; not till she was fully trained in their art. The last thing Ọwa wanted was to be discovered by the fearsome duo that ruled The Cold Realm. That would be self-murder and she was no fool.

Walking-Grave and Corpse-Maker were aware of her nocturnal visits to her mother. They would give a hundred souls to catch and entrap her in their dark realm. But she'd always timed her visits to coincide with their absence, during periods of human tragedies, fatal accidents, bus crashes, plane crashes, boat capsizings, petrol pipe explosions, ethnic clashes and border wars, deadly outbreak of diseases and epidemics, Ebola, Lassa Fever, Cholera, Yellow Fever; natural calamities, floods, quakes, wild fires. The rogue death deities would never be found in their realm at such times of human anguish. Their greed for blood would not allow them to miss an opportunity to collect more unready souls.

'Mama, I have to go now,' Qwa's voice was rushed, hushed. 'Stay strong for me, okay?' Her grip on Xikora's hand was tight. Her face grew hard, blue eyes dancing cold. 'If it's the last thing I do, I'll yet get our Earth Mother to forgive and set you free. With each day that passes, I extend myself, grow my powers in her service. My life is a sacrifice to her and surely, a faithful servant deserves a reward. Have faith, Mama. All will be well.'

With a final merging of souls, Qwa hugged her mother goodbye and floated upwards towards the soil-sky of *Mbana-Oyi,* frantically trying to hold onto the fading blue light in her left palm. Already, her right arm felt numb, lifeless, deprived of the light of life. She felt dark rage rising from the pits of her stomach, rage against her careless daughter who had allowed her concentration to lapse, jeopardising her life. She pushed back the fury, fought off the malignant influence of *Mbana-Oyi* that would poison her love for her daughter. She pushed upwards, rising, surging. Just as her arms reached out to the dark soil-border of the realm of man and death, the blue light in her left hand winked out and a pair of cold, freezing claws grabbed her feet, pulling her down, lower, deeper.

Qwa felt a chill, the like of which she'd never imagined, crawl into her bones, numbing her marrow in seconds. It was a chill of terror, the cold of nightmares, fear beyond anything the human mind could conceive. Death's claw was a touch no human should experience, even a medicine-woman as herself, steeped in the mysteries of the underworld. All her life she had flirted with death, roamed its realm, raged against its evil. And now she was finally touched by it, Qwa realised how pitiful her powers were, how puny her spectral body was, how fearful her heart was, how unprepared she was to challenge the fearsome death siblings of *Mbana-Oyi*.

Qwa began to pray. She prayed as she had never done in the entire forty years of her existence. She called to the only god she had ever known, the one deity to whom she had dedicated her life and soul. She screamed out *Aná*'s name, her deep voice hoarse, its resonance stolen by terror. The temperature plunged even lower, raising grey vapours from the blood sludge. Below, she heard her mother's terrified screams raging against the Earth Goddess.

'Fight, daughter; fight!' Xikora shouted. 'Summon all the powers, all the knowledge I've ever given you and fight for your soul. Don't waste your breath calling our heartless deity. She will not save you from these vile demons. *Aná* is a goddess without a heart, a mother that will let her children suffer and die without shedding a tear. The god you serve is a deaf god. Trust only in yourself, in your powers, never in *Aná*.'

The victorious shrieks of the gruesome duo, Walking-Grave and Corpse-Maker, drowned her mother's screams. Qwa ignored

Xikora's shrieks and continued to call on the Earth Goddess. The darkness grew denser, stealing her sight, clouding her mind. She was none-flesh, a spirit being in the realm of the dead. Yet, Death's touch killed her senses as if she still wore the flesh of mortality. The end was near and there was nothing she could do to save herself. All her life, she had yearned for a chance to avenge herself on the deadly duo that stole her mother and her little brother and left her an orphan at an age every child should be with a loving parent. Yet, now she had finally come face-to-face with them, she was as helpless as a day-old chick against a killer eagle.

A fly buzzed in her ear. It was a sound so alien to *Mbana-Oyi* that it took Ọwa a few confusing seconds to register what the sound was. A second fly grazed her forehead and Ọwa's heart soared. She smelled the presence before she heard the voice. It was the smell of wet soil after the rain, of dry dust in the harshest Harmattan, of tree roots and green leaves, ripe fruits and decayed foliage. It was the musky odour of sweaty skin and the metallic smell of blood. Yet, above it all, it was the terrifying smell of rank decay, the cloying scent of a billion rotten bodies and bloated corpse flies.

Aná! Ọwa let out a cry of victory. *The great Earth Goddess had arrived. She had heard the cries of her servant. Aná had not forsaken her child after all!* The hold on her feet instantly loosened and the crippling chill vanished. She soared upwards once again, towards the black soil-sky of *Mbana-Oyi* and straight into the waiting arms of the Earth Mother. Her eyes were still clouded and she could not see the great deity. But she felt the soft warmth of a trillion whirling flies, the sweet sensation of moist soil and mushy leaves that was the body of the Earth Goddess.

'That soul belongs to us! She trespassed on our realm. You cannot take her away from us!' Corpse-Maker's voice was an angry shriek. Her brother, Walking-Grave, added his protest, his voice heavy with menace. 'Even you, great goddess, cannot disrespect us so in our own realm. Hand us back our feast. She belongs to us.'

'Silence, vile saplings!' *Aná's* voice thundered across the endless expanse of *Mbana-Oyi*, wreaking sudden turbulence in the blood sludge. Even the soil-sky trembled, showering Qwa with loose soil. 'You can only take what *Aná* freely gives and nothing more.' *Aná's* voice was the rumble of the earth in a quake, the shrieking of the winds in a storm, the crashing of the waves in troubled waters. It was the Earth Goddess as Qwa had never heard her before. Gone was the gentle rustling of leaves, the sweet tinkling of clear spring over white pebbles, the soft pattering of gentle paws on soft earth, the loving voice of a good mother which had guided Qwa's dreams from the day she first embraced her destiny as a child. The death deities shrank away, morphing rapidly into shadows, hiding their dark forms in the perpetual gloom of their cold realm. They became invisible to ordinary eyes, to Qwa's eyes, which were fast closing in weariness beyond anything she'd ever experienced. Sleep beckoned. It was like the sleep of death except she was in the loving arms of the Earth Mother, cocooned in safety and love, free from fear and worries. She would remain in that position for eternity if it were in her power to grant herself that wish.

Her mother's voice pierced through the terrible thunder of *Aná*'s rage. Xikora pleaded with the Earth Goddess to take her along, to free her from the bondage of the blood sludge. She begged for forgiveness, for railing against the name of the great goddess. She asked the Earth Goddess to grant her a rebirth and allow her to redeem herself once more in the service of the great deity. Qwa wanted to add her voice to her mother's own but she was too weak, so tired... *drained.*

'Woman of little faith! Even now, even after all this while, you still doubt, still wallow in your own pride. When will you ever learn?' *Aná*'s voice was the sad howl of a dying wind. It was the last thing Qwa heard before sleep cloaked her mind in a dark cloud of nothingness.

Ω Ω Ω

5

Inside The Grand Room of Mirrors

The Fat-Man stooped low and walked through the dwarf door of the mud hut that housed the shrine of *Aku-n'uba*, the deity of wealth. He groped the wooden doorframe, steadying himself as he entered the dark interior of the shrine. He kept his eyes tightly shut as he'd been instructed by the witchdoctor. For several silent minutes, Eze stood still, inhaling the unique smell of the shrine, a cross between burnt wood, fresh blood and palm wine. A sudden feeling of awe overwhelmed him, causing goose pimples to litter his flesh.

He'd finally done it! After so many months of seeking, bribing and hoping, he had finally gained access into the most secretive and infamous shrine in the entire country, the shrine of *Aku-n'uba*, the place that housed the famed Grand Room of Mirrors, the black mirrors of destiny. Eze shook his head in disbelief. A slow smile of satisfaction spread across his knife-scarred face. With unsteady hands, he slowly removed his clothes as he'd been told to do by the witchdoctor, Dibia Ogam, the guardian of the shrine. He kept a tight grip on the sealed jar given him by the witchdoctor, careful not to drop it as he pulled off his kaftan and vest. His shoes were outside the shrine. Only bare human feet were allowed into the sacred shrine. Quickly, Eze gathered his clothes and jay-walked himself across the room till his outstretched arm connected with a wall.

He stooped and placed the items on the floor, hearing the low thud made by his mobile phone inside the pocket of his discarded kaftan. Straightening again, he opened the jar of oil given him by Dibia Ogam and sniffed it. He wrinkled his nose. A foul odour filled the room, a cross between rotten chicken flesh and soured cassava. Eze hesitated, debating whether to discard the jar unused or follow the witch-doctor's instructions to the letter.

In the end, his greed got the better of him. He hadn't gone through all the trouble to gain entrance into the great shrine only to sabotage his goals with his own finicky shenanigans. With brisk determination, Eze quickly coated himself with the noxious oils, covering every inch of his massive, obese frame with the foul grease. When he was done, he allowed the jar to roll away to one corner of the room and stood for several minutes gearing himself to open his eyes. *The moment had come.* He had prepared his body for the shrine as instructed by the witchdoctor. Now, he could finally open his eyes and see for the first time a sight very few men had seen, the interior of the sacred shrine of the great deity of wealth, *Aku-n'uba.*

Eze opened his eyes and gasped. His stunned gaze took in every inch of the square box-room of the shrine. The room was dark, devoid of both natural and artificial lights. Yet, a murky glow coated the interior, a glow that allowed Eze's red-hued eyes to observe every inch and corner of the shrine. The room was bare save for a dwarf wooden stool placed right in the middle of a square raffia mat. The walls in the room, including the floor he stood on, were covered in mirrors, mirrors that glimmered with a dark brilliance that sent a sudden chill up Eze's spine. The mirrors were black, blacker than the hair that coated his head, blacker than the darkest moon-less night. Eze had never seen a black mirror in his life, never knew that such a mirror existed till he heard about it from another witchdoctor he had visited. Even then, he had doubted the veracity of the claim.

Till now. *The black mirrors of destiny!*

A sudden wave of terror shock Eze's body as it dawned on him that the black mirrors actually reflected images. In its dark smooth surface, Eze picked out the white bundle of his clothes against the left wall. He saw the discarded jar of oil where it nestled close to the dwarf door of the shrine. His eyes zoomed into the dwarf wooden stool in the centre of the room and the raffia mat underneath it. Yet, search as he could, peer as hard as he did, he could not find his own reflection in the black mirrors. From the left to the right walls, the front to the back walls, the mirrored ceiling to the mirrored floor, he could not see the massive frame that was his naked body in the black mirrors of destiny. It was as if he had ceased to exist, as if he had been devoured and nestled unseen inside a great belly. The absence of his reflection in the black mirrors terrified Eze as nothing in his life had ever done.

Then the floor began to vibrate. A gasp escaped Eze's lip. He hopped away from where he stood and landed clumsily close to the dwarf stool. The stool shook as if an invisible hand rocked it. Eze backed away from it as one would a deadly viper. The ground continued to quake beneath his bare feet, sending shafts of electric shock up his nerves. Then, the mirror-wall to his left began to glow. Eze wasn't sure if to call it a glow or a humming light. The hum was like the deep, wordless chorus of a thousand men. Images began to appear on the glowing wall, images that brought a gasp of surprise and a rush of adrenaline to his heart. Eze stared.

What his eyes beheld was beyond anything Eze had ever imagined. In the humming mirror, he finally saw his reflection. But not himself as he was, nude and oiled inside the Grand Room of Mirrors. No. Instead, the image reflected to him was that of a well-groomed man dripping in opulence. He saw himself clad in garbs he had only ever seen in high-class Nollywood films and the acclaimed *Ovation* magazine. He was entertaining guests in a house he could only describe as palatial. Everywhere he looked revealed more opulence than he'd ever thought possible. Expensive cars with personalised number plates bearing his name – EZE 1, lined up in front of his mansion. Uniformed servants and liveried chauffeurs stood to attention while countless tables groaned under the weight of assorted drinks and exotic foods. People, men and women in stupendous colourful outfits, fawned over him, hanging onto his every sentence.

Eze's breath came in rapid, hot rasps. His heart beat so fast he raised his hand to his chest, seeking to still it, calm its race. *'Chei! Chei! Chei!'* The exclamations spilled from his lips, over and over as he pounded his fists into the air. Hot sweat dripped from his head down his hairy chest, sprinkling the floor with tiny dots of salty moisture. Even as he shouted in triumph, the images began to fade. Figures winked out of the mirror-screen one by one, till only the large reflection of Eze's doppelganger remained in the mirror, staring sightlessly into the room. Soon, it too winked away and the mirror went black. Eze groaned. He hadn't seen enough. The awesome vision ended too soon.

Then, the right mirror-wall began to glow with a piercing whistle that sounded like the shrill of a million crickets. Eze's heart leapt. Joy blazed in his eyes. He quickly turned to face the wall, this time without the fear that had accompanied the first revelation. He could barely wait to see what awaited him in the right mirror-wall. And like the left mirror, this mirror did not disappoint. The pictures began to unfold. Eze saw himself engaged in an intense conversation with none other than the president of the country and his innermost cabinet at the impressive presidential house in *Aso-*

Rock. He saw himself signing multi-billion contracts, international crude oil agreements worth billions of *Naira* currency. On the walls above him, photos of presidents, past and present, smiled benignly down at him. The image changed, like instant polaroid pictures pushed out of ready cameras, as the next segment segued into the screen. He saw himself drinking celebratory glasses of Champagne and shaking hands with foreign diplomats. A flash of lights on the mirror-wall revealed yet more scintillating images; resplendent depictions of himself conducting tours of several massive manufacturing factories, head bent in intense private discussions with Chinese and Arab men in flowing white garbs, giving terse orders to thousands of employees and boarding private jets to exotic destinations. A motorcade of police escorts, lights flashing, followed his every move.

'*Chei! Chei! Chei!*' Again, Eze was robbed of speech by the visions flashing across the black mirrors. Little giggles escaped his lips like the secret titters of a teenage girl after her first romantic encounter. He wanted to shout, share his glorious knowledge with the whole world. Instead, he forced himself to restrain his glee till the revelations were over.

The wall in front of him, the one nearest to the door, began glowing with its own special music, whispered echoes that sounded like soft breaths, deep sighs, gentle moans. Eze awaited its revelations with excited impatience. And when it came, it dazzled him as nothing else that came before had done. On the mirror screen, he was sprawled on a circular king-size bed inside a room with walls of red paint and tasselled curtains of the purest gold. But he wasn't alone in the bed. With him were the most beautiful women he had ever seen. They were all over him, doing things to his body he never knew were possible, titillating things which even his third wife, Oge, couldn't do for all the *Naira* in the world. There were black women, white women, Chinese women, Indian women, mixed-race women, every variety of exotic womanhood playing out their fantasies on his supine body. He was a ram, a bull, a Viagra-defying wonder, satisfying the lust of the women with indefatigable stamina.

As he stared with rapt attention at the erotic images playing out in the mirror in front of him, Eze felt himself hardening. His breath rushed out of his open mouth and hot sweat dampened his oiled body. His mind silently screamed the habitual *"Chei!"* but his tongue clung drily to his mouth, killing his speech. All he could do was make soft moaning sounds similar to the noises that accompanied the glow of the mirror-wall.

Then, like the previous images, the mirror winked out the women just as the sound of beating drums rose from the mirror to his back. There was something unsettling about the steady low beat of the drums that sent the sudden chill to Eze's heart. Suddenly, he did not want to see that final wall; didn't want to look into its black surface and see what it had to reveal. The drums maintained the steady low beats of a dirge, filling his heart with terror. With great effort, Eze turned his large bulk around to face the only wall he had yet to see.

He frowned. Puzzlement coated his pupils. The last mirror was blank. Its black sheen revealed nothing, not even the wooden stool or raffia mat in the room. A dim glow emitted from the wall, a glow that was like the murky light of the shrine before the mirror movies lit up the room. Eze stepped forward for a closer inspection. Perhaps it wasn't a mirror after all, just a wall painted with glossy black paint, giving the false impression of a black mirror. He reached out a hand to touch the wall and in that instance, the room went black and the drums ceased. Every vestige of light vanished from the shrine. *Bloody NEPA!* Eze cursed the Nigerian Electricity Power Authority, NEPA, who were able to generate electricity supply to every neighbouring African country except to Nigerians. He turned and groped his way towards the wall where he had placed his clothes. He bumped into the wooden stool and grazed his knees. Another loud curse spilled from his lips. He went on hands and knees till he finally made contact with the soft fabric of his kaftan. A sigh of relief replaced the curses. He pulled out his mobile phone from his pocket and switched on the torch. The phone lit up, casting the room in a dirty yellow glow. Eze hurriedly pulled on his trousers, uncaring whether they were inside out or normal. He had seen what he came to see, his future, his incredible, wonderful future. The Grand Room of Mirrors had lived up to its reputation. He would gladly pay its guardian, Dibia Ogam, his fee and return to his house to await the realisation of his amazing future.

The thought of returning to the storey building he had inherited from his late father dampened Eze's spirits. After the visions of opulence he'd just witnessed, even driving his trusty Peugeot car now filled him with disgust. The sooner he found out from the medicine-man how quickly his vision would manifest, the happier he'd be. He'd go crazy if he had to wait any length of time for it to materialise. He wouldn't mind paying Dibia Ogam extra to speed up the process. Eze turned towards the direction of the door to exit the room. He paused, deep furrows burrowing into his forehead. He could have sworn the door was towards the right wall. In fact, he was positive the witch-doctor had led him to a dwarf door positioned at the very spot he was staring at. Except there was no door there anymore. All he saw were blank walls of black mirrors each direction he turned.

His mobile beeped a warning sound; his battery was running low. Eze cursed both mobile and witch-doctor and began banging on the mirror walls, shouting out to the witch-doctor. He paused to listen, just in case Dibia Ogam was letting him out. *Nothing.* Just then, his mobile beeped a frantic succession of warnings and died out, as if drained of power by a vampire appliance. It plunged the shrine into a darkness that was as total as the silence in the room. Eze was fast running out of curses as he resumed his knocks, wincing as his knuckles absorbed the hard, cold surface of the mirror walls. A sudden thought worked its way into his mind, halting his actions. *What if it was a trap? What if Dibia Ogam planned to rob him, trick him with fake images and then use him for human sacrifice for his nefarious art?* Eze wasn't born yesterday. He knew how these things worked; human body parts harvested for potent *Juju* medicine. After all, he was in the system, a part and parcel of the dark arts. His last election victory had been down to the exorbitant sum he'd paid for a pair of women's breasts, which his witch-doctor used to work his magic. Nobody, not even his highly-educated opponent, had expected him, a mere illiterate rice trader, to win, Yet, he had defied the odds at the poll on election day. And it had all been down to the efficacy of the powerful *Juju* brewed by his *Dibia.* His "Thank You" envelope had been very generous, in fact, so generous that his witch-doctor had moved the heavens to secure him this highly-coveted audience inside the famed Grand Room of Mirrors.

Recalling everything calmed Eze's racing heart and frenzied thoughts. He trusted his own *Dibia* with his life. The medicine-man would never send him anywhere that was detrimental to his safety and well-being. Theirs was a relationship sealed in blood, going back years too numerous to count. The Grand Room of Mirrors had shown him things that were beyond magic. He had seen his future, a wealthy and powerful future, not a future as the sacrificial body for a witch-doctor's brew.

Eze fumbled his way to the low stool and sat down. He would wait out NEPA and the witch-doctor and whatever else was to come. Dibia Ogam knew where he was and would come and let him out at the right time. He fiddled with his mobile, hoping for a signal. He peered into the darkness, just in case the dwarf door reappeared as miraculously as it had disappeared. He rubbed his sore knuckles, swearing once more at the witch-doctor. *Rubbish man had better not have left him trapped inside the shrine while he was off somewhere drinking palm-wine with his cronies.*

Eze shut his eyes and allowed his thoughts to drift. His mind's eyes re-lived everything he'd seen on the black mirror walls. For several silent minutes, his heart pulsed with a steady joyful beat as he recalled the glorious images he had seen inside the shrine. An unfamiliar peace descended on him. The tension in his temples slowly ebbed and the tight knots around his neck loosened. His eyes felt heavy and his breathing slowed to the deep lull of approaching slumber. He inhaled deeply, exhaled loudly, dropped his chin to his chest and allowed his eyes to close in grateful sleep.

***

The cold woke him up, the sudden chill that hit the room with the fury of a tempest. The Grand Room of Mirrors shrieked with the sound of a major hurricane. Gusts of icy winds lashed his face, sending him flying from his stool. Eze crashed to the floor with a loud shout which was drowned out by the shrieking winds. He was dragged across the smooth mirrored floor and smashed against the hard, black walls. He was a big man, weighed over three hundred pounds. Yet, the freezing wind tossed him about as if he weighed no more than a chicken feather.

Just when he thought he couldn't endure another second of pain, that his body could not survive the battering assault a minute longer, the fury died. Without warning, as rapidly as it had begun, the hurricane ceased. Eze found himself cradling what felt like a broken left arm on the icy floor of the shrine. The silence was once more as total as the darkness, broken only by his harsh sobs and hard breathing. He crawled across the room on his knees, moaning softly as his broken arm banged against his thigh. He shouted again, screaming that he was hurt, that he needed desperate medical attention, that he was dying. He held his breath and cocked his ears. Nothing moved, either inside or outside the shrine. He wasn't getting rescued. Eze tried to stem the rising terror in his heart, the fear that he might never leave the Grand Room of Mirrors alive. He was trapped in a supernatural chamber, haunted by unknown entities whose intentions seemed to him as malignant as the pitch darkness of the room. A sound pierced through his panicked thoughts, a choking sound. It came from his open mouth. He was slobbering like one of his three wives after he'd given them a good thrashing, snot and tears trailing the hot skin of his face. He halted his sobs, mortified by his weakness. He scrambled across the smooth mirror floor, seeking his mobile phone.

His hand connected with something smooth and hard. It was the jar of *Juju* oil the witch-doctor had given him. He pushed it away with an angry oath. His feet hit something, kicked it away. He scrambled after it, left out a loud shout of relief when his hand held the familiar rectangular shape of his mobile phone. Miraculously, it had survived the hurricane's assault, more than he could say for himself. He slumped back on his bottom, cradling his mobile phone like a dying sinner clutching his priest's rosary. His thumb pressed the device from habit, hoping… praying it would have miraculously recharged itself. But it lay in his hand as cold and black as the floor he sat on.

Then, someone touched him. In the darkness, a hand touched his left shoulder, an open palm so icy it burnt like the reddest flame. It happened so quickly that Eze barely had time to register it before he was writhing on the floor, wailing, wracked with pain that was beyond anything he'd ever felt. He howled, reaching up a hand to feel the spot where the icy hand had touched. Again, he screamed as his hand encountered the charred skin of his shoulder.

He scrambled in the dark, blindly, like a stunned cockroach seeking escape from a housewife's broom. His head bumped into the hard surface of the mirror wall. He groaned and slumped against the wall, cowering in terror, offering prayers and promises to his known and unknown ancestors, pleading for forgiveness for sins remembered and those forgotten.

For the first time, Eze found himself dealing with something he could neither kill nor order his thugs to kill, an entity he could neither see nor touch, a malignant power that terrified him as he'd never experienced in his fifty years of violent existence. Eze began to sob anew, pride and strength sapped from his body like the hot piss that dampened his trousers. His huge frame shook like wind-tossed leaves in the midst of an African thunderstorm.

Ω Ω Ω

6

The Black Hand

The door opened with a long, slow creak, bringing shards of golden sunshine into the shrine. It pierced through the black iciness of the room, turning the black mirrors into a glorious blaze of light. They sparkled, leaving pin-dots of rainbow all around the room. Eze gasped in surprise, stifling a sob. His eyes pooled again, this time with tears of relief. He struggled to his feet and stumbled towards the open door, the same dwarf door he recalled entering and yet, had inexplicably vanished during his terrifying ordeal in the Grand Room of Mirrors. The stench of his fear-piss followed him out of the room.

'Ah! You're out,' the witch-doctor called out to him from his high-backed chair at his veranda across the shrine. He looked so calm and cool underneath the blazing mid-day sun that Eze instantly saw red.

'Ha! *Ekwensu!* Devil! I am out and no thanks to you,' Eze yelled, his eyes burning with rage. He stumbled towards Dibia Ogam, menace in every limb of his massive frame. The shrivelled witch-doctor watched his approach with an impassive face. His small eyes revealed neither fear nor anger. He maintained eye contact with Eze as the big man drew nearer, his right arm raised to

94

strike a devastating blow. The witchdoctor shook his head, weary contempt icing his dark pupils.

'You are truly a blind man,' Dibia Ogam said, his voice quiet, like a disappointed teacher to a wilful pupil.

In a blink, the world went black. Eze's eyes rolled back, retreating into his sockets till only the whites showed. His arm, raised in attack, fell to his side as he let out a loud shout, rubbing his eyes furiously to clear the sudden black fog clouding his vision. He stumbled, tripped on his feet and fell to the ground, hitting the hard cement of the veranda with a heavy thud. He howled in agony as his broken left arm cracked in two new places. His humiliation was complete, sprawled out in blind indignity on the dirty floor of the witch-doctor's veranda, covered in his own piss and bawling like a little boy having his circumcision ritual. In his black haze, Eze suddenly saw the light of wisdom, realised the awesome powers of the forces he was dealing with. For the first time in a lifetime of megalomania, he discovered true humility and reverence.

'*Oke Dibia!* Great medicine-man! Forgive!' Eze's voice was hoarse, almost a whisper. 'Forgive this stupid, rice-brained chicken that dares to mistake his puny feathers for an eagle's mighty wings. Pardon this worthless kitten that dares to raise his tiny paws to the great lion's claws. What am I but an ignorant fool? Look, my knees are on the floor. Forgive, powerful *Dibia*. Your will is my will.' Eze scrambled to a kneeling position, turning his head from left to right in search of the witch-doctor. His sightless eyes were wide with terror and confusion.

A chair scrapped on the cement floor. Firm footsteps drew closer to him. A faint odour of tobacco snuff and palm-kennel oil wafted up his nostrils. Eze felt eyes boring into him, a powerful mind burrowing into his brain, probing, seeking out his true thoughts, searching for mendacity, pride, anger. But his head was free from treachery and vanity. He knew he was in the presence of a power superior to his own. He felt a burning sensation on his skin as a chaffed hand touched the tender spot on his shoulder, the same spot where earlier, another hand, an icy hand, had scorched inside the Grand Room of Mirrors. He winced, forcing himself to withhold a cry. He didn't want to disgrace himself any further before the powerful medicine-man.

'Aahh! It's amazing how bright *Amadioha*'s sun can be on a hot afternoon,' Dibia Ogam's voice was warm. 'Open your eyes and see the great wonders of the gods all around us.' Eze felt the warm tears of joy flow down his cheeks as the dense fog in his eyes suddenly cleared, leaving him blinking from the blinding brilliance of the afternoon sun. Dibia Ogam reached down a hand to help him to his feet. His grip had a surprising strength, the strength of two young men in the body of the withered, old medicine-man. '*Enyi*, good friend, come and share *Oji*, Kola-nut, and some palm-wine with me,' the witch-doctor said, making his way back to his high chair. Eze followed him, his gait unsteady, sweat pouring down his fleshy face. Dibia Ogam pulled up a chair for Eze and he collapsed into it, careful not to bump his injured arm on the wooden arm-rest. Dibia Ogam poured foamy *Nkwu-ocha,* palm-wine, into tin cups and passed one over to Eze.

'This palm-wine was tapped fresh from my favourite palm-tree this morning. So, it is as sweet and potent as you can expect. Not like the rubbish, water-diluted brand you city folks drink,' Dibia Ogam flicked off a couple of dead flies from his cup of palm-wine. Eze drained his cup before the witch-doctor could recite the obligatory salutations to the ancestors that went with the ritual of palm-wine drinking.

'Sorry,' Eze mumbled, his eyes lowered in embarrassment. He passed the empty cup back to Dibia Ogam. 'I was very thirsty, you understand... after everything that happened in the Grand Room of M...mirrors.' He could barely get himself to mention the word, "mirrors". Such was the terror that his ordeal still brought to his heart.

'No need for apologies, my friend,' Dibia Ogam smiled kindly at him, refilling his cup. 'Even the greatest warrior can be felled by the bite of something as tiny as a mosquito. Drink till your thirst is slaked. Not everyone that enters that shrine comes out alive or with all their senses intact. And even more significantly, not everyone that enters the Grand Room of Mirrors is touched by The Black Hand of destiny. You are truly a great man; for only the great are touched by The Black Hand.' Dibia Ogam reached down his side and pulled up a raffia bag, faded and frayed with age. From inside the bag, he brought out a square framed mirror. He held it out to Eze. 'Look at your shoulder, friend. Look and see for yourself the mark of The Black Hand, the seal of your destiny.'

Eze took the mirror and raised it to his naked chest. He looked at his reflection in the mirror and his eyes widened. '*Chei!*' His voice shrilled with a mixture of terror and awe. In the mirror, he saw the plump, smooth skin of his left shoulder, and the clear imprint of a black hand stamped on it like the dark drawing of a lunatic mind. Four giant, black fingers reached down to his chest while a thumb crawled into his collarbone. They were all linked to a large black palm that seemed to cover the entire curve of his left shoulder. Eze stared with open-mouthed shock at The Black Hand and turned his stunned gaze to the medicine-man.

'What is this? Great *Dibia,* what is this terrifying mark on my shoulder?' His voice had the scratchy quality of a malaria patient. 'I recall something touching me inside the shrine; I felt its icy touch, an ice that burnt with the heat of fire,' Eze could not suppress the shudder that convulsed his massive frame. 'Whose hand is it? What does it mean? Tell me without delay, great *Dibia,* for even a thirsty man can die in the midst of an ocean. My patience is that of a new baby in search of its mother's breast. Please quench my thirst and satisfy my curiosity.'

The medicine-man smiled. 'Let us finish our Kola-nut first and feed our ancestors and then I will tell you all; for, only a bad son keeps his father waiting for his palm-wine.' Dibia Ogam got up from his chair and walked to the sandy ground of his compound, till he reached a couple of gravestones. He paused before the graves and bowed low. Eze mimicked his actions. Dibia Ogam poured some palm-wine atop the graves and into the earth, watching the dry soil soak up the liquid with greedy speed. 'Aahh! See how our forefathers like this wine! See how they just drink it all up,' he crowed, pouring more wine into the soil. He topped up his cup and handed it to Eze. 'Your turn.'

Eze did as the witch-doctor had done, emptying the cup of palm-wine in the sandy soil and over the graves. And all the while, the medicine-man called on the great ancestors, each by their unique names, *Agu, the killer of lions, Ike, the one with bones of steel, Ofor, you with the heart of justice, Ogu, mighty one that will always avenge a slight.* The witch-doctor praised *Ndichie*, The Old Ones, for their prowess and wisdom, asked for their protection and blessings and finally demanded for their vengeance upon his enemies and detractors. When he was done with the libation, Dibia Ogam led the way back to the cool shade of his veranda. Once seated, he began to break the red Kola-nut into segments, reciting the *Ofor n'Ogu* ritual that accompanied the breaking of Kola-nut in traditional *Igbo* custom.

'To the chicken perched high on the coop and the chicken huddled on the floor of the coop. May they remain equals within the enclosure of the coop!' The medicine man broke off a segment of the Kola-nut.

'*Ise!* So be it!' Eze responded with fervour.

'The eagle flies just as the kite flies. Should any one of them tell the other not to perch on a tall tree when they're tired, then may lightning strike it dead,' he broke off another segment.

'*Ise!* So be it!' Eze repeated the chorus.

'The stubborn chicken that will not stay inside its coop soon learns its lesson inside the soup pot of a wretched widow.'

'*Ise!* So be it!'

'The grasshopper that is killed and eaten by the noisy bumbling bird, *Okpoko*, must be a very stupid grasshopper or a deaf one.'

'*Ise!* So be it!'

'The termite can fly up and it can fly down but in the end, it has to fall into the greedy tongue of a fat frog.'

Ise! So be it!'

'The fly without good advise follows the corpse to the grave'
Ise! So be it!'

'When a child washes his hands very well, he earns the right to sit down amongst his elders and share their meal with them.'

'*Ise!* So be it!'

The witch-doctor broke the last segment of the Kola-nut and popped it into his mouth. Eze copied his action, chewing his Kola-nut as lowly as Dibia Ogam, savouring the slightly bitter taste of the sacred *Oji* nut. The witch-doctor spat into the soil and turned to Eze.

'Today my friend, you have become that favoured child that washed his hands very well. Today, you entered and survived the trials of the Grand Room of Mirrors and now, you shall reap the fruits of your labour,' Dibia Ogam fixed fierce eyes on Eze. 'Are you ready, my man? Answer me with a warrior's voice. Speak like a man. Roar like a lion. Are you ready?'

'Yes! Yes!' Eze's voice rang almost beyond the five compounds that bordered Dibia Ogam's white-washed bungalow. There was a feverish glint in his permanently red-hued eyes. The jagged scars on his face were stark in the noonday sun. His heart raced with excitement. *This was it; what he came for, finally within his grasp!*

'I will need the heart of an albino to make you the Juju that will bind the hearts of your voters and ensure your success in the upcoming election,' the witch-doctor said, his eyes like flints, all warmth and friendliness vanished with the speed of the fast-receding sun. 'You must bring me the hand of an albino for the

Juju that will make you fabulously rich through government contracts signed over to you. Are you listening?'

Eze nodded, his heart pounding. He tried to swallow but his throat was as dry as his mouth.

'Finally, I will need the nipples of an albino woman to make you the Juju of prowess, the powerful medicine that will make you irresistible to women regardless of your looks,' the witch-doctor's eyes scanned Eze's fleshy bulk and scarred face with a wry smile. 'Albinos are not easy to catch, just like dwarves and white men. But their body parts make the most potent Juju as everyone in the trade knows.'

Dibia Ogam picked up the mirror again and held it up to Eze.

'Take a good look again at The Black Hand of destiny,' he said, motioning to Eze's shoulder with a nod. 'You see how black it is against your skin? That is because it has fed on its first blood, your blood. From now onwards, you must keep it fed on an annual diet of blood otherwise, it will vacate your body for a better and more deserving one. The Black Hand will be your guide. It will tell you when it needs to be fed by its colour. It will turn an ashy grey colour which signifies it needs a blood sacrifice. So, nurture it well, for the day it vanishes from your shoulder is the day you will die.'

Eze gasped! His body began to tremble as hot sweat suddenly drenched his skin, staining the white cotton of his kaftan.

'Oke Dibia! Great medicine-man! What is this you say, eh? That I will die if The Black Hand disappears from my shoulder? Why? What kind of blood sacrifice will it need? I did not come here to die. Please, take away The Black Hand; return it to wherever it came from.' Eze cast another terrified look at his shoulder, feeling his skin crawl as he saw the sinister mark in its malevolent black glory. *Was it his imagination or had the hand suddenly grown larger, blacker, thicker, seeming to burrow deeper into his skin?*

The witch-doctor laughed. His dark pupils gleamed with mockery and malice. 'Just listen to yourself,' he sneered. 'Take The Black Hand away, I don't want it,' Dibia Ogam mimicked, his voice pitched like a woman's. He leaned over his chair and spat again into the soil. Then, his face hardened. 'I neither give nor take away The Black Hand. Did you not hear anything I said to you or are your big ears just there to decorate your ugly, fat face? Let me repeat myself again; you have been touched by The Black Hand of destiny, the hand of the great deity of wealth, fame, power, success and prowess.' The witch-doctor fixed glowering dark eyes on Eze. 'You think everyone is fortunate enough to be touched by The Black Hand, eh? You think I am happy just sitting in this shack of a house, serving the great deity day in and day out and yet, get passed over, ignored, deemed unworthy to be touched by the very god I serve? Ha!' The medicine-man barked a laugh, a bitter laugh laced with sudden rage. 'You chose to come to the shrine of *Aku-n'uba*, the deity of wealth and fame,' he jabbed Eze's chest with a dirty fore-finger. 'Nobody dragged you here. You sought me out. Let me tell you, many that came here before you, left that Grand Room of Mirrors as walking corpses, their faculties permanently ruined by the dire images they saw in the black mirrors of destiny, images of death, torture, destitution, sickness persecution, madness, curses beyond what the human mind can conceive. But you, you and a handful of men and women... yes, women too... you have been blessed by the shrine, deemed worthy for whatever reason to receive the seal of the great deity of wealth. And you sit there and whine like a stupid woman, "take The Black Hand away; return it to wherever it came from," as if I have nothing better to do than waste my time with a fool like you, ha!'

The *Dibia* spat, the perpetual brown spittle formed from an addictive intake of Kola-nut and tobacco snuff powder. 'Listen to me and listen very carefully because I will not repeat myself.' He leaned back into his chair and shut his eyes, sighing deeply, as if garnering the energy to speak to an *Onukwu*, a dimwit. When he next spoke, his voice was low, so soft that Eze had to lean forward to catch his words. 'You saw images of your future in the black mirrors of destiny. The mirrors never lie. The Black Hand of our great deity, *Aku-n'uba*, will secure that future for you; a future of immense wealth and power, a future of fame and success beyond

104

your wildest imaginings,' the *Dibia* paused to stuff more brown tobacco snuff into his back molar, waiting for it to numb the habitual toothache. Again, he spat out the brown tobacco spittle before returning his attention to Eze. 'As I said, The Black Hand has given you its seal of approval. You will own the world. When you speak, men will quake and women will fall. Your name will be one that will instil fear and respect in mankind. Your legacy will endure beyond ten generations. That is what The Black Hand will give you as long as you feed it its diet of blood. You ask me what the diet is, what blood it wants. The answer, which should be clear to even a young child, is human blood, human sacrifice. The Black Hand is not greedy, considering the incredible gifts it bestows on its chosen few. It demands just one human sacrifice every year. It's not even choosy. It will accept any blood, man, woman, child and even an idiot like you, provided it is human blood,' the witch-doctor hooted, a derisive laugh that sent a sudden chill to Eze's spine. A sudden phrase entered unbidden into his head, a famous *Igbo* proverb – *To dine with the devil, ensure you have a long-handed spoon, in case you need to make a speedy escape.* The shrivelled *Dibia* was starting to assume the form of a mammoth demon to him.

Dibia Ogam leaned forward. 'Listen and listen well,' he said, his eyes hardening to flints. 'The Black Hand's gifts are commensurate to the quality of the blood you feed it. Offer it an ordinary human sacrifice and your destiny will still be great, ordinarily great, for The Black Hand always delivers. It has promised you greatness and greatness it must deliver. However, offer it quality blood, the blood of the innocents, a child or a virgin, and see the heavens open up for you. Those ones are the blessed of the gods and the ancestors, virgins and children. They're the special ones who are always guaranteed a blessed reincarnation when they die. So, say you choose to sacrifice your own son, you will have that child reborn to you, right into your own family in your lifetime,' the witch-doctor smiled as Eze gasped, horror widening his eyes. Dibia Ogam nodded his head. 'It's ok, I'm not telling you to sacrifice your son… not yet. There are even better choices. You could equally feed it the blood of the un-naturals, those unfortunates who become *Ozu nwulu-awu,* dead corpses, when they die. They are the cursed ones without hope of reincarnation, such as the albinos, dwarves, twins, babies born with teeth or extra limbs and fingers, or even better, *Oyibo,* a white man. For what ancestor would wish to return such abominations for a second rebirth into their bloodline, eh?' Dibia Ogam shook his head sadly, taking a long sip of his palm wine. He raised the gourd to refill Eze's cup but Eze shook his head. His throat could barely swallow his own spit. 'Those poor un-naturals have been created as food for the super-naturals, the great deities. When they die, they die. As I said, they're just dead corpses. If you sacrifice

106

them to the deities, you need not fear retribution or hauntings from them because they do not live beyond the grave like normal corpses do. But as I mentioned, they're not easy to catch. However, should you succeed in getting one of them for blood sacrifice, then believe me, your body will not be sufficient to withstand the assault of abundance that will be your reward from The Black Hand.'

The *Dibia* leaned back into his chair and shut his eyes again, as if shutting out the sight of something repugnant. His lips twisted in a downward curve and a deep frown furrowed his brows. 'I'm done with you. Our paths will cross only once a year when you bring me the blood sacrifice to offer *Aku-n'uba*, our wealth deity. I will receive your first offering in two market weeks from now. The Black Hand will let you know when the next blood sacrifice is due next year. As I said, its colour will turn an ashy grey on your shoulder when it needs its next feed. We're now done. Goodbye.'

Eze stumbled out of his chair. His knees were so shaky he feared he would collapse in another undignified heap before the witch-doctor, whose contempt had already destroyed what was left of his self-esteem. His heart pounded so hard he feared a cardiac arrest. The hand clasping his kaftan and mobile phone shook like a coward's heart. *Surely, instant death was preferable to the terrible burden he now bore, despite the promised benefits.* His head throbbed as a phrase whirled in his mind like tornado circles – *I*

107

have to kill a person every year, I have to kill a person every year... The image of his little son, Caesar, flashed in his mind, a boy of five years who was his replica in every way, right to his little fingers. Eze shuddered. He would rather die than offer The Black Hand the innocent blood of his child... *never!* He searched his brains for the last time he had seen a dwarf and nothing came to mind. *Albino! Amadioha in his great heavens! The girl, Aku, the young albino girl he had grabbed on her way to school only a week ago! And he would set his last Naira bank note that she was a virgin too!*

Eze let out a loud shout, a cry of triumph. Suddenly, his legs firmed up, his step lightened and his stride lengthened. The pounding in his head eased and a dark fog lifted from his mind. He had himself his first sacrifice for The Black Hand and he hadn't needed to search far for it. His fortune was about to change with the speed of lightning. The thought brought an impatient glint in his eyes, an excited racing to his heart. A brief thought flashed in his mind, the image of the girl's mother, the famous medicine-woman he had once visited to his eternal chagrin. *Owa.* He had gone to her to request *Juju* to kill his main political opponent, the local government chairman. But, the woman had literally chased him from her shrine with a broom. She had called him all kinds of derogatory names underneath the sky and warned him never to sully her compound with his feet again. But for her art and status as a *Dibia*, Eze would have squashed the tiny albino witch with his mighty right arm.

Instead, he had decided to hurt her where it mattered most, seduce her only daughter, Aku, a young girl it was said the witch-woman loved more than her own life. He had never slept with an albino and was looking forward to the experience. But for the intervention of that idiot priest, Father Ike, he would have had his way with the girl and put her in the family way that day. The rubbish priest was well-connected with the state governor. It would've been political suicide to challenge him. So, the witch-woman's daughter had had herself a very lucky escape that day. But clearly fate worked in mysterious ways. What he had cursed as bad fortune on the day had turned out to be his good luck. Not only was he getting himself an albino for The Black Hand, but also a virgin sacrifice; two quality blood in one young body for the great deity of wealth.

Again, Eze hooted. He wasn't afraid of the albino medicine-woman. She could not harm him, not now. After all, he'd been touched by The Black Hand. Even with all her powers, she would be no match for a deity as powerful as *Aku-n'uba*. The girl, Aku, was his and his future was already shinning with a brilliance that rivalled the full noonday sun blazing across the vast skies. By the time he returned to his Peugeot car parked underneath the great

Ngwu tree in the *Dibia's* compound, Eze had ceased to notice the painful throbbing of his broken arm.

Ω Ω Ω

7

Killing Encounter

The village market was located inside a vast square surrounded by multiple small shops and kiosks catering for the various needs of the growing community. The small music store blasted gospel music from massive loudspeakers located at its crowded entrance. Next to it, the larger store that catered for everything female, bags, hats, shoes, make-up, shiny cheap jewellery, sunglasses, cheap perfumes and colourful clothing, sparkled with bright Christmas lights which kept it in a festive mood all year round. A small internet café sold everything techno, from sim cards to mobile phones and even access to a Mac computer when there was electricity, which was as infrequent as the full moon.

But the most important store in the village square, the social hub of the community, was the wooden shack that was both the village bar and news broadcasting station, run by the mammoth proprietress, Mama Ten and her useful litter of nine daughters. It was in this ramshackle joint that the village men gathered to drink palm-wine, eat assorted bush-meat from antelopes to squirrels and share the latest gossip circulating in the community and neighbouring villages. The little black radio mounted atop the wooden beam blasted every kind of information courtesy of the

BBC World Service. Mama Ten's nine daughters kept the clientele well fed, wined and entertained, allowing their bottoms to be pawed by the men as an enticement to keep them spending. Mama Ten would feign blindness to their shenanigans until a roving hand strayed too far and the owner soon felt the hard bash of her wooden pestle on their shoulder. Her customers knew how far they could go with her daughters and rarely crossed the unspoken boundaries set by the massive bar-madam.

In the noon-day bustle, Aku and Ego wandered from store to kiosk, browsing through the various displayed wares, enjoying the unexpected holiday from their studies. The deputy principal had announced at the morning assembly that Father Ike had been ambushed by armed robbers on his way to the school and was fighting for his life at The Teaching Hospital in the big city. The students were dismissed early for the day after Mass and Novena were recited for their injured principal. Aku had prayed especially hard for their principal. She owed the priest not just her life, but also her soul. But for him and the secret baptism he'd given her, there would've been no place for her soul in either purgatory or heaven, thanks to her pagan heritage. She was the only teenager who didn't have a mobile phone in the village, all because her mother believed it was an avenue for evil spirits to possess humans. They neither had a radio nor a television in their house even though Aku knew her mother could afford those items.

But again, all the pagan beliefs linked to the Earth Goddess prevented them from joining the twenty-first century. In fact, the thought of returning to their small bungalow, junked up with the various occult materials used by her mother, had been enough to drive her to the village square in the company of her best friend, Ego. She would rather endure the cold contempt of the villagers than spend an hour longer than necessary under their stuffy, dark bungalow.

'There they go again, staring at you as if they've seen a terrifying *Ojuju Calabar* masquerade, the idiots,' Ego's voice had its habitual biting sting.

'Let's just ignore them,' Aku said, her voice low, as if afraid of being heard. 'After all, the market square is nobody's inheritance or their father's compound. I have every right to be here just like all of them.'

'Look at that fat pig, Boniface, with breasts the size of a woman's own,' Ego sneered. 'See how his eyes are almost popping out of their sockets, the fat fool. Hey! Fat fool Boniface! What are you staring at?' Ego shouted.

'Sshh! Ego, don't! You'll only draw more attention to us,' Aku said, anxiety glazing her pale eyes behind their dark glasses.

'So? Let the market burn! Who cares? I keep telling you that you must stick up for yourself, Aku. Don't let your mum hide you away as if you've committed some heinous crime just by being the way God made you. Everyone shits and farts and bleeds red blood regardless of their skin colour.'

'It's easy for you to talk,' Aku's voice was tinged with bitterness. 'You have no idea how hard it is to keep going when you know everyone detests you and considers you less than human. You take your dark colour for granted, Ego. You don't realise how blessed you are to be born black, with the right skin hue. It's your black skin that gives you the confidence to talk to anyone, the fearlessness to go anywhere you like, the security to be seen, be heard, be recognised and be accepted. I wish you could wear my skin for just one day and see what it is to be me, an *Aghali* albino girl, worse, an *Aghali* girl who is unfortunate to also be the daughter of an *Aghali* witchdoctor.'

'Sorry,' Ego was immediately contrite though her face still wore a combatant look. 'I know it's hard for you. It's just that I get so angry with them. They're all bullies, that's what they are. You should have seen how they treated my mother and I when my father died, just because I'm a girl and not a rubbish son. My uncle now lives in the house my father built, while my mother and I have to make do with that shack he put us in. I tell you, I can't wait to leave this rubbish village once we graduate. I've told my mother she must leave this place and join me in the big city when I get my flat there. The only time they'll see me in this idiot village after that is when I drive back in my big Mercedes Benz car.'

115

Aku laughed. 'See how you're talking as if we're already rich. Anyone hearing you will think we already own a successful business and making big money.'

'But we will have one, you watch and see,' Ego's voice ringed with conviction. 'You're going to make use of your mother's powers for once and get us some special *Juju* that will make people troop to our shop and spend, spend, spend once we open it.'

'Ego!' Aku's voice was shrill, a scandalised look on her face. 'What kind of Catholic are you to talk about *Juju,* good or bad? You know how much I hate all that stuff. Imagine what Father Ike will say if he hears us talking about all this pagan business!'

'And who's going to tell Father Ike about it? You? I?' Ego snorted. 'That's the trouble with you, Aku. You have no appreciation of the gift you've been given because it's come so easy to you. I swear, if my mother had just a tenth of the powers your mother has, I would own the world by now and make sure all my enemies, especially my rubbish uncle and his fat wives are cursed with painful deaths,' Ego shook her head, giving Aku a look that was both contemptuous and pitiful. 'Just look at you,' she continued, reaching out a hand to pull a strand of Aku's thin long braids, making her gasp. 'See how you cower with your head down, your shoulders slouched and your voice hushed just because you're afraid of these rubbish villagers. And yet, your mother has the power to ruin them all if she wants. You think I don't have ears to hear or eyes to see? Everyone knows what your mother can do but you two are the same, two scared mice. You've allowed the villagers to frighten you so much just because you're *Aghalis*, that now, your powers are worthless. If your mother was anything like your late grandmother, Xikora, by now, you'll be riding a Mercedes Benz and living in luxury like your cousin, Enu.' Ego hissed. 'I swear, I just hate "money-miss-road". Good things always go to people who don't deserve them and have no inkling how to enjoy or appreciate them.'

'You're more than welcome to my life,' Aku mumbled, her eyes pooling. Ego's words had stung. 'I'll be happy to switch any day with you. You can take my skin, my name and my so-called heritage while I'll happily take your dark skin, vile uncle and all,' Aku's eyes darted in distressed frenzy. 'I keep telling you, you have no idea about my life, Ego. No idea at all. Yes, I hate this village and all their meanness but at least, I'm safe here; well, as safe as anyone can be in a place like this,' she gave a little laugh, a bitter laugh. Her voice had an uncharacteristic harshness to it. 'Like you, I also dream of escaping to the big city. But I also dread the prospect because one hears terrible stories about the fate of *Aghalis* in the big cities. They say that politicians, armed robbers and even church pastors hunt us for our body parts to make powerful *Juju* medicine. They say that no *Aghali* is safe there, even the dead ones buried in their graves. They dig up their corpses just

117

to harvest their body parts.' Aku quickly swung her arms over her head and clicked away the evil from her body. 'I just know I'll not survive for a week in the big city if all the stories I hear are true. I'll be amongst strangers who wish me harm just because of my skin colour. At least, here in our village, they know me. They've watched me grow up. They know my family and even if they hate us, I don't feel the need to look over my shoulders in fear of one of them decapitating my head or severing my arm with a machete. Tell you the truth, apart from The Fat-Man who wants to molest me, I don't really fear that anyone here will kill me. Maybe they'll hit me or spit at me as they've done in the past but they certainly won't go slaughtering me as they do to people like me in the big city.'

Ego's eyes clouded with dark suspicion. 'So, are you saying that you won't be following me to the big city when we graduate, eh? Is that what all this is leading to?' Ego's voice rose with anger. 'All these years we made our plans together. You know how desperate I am to get away from this rubbish village. I thought you'll be happy to ask your mother to help us succeed. But now, the wind has blown and I've seen how filthy the chicken's anus is. You've just shown me your true colours. All this time, you've been playing along, knowing you had no plans to leave this useless village. You're nothing but a coward, Aku. I think you deserve everything you get from people. All you do is moan about your

Aghali skin and yet, you're not ready to do anything about it. Thanks to you, I now have a bad headache. See what you've gone and done to me now. I'm going home to rest. Bye. I'll see you at school tomorrow.'

Ego stormed off, leaving Aku in the middle of the market square holding tight unto her umbrella and school satchel. Hot tears pooled in her eyes. *It wasn't true what Ego just said about her,* Aku thought, her pale eyes darting wildly behind her dark sunglasses. She wasn't a coward...*she wasn't.* Ego didn't know what it was to be an *Aghali,* the pain of her skin colour, the dangers and terrors that accompanied her albinism.

Aku looked around her, trying to still the sudden panic in her heart. She wasn't afraid...*she wasn't afraid.* No one in the village would kill her... *surely, they wouldn't.* Just that she'd never been to the market square by herself, never had to walk all the way from the village market to her mother's house at the edge of the village. She had done a foolish thing by following Ego to the market square when they were let off school for the day. The earlier thrill of the adventure evaporated into the dark mist of anxiety that suddenly shrouded her.

Aku started to walk towards the direction of the police station which led out of the village square. As if the sky had seen her tears and wanted to share her misery, it opened its bowels and released a sudden downpour of hard rain, which pelted her like cold, wet

119

pebbles. Her umbrella was little help against the ferocity of the thunderstorm and in seconds, her dress clung to her skin like cling-film. She was sobbing with deep gulping hiccups as she walk-ran along the muddy path that led to the sole tarmac road in their village. The pot-holed road led directly to her mother's house, just a two-mile walk.

Aku's shoulders continued to heave with the violence of her tears. She had no idea why she was crying. It wouldn't be the first time she had fallen out with her best friend. Ego's temper was notorious in their school. Her tongue was brutal when she got into one of her fits but her heart was good, free from malice. Yet, the tears would not stop. A deep sadness welled in her heart, washing her with dark despair. Her steps slowed till she was almost snail-walking. Thoughts raced through her mind, draining her strength. *What was she rushing home for? Why was she even studying in the first place? What hope did she have for anything good in life? What man would want to marry her with the curse of her heritage and the scourge of her skin hue? Where can she feel safe apart from her mother's wretched house? Here she was, almost eighteen years, trembling with fear like a two-year old let out of her mother's sight, just because she was born with a skin colour that made her a target of hate.*

A horn honked and a car pulled up next to her. Lost in thought, Aku didn't realise the car had stalled till a voice called out to her.

'Aku! It's Aku, isn't it? That's your name, yes?' The voice was female, authoritative. Aku turned to look in the car and her heart missed a beat. She recognised the person behind the wheel. It was her second cousin, Enu, a family member whose hatred was worse than that of the entire village combined. Enu was their rich relative who had never bothered with Aku and her mother. She didn't consider them worthy of her attention and publicly rejected all claims of kinship to them. Enu's dark skin and wealth gave her the freedom and security her albino cousins never enjoyed. Aku wanted to ignore her but she didn't dare. Tradition and upbringing held her hostage by the wet roadside. Enu was a much older cousin whose superior age and kinship conferred the right to demand and receive Aku's reluctant respect.

'Good afternoon, Auntie Enu,' Aku's voice was low. Her eyes darted wildly behind her dark sunglasses. 'Yes Ma, it's Aku; I'm your cousin Owa's daughter.'

'Of course, I know whose daughter you are,' Enu snapped. 'How many *Aghalis* do we have in this village? Get into the car let me drop you home. No need you walking and getting drenched in this downpour. Family is family after all,'

'No, thank you, Auntie. I'm fine walking. It's not far to our house,' Aku tried to keep her voice steady. Her earlier sobbing, coupled with the intimidating presence of her older cousin, had brought the trembles to her voice. She heard some voices and saw a man and woman watching her from the dry safety of their veranda across the road. They called out a friendly greeting to Enu, who waved back carelessly with a muttered hiss. Soon, a few nosy neighbours joined the onlookers, staring at the cousins with shameless curiosity. Their attention flushed Aku's skin red with embarrassment. She looked away, fiddling with her sunglasses and lowering her umbrella till her face was almost invisible to the watching villagers.

'Just get into the car and don't argue with me,' Enu's voice was impatient, a dark frown on her heavily made-up face. 'I've got better things to do than stay here arguing with you.' The authority in her voice brooked no challenge. Aku scuttled into the car, sitting as if she had a brood of vipers squirming underneath her bottom. She squeezed herself as far away from her cousin as the small interior of the car allowed. Her shoulders were tense and her heart thudded against her chest, fast and hard. Her earlier tears were instantly dried up by nerves. Wild thoughts rushed through her mind. *Why in Jesus' name did her cousin suddenly decide to give her a lift in her car? She hated cars, she really did. All that cars brought her were misery and fear. Maybe she'd been killed by a car in her former life. Worse, what would she say to her mother when she got home?*

There was no love lost between the cousins. Aku had grown up witnessing the frequent humiliations and insults heaped on her mother by Enu and her group of spiteful, village women. They were the only people who still called her mother by the derogatory childhood nickname, *Nwa-Ntu*, Ash-Child. The few times she'd heard her mother mention Enu's name, it had been said with pure venom. Aku didn't want to be caught in the middle of their life-long feud. Her mother would be furious at her for accepting the lift but how could she say "no" to Enu?

'Put your umbrella on the floor of the car before you ruin my car seat with the water dripping from it,' Enu's voice cut into her dark thoughts. Aku hurriedly obliged, putting her satchel next to the umbrella. The wiper raced at manic speed to clear the rain from the windscreen but its efforts were in vain. Enu leaned forward to peer into the road, hissing and swearing as she drove.

Suddenly, she veered off the road into an untarred path.

'Auntie Enu, our house is just down the road,' Aku said, reaching down for her satchel and umbrella. 'I can get off now and walk the rest of the way. Thank you for the lift, Ma. I am grateful.'

'Don't be silly. I'm not letting you off in this downpour,' Enu's voice was friendly, kinder than Aku had ever heard it in all her seventeen-plus years. 'My house is just down this path…here we are…I need to urinate desperately and can't do it by the roadside.' Enu laughed, easing her car into a nice compound filled with flowers, hosting a posh bungalow which seemed to be built entirely of glass windows. Aku stared open-mouthed. She had never been to her cousin's house. She'd heard stories about Enu's wealth but never knew she lived in such a house, that such a property even existed in their village. As far as she was concerned, Enu's house was better than their chief's own and even better than the one The Fat-Man lived in, a storey-building which she heard he'd inherited from his late father, Agu of Onori clan. It had been the very first storey-building in their village before a few other villagers began to vertically upgrade their bungalows.

'Come inside and have a drink while I use the toilet,' Enu invited. Aku began to shake her head but curiosity got the better of her. She wanted to see what the house looked like inside. *Wait till she told Ego what she'd seen!* Just seeing the house was making Aku change her mind about relocating to the big city with Ego. *What wouldn't she give to own a place like this?*

The interior of the house was everything Aku had expected and more. The flowers outside seemed to have been imported into the large living-room with decorated ceramic pots. A large chandelier hung low from the high roof. Aku had never seen a chandelier, never knew such a thing existed. She stared at the bright rainbow sparkling from the faux-diamonds of the chandelier with eyes rounded by wonder. Everything in the large bungalow seemed to be made of glass, from the side tables to the shining white marble flooring. A giant-sized plasma television was mounted high on the wall. Aku had seen televisions, both at Ego's house and at the market square. But she had never seen one as large as her cousin's own.

'Sit down and wait for me. I'll be back soon,' Enu waved her to a black, leather sofa with a languid flick of her hand. Several gold rings winked on her fingers, while bangles jangled on her wrist. Aku hesitated. She glanced uncomfortably at her wet dress and clenched her hands at her side. Enu smiled.

'Don't worry, the chairs are leather. They won't be ruined by your wet dress. Go on, sit down and I'll be with you in minutes.' Enu walked through one of the numerous doors that led off from the living-room. Aku sank into the plush softness of the sofa. She let out a deep sigh. She had never sat on such a chair and wanted to sink herself into it, rub her face against it, just like a cat. *Wow! Who can believe that people lived like this, and her own cousin no less? If only her mother wouldn't be so righteous about her goddess and use some of that money she dumped into earthen pots in the shrine to beautify their home. What wouldn't she give to have chairs like these at home. Wow!*

Aku knew that customers paid her mother handsomely for her services even though she demanded no fees for her work. Qwa simply chucked the money into the earthen pots and forgot about them. She called the money *Ego-Aja*, sacrifice money, which belonged to the Earth Goddess and the shrine. They lived off their farm and the money Qwa received as farm rent from the people tilling the various farmlands Ọwa inherited from her late mother, Xikora. Unlike Ọwa, Xikora had held no scruples about charging exorbitant fees for her services and demanding farmlands when her customers had no ready cash to pay. By the time she died, she had amassed an impressive horde of farmlands which passed to Ọwa when her grandmother died. Enu's mother had inherited the homestead, being the older twin. In fact, if Aku recalled, she was sitting right inside that old homestead which had been demolished to build this grand bungalow.

'Here, I've brought you a drink,' Enu walked back into the room, bearing two glasses filled with what appeared to be Cola drink. She held out one glass to Aku, the one in her right hand. Aku's heart sank. She had been warned never to accept food or drinks from strangers in case of poisoning, never to accept items of clothing in case of demon possession. How could she turn down Enu's generosity without appearing rude? 'Aahh! I see your mother has trained you well,' Enu's voice was a mixture of mirth and contempt. 'You think I'll poison you, don't you? Here, take my own drink…in fact, let me drink from both of the glasses to show you they're not poisoned.' Enu raised the glass she had been holding out to Aku and drank from it. As she raised the other one, Aku reached out to take it from her.'

'It's okay, Auntie, Thank you. I wasn't thinking of poison. Just that I didn't want you to go to any trouble on my behalf. You've already done too much for me,' she raised the glass to her lips and drank. It wasn't Cola. It was Holy Communion wine, the blood of Jesus! Aku gasped and starred down at her glass. Her eyes danced merrily behind her sunglasses. If she ever had any doubt about her cousin's wealth, this laid it to rest. Only someone very rich or powerful could lay their hands on Holy Communion wine so easily and offer it to people as if it were plain water from the stream. She took a longer sip and almost drained the glass.

'You like it, eh?' Enu laughed. 'It's red wine. I hope you're old enough to drink it. How old are you, by the way?'

'I'll be eighteen years this weekend, Ma,'

'Eighteen!' Enu seemed surprised. 'You look older than your age. You're quite tall, aren't you? Must take after your father whoever he is, since your mother is closer to the ground than to the ceiling,' Enu's eye ran over Aku like one inspecting a strange insect. 'You're a pretty girl alright, a pretty girl, despite being an *Aghali*. You should make good use of your looks and better your life instead of letting your mother chain you to that shrine of hers. I bet you've never drank wine before today.'

'I have,' Aku didn't want to appear even more gauche than she already felt before her cousin. 'It's the same wine we have for Holy Communion every Sunday at Mass.'

'Aahh! Mass! I forgot. You mean your mother allows you to attend Mass? I thought you're training to take over from her as the high priestess of *Aná?*' There was a biting edge to her cousin's voice. The earlier friendliness seemed to have vanished. Suddenly, Aku didn't want to linger in the house anymore, even with the gripping Nollywood film airing on the large plasma television.

'Thank you, Auntie, for the nice wine,' she gave a nervous little laugh and drained the last of the red wine. 'I think I should start getting home now otherwise my mum will start to worry. She doesn't like it when I stay out too long,' she started to get up from the sofa but her legs collapsed underneath her. She frowned and made a second attempt. This time it was worse. Not just her legs, but her arms had also turned mush on her. In fact, her entire body appeared to be numbing on her.

'Au....Aun...I...' Aku's heart began to pound with terror. Even her tongue had frozen on her. She could see everything as clear as a mirror, see the gloating look in her cousin's eyes which observed her struggles with cold detachment. She could hear everything, including the sudden doorbell song which announced a visitor to the house. Aku's heart soared! *Her cousin could not harm her now.* Whoever it was ringing the doorbell must have seen Enu's car and the blazing lights in the house. Enu must receive the visitor and Aku would try to make her plight known. *Holy Mary! Trusting fool that she was! After everything her mother had tried to teach her, she had ended up falling into the exact trap her mother had feared. She was a fool, an idiot fool, a proper fool.*

Enu walked to the door and flung it open as if she were expecting the guest. Three men walked into the house and Aku's blood chilled in her veins. Her heart dropped to her feet. Her breath rushed out in short, hot gasps. *The Fat-Man! Chief Eze and his two thugs! Oh Mary Mother of God! What evil did her cousin and The Fat-Man plan for her?*

'*Eze-nwanyi!* King-woman!' The Fat-Man hailed her cousin and engulfed Enu in a big hug. 'She that delivers what she pledges, just like a man! *Agu-Nwanyi!* Lion-lady that devours warriors! I hail you, I bow to you,' Eze made several exaggerated bows in Enu's direction before walking towards Aku where she half-lay on the sofa like a seal stranded on a sandy beach. He stood in front of her, towering over her like a colossal demon. His little eyes glinted with triumph as they roved over Aku's paralysed body.

'Don't worry, she can't do or say anything,' Enu said, joining The Fat-Man. 'The herb I used will ensure she sees, hears and understands everything but her body will be like a stone statue for several hours. She can neither speak nor move,' Enu barked a harsh laugh. 'They think they're the only ones with power and knowledge just because the Earth Goddess favoured their half of the family. But they forget that we still share the same bloodline and the knowledge is there for those of us who will seek it out. I used a special herb which no doubt her mother knows about but never taught her, otherwise, she would have recognised the

129

distinctive taste as soon as she took her first sip of the wine. Teenagers!' Enu hissed, kissing her teeth. 'Lazy things. No knowledge or willingness to learn. Oh well. I can't be blamed for her ignorance,' Ego turned to The Fat-Man. 'Have you got my money?'

'Boys!' The Fat-Man motioned his thugs over. The one with the dark sunglasses like Aku's own, dashed forward with a black briefcase. He opened it and Aku stared with shock at the wads of *Naira* banknotes stuffed inside the briefcase. She couldn't even try to guess how much was in that briefcase. It was surely enough to build a house. Her cousin had sold her to The Fat-Man for a very handsome fee. Aku watched as Enu meticulously counted the wads of money. There was nothing rushed about her actions. The Fat-Man waited patiently, his eyes fixed on Aku. Then he smiled, the same oily smile that had so repulsed her the first time she met him.

'Aku… Aku,' he shook his head, false pity in his eyes. 'See what you've gone and done to yourself. I offered you everything but you turned me down, made me look bad before your stupid priest. Now, where is he?' He turned to his thugs. 'Boys, you did a good job on that stupid priest today. You will get your reward when I receive news that he's died of his injuries at the hospital. You weren't supposed to leave him alive but then, I guess you did your best under the circumstances. Hopefully, he won't live long enough to point fingers,' he turned back to Aku. 'You see what happens to people who challenge me? When I'm done with you, your mother will also know what it means to insult me. I don't take insults lightly as you'll soon discover,' he turned back to his thugs. 'Boys, tie her up and put her into the car boot. We have a long trip ahead of us and I don't want any stupid police at the check-points to disturb us. Make sure you have the check-point bribe money ready at hand.'

'*Agbalaka!* He that acts with the speed of lightning and thunder! I thank you for your generosity,' Enu's face was all smiles. 'This is much more than I expected.'

'And there's even more in store for you when we're done with our job. You're a good woman to do business with and I'll not forget you when I become governor of this state.' Eze hugged her cousin again as Aku felt herself trussed like a chicken, her hands and feet bound with a cord rope. She was hauled up from the sofa and carried out of the room by the two thugs. She wanted to scream, to curse her cousin and swear at The Fat-Man. But her tongue was frozen inside her mouth. The most terrifying aspect of her predicament was her total awareness of everything happening to her and yet, her total paralytic helplessness. Her terror killed every discomfort she felt as she was dumped into the dark claustrophobic boot of the white Peugeot.

She thought she would die, that she would not live through the next seconds after the boot slammed down and killed her oxygen.

She started to choke, cough and sneeze, all at the same time. Great hiccups of sobs brought a gripping pain to her chest. Every pore in her body hurt, bruised by unknown sharp edges and bits in the boot. She wished she could make herself comfortable, stretch out her legs. But even if she had not been drugged, the boot space was just enough for a midget goat. The smell of dry oil, rubber and dust, stole her breath and vied for her sanity.

After what seemed like hours, she heard the engine start. The car went into bumpy motion. Her body bounced about in the tight confinement of the boot, bringing soundless whimpers to her throat. Hot tears rolled down her cheeks, staining her already rain-soaked dress. Her body was wracked with shivers, chills of terror, as her mind conjured all kinds of scenarios. Top on the list was rape. She knew she was going to get raped by The Fat-Man. That was what he had always wanted. *But why pay so much money to her cousin to abduct her? What did he mean about making her mother pay for insulting him? Did he plan on getting the two thugs to molest her as well, just to make her ruin complete? Worse, will he let her live after the attack, knowing that she would tell her mother?*

Aku's heart raced, terror-charged. She'd promise him her silence and keep that promise if it would spare her an early death. She'll even keep quiet about Enu's involvement if The Fat-Man demanded it. She would do anything to live...*anything*. She didn't want to die, didn't want to think about the pain of dying, never seeing her mother again, never seeing the world, hearing music, eating nice food, never getting married, knowing love and having her own children. She didn't want to die...*oh Holy Mary Mother of God, SHE DIDN'T WANT TO DIE....Mama...Mama...please save me, find me, Mama... don't let me die... Mama... Mama...*

***

The car stopped and the boot opened. Rough hands lifted her out of the boot. She screamed and was shocked to hear her own voice. The thugs were equally stunned. They dropped her on the ground like a sack of *Garri* cassava flour. She screamed again, louder, longer. Her limbs were moving, free once more to struggle against her ropes on the grassy soil. Sunglasses fell on her, covering her mouth with his hand. She bit him, hard. His blood tasted salty on her tongue. He punched her, harder. Her blood tasted saltier in her mouth. She kneed him and rolled away, fighting the ropes. Several feet kicked her, in her stomach, her head, her thighs. Her screams turned to moans, then whimpers.

'Boys, enough. Let her be. We want her alive till we know what Dibia Ogam wants us to do,' The Fat-Man's voice drifted down to Aku from a pain-hazed distance. His words chilled her to the bones. The pounding in her chest grew louder, tighter. The word, *Dibia,* told a gruesome truth, a fate she had dreaded all her life, the dark shadow that had been her companion from the first day she realised what it meant to be an albino amongst dark-skinned neighbours. The fear was so great it became a physical being, a heavy burden squashing her chest, her head, her stomach. It stole her breath and her thoughts. Then it stole her mind.

Aku fainted.

***

She woke up screaming. The pain was like nothing she had ever felt. It washed over her entire body before settling on her right arm. She turned her head to look. Her hand lay by her arm, a few inches away from her wrist. At first, her eyes refused to accept the truth of what they were seeing; the bleeding stub of her right arm, the twitching fingers of her severed hand, still frantically scratching the floor as if searching for the arm they used to be attached to. Thick blood gushed from her mutilated arm into the hard mirror floor that was identical to the walls of the room, walls built entirely of black mirrors.

Aku screamed and gaped at the two men staring down at her inside the lamp-lit room. Her pain-glazed eyes recognised one of them. *The Fat-Man.* He was naked, his bloated body oil-sleeked and damp with sweat. The other, she also recognised even though she'd never met him in her life. His macabre attire of chicken feathers, face-paint and beads, proclaimed his title. *Dibia,*

Witchdoctor! A sharp blood-drenched machete was still clenched in his hand. *Her blood... her hand...* Aku tried to scream again but the sound that came from her mouth was the whimper of a kicked dog.

'*Bi...Biko...*Pleea...please, let me go,' her voice was a whisper. Her throat was so dry it hurt to swallow. 'I'll not tell anyone about this...I swear...*Biko*, let me live...please...' The pain cut off her words. She began to convulse on the hard, mirror floor of the room. Thick, black clouds attacked her head in waves. She gave in to them with gratitude, allowed them to swallow her mind and sight.

The next time she awoke, she was dying. Aku knew she was dying because she saw her great-grandmother, standing by her side, smiling down at her. *Nne-ochie* looked exactly as her mother had described, tall, dark, kind and beautiful. Ironically, she looked almost identical to her evil cousin, Enu, except her eyes were kinder, truer, loving. Her great-grandmother smiled at her again and Aku smiled back. A feeling of peace descended on her. She heard voices and followed their source. The Fat-Man and the *Dibia* conversed in hushed tones. Aku looked at The Fat-Man and the *Dibia* and there was no fear any more in her heart. There was nothing in her heart because her heart was in the *Dibia*'s palm. Her life-blood still pumped from the organ, soaking the *Dibia*'s hand, dripping to the mirror floor which was already drenched with her blood. In his other hand, the *Dibia* held a bowl containing her severed right hand and two little, dark red pebbles. She stared up at The Fat-Man and he stared down at her, her still face, her unmoving eyes which no longer danced their familiar darts, her two bleeding breasts devoid of their dark red tips, the gaping hole in her exposed chest which once housed the heart the *Dibia* held - her life.

She felt herself engulfed in a sweet embrace. Her great-grandmother's eyes smiled into her own, filled with warmth and love. Aku turned to look at her mutilated corpse on the mirror floor but her great-ancestor turned her head away, shielding her gaze from the horror. Just then, Aku saw them, two terrible figures whose visage filled her with more terror than her mind could endure. They emerged from the mirror walls, filling the room with ice air. Her great-grandmother screamed and cursed at them. She started pulling Aku towards the bright light glowing at one corner of the mirror room, a light so dazzling it blinded her. The *Dibia* spoke urgently to The Fat-Man and they both rushed out of the room.

The two mammoth shadow beings advanced closer to Aku. She cowered in terror, clinging tight to her great-grandmother's arm. *Nne-Ochie* tugged Aku's arm with panicked desperation, trying to get her to the bright light, away from the malevolent entities gliding ever closer. Each time, an invisible wall rebuffed her, a wall that would not let her through, only her great grandmother. But, *Nne-Ochie* would not leave her, would not let her go. She wailed and cursed, pulled and fought, even as she realised the futility of everything.

A cold hand touched Aku's leg and turned her into an ice statue. Her great-grandmother howled, a wail of agony and loss. Then, she vanished. By the time the second hand touched her head, Aku had ceased to feel. All was silent, numb, dead. All was nothing and she too, she was nothing.

Ω Ω Ω

8

Missing

Ọwa saw the women before they saw her. Her chest tightened and her breathing quickened. Every muscle in her body tensed, bringing a red flush to her pale skin. Her body broke out in the familiar warning rashes, bringing the burning itch that turned her skin into red sores. She halted her steps, scratching her arms with manic frenzy, her face, her neck, debating what to do, whether to walk past the gathered women with a false smile or avert her face, feign sudden blindness and un-exist them. She might turn back, pretend she had forgotten something in her house, lurk in the bushes till they dispersed; cowardly perhaps, but prudent. The urge to coat herself in ashes once more was very strong. She had not used that escape route since her childhood days, when she was known by the cruel nick-name, *Nwa-Ntu,* Ash-Child.

The women ruled the day while she ruled the night. Their collective spite and ostracism always aroused those unwanted feelings of exposure, vulnerability and even fear. They raised submerged memories to the fore, lifelong recollections of rejection and exclusion by the very community she called her own. They reminded her that she was different, badly different, fearfully different, just as she was in her childhood, when she went from hearth to hearth, collecting ash to cover her detested skin and hair, cloak herself in blackness so that people would not see her albinic difference and accept her, maybe love her.

The women saw her and stared – as always. Their chattering voices died out with the speed of a radio unplugged from its socket. Owa thought she saw something furtive in their faces but perhaps she was mistaken. In unison, they turned their backs on her as one would something repulsive. Some of them weaved their arms across their shoulders in frenzied signs of the cross. Others spat into the soil and snapped the evil over their heads, their fingers clicking noisily in the sudden evening lull. Owa's head pounded, shame and rage warring in her heart.

There was Mama Uche, the obese wife of the village wrestler, who had made several nocturnal visits to Owa's hut in search of a charm to chain her husband's heart to her own. Her husband was a handsome man, a favourite of the spinsters, especially on wrestling nights, when his oiled and muscled body drew the gasps of passion from the lips of the desperate women eager to offer their bodies to him with shameless abandon. Owa felt pity for the obese woman that wailed bucket-loads of tears in her shrine. She had given Mama Uche a phial of *Mmili Echezona,* the forget-me-not water that flowed in the secret springs of Udi, known to only the most powerful medicine-women in the land. Mama Uche now swaggered with the confidence of a well-loved woman, her face plump with contentment. *Mmili Echezona* had worked its mystical magic on her husband. His eyes were now blind to every woman save his obese wife, whom he now addressed lovingly by the pet name, *Nku*, Feather.

Yet, there she was, crossing herself with piety, pretending Qwa was a cockroach that crawled into her bed in the dead of night. Next to her was One-eye Theresa, who would have been No-eyes Theresa but for the powerful herbs Qwa had treated her with after a cobra spat into her eyes. Her right eye was now a permanent milky orb, dripping salty water, totally ruined by the reptile's venom. Yet, with her good left eye, the single eye Qwa had saved and spared from blindness, the woman still managed to convey her loathing for her albino saviour. Hers was the first spit to hit the dusty soil at the sight of the diminutive medicine-woman.

Qwa felt the dark rage rise in her once again, obliterating her earlier fear. *What right did they have to treat her and her daughter like pariahs? Who were they to feel superior to her, the one person that was privy to their deepest fears and darkest secrets? What had she ever done to them except help them with the powers given her by the Earth Goddess? What was it about her skin that they found so repulsive? Was it the fact that she burnt a red hue when she stayed too long under the sun; that she carried a large umbrella come rain or shine to shield her skin from the damages of nature; that her blue eyes danced a hurting motion when they were*

142

unshielded behind dark sunglasses; that her hair glowed a bright yellow sheen that differed from the standard black thickness of her race? What was it about her and her daughter that they found so hateful despite everything she had done for them?

Ọwa took deep breaths, forcing the rage to abate. She was as *Aná* made her and her lineage. She could not alter any facet of her appearance if her life depended on it – which it did with every breath she took. She knew that her albinism was not the only grouch the women held against her in the village. Her lifestyle did not endear her to them. In a way, she could understand their contempt. She was an unwed mother in a fanatically Christian community that held tight to the tenets of the Roman Catholic Church. She was the harlot of Babylon, the immoral corrupter of souls. The priests branded her art evil, demonic and barbaric. They preached that her powers were of Satan, not from their God, Jesus. They called the good earth-mother, *Aná,* evil.

Worse, nobody knew who her daughter's father was, not even herself. He had been chosen by the Earth Goddess, a strange man from a different tribe, who had wandered into her shrine in search of some charms to cure the malaise in his cattle. He was a *Fulani* man from the nomadic tribe in the northern part of the country, tall, light-skinned and slender, as was the norm with that caste. The Earth Goddess had shown him to Ọwa in a dream. She had guided Ọwa to the charmed potions that distorted the man's mind and

143

seduced his eyes. Theirs had been a coupling of hot bodies, not of warm souls. When it was over, she had dismissed him with the cure for his ailing cattle tucked inside his worn satchel. He'd left her house with a bemused, yet, happy smile and that was the last she ever saw of him.

His seed germinated in her womb and nine months later, she presented the Earth Goddess with the greatest gift she could give, another special albino, her beautiful daughter, Aku. There had been no birth-aiders to assist her. She was after all, the only birth-aider in the village since Efuru's death; the person everyone depended upon to deliver their babies when they went into labour. In her entire time of assisting births, no mother or child had ever lost their lives in the birthing ritual. The Earth Goddess protected all that came into intimate contact with her high priestess. That was one of her gifts from the goddess, that no birthing mother or infant would die at her hands, even twins in the deadly breach position.

Qwa had delivered her daughter alone inside the dark shrine of the Earth Goddess and cut the umbilical cord that bound their souls to each other. She had burnt the afterbirth placenta in sacrifice to the Earth Mother and branded her daughter with the mark of the *Nshi* women, the three tiny razor cuts at the side of her right brow. The villagers wondered who the father of her child was. The women worried that it could be their husbands, their sons, their brothers or their fathers. They feared that the medicine-woman had hexed their menfolk with her powerful *Juju* and produced the bastard albino child that could well be related to any of them by blood. Their fear grew, together with their hatred. Still, they would seek her out in the dark of night, offer her money she didn't demand for her services. They would call on her for the slightest sicknesses and the biggest worries, a missing relative, a blighted farm, a soured womb that would miscarry every pregnancy, sudden possession of the mind by the madness demon, a viper bite at the farm or simply to aid another birth. And each time, Owa answered their pleas and offered her services. But for *Aná*'s laws, she would turn them away from her door, deny them her services, watch them suffer in pain as she did, do to them as her late mother did.

Xikora had shared none of Owa's reticence in her lifetime. Her enemies had felt her fury where it hurt them the most. Owa could remember a few of them still; Chioma, whose womb would never again hold a pregnancy to its full term after she maligned her mother's pregnancy; Oguchi, whose farm would never yield any crops, permanently decimated by a plague of locusts that mysteriously attacked only his farmland every harvest season; Ezugo, who fell from the same palm tree he had climbed for over twenty years and never walked again after swearing at her mother; Adamma, the most beautiful woman in the twelve villages, who would never hold the heart of any man in marriage after mocking Xikora's sun-burnt skin in her thoughts. The foolish woman had forgotten that Xikora was the queen of the mind, that no thoughts within half a mile of her vicinity was hidden from her view. In punishment, Xikora ensured that when men looked at Adamma, they saw only ugliness and evil in her beautiful face. Adamma had aged childless and alone, her famed beauty faded to withered bitterness.

The list was endless, people her mother had cursed and hexed. The people had lived in terror of Xikora, yet, they had respected her too. *Igbo* people respected power and strength. They had no time for weakness and Qwa knew she was unanimously perceived as weak in the village, an unworthy successor to her powerful mother. But she knew what nobody else knew about her mother. She had seen how the Earth Goddess dealt with those that would abuse her powers for their personal gain. No; she would never end up in the blood sludge as her mother had done, just to impress the unworthy community that treated her and her daughter as scum. The Earth Goddess was the mother of all. Her gifts were to be given freely to all and her powers must never be corrupted.

Qwa felt her fury slowly recede, retreat into the locked place behind her heart where the old pains hid, where the bad memories slept. It was a sanctuary weaved in her early teenage years when she could no longer hide herself beneath the dark ash; a solace from the hatred and rejection that had followed her like evil twins from the day she was born into the notorious *Nshi* clan, an albino daughter of an albino medicine-woman, feared and reviled across the twelve villages of their tribe. Her mother's notorious death was now part of the local lore, a horror tale told by parents to their troublesome kids as a warning of what would happen to those that abandoned the cross of salvation for the graven images of heathen idols.

The wretched birth-aider, Efuru, had not helped her mother's reputation either. By the time the woman was done telling her story for the thousandth time, the two death-deities had become a multitude of demons, her mother had died and resurrected a hundred times, the baby had spoken in ten different tongues and the birth-aider had single-handedly vanquished the demons with the power of her cross, her rosaries and her bible. And with each recount of the infamous birth ritual, the word "*Aghali*", albino, was repeated like a vile curse, a monstrous state without grace or redemption.

As the child of the notorious albino medicine-woman, abuse and violence followed Qwa like corpse flies to rotten flesh. *Yellow paint, banana, earth worm, bat-eyes, rotten mango, vomit face, tomato midget…*Qwa lived with the bad names, initially with tears, then with hate and finally, with nothing. The pain was locked in the barricaded place inside her heart, where no emotions were allowed to flower or flourish. Except for times such as this, times when she came across her painful past, her childhood tormentors.

'*Ndewo,* greetings,' Ọwa called out as she came closer to the women huddled together in aggressive silence. She raised the pitch of her voice while softening the tone, attempting to kill the masculine resonance that terrified and repelled most people. She needed their help and would do anything for information. 'Have you seen my daughter, please?' Ọwa removed her sunglasses, squinting in the unfamiliar glare of the dying sun, trying to focus her dancing gaze on the women's hostile faces. 'Aku hasn't returned from school today and it's very unusual for her to stay out this late.'

The itching of her skin intensified as she spoke, setting her entire body on fire. She tried to resist the urge to scratch but it was as if a colony of ants had invaded her body. She was almost dancing in frenzy, her hands all over her body, the terror in her heart growing with each second. *Evil was everywhere! She was surrounded by great evil! The warning itch had never been this bad, ever.* The women looked at each other, debating what to do, if to feign deafness to her voice or blindness to her form. Again, Ọwa observed the furtive expressions on their faces, save for one of them, Mama Ten, whose face bore a look of pity and embarrassment. Ọwa had delivered each of the woman's ten children, all daughters, save for the tenth child. Mama Ten was a devout Christian whose faith in her Christian god had been sorely tested when her husband decided to take a second wife to produce the much-needed son for his lineage. Her desperation destroyed her long-held belief in the power of her Catholic rosaries.

Mama Ten had made an unexpected nocturnal visit to Ọwa's shrine one night, asking for a son. Ọwa had given her the special herbs that worked together with the will of the Earth Goddess. Even before she was summoned nine months later to deliver Mama Ten's tenth birth, Ọwa had known it would be the long-awaited son. Mama Ten's gratitude was the only genuine one Ọwa had received in her long years of birthing infants in the village. Ọwa knew the woman bore her no ill-will despite being in the company of her foes.

All eyes turned to one of the women, a tall, dark woman with long hair extensions, loud jewellery and garish make-up. It would be up to the red-lipped woman to decide what collective action they took. Owa's heart plummeted. She knew the woman; Enu, her cousin - and her worst adversary. She should have paid more attention to her itch, avoided the group like one would the Ebola virus had she known Enu was amongst them.

'*Nwa-Ntu*, Ash-Child, what makes you think we have nothing better to do with our time than to look out for your bastard daughter? And stop that stupid scratching before we do it for you,'

Enu's voice was as it had always been from the time they were kids in the playground, spiteful and mean. The envy which their grandmother had tried to beat out from her, marred her heavily made-up features. They shared the same grandmother, Enu and herself. Their mothers had been sisters, hatched in the same womb, twin girls, as different to one another as the sky was to the earth. The albino heritage, together with the gift of the Earth Goddess had gone to one twin, Xikora, Ọwa's mother. The older twin, Chika, Enu's mother, had been born with dark skin and without the yoke that came with the calling of the Earth Goddess. Yet, she had resented her younger sister's powers and constantly spread malicious stories about Xikora.

Ọwa could recall her mother raging against her twin sister, saying that save for the fact that they'd shared the same womb, she would have inflicted some terrible deformity on Chika. At those times, Ọwa would feel herself quake with fear, even though her mother's fury was not directed at her. It was the deadly blackness she saw in her mother's normally pale eyes that struck the chill of terror in her.

Her grandmother, *Nne-Ochie*, tried her best to beat the envy out of her dark-hued daughter. She'd failed. The green poison had travelled through the blood to the next generation, tainting the daughter, Enu, with the same jealous streak as her mother. Once Xikora died and her protection ended, Ọwa had endured the brunt of both her aunt and cousin's venom. Enu's taunts had been the meanest in their childhood, her tricks the nastiest and her tongue, the most vicious. Their grandmother would scream at Enu and rock

Ọwa on her laps, dry her tears and ask her not to hate her cousin. It was all envy, just plain envy for the awesome powers Ọwa had inherited from her mother, powers granted by the great Earth Goddess to the daughters of the *Nshi* clan, the albino daughters only.

Despite her grandmother's words, Enu's spite still hurt, especially when she organised a gang of tormentors, little girls who called Ọwa vile names and chanted horrible songs about her colour. They would surround her in the playground, smash her dark sunglasses and expose her eyes to the hurting brightness of the sun or break her umbrella and leave her skin in painful blisters. Then, they would laugh as she cried, sing the detested "yellow banana" song at her before consigning her to ostracised non-existence. Those were the days that her *Nwa-Ntu,* Ash-Child, habit was at its peak.

Adulthood had not minimised Enu's spite. If anything, it made it bigger, meaner, especially with the birth of Ọwa's daughter, Aku, another *Aghali* daughter who would eventually inherit the powers of the Earth Goddess. Enu was yet to have any children of her own, male or female. The men would not offer her marriage even though they willingly offered her money and sex. The reputation of the *Nshi* women, even to the tenth generation, preceded them. It was no news that the *Nshi* women did not birth living sons; just daughters, girls that might be born with the dreaded albino colour. No man wanted a wife who might taint the colour of his lineage or worse, not bear him strong sons and ensure the family name did not die out. Enu languished in luxurious discontent, milking the men for all they could give, which included a flashy red car, a lavish bungalow and a healthy collection of clothes and gold chains from Dubai. Her wealth earned her many friends, including her childhood gang of tormentors. They looked to her to make the rules of their association, as well as the rules on how to treat her poorer cousin and her bastard daughter.

And now, Enu did not disappoint. Her red-coated lips twisted with contempt as she looked down on her shorter cousin from her impressive height.

'*Aghali Akakpo,* albino midget, I thought you have the powers of the Earth Goddess in your dirty palms?' Enu mocked. Her pupils gleamed like black ice. 'Why don't you sprinkle some of your *Juju* powder and summon your daughter wherever she is,' Enu hissed and turned her face away. The other women, save Mama Ten, giggled and twittered.

'Enu, I swear your cousin has not grown an inch from our primary school days,' one of the women said, her eyes wide with mock wonder. Ọwa recognised the speaker. It was Agnes Bow-legs, the mother of the troublesome twin boys, Miracle and Marvellous. Ọwa had saved her sons' lives, not once but twice, both times for infected sores from the lashes they received from

152

the elders as punishment for theft. The boys were born with the curse of kleptomania, an ancestral curse that had blighted their lineage for centuries.

'Don't call that midget my cousin,' Enu snapped, her face clouding. 'Do we look like family to you, eh? Don't our people have a saying, *"nwanne di na mba"* - the best family is found amongst strangers? Are you women not more of a family to me than this dwarf albino witch? What has she ever done for me except to use her vile *Juju* to ensure I never get married?'

'That's a lie and you know it,' Qwa protested, unable to remain silent in the face of her cousin's false accusations. 'You know as well as I do why you're not married and I don't need to spell it out for you. I'm sorry I bothered you all. I shall continue my search for my daughter.'

Qwa turned and walked away from them. Enu's furious curses and the women's spiteful laughter followed her. Her chest felt tight, as tight as the lump behind her throat. *She must not let them get to her; she mustn't let anything distract her from her mission.* She forced back the tears and rage. Aku was all that mattered. Finding her daughter was all that mattered, not the baseless lies of a frustrated spinster and her band of worthless minions. Once again, Qwa wished she were more like her late mother, reckless and ruthless. Then the women would truly fear her. The entire village would quake in her presence. She had the powers to destroy every single one of them, bring them unspeakable pain. But as her grandmother always said, "the fully-manned lion need not roar for even the bravest warrior to quake in its presence". True power lay in knowing one's strength and refusing to use it in pride.

Ọwa nodded her head, once, twice, slowly. She would let the insult ride, swallow her humiliation and what was left of her pride. Her time would come when the rooster crowed away the dying sun and the night owls hooted the bats out of their dark caves. Then, the same women that mocked her in the daytime, save her cousin, would come crawling into her shrine, pleading forgiveness, begging for her help, asking not to be cursed or hexed, accusing each other, and revealing secrets meant for dark closets, in order to curry her favour.

Those were the toughest hours for Ọwa, the times when she required all the discipline of her art to resist the burning urge to exact vengeance on them. At those twilight hours in the dark secrecy of her hut, she could easily wreak unspeakable horrors on her tormentors and gorge them with the same pain and hatred they fed her every day of her existence. No one would know and even if they did, none would dare lift a finger against her. For then, they would truly know the terrors of her powers and fear her as they had feared her dead mother, Xikora. *Except the Earth Goddess would know*. She that sees everything underneath the sky would know how Ọwa had abused her powers and would make her pay for her pride. A true servant of the shrine was without pride; for every power she has, is but a poor reflection of the true source of that power. As her grandmother drummed into her ears in her apprentice days, it is a foolish slave who mistakes the honour given to his master as his own and a foolish king who mistakes the honour given his crown as his personal glory. She would wait and endure. Patience is a gown weaved with hope. The Earth Goddess would take vengeance for her. One day, one glorious day soon, her time would come.

With her shoulders slouched underneath her umbrella, Qwa walked on, the tight knot in her throat as painful as the bone-band gripping her heart. *Aku…Aku…where are you, daughter? Speak to me… find my soul and lead me to you…*

***

The village police station was located near the Eke market square, a few yards from the notorious dry water well that had propelled the arrival of the police to the village five years earlier. Prior to the dastardly event that took place in that well, there had been no police presence in the village. The only time the police had entered their village was on the fateful day, long before Qwa's birth, when the murderous widow of Agu of Onori clan was freed from under The Tree of Truth. The woman was never seen again and the matter died out eventually.

The village head, Chief Igwe, who was also of the Onori clan, together with the elderly *Ozo* peer group, arbitrated in most matters that could not be settled within the extended family circle. When they failed and conflicts could not be resolved amicably, they sought Qwa's help for a consultation with the oracles and *Ndichie,* the great ancestors. Cases involving missing people, major theft, farm destruction, birth of babies with unusual defects, inexplicable illnesses and sudden deaths were all brought to Qwa's doorsteps by the village representatives during the twilight hours. This was the time she carried out her night diplomacy with The Old Ones, the dead and the undead.

The notorious event that dramatically changed the lives of the villagers took place in glaring daylight when the sun was at its brightest and the market at its busiest. A vertically-challenged man, Okoro, famed for his vile disposition, had heard rumours about his wife while drinking at Mama Ten's bar. A fellow drinker had joked about his wife having a taller and more educated lover than Okoro, seeing as the woman was amongst the few educated females in the village. Suspecting his wife of infidelity, Okoro had organised a brutal revenge against her. He had bribed the members of the fearsome teenage age-group, The Ikenga, and instructed them to kidnap his wife and humiliate her in every way imaginable. The wife had just returned home from a long day at the Catholic secondary school where she taught, when the young

156

men burst into her home and dragged her off to the village square, accompanied by her husband and his clansmen. The woman's daughters screamed at them and tried to protect their mother but were violently manhandled by both their father and his male relatives.

As the villagers watched with glee, Okoro's wife was stripped naked and her hair shaved down to the scalp with some blunt instrument that left a trail of blood on her bruised head. The woman howled and cursed her husband and his clansmen, calling them every vile name under the sky. Her anger was proof of the arrogant pride and haughtiness her husband's family had always accused her of. They urged The Ikenga to deal ruthlessly with the woman. And they did.

The boys pounded her body with fists and sticks before dumping her into the dry village well. They then proceeded to spit, urinate and defecate on her naked body in turns. The more ingenious amongst them took recordings to upload on *YouTube* while others took photos of the abuse on their mobile phones. All the while, the gathered villagers jeered at the woman and cheered for her abusers. Then, The Ikenga boys broke into an impromptu celebratory dance around the well, chanting vulgar songs about the semi-conscious woman and praise songs about her husband. At the periphery of the gathering, the woman's two daughters bawled out their eyes at the unspeakable acts perpetrated against their mother.

157

One of them, the older girl, was on her mobile phone throughout the duration of the attack on their mother. Her rushed words into her phone were swallowed by the loud chants from The Ikenga, who were soon joined by the villagers and the jubilant husband, Okoro.

As The Ikenga celebrated their dastardly deed, a troop of policemen arrived in a black van, armed with tear-gas, handcuffs and guns. They were led by the abused woman's brother, who was a senior police officer in the big city. His niece had alerted him to what was happening and he had arrived just in time with his men. The villagers stared in stunned surprise at the sight of the policemen, unsure of what action to take. The streetwise amongst them quickly dispersed to their compounds while the ignoramuses stared at the officers with open-mouthed curiosity till the first bullet was fired into the air.

Then, it was pandemonium, as the villagers scattered in all directions, tripping over displayed wares in the market in their panic. Okoro was the first to be thrown into the Black Maria van. He never returned to the village alive. His bullet-riddled body was brought back to the village a few days later. He'd been shot while trying to escape from the police cell. That was the official version of events the police released. Everyone knew an alternative fact, that the woman's brother had exacted a terrible revenge on the brutal man that had publicly abused and humiliated his little sister to near-death. The entire membership of The Ikenga were also rounded up and locked up without bail at the city police station for several months. They were systematically tortured by the police till eventually, their families sold everything of value to raise the exorbitant bail-cum-bribe money demanded by the police for their release. And exactly a week to the day the last of them was released, the village police station was imposed on the community.

The state police commissioner served the village chief with papers and forced him to allocate a building to the police force. Within days, the bungalow was coated with white and blue paint and a large signboard with the inscription, "Ukari Community Police Station" was mounted. That same week, five new arrests were made in the village for minor offences that would have previously been settled within the community or by the extended families. A new era had dawned on the community, an era of outside interference and accountability, an unwanted external influence that would bring sweeping changes to their hitherto insular lifestyle, all thanks to the actions of one jealous husband and his bumbling clansmen.

***

Qwa paused at the open door of the police station, pressing herself against the white-washed wall, waiting for the sudden pounding in her heart to cease. The light bulb above the signboard was bright in her eyes. She adjusted her dark sunglasses and hugged the back of her neck with her hands. Her palms felt clammy and hot on her skin. Her head pounded and her stomach hurt as if hard pincers were gripping it. She had never been inside the village police station, had never had any contact with the police since they arrived at the village. All she knew about them was what she heard from people, stories about their guns, their brutality, their powers and occasionally, their knowledge. She'd heard that the police had secret powers, secret methods of finding things no one else could, some powerful knowledge about the minds of criminals which made it easy for them to track down bad people. It was this aspect of the police that now brought her to the station, her last resort in finding her daughter.

Qwa could no longer deceive herself about her daughter's whereabouts. The ticking on her lower lids now twitched in spasms, indicating she would have cause to weep and grieve. The warning itch on her body had never been so severe. It was now a manic possession. She gorged her skin to alleviate her distress. The sense of evil and doom was all pervading. She was trying to stay sane, stop her mind from straying to the one place that would destroy her, a terrible dark place with a deadly truth she would rather die than accept. Hope was all she had left. She could not afford to cut that thin vein of salvation. The police would find her child. *They had to...they just had to....*

She dragged herself away from the wall and shuffled into the station, her head down, her eyes dancing frantically behind her dark sunglasses. There were several people in the station despite the late hour. As soon as she stepped into the small waiting room, all sounds ceased. Voices died out and every eye turned towards her. Then the whispers started, growing louder till every ear in the room and beyond could hear multiple thoughts that were meant to be hidden but voiced with reckless abandon – *It's the albino witch-doctor... what is she doing here? Maybe she's finally killed someone with her Juju....no, I think I heard that her daughter is missing...oh yes, she has a daughter doesn't she, another albino just like herself... makes you wonder what kind of man will want to sleep with her. Just look at that skin, see how she's bleeding all over like a chicken whose feathers have been plucked while alive... Shhh, she can hear you. You don't want her to hex you and make you blind or worse, turn you crazy...*

'Woman, what can I do for you?' The loud voice pierced through Qwa's befuddled mind. It took her a few seconds to realise that the voice was addressing her. It came from the tall uniformed man behind the counter. His eyes were black, indifferent orbs that appraised her coolly underneath bushy brows. Qwa scurried over to him, her footsteps falling lightly on the dusty cement flooring.

'Good evening, sir,' her voice was low, almost a whisper. She didn't want the policeman to judge her and despise her because of her deep masculine voice. There was little she could do about her colour. She would just have to pray to the Earth Mother that the man had a heart beneath the daunting black uniform. She glanced behind her fearfully, craving privacy, wishing no one was about to witness her humiliation. Insults were a daily aspect of her life but it was insults from the familiar, her community and family. She was used to that. She just didn't want the humiliation which she knew was coming from the policeman, a total stranger, to be witnessed by others who would spread it across the villages. 'Please *Oga*, master, help me find my daughter, please. She has not come home since she left the house for school today. She has never failed to come home, never. Please help me, *Oga* police, help me. Aku is all I have... my only child... she's my only child... everything. Please... please... help me... please sir...'

Owa began shaking. Her whole body was one massive quake. It was as if voicing her fears had finally made them real. Tears she had fought so long to withhold poured from her eyes, streaming underneath her sunglasses. Her harsh sobs reverberated in the small crowded room. She clasped herself, wrapping her arms around her body, tightly, trying to halt the rocking motion that threatened to topple her to the hard floor. No one came to her comfort, not one among the several villagers in the room. She was lost in a dark place, a terrible lonely place without light, without hope.

162

A strong arm enveloped her shoulder, held her close, a human arm, a caring arm. The shock halted her sobs. Qwa glanced up to see the tall policeman she'd been speaking to minutes before grief overwhelmed her. His eyes had lost their aloof indifference. They were warm with compassion. She wasn't sure who was more stunned, herself or the goggle-eyed villagers.

'Come,' he urged. 'Come and sit down, ok? Don't cry. Your daughter is ok. We'll find her for you.' He guided her to a wooden bench occupied by some of the villagers. 'Get up, you idiots,' he shouted at them, lowering Qwa onto the bench as it was vacated with panicked alacrity. The villagers didn't need the policeman to scare them away from the bench. No one wanted to share a seat with the albino witch. One never knew what evil entities clung to her in the guise of flies or bedbugs, which might leap from her body and possess the unwary.

Qwa removed her glasses, wiping her eyes with the edge of her wrapper. She kept them shut, wary of the bright glare of the florescent bulb overhead. The policeman left her briefly for his desk. He soon returned with a sheet of paper and pen and sat close to her. Qwa hurriedly replaced her dark sunglasses, unwilling to look into his eyes, afraid of what she might read in them, of what she might *not* read in them.

'Brother, I'll advise you not to seat near the *Aghari*,' a male voice advised from across the room. 'You're a stranger here and not even from our tribe. So, you have no idea what that thing you're sitting next to is. Take it from us who know better and care for your wellbeing, you'd better send that thing away and focus on us real humans.' Qwa saw a dirty middle-aged man whom she recognised as the husband of One-eye Theresa.

'Shut your filthy mouth before I throw you into the cell,' the policeman thundered, his eyes blazing.

'Brother, calm down, you hear? The man is only trying to help you because we know you're not from our parts and don't know about the *Aghali* woman or the risks you're taking by sitting next to her.' The voice was female this time, a wheedling, obsequious voice. Others joined in till the waiting room was as noisy as a Pentecostal church service in full steam.

'Out! All of you. Get out now and don't let me see your faces again this night, otherwise, you'll all spend the night in the cell and your bail will be set at ₦2000 each,' the policeman threatened, standing up from the bench. He didn't need to repeat his threat. The villagers rushed out of the station as if chased by angry bees. The mention of bail money was enough to send them packing. Everyone knew that where bail money was concerned, the police were ruthless. The villagers could barely afford three meals a day much less forking out ₦2000 bail-bribe, and all because of the albino witch. If the *Yoruba* policeman wanted to kill himself, then that was his prerogative. He wouldn't say they hadn't warned him.

164

Yoruba people always think they're smarter than everyone, especially when you dress them with the power of a police uniform. It was his funeral. They'd done their bit and fulfilled all Christian righteousness. The stupid grasshopper killed for breakfast by the very noisy *Okpoko* bird can't say it wasn't warned unless it was deaf or suicidal.

'Are you okay?' The policeman sat down again next to Qwa. His voice was unchanged. It was still kindly, laced with sympathy despite all the dire warnings from the villagers. Qwa felt something inside her collapse, the locked place behind her heart. Unfamiliar emotions coursed through her body, emotions long buried since the death of her grandmother, *Nne-Ochie,* the only person that had loved her unconditionally before the birth of her daughter, Aku. Gratitude, relief and security all rushed to the fore, warring with other equally powerful emotions of uncertainty and fear; anxiety that it might all be a fluke, that the policeman was playing a trick on her like everyone else, that he might not have heard what the villagers said about her, that he might soon come to his senses and see her as everyone else saw her, something loathsome, unnatural, unworthy to be called human. His compassion had flowered something within her, a fledgling trust in humanity, a budding belief that perhaps, there were people who didn't hate her kind as her tribe did, people who might accept her right to existence as a full member of the human race.

'Thank you, sir... thank you,' her voice was deep with its natural male resonance. She was bone-weary, tired of hiding herself. All she wanted to do was to curl up on her mat and sleep and never wake up; unless she was waking to the blissful sound of her daughter's voice. '*Oga*, please help me find my daughter. I know something is wrong. I sense it in the people. They know something but nobody is telling me anything. Maybe they will talk to you, tell you where my Aku is. I'm not evil as they say... I swear. I have never harmed any of them. My daughter is a good girl. She's a good student too. Ask them at the Catholic school and they'll tell you she is respectful. She's all I have in this world. My life is worthless without her. If you can't help me I...'

Owa halted her speech, abruptly, as if her mouth was plugged with glue. She sat quietly, tensed with an unnatural stillness that made her appear like an alabaster figurine. She'd never been much of a talker, save when she chatted with her daughter and consulted with the oracles in the shrine. She was surprised by how much she had said to this stranger, a policeman no less, one of the very people she'd heard talked about with so much negativity. Owa gave herself a mental kick. *She of all people should know better than to believe everything she heard from the villagers. After all, wasn't she a victim of their lies and vicious rumours?*

'Tell me everything, right from the start,' the policeman said. 'Don't leave anything out, no matter how insignificant it may seem to you. Start from the last time you saw your daughter. In fact, start from a week before the last time you saw your daughter. Tell me everything about her, who her friends are, how she behaved for the week preceding her disappearance, what you suspect about the villagers and why you suspect it, who your enemies are in the village…no, don't bother with that last bit. I think I already know how things stand with you here. You don't need to tell me.' The policeman made a wry face. 'My father was also the *Babalawo* of my people, just like you. So, I have an idea how superstitious people can be about the art and its practitioners,' the policeman laughed, a sound that again brought a flowering to Qwa's heart. *Surely, this must be a gift from the Earth Mother*, she marvelled. How else can one explain the coincidence that the very policeman she'd turned to for help happened to be the son of another servant of the gods, a medicine-man, just like herself?

'Which god does your father serve?' She asked, looking fully into his eyes for the first time since she entered the station. His pupils were dark and warm, his features, rugged and strong. It was a face she could trust.

'*Orisha Orinle*. My father was a servant of the deity, *Orisha Orinle*, he of the forests and oceans, the hunter deity. I grew up in the art and was raised to take over from my father. But as we know, the gods don't always give us the wishes of our hearts. My father is now dead and I am here. And you, who do you serve?'

'*Aná*, the Earth Goddess. My clan have always been the high priestesses of *Aná*. My mother was one before her death. I took over from her.'

'It's the same with my family. My great-grandfather right down to my father, were all servants of *Orisha Orinle*. My little brother inherited the gift despite my father's hopes for me. So, I joined the police force instead for a different kind of power,' he laughed, a warm sound that brought an unfamiliar knot in Qwa's stomach. She marvelled yet again about the incredible situation she found herself in. He was the first male she had fully engaged in conversation which didn't revolve around occultic remedies for mysterious troubles.

'I think the gods must like younger siblings. *Aná* also chose my mother, who was the younger twin. I don't think her sister ever forgave her for inheriting the power. Were you upset when it went to your younger brother?'

'Not at all. In fact, I was very relieved. I don't think I would have made a good shrine-servant. I'm too independent and want to do things my own way.'

'We're as the gods make us. They know our talents and weaknesses before we are born and give their gifts to those they think will serve them best. It doesn't mean they don't love the others. In fact, they seem to favour the ones they don't yoke with their powers.'

'You're right. I consider myself blessed. My little brother never gets any rest. Just as people come to me with their troubles when I'm on duty, they pester my brother day and night with everything. You know how it is. No day off or rest for you shrine-people,' he laughed again. 'Incidentally, my name is Femi, Detective Femi. I already know your name. You have no idea how many times your name comes up during my working hours,' he laughed once again.

'What do they say about me?' Owa couldn't resist asking, even as she knew she wouldn't like what she heard.

'The usual.... the albino witch has hexed our crops, our health, our marriage. Our enemies are getting powerful *Juju* from her to harm us. Arrest her, arrest them, the usual nonsense.'

'I have never used my powers to harm anyone, I swear in the name of *Aná*,' Owa was desperate to clear her name before Femi. For some reason, his opinion of her mattered more than it had ever done with anyone. 'All I do is heal them with special herbs that benefit them, engage in divination with the ancestors and my goddess on their behalf, bring out their young from the womb and prepare their dead for the ritual of departure into the realm of the ancestors. My powers are not for evil. *Aná* would take her gift from me if I used it for evil. My mother lost her life because she used it in ways which the Earth Mother didn't like, not evil as such, just a bit excessively, if you know what I mean. I would never make the same mistake.'

'I understand. You don't need to explain. Their problem is your colour, that's all. Every sentence that comes out of their mouth when they talk about you is prefixed with the word, "albino witch". I tell them to bring me proof and I'll arrest you. We policemen deal with facts, not superstitions. Which is why I want you to tell me every single fact about your daughter's disappearance. I promise you that I'll not let you down. I'll work on this case as if it's my daughter that is missing and we shall find your daughter for you very soon.'

'May the Earth Goddess shower you with her blessings,' Qwa's voice was fervent. She clasped Femi's large hand with her own. 'I will never forget your kindness. Never! My powers are at your disposal. Day or night, I will do anything that you ask of me. Thank you, thank you.'

'Don't thank me. I'm only doing my job. Now tell me everything you know.' Femi raised his pen and waited for her to speak. Qwa paused, unsure where to start. So many things had happened, things she should have paid greater attention to but didn't. Perhaps she wouldn't be in this situation had she been more focused on the omens rather than her art. She would tell Femi everything, every tiny fact, beginning with the dreams that started three nights ago, dreams about *Mbana-Oyi*, The Cold Realm, a place she used to visit during her night diplomacy, till the night the rogue death deities almost trapped her in their blood sludge.

But for the Earth Goddess, Qwa would have lost her soul and never returned to her prone body inside the shrine. As it were, she had made the journey back, brought home by the Earth Mother, waking to find the unconscious body of her daughter who had been overcome with terror at her first sight of the great Earth Goddess. That night was the last time Qwa visited *Mbana-Oyi* to see her dead mother. The Earth Goddess had banned her from returning to The Cold Realm.

Yet, for three nights in a row, she had dreamt of returning to that dark, soulless void. Each time, she saw her mother as always, stuck to her midriff in the blood sludge, railing against the fearsome guardians of the realm, Walking-Grave and Corpse-Maker. But in her dreams, her mother was no longer alone in the blood sludge. Another doomed spirit shared the sludge prison with Xikora, a figure whose face Qwa could never see in her dreams, no matter how hard she tried. She had discussed the dreams with Aku, tried some divination to reveal the meaning. All in vain. In the end, she had pushed it to the back of her mind. It was just her guilt about her mother that was haunting her dreams. The other figure in the blood sludge was none other than herself, visiting her mother as she wished with every breath in her body. Which explained why she couldn't see her own face in the dreams.

Then the body itching had started, without warning. Normally, she would get the itch when she was in the presence of someone or something bad, evil. Her whole body would start to itch as if infested with a colony of soldier ants. The itch was her guide, her early warning mechanism. Just like when The Fat-Man came into her shrine for a consultation. She had never met him prior to that night when he turned up at her door. She knew him only by name, Eze son of Agu of Onori clan. He was the only surviving son of his late father. Rumour had it that Eze's father and brother had been murdered by his stepmother, a foreign woman with the strange name of Desee, because she couldn't have children – at least, that was the story Owa had heard as she grew up in the village. The terrible crime had happened long before her time, in the years when the Tree of Truth still stood, tall and foreboding in the forbidden forest. They said that the wicked stepmother had been force-fed the corpse water used in washing her husband's decomposed body. She was also forced to spend three nights with her late husband's corpse underneath The Tree of Truth to prove her innocence in her husband's strange death.

Owa heard that the murderess had been at the point of death before she was miraculously freed by the policemen brought by her sister, who was a political bigwig at the time. Several villagers had spent long incarcerations at the prison in the big city because of that terrible event which eventually led to the felling of The Tree of Truth by the Government Forestry Ministry. Eze was born a few months after the nefarious events that took place in the forbidden

172

forest and had been raised by his mother and clansmen in the village before making it big in the city.

When Ọwa heard that he wanted a consultation with her, she had agreed to the meeting. She had no idea what he wanted from her. She was aware that he had three wives and that only one of them had given him a son. It would appear that the problem his late father experienced, had also followed Eze into his matrimonial home. Males were certainly a scarce commodity in the Onori sperm-holder. Perhaps he wanted some herbs to make his wives birth sons for him. Ọwa would let the Earth Mother guide her.

To her horror, her body had begun itching the second The Fat-Man walked into her shrine. Looking at his face, there was nothing particularly evil about the fleshy scarred features with the unusual thin lips. Yet, Ọwa's body crawled as if it had been in contact with squirming snakes. She immediately steeled her mind and guarded her spirit. This was a bad man regardless of appearances, despite the aura of benign geniality he exuded.

Their meeting was brief and terrible. Throughout its duration, Ọwa scratched her body like a demented fool. Her instincts had been right. As soon as he sat on the shrine floor, The Fat-Man had asked for *Juju* to eliminate a political opponent. He wanted a powerful curse that would not only impoverish his enemy but also drive him to lunacy. The Fat-Man demanded that Ọwa inflict his enemy with the *Leloolé* curse, the rotting-flesh death, a terrible curse that struck the body with festering maggot-infested boils. The accursed would become a walking corpse, stinking from putrefaction as his body slowly rotted from inside. A swarm of grave flies would follow the doomed victim like a black cloud, feeding on the weeping pustules. Eventually, he would be ostracised by all. When death finally came calling, it would be a merciful release. The *Leloolé* curse was a fearsome one reserved for the truly wicked. It had been the chosen weapon of her late mother, Xikora, in her lifetime.

Yet, this was the kind of evil that The Fat-Man wished for his political opponent, just because the man had beaten him to the top spot at the local government elections. With his opponent dead, Eze, who was his deputy, would automatically assume the seat of the chairman of the local government.

Qwa had not spared him her vitriol and rage. She'd chased him from her shrine as if he were a black viper. She hooted at him as he dashed out of the shrine to his car, determined to shame him. In seconds, the headlamps from his car flooded the night with light. Just before he drove off, he had fixed her with a look she would never forget, a cold look that would have sent the chills of fear to her spine had she not known her own powers. He had spat at her and promised retribution.

She could still hear his voice as he told her to sleep with one eye open from that night onward. Qwa had dismissed his threats as the baseless bluff of a humiliated man. Now, she wished she had not been so cocky, so unprepared. She wished his stepmother had murdered him together with his father all those years gone. Something told her that The Fat-Man was somehow involved in her daughter's disappearance. She had no proof but every instinct in her body screamed out his name and she knew that her instincts never lied.

It was that same instinct that had suddenly driven her from her house to her daughter's school at midday, even though Aku was not expected home till late in the afternoon. But she couldn't wait for school to be over. Her body had suddenly started itching like crazy for no visible reason. Her lower lids had started twitching violently at the same time, a sign that she would have cause to shed tears in grief. The last time her lower lids had ticked was on the day her grandmother died, a terrible day that wrought an equally terrible change to her fate, the day she fell into the wardship of her auntie, Chika, as a young teenager. Otherwise, all the twitches she got were on her upper lids, which simply signified rain or a storm.

The sudden chills that coated her body with cold sweats finally decided her. She was not one to get ill, had never suffered from even the common malaria which everybody in the village endured at frequent intervals. The Earth Mother kept her servants healthy and strong to do her work. So, when the first shivers hit her body, Qwa knew it was a bad omen, just like the body itch and eyelid

175

ticks. Without delay, she changed out of her home wrapper and tied her market wrapper. She would bring Aku home from school early till whatever evil was lurking in the shadows passed away.

Her trip to the school had been uneventful even though she noticed that she got more curious looks than usual from the villagers. She was used to their stares and their taunts. At least they never used physical violence on her, not since her childhood days. She always thanked the Earth Goddess for her gift, as she knew that it was her powers that kept her and her daughter safe. Her skin-kin in other lands did not fare as well as she did. At least in their village, all they had to endure was contempt and exclusion, not violence and death.

The school gate was open when she got there. Owa could count in one hand the number of times she had been in that Catholic bastion of learning. She hated the school and everything it stood for. But the Catholic priest was an influential man and insisted that every child in the village attended school. He was backed by both the village chief and the state government. Worse, her daughter, Aku, liked the place. But for Aku's tearful pleas, Owa would have never allowed her daughter to step foot in that place of false teachings.

Owa had been surprised to find the school deserted save for the old man that acted as the security man for the principal's office. He informed her the school was closed for the day as the principal,

Father Ike, had been attacked by armed robbers on his way to the school that morning and was hospitalised. The students had all been sent home as a result.

Ọwa segued across the schoolground, shouting out Aku's name. By the time she'd searched every classroom and realised that her daughter was anywhere but in the school premises, her heart had started thudding painfully in her ribs. The itching had turned her into a hopping, dancing maniac and her eyelids were in spasms. From that fateful time, she had not stopped her search for her daughter. Ego, her daughter's only friend, had been in tears, blaming herself and insisting on joining Ọwa in her search. She had welcomed the companionship of someone whom she knew cared almost as much for Aku as she did. Their search had yielded nothing and as the day lengthened into evening, Ọwa would see the same furtive look her cousin had worn on the faces of several villagers that day.

Femi's pen raced across the pages of his notebook all the time Ọwa talked. When she finally went quiet, he took a deep breath and let out a loud sigh. Once again, he reached out an arm and hugged her close, in silence, with deep empathy. Then he stood up from the bench. Ọwa marvelled at his great height and the muscled strength of his body.

'You've done well,' he said to her, a hard look in his eyes. 'Come, go home now and rest, ok? I'm guessing you have not eaten anything all day. There's nothing more you can do this night except to try and catch some sleep,' Femi paused, as if choosing his words with care. 'Just a thought. Have you asked your goddess for help?'

'Not yet. There's been no time. As I said, I've spent all day searching for Aku, walking everywhere in the village, asking people questions, calling out her name, returning home again in case she was back. My daughter is my helper, my link-chain to the underworld. Without her, all I have is the shrine-goat, which I haven't used in a very long time, not since Aku learnt how to conduct my spirit during night diplomacy. I usually consult the Earth Mother at night, during our *Áfá* ritual. Now I'm done here, I'll go home and seek her help, even though I believe she is already helping me without my asking. See how she sent you to me. The Earth Mother, like all the gods, is all knowing and all loving to her servants. Praise be her name.'

'Amen,' Femi said.

'Our people say, "*Ise,*" meaning, "So be it!" It's the church people that say, "Amen",' Ọwa laughed, a hoarse sound that stunned her by both its sound and its occurrence. She could not remember the last time, if ever, that she had laughed with a man; she could not remember ever having met a man such as the tall detective, whose quiet strength and warm gaze filled the cold place in her heart with hope and something else she could not name.

Except it was something good, even beautiful, a strange feeling that made her want to wrap her arms around herself to keep it safe, savour it and never let it go.

Ω Ω Ω

9

The Search for Justice

Mama Ten came to visit her that night. She arrived a few minutes before midnight when Ọwa was preparing to commune with the Earth Goddess. The knock at her front-door was low, tentative. Owa heard it from the gloomy silence of the shrine. The shrine-goat stirred at its post by the door but stayed put, chewing on dried yam peels on the floor. Ọwa's heart soared as she rushed out of the shrine towards her hut. *Aku! Her daughter had returned! Finally! Earth Mother be praised!*

Mama Ten waited outside her shut door, her features invisible in the darkness. But Ọwa recognised her mammoth form and every line on her face. At night, her vision was as sharp as a cat's. It was only the sun that killed her sight. Her heart sank as her former joy turned to weary resignation.

'Mama Ten,' Ọwa's voice was dull, drained. 'What brings you to my hut this night? It is not a good time for me, as you know. I have a bigger burden that demands my attention.'

'That's why I've come, to lift some of that burden for you,' Mama Ten said, her voice a whisper, her face coated with fear and pity. 'My mission will bring you no joy but maybe it might give you some answers.'

'Come, come inside and rest your legs,' Owa offered, opening her front-door. But Mama Ten did not accept the invitation. Her body exuded anxiety as she kept glancing over her shoulder and fidgeting with her wrapper. The smell of fried food clung to her like a second flavoured skin.

'I'm sorry I can't accept your invitation, not tonight,' Mama Ten said. 'I'm praying no-one followed me here. But I couldn't rest in all Christian conscience after what I heard at my bar this evening. You know how the men like to come and relax at my bar after work. Sometimes they drink too much and their mouths leak like baskets. Secrets spill, some good, some bad,' Mama Ten laughed, a loud, jarring sound in the dark solemnity of the night. She caught the laughter in her cupped hand and glanced behind her with the same fearful look her eyes had worn since her arrival. 'Anyway, as I was saying, drink can drag out strange things from men's mouths and tonight, a bad secret spilled from the lips of one of the young men who works for Chief Eze - you know, The Fat-Man, son of the late Agu of Onori clan. He's the deputy local government chairman and a big name in politics. Anyway, the boy, Uche, a silly lad who will insist on wearing sunglasses even in the darkest night...God knows there's nothing wrong with his eyes. It's not as if he needs sunshades like you do. Still, each to their own. I just think he looks silly in them at night,' Mama Ten's lips curved in a disapproving sneer.

'Yes, yes, I know. So, what did he say? What bad secrets did he spill?' Qwa's voice was impatient. Her heart thudded in a frantic beat. *Her instinct had been right! The Fat-Man had a hand in Aku's disappearance!*

'Well, he came into my bar to drink with another one of his colleagues, a boy called Donatus, not a bad boy but easily misled. It's terrible when our children fall into bad company. Mind you, I blame it on the parents, who should tie a stronger rope around their children to stop them falling into Satan's temptation. I don't care what anyone says but that kind of work is no good for any decent young man. Being a thug is as bad as being a policeman in my opinion. I...'

'Mama Ten, tell me what the boy said,' Qwa's voice was almost a scream.

'Yes, sorry, of course,' Mama Ten looked apologetic. The look of fear returned to her plump features again. 'The boy, Uche, the one that always wears the dark sunglasses, he got very drunk and began to boast about how his *Oga*, master, will soon be coming into a lot of money and power. He said Chief Eze had your daughter, Aku, to thank for his incoming abundance. I asked him what he meant and he said it was a secret and his friend, Donatus, who wasn't as drunk, scolded him and hushed him up before he could say anymore. But I thought you should know what he said. I mean, why in Jesus' world would he say Chief Eze has your daughter to thank for his incoming wealth when everyone knows your daughter went missing today? Also, I've heard quite a few people whispering Chief Eze's name together with your daughter's. I won't mention names but several people in the village know secrets they're not telling. Anyway, I must leave now. I've told you what I heard. My conscience can now rest. I owe you a lot and want you to know that my heart cries with your heart and I will light a candle for Aku at Mass tomorrow. *Kachifo,* may morning come.'

Mama Ten hurried away into the night, her fat body rolling like a pregnant cow on the run. Qwa remained immobile by her front-door. The pounding in her heart had travelled to her head, weakening her limbs, stealing her strength. Every vein in her body reacted to the terrible words Mama Ten had spoken. Her heart rejected them even as her mind screamed the dark truth of the news. *Aku! Her daughter had fallen into the hands of The Fat-Man and been used for evil rituals! The Fat-Man had made good his threats and murdered her only child to attract wealth to himself! The dark terror she had lived with from the day she cut the umbilical cord binding her infant to safety, had finally descended on them.*

Qwa was a medicine-woman and an *Aghali*. She knew how those things worked, how unscrupulous witch-doctors harvested the body parts of albinos for their nefarious arts. She had thought her art kept them safe in their village, as it had done through several generations. But now, that safety net had been torn. Evil had crept through the barrier and into their lives. The Fat-Man, Eze, son of Agu of Onori clan, had carried the evil that had tainted his late father's house into their lives. *Her daughter... Aku...her beautiful daughter... Aku... Aku...*

Ọwa began to howl! Her cries echoed into the night, halting the hoots of the owls and the chirps of the crickets. Mama Ten heard the keening and hurried her steps, crossing herself and warding off the evil. A sudden shadow, a dark and terrifying shadow seemed to have descended on the silent path, sending chills to her spine. She wondered if she had done the right thing in telling what she'd heard, if she had unwittingly released a darker evil by her nocturnal visit to the medicine-woman's remote bungalow. But, she owed it to her conscience to speak up. Regardless of what anyone in the village said, Ọwa had never done her or any of them any harm, unlike her late mother, Xikora. The poor woman had been badly ostracised by all just because of the vitriolic campaign waged against her by her cousin, Enu and her gang of petty village women. She prayed the child, Aku, was safe; that no harm had come to her. The girl was all that the poor thing had. Without her daughter, Mama Ten feared the woman might go crazy. As a mother, she knew it would kill her if any harm ever befell any of her ten children. *Jesus Christ forbid!* Again, Mama Ten crossed herself and warded the evil away as she hurried towards her house. Behind her, the deep wails of the keening mother followed her like the death knells of a funeral bell.

***

Ọwa made her way to the house of the village head, Chief Igwe. Her eyes were swollen and red-rimmed. Tear stains crusted on her cheeks. Her feet were bare, free of shoes. They were dust-coated and sore from the endless hours of walking she had endured, searching for her daughter. In the deep gloom of the night, the fear of snakes or scorpions was the last thing on her mind. Two names rang in her head. *Aku. Eze.* Like the repetitive speech of the village tailor, Stuttering Linus, the names ran in her mind with incessant urgency. *Aku. Eze.* One name was loved, the other loathed. The village chief would give her justice, Ọwa thought, as her steps drew nearer to the story building that housed the peer.

Chief Igwe was respected by the demon man, Eze, who was from his clan. The chief was also the only man that could confer Eze with the coveted *Ọzọ* title, which all wealthy men sought to cement their status in the wider community. The chief had the power to summon Eze and demand answers. He was the final arbiter in the village before even the police. Had she known what she now knew, Ọwa wouldn't have gone to the police station for help that evening. Some things were better resolved within the community when one knew the players involved. She now had irrefutable proof that The Fat-Man was involved in her daughter's disappearance. She would lay her case before their village head and it would be up to Chief Igwe to give her justice.

The gate at the chief's house was locked. Qwa banged on the high metal shield. The sound of her knocks was like raucous laughter at a dirge. It shattered the silence of the night, dragging the gate-man from his sleeping mat and sparking bright lights into the darkened windows of the main house. Before the sleepy-eyed gate-man could open the gate, an angry voice boomed from an open upstairs window in the large house.

'Who is it that dares bang on my gate at this unearthly hour? May *Amadioha*'s thunder render them deaf if their mission is not important enough to warrant this intrusion,' Chief Igwe's voice boomed with rage. '*Aboki,* gate-man, where are you? Open that gate at once and see who the mad person is that dares disturb my sleep.'

The gate-man fiddled clumsily with the heavy padlock before drawing the metal panel inches apart. He pushed a torch-welding hand through the narrow opening and peered out at Qwa. She blinked and shut her eyes, blinded by the harsh glare. On recognising the visitor, the gate-man's face twisted into an ugly mask.

'Albino woman, you be craze? What you want here at this hour? You not fit wait till morning to see the chief? Instead you come disturb the sleep of peaceful people like myself, banging at the gate as if the house belong to your Papa,' the gate-man hissed and spat into the soil. His pigeon-English lingo, together with the deep blade marks cut into his dark skin, singled him out immediately as an *Hausa* man from the far north of the country. A lot of wealthy *Igbo* people employed Hausa men as their gate-keepers in the belief that it would be more difficult for enemies to bribe them and gain entry into the house to do harm. After all, a man's deadliest enemy was the enemy that shared the same mat and cooking pot with him.

'Let me in, please. I must see the chief immediately. My mission is not one that can wait till morning,' Qwa tried to push her way through the gate. The gate-man resisted her with his arm.

'Who is it?' Chief Igwe shouted from the open window. 'Let the person in so I can see who the idiot is that has no respect for his superiors.' The absence of a car parked outside his gate assured the chief that whoever his visitor was could not be a wealthy and important person worthy of his respect. The gate-man let Qwa in with a muttered curse and returned to his small shack by the gate. His job was done. He had no curiosity about the albino woman's visit. He knew her, of course – who didn't? The one the villagers called "the albino witch". But he could neither understand nor speak the *Igbo* language even if he wanted, to follow the conversation between his master and his midnight visitor.

'*Dibia* Qwa of the *Nshi* clan!' The chief's voice was filled with incredulity at the sight of the medicine-woman. She was clearly the last person he expected to see. 'What brings you here tonight? Have the oracles spoken to you concerning any matter dear to my heart or pertaining to the welfare of our village? It must indeed be urgent for you to come to my house for the very first time if my memory is correct, and at this unearthly hour. Come closer, woman. I will be downstairs with you in minutes.' The chief's fleshy face disappeared from the window before Qwa could speak.

The front-door opened and Chief Igwe motioned her inside his front living-room where he received the poorer masses. The inner plush living-room was reserved for his important guests. He ushered Qwa into one of the wooden benches lining the walls of the room. Qwa shook her head mutely, her pale eyes darting wildly in her agitation. Her skin began to itch, a burning itch she hadn't felt since leaving the police station earlier that evening. She forced her hands to still, to resist the manic urge to scratch.

'Chief Igwe, I come to you for justice,' her masculine voice rang even deeper in the sparsely furnished room lit up by a dim bulb. 'My daughter has been kidnapped for evil *Juju* by Eze, son of Agu of Onori clan, your clansman. She went to school today and never came home again. I am begging you to summon Eze

190

immediately and make him return my daughter to me. She is all I have. Without her, my life is worthless. Help me, please. Help me.' Qwa reached out to take the chief's hand. He flinched back as if she were a viper, pushing his hands into the pocket of his white kaftan. His face wore a cloudy look.

'Are you telling me that the only reason you've come here at this time of the night is to lay false accusation against a respected son of this village, a man who has brought honour and pride to our community despite the tragedies that marred his childhood, my own clansman and friend?' The chief's voice rose with each syllable he uttered. 'Are you crazy, woman? *Chei*! That I, Chief Igwe, should live to see my throne so disrespected just because of my good nature and generosity!' The chief pounded his chest with his fist. 'Woman, if you know what is good for you, leave my house at once and never step foot into this compound again, even if my late father speaks to you from our ancestors' realm, do you hear me?'

Qwa fell to her knees and gripped his ankle. Fresh tears flooded her face. 'Chief, please do not send me away without giving me justice,' she sobbed, giving in to the itch, scratching her face, her throat, her arms. 'You are our village head. It is to you that we all come for justice. Despite his status, Eze, son of Agu of Onori clan respects you like everyone else does. As you said, he is your clansman, an Onori man like yourself. You are his elder and he will do as you tell him. You are a parent like I am. You must know the pain I'm going through right now. It will take nothing off you to demand answers from Eze, make him return to me that which he has unjustly taken. Please Chief Igwe, help me. Don't send me away without giving me justice...justice...' Qwa's voice choked behind her throat as her body shuddered with the violence of her sobs. Chief Igwe shook her hands off his ankle and stepped further away from her.

'I've heard enough of your ramblings,' he thundered, a deep frown furrowing his brows. 'I have a good mind to call my gate-man to throw you out of my house immediately. But I'm a generous and righteous man and will grant you justice if you give me proof that Eze is behind your daughter's disappearance,' the chief glanced quickly at his watch. 'I can spare you just five minutes, so make it brisk. You've already disrupted my sleep long enough. Speak. Who told you that Eze kidnapped your daughter?'

'It was M...' Qwa paused. Mama Ten's frightened face flashed in her mind. She couldn't take the risk of getting the woman into trouble with The Fat-Man and his violent thugs. 'I consulted the oracles. They gave me his name.' Qwa lied for one of the few times in her life. The lie stuck in her throat and her face flushed with guilt. She had never learnt the art of subterfuge. Her meagre social interaction with people had given her little preparation in the art of deceit. The chief saw the lie for what it was in seconds. A deep frown furrowed his brows. He scowled down at Qwa from his imposing height.

'You are lying and you know it as well as I do,' his voice was a contemptuous sneer. 'It is a shame when a high-priestess of the oracle uses the position for her own questionable ends, just to injure another innocent party. Leave my house at once and don't dare spread any more malicious stories about my clansman otherwise, you'll know the full weight of my justice which you so loudly demand. Go now; and keep your peace to yourself.'

Chief Eze walked towards his front-door and flung it wide open. Qwa scrambled to her feet, retying her wrapper which had come loose while she knelt before the chief. She wiped her wet face with one end of the cloth and tucked it in again. With slow deliberation, she untied her head scarf, exposing the bright, yellow lushness of her braided hair. As she squeezed past the bulky frame of the chief, she stooped and laid her headscarf on the floor at his feet.

'I bare my head before you, Chief Igwe,' Qwa said, her voice hard, bitter. 'I leave all my thoughts and my pain in my scarf at your feet. Step on it as you have stepped on my heart tonight. Fling it away as you have flung away my pride and my hope. Destroy it as you have destroyed my life with your words and actions. What are we but mere mortals? In the end, justice belongs to the gods. I will return to my Earth Goddess to seek justice for my child. *Ndewo,* goodbye.'

Ọwa walked out of the house and made her steady way to the gate. Behind her, she heard the chief's voice shout her name, demand that she take her scarf with her. She ignored him. Her thoughts were far away from the place. His voice was an irritant that intruded into her musings. She walked through the open gate, gazing through the gate-man as if he had ceased to exist. She caught the startled look on his face, a sudden fear in his eyes as he followed her progress.

A subtle change was taking place inside Ọwa, a change that was yet unknown to her but cloaked her with an unsettling quality. A wild fire blazed in her eyes, a flame that burnt with resolve and hate. The rage that had lain dormant within rose to the fore. She had paid her dues to the mortal authorities. They had failed her. Now, she would seek the greater authority, call on all her powers for justice. After all, what justice can be deadlier than the pure justice of the great Earth Goddess, *Aná*?

***

Ọwa returned to her hut and headed straight to the small hut that housed the shrine of the Earth Goddess. Inside, the white shrine-goat, the one she fondly named Ebele, stumbled to its feet at her entrance. She stroked its head, her actions tender, yet distracted. She stripped herself of every item of clothing, her movements deliberate, unhurried. Then, she covered her skin with the special kennel-oil of divination before sitting cross-legged at the base of the imposing black statue of the Earth Goddess. She took several deep breaths, forcing focus and calm into her raging mind. Soon, she began to mutter words to the deity, her voice growing in volume, till she was screaming her pain with unleashed fury.

For several hours, Ọwa alternated between wailing and shouting, mumbling and whispering, pounding her head with her fists and pulling her hair with manic fingers. The shrine goat fidgeted, restless, yet too greedy to abandon its meal.

Suddenly, Ọwa stilled. Her head cocked, as if listening to a silent voice in her head. Her nude body glistened with hot sweat underneath the poor light of the lamp. Soon, she rose to her feet and began rummaging in her raffia bag. She collected several white *Nzu* chalk sticks which she proceeded to ground into fine powder with the grinding stone by the hearth. Then she collected some charcoal from the burnt wood in the fireplace and ground them into powder as well. She made a deep cut in her thumb and squeezed tight. Her blood, thick and dark, dropped into the small calabash of water she held beneath her thumb. She watched the water turn a bright red. Then she poured some of the blood-water into the ground ash and the rest into the chalk powder.

When she was done, Ọwa covered one half of her face with the black ash paste to signify the mourning of her child. Then she coated the other half of her face with the *Nzu,* white chalk paste, to signify the protective presence of the benevolent spirits and ancestors. Finally, she wrapped a couple of *Igu,* palm fronds, around her head and gripped more of them between her teeth to signify *Ofor n'Ogu,* clean hands, justice and karma. She stood up, bowed to the statue of the Earth Goddess, patted the shrine-goat once more on its head and collected her discarded clothes by the door. She dressed up, this time with haste and shook the dust off her feet. She was now ready for the first phase of her war against the foul man that had murdered her only child.

***

For two days and two nights, Qwa camped outside the storey building built by the late Agu of Onori clan who was murdered by his first wife after he brought in a second wife into their home. That second wife was Eze's late mother, Enu, a woman who had been as huge and violent as her son. Eze now resided in his late father's house, together with his three wives and his nine children, all daughters, save for one, his only son, Caesar, a boy of five years. Qwa had seen the child several times, a carbon image of The Fat Man in every way, albeit, his height was closer to his late grandfather's small stature rather than Eze's imposing gait.

On arriving at Eze's house, Qwa knocked on the gate, several loud knocks that awakened the entire household. Several voices were heard from inside the main house, woman and children's fearful voices, panicked shouts of armed-robbers and burglary. Eze's gate-man was the first to rush out, quickly followed by Eze himself when he heard the loud scream of his gate-man. On seeing Ọwa in her full *Dibia* attire of war, they both rushed back into the compound. The gate to the compound remained tightly shut against Ọwa. Eze and his gate-man hurled curses at her from the safety of the locked gate, both refusing to step foot outside the compound while Ọwa kept sentinel. Her deep voice howled out Eze's name at regular intervals, repeating her mantra.

"Eze, son of Agu of Onori clan, where is my child? Give back that which you have unjustly taken. I come in the name of *Ọfọr n'Ogu*, clean hands and justice. Eze, son of Agu of Onori clan, give me back my daughter."

Through the long night of moonless skies, Ọwa's deep voice rang out, stealing the sleep from the eyes of all who heard her. Halfway through the night, the thugs, Uche and Donatus, arrived, summoned by their boss. They swaggered up to Ọwa, violence and menace in their demeanour. She turned at them and snarled, raised her hand and pointed at them. They fled before the curse could spill from her lips. Like their master and his gate-man, they cowered behind the locked gate of the house.

By morning, the villagers started gathering outside Eze's compound to observe the antics of the diminutive medicine-woman. Word had spread across the hamlets that Ọwa had armed herself with *Qfor n'Ogu* and was accusing one of the village's most important sons of murder. They said that Eze and his family and thugs were cowering behind their locked gate, terrified to venture out of their house while the albino *Dibia* waited and watched.

As the crowd grew, Eze's thugs, led by the lad, Uche of the perpetual dark sunglasses, tried to make a show of bravery by threatening the villagers with shouts and curses. The crowd returned insults for insults and threats for threats. Their superior numbers cowered the henchmen into sullen silence. From his upstairs window, Eze watched the rowdy scene unfold. There was an ugly air amongst the gathered villagers which threatened the safety of his shut gate. He scanned their faces to see if any of his allies were amongst them. All he saw were the usual pinched faces of poverty and envy, the dregs of the village society, the ones that gathered at the village square most evenings to exchange petty gossip and spread false rumours about the rich and powerful. They had little love for the *Aghali* witch, but nonetheless, wished for his downfall because they envied his success. It was at times like these that Eze wished his mother still lived. Taller than most men and with a voice and temperament like thunder, his mother would have sent them all scurrying back to their hovels. But she was gone and he was stuck inside his house, waging a war of attrition against the albino witch as suggested by his clansman, the village chief.

Chief Igwe had told him about Ọwa's accusations. There had been no need for denials or explanations. The chief already knew every step Eze took regarding the matter of The Black Hand. They had been friends for almost as long as they'd been clansmen and Eze's success had benefitted the chief. It was due to Eze's political connections that Chief Igwe had beaten his opponent to the village throne, a post conferred by the people but only ratified by the state governor. His opponent had been the people's choice but with some bribery and political wrangling, Eze had managed to get Chief Igwe's name ratified by the state governor. In return, the chief was already making plans to confer Eze with the coveted *Ọzo* peer title, which would cement his name in the society and make him a true man of respect.

When Eze called the chief to inform him of Owa's vigil at his house, the chief had suggested they let the albino woman shed her grief outside Eze's gate. There was only so long she could go without food and water. Sooner or later, she would tire and return to her hovel at the edge of the village and everything would die down and return to normal. So, against his better judgement, Eze had concurred and held his hand. But, as he watched the restless crowd grow outside his gate, his patience snapped. He picked his mobile phone and dialled the number of the Divisional Police Officer, DPO, in charge of the village police station, amongst others. He was another friend who had benefitted from Eze's largess in the past. Eze knew he could count on the DPO to come through for him.

The DPO did not disappoint. He asked Eze to send down a vehicle to the head office in the big city to pick some officers. The crowd booed as Eze's car almost ploughed through their midst as it sped out of the compound. They peered through the windows and saw only the driver and Uche, the head thug. Ọwa's voice rose once again, deep and loud.

"Eze, son of Agu of Onori clan, where is my child? Give back that which you have unjustly taken. I come in the name of *Ọfọr n'Ogu*, clean hands and justice. Eze, son of Agu of Onori clan, give me back my daughter." The crowd shivered, hushed into sudden silence by the chilling threat behind the words.

Within hours, Eze's white Peugeot returned, packed with black-uniformed and armed policemen. The first officer leapt from the car and fired a shot into the air. The villagers dispersed in screeching panic. Some of them, the ones infected with the dual viruses of curiosity and gossip, lurked in hidden corners and nearby bushes, watching the drama unfold. Ọwa remained still at her post by the locked gate, howling the now familiar chant, her voice going hoarse from endless hours of shouting.

Seeing her demeanour and the terrible visage of her painted face and palm-fronds, the policemen hesitated, uncertain how to approach her. They'd been told they were there to disperse an unruly crowd and a mad woman. No-one had said anything to them about dealing with a *Dibia*, medicine-woman. None of them wanted to be the first to approach the woman, each fearing a *Juju* hex. Finally, the bravest amongst them, a born-again Christian with a fanatical zeal in his eyes, made the first move.

'Woman, move your body now otherwise we will move it into our motor for you and all your *Juju* will not fit bring you out of the metal barricade of our police cell,' his voice was harsh, his stance, threatening. Owa looked at him, through him, her ears deaf to his words. Her voice rang out in the evening gloom, hoarse, yet deafening, dark rage underneath each syllable of her chant.

'Eze, son of Agu of Onori clan, where is my child? Give back that which you have unjustly taken. I come in the name of *Ofor n'Ogu*, clean hands and justice. Eze, son of Agu of Onori clan, give me back my daughter.'

A deep unease descended on the policemen. Uncertainty and fear cloaked their black pupils. The unnatural deep tones that issued from the lips of the statue-still figure of the albino woman stunned them into silence. Her words, chilling and terrible, filled them with disquiet. Who didn't know the stark message behind the phrase, "I come in the name of *Ofor n'Ogu,* clean hands and justice."? Only a fool would tamper with a business where those dark words had been invoked, especially by none other than a medicine-woman. The state police force did not pay them enough to sacrifice their lives. The officers looked at each other and took several involuntary steps away from Ọwa. Even the passionate Pentecostal officer took a backward step.

'We've done our job here,' he said. 'We've dispersed the crowd as instructed. I see no mad woman here. Nobody said anything to us about a medicine-woman.' He turned a baleful eye at Uche, who wilted behind his dark sunglasses, slinking back towards the compound. The police halted him. 'You! Get your driver and take us back to the station at once. Hurry up, you fool, before we shoot you for obstructing police business.' Uche turned around and shouted at the driver in turn. Together, they ran towards the parked Peugeot and in seconds, the engine was running. The policemen jumped into the car as if the ground burnt underneath their feet.

As the car sped off, the villagers slowly emerged from their hiding places. A look of awe descended on their faces. None of them had heard the exchange between Ọwa and the policemen. They had been too far away to hear. But what they had seen was the dreaded policemen scuttling away from Ọwa without arresting her or chasing her away. A new respect and fear entered their eyes. Soon, the whispering grew and the rumours flew across the market square and compounds, through the farms and the darkest bedrooms. A terrible change had befallen their hitherto timid medicine-woman! People shuddered behind the closed doors of their homes. The harmless chicken had grown teeth overnight, they whispered. Qwa had morphed into her dreaded mother, the fearsome Xikora of the *Leloolé* curse! Her daughter's loss had finally released the hidden monster that had lain dormant inside the tiny albino body of the village medicine-woman. Thanks to the pompous idiot, Eze, no-one was now safe in the village. If Qwa could easily dispatch the dreaded police, what else could she do...*couldn't she do?*

And from his sanctuary behind his shut window, Eze asked himself the same question. His hand reached up to his shoulder, seeking the familiar embossed solidity of The Black Hand. It connected with flat skin. Eze frowned and hurriedly pulled off his kaftan to investigate. The Black Hand with the splayed fingers was still imprinted on his left shoulder. But, it was no longer raised and the blackness was turning to a sickly grey colour.

Eze's heart began to pound. *This wasn't supposed to happen.* He rushed to his mirrored wardrobe to get a closer look. The image was even worse than he had thought. The Black Hand was fading from his shoulders with the speed of a slithering snake. Dibia Ogam had promised him a year for the first sacrifice, a year of the dark companion of the seal of wealth. A cold shiver shook his huge frame. *The Aghali witch!* She was behind the catastrophe. He had known that her presence outside his house spelled misfortune for him but had allowed himself to be swayed by Chief Igwe. Now, it was almost too late. Even the police couldn't help him. There was only one thing to do.

Eze pulled his Kaftan back on and picked his wallet and mobile phone. *Fuck the witch woman.* Dibia Ogam had some answers to give him and quick. It was okay asking him to wait for the *Juju* to take effect and money to flood in. But to have The Black Hand vanish from his shoulder within weeks was another matter altogether. Without one, the other could not materialise. The Black Hand and his future wealth went hand-in-hand. He had not gone to all this trouble for nothing. It was time to get results and put an end to all the recent troubles.

***

Ọwa watched as Eze sped out of his compound, accompanied by his two thugs. He neither spared her a look nor a word. She gave a grim smile and nodded. She had completed the first phase of her vengeance. It was now time to complete the cycle. She turned and made her way back to her hut, oblivious to the greetings she received from the villagers, people who till that day had never given her the time of the day. Her skin still itched in their presence so their goodwill was suspect. She quickened her steps, resisting the urge to scratch.

Later that night, Ọwa was arrested by a team of policemen led by the DPO himself. They hauled her into their black police van and sped off to the village police station. No one told her the nature of the offence she was charged with. All she knew was that the new bunch of officers that came for her were brutal. They manhandled her with vile ruthlessness. When her skin began to itch in the van, they laughed at her manic scratching and forced her to strip to her underwear. She was frog-matched semi-nude into the police station from the car.

The stunned look on Femi's face when he saw her calmed her rage. He quickly looked away, embarrassed by her near-nudity. But not before she saw the rage in his eyes, the fury that confirmed to her that he had been kept in the dark about the raid at her house. The command had come from his superior, the hard-voiced DPO who had ordered her to be stripped and beaten. Having her nudity witnessed by Femi was the worst aspect of her ordeal. Of all the people in the world, she would wish her shame to be hidden from him. For him, she wished to be the greatest of beauties, the cleanest of womanhood, a respected and loved person worthy of his special attention. She had no idea what she would do with that special attention if she ever got it. All she knew was that her heart and every bone in her body yearned for it.

It was clear to Qwa that the magic Femi had cast on her heart the first time she met him at this same station was still potent. But for the goodness of the feeling, she would've been convinced he had charmed her with some special *juju* similar to the mystical

Mmili echezona she had given to Mama Uche to chain her wandering husband's heart to her own. No one had prepared her for this feeling, this turbulent churning in her heart that was almost as powerful as the other pain tearing her heart to shreds. She wished she could seek out the Earth Goddess' wisdom, get some clarity about the man, Femi and the feelings he aroused in her. But the subject of a man's place in the life and heart of an *Nshi* woman was taboo to the ears of the great deity.

Owa wrapped her arms tighter across her chest, resisting the intense desire to scratch her skin and make them redder than they already were. Through the swollen bruise of her left eye, she saw Femi remonstrate with the DPO about the arrest and her treatment.

'Sir, this arrest should have been orchestrated by this station which oversees the village affairs, as you know. No one informed me about it.'

'It was a serious case that required urgent action. My presence here is enough to tell you how serious the case is,' the DPO's voice was dismissive.

'If this is in regard to this woman, then I think you have the wrong criminal, sir,' Femi's voice was firm, tinged with anger. 'This woman was here yesterday to report her daughter's disappearance. I've personally been investigating the matter. Surely, sir, arresting a grieving mother is the last thing the police should be doing at this time. I have my report on her case if you

206

want to go through it.' Femi turned towards the raised counter, reaching behind it for a thick, blue file which he gave to his boss. The DPO looked at it as if it were a piece off dog turd and tossed it on the counter.

'Are you questioning my authority, detective Abayomi?' The DPO's voice was laced with threat. 'Let me remind you that I have the power to arrange your immediate transfer from this station to another one.'

'I mean no disrespect sir,' Femi's voice retained its hardness beneath his polite words. 'However, I believe that an injustice is being done here and that someone else should be under arrest, not this woman. No one is above the law. As I said, I have my report ready and if you'll bother to read it, sir, you will discover the identities of the people we should be arresting now. The last thing we want is for a judge to question the integrity of the police force should this woman's daughter end up murdered and the case ends up in the courts.'

Owa saw an uncertain look enter the DPO's eyes. He looked like a mouse trapped by a cat.

'Get me the report at once,' he ordered. 'I'll take it home with me tonight and go through it. In the meantime, this woman will remain behind the cell till I make a decision tomorrow.' He turned to his policemen. 'Throw the woman into the cell and get the car ready for our journey back to the city.'

'That's not possible, sir,' Femi said. 'That cell is already crammed to capacity. The villagers are afraid of this woman. They'll rather hang than share a cell with her. I don't have enough officers here with me to handle a riot, not at this time of the night.'

The DPO frowned. He fixed a hard stare at Femi, who returned his glare with a calm, yet, resolute look. A silent tussle of power appeared to be going on between the two men. The DPO's eyes turned ugly.

'Where is your office, detective Abayomi?' He asked. Femi pointed towards a shut door at the end of a small corridor. 'Does it have a key?' The DPO barked. Femi nodded. 'Good. Men, throw the woman into the office and lock the door. The detective will have to forfeit his office for tonight.'

'Sir, with all due respect, I must protest this action. My office is where I carry out my work and it can't be used as a police cell. Surely you can let this woman go for the night and bring her in for questioning tomorrow,' Femi protested, turning to look at Owa. She saw the hidden reassurance in his eyes, understood that his protest was mere lip service. The DPO would never let her return to her house that night. They both knew it. Femi was happy to have bought her some privacy away from the hostile company of the villagers held in the crowded station cell. She thanked him with her eyes. Her respect for him increased beyond the largest yam barn in the twelve villages.

'I will not argue with you, Abayomi. You will obey my orders and hand over the key to your office to my men at once,' Owa saw the spite in the DPO's eyes. Femi drew the key from his pocket and gave it to the nearest policeman. 'In fact, I have decided that I will leave my men at the station for the night to ensure my orders are followed. It is a bad thing when a DPO can no longer trust his officers to obey his instructions. I'll be looking at your file this week, Abayomi, and will make my decision about your future.' The DPO grabbed the blue file, turned and stumped out of the station.

The four policemen dragged Owa into Femi's office and locked the door behind her. Owa listened to the melee going on in the waiting room of the station, as Femi and the policemen exchanged heated words. The initial fear that had gripped her when the men initially burst into her hut, had evaporated. It was replaced by a quiet resolve that brought a fierce light to her pale eyes. She stood up and pulled off her bra and knickers, the only items of clothing the police had left her with. The men had sought to humiliate her, instead, they had made it easier for her to communicate with the Earth Goddess without undue questions or delay. To commune with the goddess of nature, one must approach her in their most natural state, the condition in which they entered the world, the state of total nudity.

Ọwa sat crossed legged on the cold floor of the dimly-lit room and began to call upon the name of the Earth Goddess. She allowed her mind to sleep, her thoughts to die and her body to still. Several minutes passed and still she waited. Her brows furrowed in a tight frown. Soon, sweat began to form on her pale skin, building, swelling, till her body was as wet as that of a rain-drenched pedestrian. A slow smile spread over her face. It was time.

Ọwa began to hum, slowly, quietly. Her body swayed, gently, left and right, forward and backward. Gradually, the tempo built, as she sank deeper into the trance of divination. The temperature in the room heated up, draining her body of moisture as salty sweat covered the linoleumed floor like hot piss. A familiar smell filled the room, the smell of earth and rank, of flies and trees, of corn and corpse, of sweat and damp.

The first fly settled on her right shoulder. Ọwa's heart soared! *Anā was near.*

Her humming became louder, her voice growing guttural, almost inhuman. The second fly settled on her forehead, then a third, fourth. She heard them arrive, every single harbinger of the great Earth Goddess. Soon, her makeshift cell was a vortex of buzzing, heaving cacophony. Darkness descended in the room, a solid blackness that was formed from the mass of swirling flies that coated every inch of the room, including the tiny light bulb on the ceiling.

Their unearthly buzz penetrated the walls of the room into the waiting-room. The policemen looked at each other and rushed towards the office, all save Femi, who had an inkling of what was happening behind the brown wooden door of his office. The sudden clap of thunder cemented his conviction. The night had been as quiet and calm as an ancient grave before the arrival of the medicine-woman. Now, it was in a violent turmoil, brewing a thunderstorm that would rival the worst tornado imaginable. Femi knew who was responsible. He had tried to warn his corrupt DPO that some powers were better left unprovoked but the man would not listen. Now they would all pay the price, the guilty and the innocent alike.

The policemen burst into Qwa's cell and screamed. The swarm of black flies engulfed them like a wave of black sludge. It was impossible to see where the men started and the flies ended. Everything was swirling mania. Screams were choked off by mouthfuls of buzzing flies. Eyes lost their sight and ears their sound. Breaths were choked in their nostrils by the sudden infusion of raging flies into broad and high noses. In seconds, Qwa's cell had become the graveyard of four able-bodied policemen, who moments earlier had been prime examples of striding, strapping manhood at their very brutal peak. By the time the first wind ripped the roof from the building, they were all cold corpses.

Qwa allowed the flies to guide her in the darkness, their glassy eyes as a million black stars. Walking across the room was like walking through a soft mire of wet earth, such was the invasion of the grave flies. Walls collapsed around her as the station was demolished in seconds. Wild winds howled like the keening of a night demon. The villagers held in the crowded cell rushed out of the station as the cement blocks fell like paper bricks around them. They joined Femi, who stood outside the ruined remnants of what was once his proud police station, staring with open-mouthed disbelief at the carnage unfolding before his eyes. Everyone, to the last man and woman, crossed themselves, mouthing silent and loud prayers to a multitude of deities and Jesus.

What held them in awe was the fact that the storm raged solely above the police station. Its fury was concentrated on the small piece of square land that held the high priestess of a powerful deity. Otherwise, everywhere else, every part of the village, remained dry and calm. And as they watched, they saw a sight that filled them with even more terror. A figure clothed from head to toe in buzzing, swirling flies, floated out of the ruins of the police station, as if borne high by unseen wings. It was a tiny figure with the shape of a woman, a shape whom they all recognised for who it was...*what it was*. They hurriedly moved aside for it, their skin

212

peppered with goosepimples. Some of them bowed low in obeisance. Others took to their feet in flight. The great Earth Goddess was leading her high priestess home.

***

The DPO's face was ashen when he arrived towards dawn, having been briefed by Femi. The sight of the flies-bloated bodies of four of his officers filled him with a terror beyond anything he had experienced in his twenty years of policing. Villagers gathered to stare in hushed awe at the wreck of the police station and the dead officers pulled from the rubble. Everyone knew what had occurred. It was as they had feared. Eze, the foolish son of Agu of Onori clan had awakened a dark terror that had lived amongst them in peace. A force that could reduce to rubble a solid building at will, and dispatch four strong policemen to their ancestors' hell, was one that brought the chill of terror to their spines. Femi wanted to crow, "I told you so," at the DPO but he was too shocked to speak. In any case, he didn't need to say anything. The man was clearly going through his own private terrors. Femi saw the fear in the DPO's eyes. He could almost read his thoughts. *Will the albino medicine-woman come after me also? Will I ever be safe from her wrath?* Femi wanted to tell the man that Ọwa was not evil, that she would not deliberately go out of her way to harm anyone, that it was only people that had driven her to the walking terror she had now become, but he doubted his words would carry any conviction. His mind still played back the picture of Ọwa as he had last seen her, a terrifying, inhuman entity, emitting malevolent power, clothed in deadly flies as she glided away from the debris of the building she had toppled in minutes. A helpless woman brought into the station in shameful nudity had floated out cloaked in a glory of flies.

The fledgling attraction he had felt for the tiny victimised woman, blossomed like a blazing flame in his heart. He had seen her in her true glory and it was a sight that filled him with respect and awe. To think she had such powers all this while and refused to use them to defend herself against her enemies. Femi was no stranger to the powers of the occult. He had grown up in a home infused with the supernatural. His brother had demonstrated powers that sent shock waves in their community. Yet, never had he seen anything as spectacular as what he had witnessed that night. Femi swore to himself that he would find Ọwa's daughter, alive or dead. He would bring her the solace that may yet warm her heart towards him. Suddenly, nothing mattered more than gaining Ọwa's trust and affection. Something told Femi that he had finally found the one woman he could truly call his first and last love... if she would have him.

Ω Ω Ω

10

The Wrong Corpse

❖

Eze parked his car under the great *Ngwu* tree that grew in Dibia Ogam's compound. He got out of the vehicle and ordered his two thugs to keep watch as he lumbered towards the white-washed bungalow that housed the famed witchdoctor. In his haste, he failed to marvel as everyone did, the wonders and mysteries of the great *Ngwu* tree which could never be planted but sprouted where it willed. The *Ngwu* only grew in the hamlets of great witchdoctors and great men. Even in the poorest families with no visible signs of greatness, the sudden appearance of an *Ngwu* tree would bring new respect to them, as people instantly recognised the significance of the tree's appearance - future greatness would be born in that family.

Dibia Ogam was seated on his usual armed chair, fanning himself with a brown raffia fan. It was a muggy evening and the clouds hung low and dark, a sure sign that a thunderstorm was brewing in the skies. Already, several clasps of thunder shook the still air, causing Eze to look up at the sky with wariness. He didn't want to be caught out in the storm. It was a long drive home from the witchdoctor's village. A couple of determined chickens scrambled for worms in the dry soil, even as the other domestic animals, the goats and pigs, cowered in their sheds, terrified by the brewing thunderstorm.

'*Enyi!* Friend! May these eyes I see you with never go blind,' Dibia Ogam called out as Eze drew closer to his veranda. He spat into the soil, brown tobacco sputum.

'Great *Dibia*, my knees bow to greatness,' Eze bent his right knee slightly as he climbed the three steps that led up to the veranda. His breathing was heavy, his forehead dotted with sweat. He swiped a quick backhand across his face.

'Good friend of the broad buttocks, my chair welcomes your backside. Take the chair and break kola-nut with me,' Dibia Ogam passed over a cluster of red Kola-nut to Eze. He picked a segment of the nut with impatient distraction and pushed it into his mouth, chewing it as if he was chewing on rubber. 'So, what brings you to my humble abode so soon after our last encounter?'

Eze looked around as if afraid of watching eyes. Then he leaned close to the *Dibia*.

'Dibia Ogam, all is not sweet in the bedroom of the new groom,' Eze's voice was a rustled whisper.

'*Tufia!* May the heavens forbid!' Dibia Ogam clicked off the demons and spat into the soil again. 'Is the groom not mightily endowed?'

'He is…at least, he thought he was,' Eze began undoing his shirt buttons. 'Was the gift not worthy enough? Was it not of the

217

best quality? Why then does the bride turn her face away and reject the groom?'

'What makes the groom think his bride rejects him? Perhaps, she wants to be wooed, she wants her groom to learn the art of patience since that makes the coupling more exciting.'

'Dibia Ogam, if it were just a matter of patience, I assure you, this groom can wait for as long as the next randy man,' Eze pulled his shirt aside and bared his left shoulder, revealing the near-faded hand mark.

Dibia Ogam gasped.

'*Tufia! Tufia! May the heavens forbid!* What is this I see?' His eyes were wide with shock. Eze thought he saw fear lurking in the little black pupils of the medicine-man. He was glad he had shocked the *Dibia* out of his smug complacency. Eze's memory was a long one and he was still to forget how the witch-doctor had humiliated him the first time they met.

'As you can see, it would appear that your *Juju* is not as powerful as you've led me to believe,' Eze's voice was biting, almost a sneer.

'My *Juju* has never failed,' Dibia Ogam's eyes flashed angrily. 'Perhaps the problem lies with the client or even his gift.'

'There's no problem with me. I did as you asked. I brought you not just an *Aghali*, but a virgin *Aghali* from the finest bloodline for this kind of business.'

218

'What do you mean by bloodline? I never mentioned anything to you about any type of bloodline when I suggested the sacrifices to offer the deity of wealth, *Aku-n'uba.'*

'You did not need to spell things out. We all know how these things work. It makes perfect sense that someone with some genealogy in the occult and *Juju* medicine would serve as a perfect sacrifice to the gods.'

Dibia Ogam blanched. His face went an ashy hue. '*Amadioha* in his great heavens, spare us!' Dibia Ogam jumped up from his chair and stared down at Eze. His eyes blazed, his rage masked by the terror that brought the trembles to his wiry body. 'This devil man! I knew you were trouble from the day you swaggered into my compound. May the gods protect me from your folly! Talk to me, you foolish man. Tell me the identity of the girl you brought into the Grand Room of Mirrors. Who was she? Speak before I put a curse on your tongue.'

Eze froze. Every limb in his body began to quake. 'She was the daughter of the *Aghali* medicine-woman in our village,' his words were mumbled.

'Tell me you're not talking about the one they call, Qwa,' there was almost a pleading quality in the *Dibia's* voice. 'Tell me that you did not sacrifice the grand-daughter of the high priestess to the Earth Goddess, Xikora!' Dibia Ogam's skin broke out in sweat. His eyes turned a red hue. He spat into the soil and began pacing up and down his veranda like a man demented. 'May the gods forgive and preserve me. The Earth Goddess must know I had no idea of the identity of your sacrifice. All the blame must lie at your door and all the punishment must equally lie at your door,' he cast a look filled with pure venom at Eze. Eze shrank deeper into his arm-chair, feeling his heart race beneath his sweat-dampened linen shirt.

'Dibia Ogam, what difference does the girl's identity make? Surely, human sacrifice is human sacrifice, human blood, just as The Black Hand requires.'

'Except you do not offer any deity the blood of the high priestess of *Aná* or the high priest of another deity, you fool. You brought me the wrong corpse. Your sacrifice will not be accepted as no deity will accept such a sacrifice without causing outright war in the realm of the gods. And you wonder why The Black Hand has deserted you! Ha!' Dibia Ogam barked a harsh laugh. 'Let me tell you a biting truth; you have become a pariah to the gods from henceforth. No *Juju* will ever work for you again because of your insult to the Earth Goddess.'

'I did not insult the Earth Goddess,' Eze protested, his voice shaky. 'The *Aghali* woman was the one that insulted me first. The way she spoke to me, you would think I was no better than a lackey,' Eze's voice got stronger as his anger resurfaced. 'In fact, I don't even know why you're making such a fuss, Dibia Ogam.

Everyone knows Ọwa's powers are minimal and her fearsome mother is long dead and can do no harm from the grave. Really my man, I think you're making more of this than is necessary. Just admit that your *Juju* did not work and stop making excuses,' Eze's eyes glittered with malice.

Dibia Ogam stared at him as if he had grown horns, feathers and tails. For a brief second, it seemed as if he might punch Eze on the face. Eze braced himself to retaliate. *Dibia* or no *Dibia*, he would not let any insult go.

'I think you'd better leave now,' Dibia Ogam's voice was weary. 'I can see that I'm dealing with a fool who is beyond redemption. My only regret is that you have implicated me in your stupidity and I shall ready myself for the consequences. I have no advice to give you because you're clearly the fool our people hold in contempt, the one we call *Eze-onye-agwalam*, "King-let-no-one-tell-me-any-better-as-I-always-know-best-because-I-am-king." He paused and stared at Eze, a long, thoughtful look. Then, he shook his head, as if shaking off a gnat – or a terrible curse. 'You will see what you will see and I will deal with whatever comes my way. *Ndewo,* greetings, goodbye.' Dibia Ogam turned towards his door.

'What about the wealth you promised me, the women, the big contracts and election victory?' Eze stumbled after him. 'I have made plans, big plans based on your assurances. I cannot afford to fail. Do you want me to bring you another sacrifice? Is that what this is all about? Tell me exactly what you need, give me the exact specification, dwarves, twins, virgins, children, and yes, even another *Aghali* albino. Tell me what you want and I'll make sure this time I bring you the right corpse.' Eze's voice was shrill with desperation.

Dibia Ogam paused by his door and looked at Eze. There was pity and contempt in his gaze. He shook his head and walked into his house without a word. Eze heard the metallic sound of his door bolt sliding home and felt the shivers wrack his huge frame. His legs turned to mushy pap as he collapsed back into the arm-chair, his breathing like one that had run a marathon, fast and hard. *This couldn't be happening to him...surely there had to be a way out of this fiasco...*Eze's thoughts were like frenzied ants. An image flashed in his mind. *The Chairman! That was it...the Local government chairman, his nemesis, the cause of all his troubles in the first place. Yes, the man had to die... must die.* That had always been Eze's original plan, get rid of his opponent and occupy the vacant post. That way he got to control the budget and improve his finances. Dibia Ogam's route had seemed the quickest. Now, it had failed, he had to resort to his initial plan. The failed assassination of the priest meant that the planned murder of the local government chairman would be delayed for a few weeks to give the police time to cool their heels. The priest had powerful connections and the police were working hard to find his attackers.

222

Killing the local government chairman would bring unnecessary attention to himself as the natural successor. A few weeks was neither here nor there, Eze decided. He would wait and bide his time. The patient bird gets the fattest worm after all.

Ω Ω Ω

11

$\mathcal{V}engeance$

The flies dropped off her body as she got closer to her hut. By the time she entered the shrine, the last of the flies had vanished into the dark night and once more, Ọwa was clothed in nudity. She barely made it into the shrine before collapsing before the giant black statue. A deep weariness stole her limbs and her thoughts. The blackness attacked in successive waves and Ọwa gave in to its dark fog, allowed it to steal her mind.

She woke up several hours later drenched in sweat. It was still dark outside and the shrine was a blacker night. She stumbled outside to piss in the farm before returning to the shrine. She fumbled for the pack of matches and lit the candles surrounding the statue of *Aná*. Then, she prepared the hearth till the woods burnt bright and red. She walked over to the shrine-goat, Ebele, and led it gently to the black statue of the Earth Goddess. She tied its rope around the statue and carried out the necessary preparations for her night diplomacy with the oils, herbs and ash of divination. With her daughter dead, she now had to rely exclusively on Ebele to guide her back from the realm of the dead. It would be an easy task tonight, she thought. The evil duo of Walking-Grave and Corpse-Maker were no doubt feasting on the four young souls at the police station. She would be in and out of their cold realm before they finished their business. All she needed was a few minutes with her mother to learn the secret of the *Leloole* curse, the one power she had deliberately refused to learn in all her years of misguided humility.

Ọwa plucked a white chicken from the small metal cage inside the shrine and slashed its throat with a blood-coated knife. She drained its blood over *Aná's* statue, singing and chanting praises to the deity. Then, she placed the dead chicken in the shrine bowl and sat before the Earth Goddess' statue, holding firm to the shrine-goat's bloodied rope. Her thoughts wandered briefly as she prepared to go into the *afá* divination mode. *She was done with humans. She had nothing to lose anymore. By the time she was done with them, they would know the true meaning of pain and fear. They would experience the same pain she was going through and share her misery. Before she was done with them, they would learn to fear her as they had feared her mother.*

Ọwa forced the darks thoughts from her mind as she readied herself for her journey into *Mbana-Oyi*, The Cold Realm. In the three days since her daughter's disappearance, it had become harder to focus, to divinate effectively without being driven by rage. Ọwa shut her eyes and allowed her mind to die.

***

She is tumbling down, deeper, right through the black soil-sky and into the familiar dark terrain of The Cold Realm. She pauses, listens, glances about to ensure all is as she expects and the guardians of the realm are absent. Then quickly, she glides across the endless expanse of the blood sludge, her eyes clear and bright, her movements smooth and confident. Her eyes scan the familiar spot where her mother is trapped waist deep in the blood sludge.

Ọwa freezes. Her heart stops.

A scream escapes her mouth. Several screams. They turn into howls, then whimpers. Shivers wrack her tiny frame.

Xikora is not alone in the red mire of the blood sludge. Trapped with her, side by side, is the figure Ọwa has seen in her dreams, the faceless figure she'd assumed to be her own, a face which is now as clear as daylight, the face of her daughter, Aku.

The sight kills her soul and steals her thoughts. She dives down to her daughter, her flight wild, frenzied. Xikora calls out to her but her ears are deaf. She only has eyes for her daughter, frozen in sightless rigidity next to her mother.

'Aku... Aku... Daughter of mine! Sweet and beautiful daughter, what have they done to you, my child? Speak to your mother, good daughter, speak to me,' Ọwa's voice is shrill with pain. She engulfs her daughter in a tight hug, a black hug that gives no light, no fusion of souls, no fire of recognition. Aku stares into the gloomy distance, her pale eyes dance-less, frozen, her face bland, lifeless.

Ọwa shakes her, first gently, then violently. She screams into Aku's ears till her voice grows hoarse.

'Daughter, hold your tears,' Xikora says. 'She can't hear or see you. She feels nothing and knows nothing. In a way, she's blessed I guess. It would have been worse if she were aware as I am, knowing where she is and the terrible fate that has befallen her. Still, she's company for me, even as silent as she is. My guess is that she's been sacrificed to a deity and has become a dead corpse, am I right?'

'My child is not a dead corpse,' Ọwa screams at her mother. 'Her fate is not going to be your fate. She is innocent and has harmed no one, done nothing to deserve this.' She begins shaking Aku again. 'Daughter, please, please, wake up. It's Mama, here to take you home. Come with me, daughter. Come now.' Ọwa tries to pull Aku from the blood sludge but she is like a statue glued to the thick mire with concrete. She holds Aku's head between her hands, tightly, as she tries to infuse memories, good memories, happy memories into her mind. But a dense, black fog blocks out her efforts, repels her light.

Ọwa takes hold of her daughter's hands to rub in warmth, infuse her with her own living heat. Another scream escapes her lips. She holds one hand only. The other is a stub, where once Aku's right hand had been. Her eyes go into a frenzied dance, wild darts of pain and fury. They scan her daughter's body, searching, *seeing the gaping hole in Aku's chest where her heart used to live, the mutilated tips of her breasts, devoid of nipples. The sight is too much, her rage too strong. Qwa flies, up, higher, eating up the thin blue link-light of the shrine-goat in seconds, smashing through the black soil-sky of Mbana-Oyi for the human real with a loud shriek of fury.*

***

She crashed into furious wakefulness inside the dark shrine, sending the shrine-goat into an unusual panic. Ebele ran towards the entrance of the hut, intent on getting out. But it halted as soon as it got to the small door, unable to leave the shrine, held within its dark warmth by invisible hands that guided its destiny. Slowly, it lowered itself by its usual spot with its unfinished meal of yam peelings and began to munch slowly, its eyes cold, unbothered by worries, least of all, its mistress' wild sobbing. The sound of its lazy chewing was drowned out by Qwa's howls.

Qwa flung herself at the Earth Goddess's feet, screaming, banging her head against the clay foot of the mammoth statue. Blood stained her forehead, her blood and the chicken blood, still warm on the statue.

'Earth Mother, hear the cries of your child, come to the rescue of your daughter, free your servant from pain, give me back that which was unjustly taken from me. Give me back my daughter.'

Over and over, Ọwa wailed her desperate plea at the unmoving effigy of the great goddess. Her voice went hoarse and her skin became bruised. Yet, she howled and called to the deity. As the night ate up the hours before the dawn could snatch them from its jaws, Ọwa remained at the base of the mighty black statue, wailing.

Midway through the night, she came to her senses and realised that there were rites to be followed to summon the great goddess. She collected herself with difficulty, forcing her rage to pause, her pain to wait. Her knees ached from the long hours of kneeling and her body throbbed from being flung about the hard earth floor of the shrine. Her mental anguish threatened to sap her breath, her life. She brushed away her physical discomforts as one would a fly. *Mere nothings compared to what her child was going through.*

Ọwa dug deep into the soil outside the shrine till she unearthed the small clay pot that contained the sacred ash, *Ntu-Ndu*, the Ash of Immortality, entrusted to the priestesses of the Earth Goddess through eternity. Cradling the ash pot, Ọwa returned to the shrine and set in down before the black statue. She picked the blood-splattered shrine knife and began to stab into her skin. The blade pierced her palm, then her arm, her chest, neck, thighs, and stomach. Her gasps and groans mimicked the stabbing motion of her hand; stab, groan; stab, gasp. In little time, her body was a bleeding mass, dripping warm blood on the red clay soil of the shrine. The pain was lightning pure, sharp and burning. It fuelled her determination. Her hand was sure and swift, without hesitation, as one slash was followed by another deep into her flesh.

Ọwa swayed. A wave of dizziness engulfed her, almost toppling her face into the ash hearth. She shook her head violently, ground her teeth angrily. *Not yet; she was not done. To get what she wanted from the Earth Mother, she must give all she has.* Ọwa stumbled towards the shrine-goat, her footsteps leaving a bloody trail in her wake. Ebele looked up at her with its usual indifference. It bent its head to its meal of dry yam peels, exposing the perfect neck for her blade.

The first stab sent the animal stumbling to its feet in flight. A frenzied bleat choked inside its throat. Blood spurted against the wall, the floor, merging with Ọwa's blood. She stabbed the shrine-goat, again and again, sobbing bitterly with each stab. Ebele had been her best friend, her trusted companion and guide. In its mute complacency, it knew her better than any human, save her daughter. They had shared many dark journeys together, she and the white shrine-goat. Its death was her death; their deaths were Aku's life. The white goat was the greatest gift she could give the Earth Goddess, barring her life. Mother Earth will not deny her plea… *must not deny her this single favour.*

Bearing the dead shrine-goat in her arms, Ọwa stumbled back to the alter of the Earth Goddess. She almost fell from the weight of the dead animal and blood loss. Her eyes were bloodshot, glazed with pain, wet with tears. Her mind was glass-clear in its goal, with a steely resolve that would not yield to man or god, not even to the great earth deity. *She had served Aná well, had dedicated her life to her calling. One favour, one righteous favour, would not be too much to ask for and expect from the Earth Mother.*

Ọwa dropped the dead animal and lifted the small earthen pot high. Her voice raised in supplication. The dawn rooster joined her cries. The skies opened their eyes and joined her tears, pelting the earth in a sudden thunderstorm.

'Give me back my daughter, great mother. I bear the Ash of immortality. Infuse it with your will that I may bring back my child who was unjustly taken from me. Clothe me with death, Mother Earth,' Ọwa's voice was as the thunder beyond the shrine, her eyes darting wild in her agitation. 'Shroud me with the cloak of death that I may get justice for my child.'

Over and over, her voice resonated in the gloomy confines of the shine. When sleep finally came, it was like a gentle breeze, a clear spring flowing over white pebbles, sweet incense and flowers, the birdsong in the silent dawn. It lulled her as a mother's loving arm rocks her infant. It whispered words in her ears, soothing words... healing words.

'Cry no more, my child,' the voice was a soft brush against her ears, honey and milk, yet thunder and wind. 'Your mother has heard your voice and shall wipe your tears. You will have four market days and four market nights with your daughter. It will be time enough to say the words you never said to her, to prepare yourself for her departure as you never had time to do. It will be precious time for you to nurture your soul and embrace the inevitable. When the time is done, she will return to her true mother, the deity they call Mary. Your daughter had long pledged her soul to another deity and to that deity she must return. I promise you; your daughter will not lay waste in The Cold Realm. You ask for vengeance and I must give it, for that is my covenant with my priestesses. For good or for bad, I must answer their call when they call on my name with blood. But, beware what you ask for; beware the price you may have to pay for it. Sleep now, sleep and dream. When you awake, you will recall your dreams and you will know what to do.'

Qwa sighed deeply. A heavy weight settled on her lids and limbs. All her life, she'd been fighting, striving, endlessly, tirelessly. It was now time to rest. The Earth Mother had spoken and her words were good. Qwa shut her eyes and slipped into the deep sleep of unconsciousness.

And she dreamed and her dreams were vivid beyond the brightest rainbow in the clearest sky.

***

He saw her before she saw him. His body was tense and his face hard. There was an air of expectancy in the way he sat hunched forward on his chair. Ọwa felt every nerve in her body tighten as if pulled by a wrench. This was a battle that she had yearned for, one she was prepared for and would fight to the finish.

'*Amosu Aghali,* albino-witch, you have finally arrived,' Dibia Ogam said, reaching down for his raffia bag, his eyes watchful, following every tiny movement of his visitor. 'I have long expected you and now you have shown your yellow face in my compound,' he rose from his chair, his voice rising, his face thunderous. 'You dare to challenge a lion in his own lair, you foolish woman. So, now you are here, I see you. What can you do?' He spat at her, missing her by inches as she side-stepped his spittle.

Ọwa pulled off her dark sunglasses. Her eyes blazed a furious dance.

'Murderer! Vile *Dibia*! Take a good look at me because your day of reckoning has finally arrived. You have spilled your last blood, you and your despicable deity. Take a good look at me because you are looking at your death,' Ọwa threw off her head scarf, exposing the full yellow glory of her hair. She placed her raffia bag on the ground, together with her scarf and sunglasses. Her heart thudded, a thud of rage. The Earth Goddess had shown her every single detail of her daughter's murder. In her dream, she had seen the plot hatched between The Fat-Man and the *Dibia;* the despicable horror perpetrated on her child by the vile one that went by the name of Dibia Ogam. The Earth Goddess had revealed the route to the medicine-man's shrine in detailed clarity and shown her where to find the body parts of her daughter. Finally, the great deity had told her the sacred process to bring her daughter back to life. It was now time for the first of the conspirators and murderers to die.

Qwa began to untie her wrapper, her movements deliberate, unrushed. As the wrapper fell to her feet, exposing her pale, knife-mutilated thighs, the Dibia shut his eyes and turned his face away.

'Shameless slut! Is this how you plan to avenge your daughter's death, by exposing your shame for all to see?' his voice was laced with contempt. 'You think I will collapse at the sight of your skinny body?' Dibia Ogam turned around and stared at her with steely resolve, mockery glinting in his black pupils. 'Foolish woman, look how you shame yourself, see how the people have gathered to watch your disgrace,' he pointed towards the entrance of his compound where a growing crowd had gathered underneath the mystical *Ngwu* tree to observe the confrontation between the two medicine titans. They had seen the unusual sight of an albino woman making her determined way to the dwelling of their famous witchdoctor, asking nobody for directions, her step as sure as that of a chicken returning to its coop. The black and white paint on her face and the white chicken feathers and palm-fronds clenched between her teeth, screamed out her status with mega-phone clarity – *Dibia*, witchdoctor.

'Dibia Ogam, take a good look at me,' Ọwa screamed, her deep masculine voice resonating beyond the compound. The crowd gasped and stumbled backwards, fear and uncertainty on their faces. Surely, a male demon spoke from the lips of the *Aghali* witch-doctor, they thought. Yet, they stayed, curiosity mastering their fear. 'Worthless piece of dog-shit, open your eyes as wide as an owl's and see me, see me, see me!' Ọwa pulled off her black mourning top and her black bra, pounding her bloodied stab-bruised chest with angry fists. 'See me!'

The first fly settled on her yellow hair like a black seed from a wind-tossed tree. 'See me,' her voice thundered. The second fly landed on her forehead. Then the third, fourth. Soon, her hair was coated with a swarm of wriggling black flies. And still she shouted, her pale, blue eyes blazing, oblivious to the flies. 'See me....'

The last item of clothing dropped from her body to the ground. She was as nude as the day she was born, save for her *Jigida* charmed waistlet, stringed black beads of sorcery tied around her waist. It would give her body the super-natural strength to carry the possession of the Earth Goddess and repel attacks from malevolent entities. Ọwa steps drew ever closer to the witch-doctor's veranda.

And still the flies arrived, in their hundreds, thousands, dressing her nudity in a heaving black coat that glittered under the intense noonday sun.

'I see you, shameless *Aghali-witch*. I see you in your filthy nakedness, just as everybody else sees and laughs at you. I see...see...ssee...' the words died on Dibia Ogam's lips.

And he finally saw her.

He saw death in all its gory, ghastly, terrible forms, shrouding the tiny body like a colossal black grave. He saw the bloated death of the drowned, the charred death of the burnt, the twisted death of the hung, the wasted death of the sick, the skeletal death of the starved, the bloodied death of the executed, the mangled death of the war-dead, the maggot-riddled death of the forgotten dead. From her soil, Mother Earth spilled out all the rotten meat she had received through the ages, regurgitating them in their foulest terrible forms for the *Dibia* to see. Her high priestess wore them all, reflected them all, shared them all with the quaking witchdoctor. In her tiny form, he saw the ghastly deaths of everyone he ever loved, his sons, daughters, mother and father; his tutor, his mistress, his brothers and his little sister. And they all died in shrieking, writhing agony, their dying eyes staring at him, accusing him, hating him.

And death laughed at the medicine-man, laughed at his flaying hands as he strove to maintain his balance, find his charmed bloodstone. Death shrieked at his madness as he tried and failed to shut his eyes and shut out the unspeakable horror that was slowly draining his life-force and his sanity. His eyes would not shut, would not look away and save themselves from the shrieking terror before him. And the final death Dibia Ogam saw before the flies dived at him in a ferocious attack, was the stunned, wide-eyed, shrieking death of the sudden dead, his own demise.

The flies filled his open mouth, choking out his cries. They blocked up his nostrils, stealing his breath. They crowded his ears, killing all sounds, even the wild cackles of death's harbinger. Dibia Ogam was a dead man before his body hit the hard cement of his veranda.

The crowd screamed and scattered in all directions, including the immediate family of the dead medicine-man. They covered their faces with their hands and ran, lest their eyes see the same nightmare that felled the most powerful witch-doctor in their village and beyond. A great wail arose amongst the people. *A mighty tree has fallen!* They had believed Dibia Ogam indestructible, his presence a reassuring constancy in their community. His fearsome reputation kept them safe from land-grabbing neighbours. Now, the true meaning of the Igbo proverb came home to haunt them – *THE greatest wrestler will one day meet the soil of the earth at the hands of THE greatest wrestler.* Their medicine-man's reign had clearly come to an inglorious end at the hands of a greater *Dibia*, a woman *Dibia* no less. Only a fool or a lunatic would dare confront a killer of demons. Only a deaf person would hear the sounds of war and refuse to run.

Even before Ọwa turned and made her way towards the thatched-roof shrine that housed the Grand Room of Mirrors, she was alone in the compound of the late *Dibia*, her sole companions, the rapidly decaying corpse of the medicine-man and some white shrine chickens wandering about aimlessly in search of food. She bent to collect her discarded clothes, return herself to the dignity of womanhood. Her nudity was for her deity and her work, not for the entertainment of ignorant villagers or vile deities like the one whose shrine she was now about to enter.

Ọwa paused at the dwarf door and took a deep breath. She felt light-headed from the latest possession of the Earth Goddess but her *Jigida* kept her strong, physically ready to face her greatest trial within the shrine of the wealth deity. Her mental state was another matter. She would have to call on everything within to come to her aid.

Ọwa entered the shrine of *Aku'uba,* the deity of wealth and fame. The black mirror walls faced her like an impenetrable forest. A sudden chill crawled down her spine, layering her skin in goosepimples. A feeling of déjà vu overwhelmed her. Everything was exactly as the Earth Goddess had shown her in the dream; everything but the smell, the overpowering smell of death, her daughter's death. In dreams, there are no smells, just sights and sounds, feelings and actions. Qwa knew where to look, what she would find. The smell of decay was her nostril's guide. Yet, her eyes remained averted, terror holding her hostage by the door. In the four days since her daughter had gone missing, she'd known that she would never see Aku alive again. But knowing was not the same as seeing and she did not want to see what lay beyond the small dwarf stool on the floor of black mirrors. It was easier to collect the earthen dish that held the body parts that would make her child whole again.

Qwa picked up the dish that contained a hand she recognised and a blood-soaked heart she did not recognise but knew where it belonged. Chipped blue nail-polish clung to her daughter's dead fingers, just as they'd always done while she lived. The two body parts that resembled black kennel nuts belonged to her daughter's breasts. She was a woman and recognised breast nipples when she saw them. Tears pooled in her eyes, bringing a hard pain to the back of her throat. The room was cold, an unnatural chill that belied the blistering heat of the noon-day sun. It was a shrine that reflected the dark soul of its deity, *Aku'uba,* unlike the Earth Mother's warm shrine. The cold kept the heart fresh, together with the hand, which now had a darkish hue. It would return to its original colour once it was re-attached to its rightful owner, the owner whose blood-soaked body lay at the right corner of the mirror-walled room, glazed eyes staring sightlessly into an unseen terror.

Ọwa fell by her child and began to wail. Her rage was swallowed by her sorrow. Pain beyond anything she had ever experienced wracked every pore in her body, cut every nerve in her veins.

'Aku…Aku…Aku…' she sobbed her daughter's name repeatedly, rocking the cold body in her arms. Guilt almost stole her breath and her life. She should have protected her daughter better, rather than the constant judging, criticisms, scoldings, tutoring; everything but being a mother in the true sense of the word. In her determination to mould a perfect priestess for the Earth Goddess, she had forgotten to be the perfect mother to her child.

She had never told Aku that she was the moon, the sun, the stars and the air of her life; had never cuddled her with love since she began attending that Christian secondary school she so loved. She thought Aku knew she was everything, her life, her reason for being. But she should have said the words to her daughter, demonstrated that love more frequently. Maybe her daughter would have chosen to remain with her rather than escape to that school which eventually became her doom. Had Aku not gone to school that fateful day, The Fat-Man would've never laid his evil hands on her.

The rage rose again, obliterating every other emotion. *Several people were going to feel the pain of her wrath. By the time she was done with The Fat-Man and his accomplices, they would wish they had remained unborn in their mothers' wombs.* Her rage was like a live flame, all consuming. Her thoughts were everywhere, anywhere, seeking escape from her head, respite, anything to avoid confronting the soul-killing sight of her child's cold corpse. *She'll deal with each of them, one by one, give them a slow painful death. They, who had thought to make her daughter a dead corpse, a cursed corpse; she'll show them that she has not served the Earth Goddess all these years for nothing. Her daughter will rise again and they'll see the power and glory of the great earth deity, the deity of life itself.*

Qwa brought out a small jar of ash from her raffia bag. She reached under her wrapper and untied her *Jigida* beaded waistlet. She broke it into four equal pieces and left them to soak inside the small jar of ash. Then, with shaking hands, she began to wipe the blood from her daughter's body with her headscarf. The blood had congealed and peeled off in dark flakes, exposing the bruised and battered skin beneath. The sight brought more hot tears to her eyes. She brushed them away with the back of her hand. She bit hard on her lips till she drew blood. *No, she'll not let her mind wander, imagine the pain, the torture, the terror her daughter must have endured. Later perhaps, after scores had been settled.*

243

She hissed and hurried out of the shrine. The intense heat outside almost knocked her to the ground. She paused, seeking the sun's warmth to banish the chill of the accursed shrine and the cold knot in her heart. Her eyes scanned the compound and in seconds, she found what she was searching for, the brown earthen pot buried deep in the soil, a prerequisite in the home of every self-respecting *Dibia*. The pot contained river water, one of the three vital ingredients for the preparation of charms, river water, earth soil and blood. She soaked her scarf in the water, scooped a cupful with the tin cup inside the pot and returned to the shrine. She did not spare a glance at the fast decomposing corpse of the late *Dibia* whose sacred water she took. The compound remained deserted as if it had never been inhabited, cold and silent like the deity whose shrine lay within its enclave.

Back inside the shrine, Owa began once again to attend to her daughter. She gently lowered Aku's lids with trembling fingers. She could not bear to see the look of terror in her child's staring gaze. She wiped off the last vestiges of blood, cleaned the bruises and redressed her child with the clothes she had brought in her raffia bag. When she was done, she leaned back and gazed at Aku. Her daughter looked asleep and at peace. With her eyes shut and her bright yellow dress on, there was nothing to show the trauma she had endured, save for the stump on the right arm where her hand used to be.

It was time.

Ọwa reached into the jar and withdrew the four parts of the beaded *Jigida* waistlet. She took the severed hand from the dish and tied it to Aku's wrist with one section of the ashy waistlet. The beads sank into the skin, their movement swift, like the slithering of a snake. There was a soft rattling sound as they joined the limbs together, leaving a bright pink circle at Aku's wrist. Ọwa's eyes were as saucers as she gazed in wonder at the miracle of the sacred ash. She had been the sentinel of The Ash of Immortality all her life, yet, she had never witnessed its power in its awesome totality.

Next, she pushed up the dress and tied another piece of *Jigida* string around the bloodied heart. She gently pressed it back into the gaping hole on Aku's chest from where it was taken. Just as before, the beads merged the heart to Aku's chest as if it had never been gouged out. She followed the same process with the withered nipples, watching with awe as they regained their fresh firmness. Ọwa sprinkled the rest of the ash on Aku's head, chest, arms and feet before starting to recite The Requiem of Resurrection, the ancient and secret words of life, spoken by the deities at the beginning of existence and shared only with the guardians of the Ash of Immortality, the chosen high priests and priestesses of the Earth Goddess, *Aná* and the Sky God, *Amadioha*.

Her voice was low, yet, intense. Her eyes were shut, tightly. Her body swayed to the chant as her voice began to rise. She felt the stirring of unseen bodies, corpses long dead but wakened by the never heard words of resurrection. Beyond the open dwarf door, she heard the clumsy stumbling of a rotten carcass, the blind seeking of Dibia Ogam's corpse as it tried to snatch back life from Ọwa's screeching chants. She heard the distant screams across the village as people saw graves, old and new, quake and rumble, spewing out their foul inhabitants. Animal and bird skeletons regrouped and walked, filling Ọwa's ears with their cacophony of wild madness.

She smiled, a cold smile. *It was not their time. It would never be their time. Without the Ash of Immortality, their resurrection was futile, a mere few minutes of re-lived bliss. They would return to their lifeless funk the minute she ceased her chant. Only one dead being would resurrect, the one coated with the sacred ash of life, her daughter, Aku.*

Inside the shrine, she heard the faint rustling by her side, a raspy sound of coughing, gasping. Her chant ceased. Ọwa caught the loud crashing of a dead corpse just beyond the shrine door. Dibia Ogam had taken his final step on earth. Ọwa opened her eyes and stared at her daughter. Aku stared back at her. Triumph blazed in Aku's eyes, triumph and glowing life. It lasted for a split second before it was replaced by confusion and fear. Ọwa gasped, her eyes darting with joy and wonder. She stooped to engulf her daughter in a tight hug.

'Ma…Mama…' Aku's voice was scratchy as if she nursed a bad cough. Ọwa's eyes pooled again.

'Daughter, sweet daughter, you are awake, you have awoken; praise be to our great Earth Mother!' Ọwa's shoulders shook with the force of her sobs. 'Come, my child; let me take you home. A car awaits us at the edge of the village. It's a good car, a friend's car. You need not fear this friend, for he is truly good, a policeman no less, sent to us by the Earth Mother. It's not a long walk to his car. I know you're tired but your Mama will guide you and keep you safe. Rise, my child. Your Mama is taking you home. All is well now. All is well.'

Aku began to scream, piercing, inhuman shrieks that was unlike anything Ọwa had ever heard. Her body jerked on the mirror floor, thrashing and flapping like a dying fish stranded on a sandy beach. And from her lips issued words that sent the chill crawling up Ọwa's neck.

'Mama… save me, Mamaaa! I don't want to die! Please, Mama, don't let them kill me… save me…'

Ω Ω Ω

12

Choices

Femi watched the arrival of the two women, a stunned look on his face. He had believed he was beyond shock after witnessing the terrifying events that occurred minutes earlier. The dusty roadside where he was parked was still riddled with the dry skeletal bones of unknown creatures that had arrived from nowhere in minutes and quickly collapsed back into lifeless dry bones for no explicable reason. His car bonnet was littered with white bones which looked like birdlife while others had distinctive animal appearances. He'd known instantly that it was all linked to Qwa. Terror and mystery seemed to follow the tiny medicine-woman like a dark cloud of grave-flies – literally.

He had called early at her house after the bodies of the dead policemen were taken to the mortuary. The DPO had given him free reign to deal with Qwa as he pleased, since he seemed to be the only policeman that was safe from her wrath. The DPO practically ordered him to pay a visit to Qwa to find out what she planned to do, if she planned to inflict more harm on the people, especially on the DPO who had ordered her arrest and abuse. Femi was asked to placate Qwa, reassure her that the police were on her side, working tirelessly to find her child. He'd been happy to comply. Any reason to see Qwa was welcomed, even though he had no intentions of furthering his DPO's corrupt agenda.

Qwa had received him as if she'd been expecting his visit. In fact, she'd more or less said so.

'*Oga* Femi,' Qwa had grabbed his arm, her grip unexpectedly strong, coming from such a small woman. 'You have arrived, praise be to our Earth Mother. I have to go and bring back my daughter and I need someone to drive me there. Please, *Oga* Femi, will you give me a ride to Lokobar?'

'Your daughter?' Femi stared at her with wide-eyed incredulity. 'Have you heard news about your daughter? Who told you? Tell me quick, Madam Qwa. I'll need to bring them into the station for questioning without delay.'

'Don't bother, it's ok,' Qwa's voice was laced with impatience. 'Let's go now. I have money for petrol if you like,'

'I have petrol. Tell me what you heard about your daughter,'

'Later, in the car. Let's go now, please,' Qwa led him towards his car, her steps rushed. The bulky raffia bag strapped across her shoulder banged on her thigh as she walked. He noticed she kept wincing, as if her body hurt. Not surprising after what she'd been through at the hands of those policemen. One shouldn't think ill of the dead but he couldn't help feeling they deserved everything they got.

Ọwa let herself into his car while he was still mulling over her words. From the rumours he'd heard, Ọwa's daughter was dead, used for ritual sacrifice by the one they called Chief Eze, the deputy local government chairman. Femi had no proof to bring in the man for questioning and anyway, Eze was very well connected, coupled with the DPO offering him police protection. There was only so much he could do without jeopardising his job. He had no idea where Lokobar village was, had never heard of the place. In his opinion, it would take a magician to know the multitude of villages these Igbos had. He didn't relish the idea of recovering a decomposed corpse but then, he couldn't let Ọwa go by herself to collect the body of her dead daughter. By his calculation, the girl would have been dead a few days. Her body should be in an advanced state of decay. With all her powers, Ọwa was still a woman underneath everything and a grieving mother too. She would need a shoulder to cry on when the time came.

The journey to Lokobar had been a long one. Ọwa had given directions with the precision of a satnav. Yet, she'd confirmed that she had never been to the place. He didn't press her on how she knew the route. He knew better. Neither did he question her actions when she began to coat her face with white *Nzu* chalk powder and black ash. He had seen the same look several times on his younger brother. She was fortifying herself for supernatural battle. *But what battle? And with who?*

It had been a two-hour journey. As they entered the village, Femi had been struck by the number of coffin-makers that plied their macabre trade in the tiny village. Everywhere he looked seemed to be occupied by shadowy stores, displaying coffins of all sizes, designs and colours. Some were made with cheap plastic while others had intricate patterns weaved into their wooded exterior. The sight of so many coffins in one tiny village sent the sudden chills to his spine. When he asked Ọwa about it, her reply had shocked him the more.

'The deity of wealth, *Aku n'uba,* is housed in this village. They all believe they're entitled to riches and it breeds envy and evil in their hearts. Anyone who displays wealth is immediately killed off by his neighbours through *Juju* magic. They see you with a new car, a new bicycle, a wealthy son-in-law, a fertile harvest, even a new wardrobe, and you're marked for death. This is one village where you'll hardly come across a storey building and if you do, rest assured the owner is dead. Soon, their lands will not contain their dead.' Femi had found himself searching out for any house that wasn't a hut or bungalow in the village and wondering if what Ọwa said was true, if the owners were dead and if such wickedness could possibly exist.

'Stop me here,' Ọwa suddenly commanded, her voice hard. They were at the edge of the village, a deserted stretch of dusty road with hardly any building in sight. All around them were bushes, dense foliage, likely teeming with dangerous wildlife. The police officer in him rejected the request.

'I can't let you go anywhere by yourself, especially in a village like this,' he said, pulling over to the edge of a thick shrub. 'I'll need to either arrest the kidnappers or assist you in bringing back your daughter.' He didn't use the word, "corpse". He didn't want to cause her more distress than was necessary. Not that she looked distressed. On the contrary, she was the calmest he had ever seen her in the few times they'd met. There was a steely resolve in her demeanour that made him both wary and impressed. Surely, she had to know she was going to discover the dead body of her only child, he thought. Yet, her appearance was like one going into battle for the greatest prize in the world, fierce, confident and pulsing with suppressed anticipation.

'What I need to do must be done alone,' she replied. There was an authority in her voice that brooked no arguments. 'I don't want to risk your life. It's better you remain here till I call for you. I will be fine, trust me.'

He had done as she asked because he had no choice, because he knew what she was capable of doing, because something inside told him he didn't want to see what she was going to see... *what she was going to do.* He was still reeling from the events of the previous night. He hadn't brought it up with her yet, didn't think it was the right time to question her, gauge the state of her mind.

That would come later. *After*. He'd watched her walk away into the distance. Then, he got out of the car to take a leak by the bushes. When he was done, he got back into his car and put on the radio. He allowed his thoughts to wander, think about all he had witnessed since his transfer to that dreadful village, Ukari.

Femi's temper had always been his undoing. He had entered the police force with what he now realised was stupid naivety. Despite being the heir to his father's considerable wealth, he didn't inherit the powers that went with it, the powers conferred by *Orisha Orinle,* their family deity, whose river flowed through their town. His younger brother, Olu, had exhibited all the awesome powers of the high priests of the great deity. Femi had felt nothing but pride and love for his sibling. He knew the terrible burden that came with such great powers.

The police force had been anything but the just and fair career he had envisaged. In no time, he'd found himself at loggerheads with his superiors for refusing to obey corrupt instructions. His roots were formed at the shrine of *Orisha Orinle*. He would never compromise his integrity for monetary gain. The result had been several promotion by-passes, multiple transfers to unsavoury locations as well as a witch-hunt by his latest DPO, a man whose corruption was phenomenal even by the terrible standards Femi had encountered in his fifteen years of police work. Everyone knew the fat bastard had a hand in the girl's disappearance…*murder*. It was no secret that the DPO and the man had a close relationship, no doubt, one built on foundations of bribery, embezzlement and intimidation. Nailing the fat toad for the murder of the young albino girl would be hard. But once he had the corpse, he would have something to work with, proof that a vile crime had been committed, rather than mere speculation. Femi geared himself for Qwa's return.

That was when the ground began to quake. His car rocked as if it were being shoved by giant arms. Things began to burst from the earth, things that looked like skeletons, soil-coated bones that stumbled about in dazed blindness, horrors that had no business being above ground, yet walked about in the bright light of noonday. The air was a fog of dust as the earth erupted to unholy life. Femi shouted as a bird skeleton hit his windscreen, a skeleton whose claws scrambled against the glass, seeking entry. He quickly wound up his window and locked the door. He started the engine and turned on the wiper, swiping away the scratching bird skeleton. Pieces of white bones littered his bonnet. He put the gear in place, intent on escape. But the ground quaked so hard he feared a sinkhole. He killed the engine and began to pray, pray to deities known and unknown. More carcasses dropped on his car, his bonnet and roof, bird, animal and human skeletons. They scratched at his doors, his windows, their bony claws brown with the grave soil. They howled and moaned, sending cold shivers down his spine. He started his car again, not caring about sinkholes and earth quakes. Some deaths were better than others. He would rather die in a car accident than be feasted upon by the walking terrors by noonday.

Femi set his car in motion, driving towards the unknown village, determined to find Owa and get them far away from the accursed village. The ground rocked beneath him and his car weaved from left to right as he strove to avoid the walking dead. His heart almost ceased its beats when an earth-coated corpse in the shape of a man stumbled onto his path. Bloated grave-worms mired the man's face. Femi screamed, swerving violently to the right. He felt his fender brush something soft, yet hard; heard the grinding, squishing sound of crushed bones and rotten flesh underneath his tyres. Femi carried on driving, praying, shouting, his body a trembling mass of terror.

He had driven less than a quarter of a mile when the earth rumblings ceased and a sudden calm descended. He slowed down and crawled to a stop. His heart was still pounding, his eyes cloaked in terror as he glanced about the terrain, searching, dreading the re-appearance of the noonday horrors. But the ground was still, as unmoving as the multitude of dead things littering the roadside. They had collapsed with the same inexplicable suddenness of their resurrection. Femi wiped the sweat drenching his face with a shaking hand. Thoughts returned to his scrambled mind once more. *What had he let himself into? What had made him imagine he could manage such an awesome force like Qwa? A person with the power to raise the dead was not one to tangle with in any way. He was not a coward but neither was he a fool.*

Femi swore again, furious with himself, his stupidity, his arrogance and blindness. He had allowed his desire for the woman to cloud his reason. The woman and the medicine-woman were one and the same. One was vulnerable and sweet while the other was powerful and deadly. Both belonged to a force greater than man, a power that would demand total loyalty and servitude. He could not dare antagonise that force by getting involved with its high priestess. He was not familiar with the deity Qwa worshipped but he was smart enough to know that each deity had its own powers which could prove deadly to any fool who dared challenge its authority. He would drive the priestess back to her village and stay as far away from her as it was humanly possible.

Femi settled himself in the car and began his wait for Qwa. It was hot inside the car but he kept the windows raised and the doors locked. He wanted to get out of the car and breathe in some deep gulps of fresh air but his fear kept him trapped within the inferno of his car. He picked up a discarded old copy of a newspaper and started to fan himself. The air was hot yet cool. It brought some calm to his racing heart. He looked around his surroundings again and suddenly his eyes widened.

Two figures were stumbling their slow way towards his car, two women of identical pale-coloured skin and yellow braided hair. One was tall and slender, the other, short and thin, almost child-like in size. Yet, in every way, the strength lay with the smaller woman, from the way she held up the stumbling figure of the tall, young woman, to the firm purpose in her stride. *Qwa! And her missing daughter, Aku!* Femi crossed himself, his actions involuntary, fevered. Cold terror washed over him afresh. *There was something wrong.* He felt it deep in his marrow. Every instinct in his body told him to flee, drive away in the opposite direction without delay. His mind told him to keep his car door locked, not to let in whatever it was that was being led into his car. The girl couldn't be alive, not after everything he'd heard. The events of the last minutes still filled him with terror.

He made to start the engine, flee from the place. But his heart held him to his seat, his treacherous heart which refused to listen to the reason of his mind. He would never forsake Qwa, not for his life or sanity. He was in this for the long haul, whatever "this" was. His heart now belonged to the tiny medicine-woman for as long as she would accept his servitude and love. He had known that she was the one, the true soulmate he had sought in his fifty years of existence. A failed marriage, several relationships, two sons and three grandchildren and he was still searching for that elusive love which he believed was the true destiny of every human being. He did not consider himself a good-looking man in any conventional sense but his tall and muscular physique, coupled with an innate self-confidence and reserve, somehow drew the women to him like moth to light. His profession also exposed him to all manner of feminine dangers, women who offered themselves to him in exchange for freedom from arrest or just for the sheer thrill of sleeping with a man in uniform. Femi spurned them with the contempt that had gradually brought the cold glint of ruthlessness to his dark pupils. Yet, as he spied Qwa at the distance, leading her daughter towards his car, his eyes lost their cold detachment and took on a tender wryness that would have shocked all who knew him, save his grandchildren.

With a deep sigh, he started the engine and drove towards the two women. He marvelled at the superhuman strength it took for Qwa to support the tall young woman leaning heavily against her. As he drew level to them, he stalled the engine and got out to assist them into the car.

'Madam Qwa! I welcome you,' his words were almost a shout, his nerves still tense after the recent harrowing events. 'I thank God you found your daughter safe too,' he quickly opened the back door and reached out to assist the stumbling girl into the car. A faint smell wafted up his nostrils, an unpleasant odour of sourness, something off; he couldn't give a name to it, though it reminded him of the death he frequently dealt with as a policeman, yet somehow different. It mixed with the surrounding smell of dusty earth, fermenting Cassava and smoke, the familiar odours of Igbo villages. Femi wrinkled his nose and lowered the girl into the back seat. Her eyes remained shut as if in sleep. She appeared catatonic, like one in a coma. A deep purple bruise coloured her forehead while her face bore signs of healing wounds, as if she'd been dragged along a rough surface. *Poor thing!* Only the heavens knew what terrible ordeal she had been through. She was lucky to have a mother who could literally move the earth to find her. So many in her shoes had not been so fortunate.

Femi could not count the number of times he'd had to recover the mutilated bodies of albinos, children and young women, used for dark, ritual purposes by evil animals that went about in the guise of human beings. His eyes did a sweeping survey of the girl. All her limbs seemed to be intact. A true miracle indeed, he thought, a slow rage burning in his heart. They had probably raped the girl and left her for dead. Left to him, that fat scum, Eze, would be executed for the common criminal he was.

Femi desperately wanted to ask Aku questions. The policeman in him demanded immediate answers to riddles that had plagued him ever since her disappearance. But he knew he would have to wait a little longer for her statement. The girl looked more dead than alive. In fact, he could almost swear she wasn't breathing. He could hear no sound of soft air released from laboured lungs neither could he see the steady rise and fall of a breathing chest. But it was surely his imagination playing tricks on him. He had seen her walk the distance into the car. No walking human could be without breath.

Femi quickly withdrew from the car and assisted Qwa into the back seat, waiting till she was nestled next to her daughter before shutting the door. He got into the car and took a quick look at the rear mirror. His eyes met Qwa's own. She smiled at him, a smile of gratitude. Weariness coated her face yet her eyes burnt a fierce light in their pale dance. Her features looked piquant underneath the faded coating of ash and chalk. Her smile brought the sudden race to his heart and a good warmth to his blood. *He would yet make her his woman one day, make himself worthy of her love.*

Just then, he caught a movement at the periphery of the rear mirror. The girl, Aku, was stirring. Her eyes opened and his gaze connected with hers. Femi gasped. Cold shivers hit his body. His neck whipped round to refute what he had seen in the mirror. The blood drained from his face as he quickly swung his body back into his seat. He wanted to shrink, hide like a child behind the safe shield of his driver's seat, anywhere he couldn't be found by the passenger sitting directly behind him in his car. His heart pounded as loud as the heavy breathing from his lungs. His hands gripping the wheel shook so bad he doubted his ability to drive. The man in him fought the child in him, demanded that he man up, get a grip, control the trembling of his hands and forget what his eyes had seen in the girl's pupils.

He had seen death. The face he'd seen in the mirror was not the face of the young girl he had assisted into his car, but a death mask, an ashy and withered corruption from the depths of the grave. In the glittery, black pupils holding his own, he had seen what no human should see, chilling death, blazing with malice. He had been unprepared for the oldness, the knowing and the fury that glowed in the pair of piercing black eyes that stared him down with a look of pity and contempt. Gone were the youth, the tiredness, the fear and the confusion he had seen on the face of the kidnapped young girl, replaced by a terror that stole the last shreds of courage from his thudding heart.

Femi wiped the cold beads dampening his forehead. He was a detective, trained to follow his instincts and the evidence of his eyes. Every drop of blood in his body screamed at him that the thing sitting in the car with them was not human. Qwa might believe it to be her missing daughter but Femi had seen its true nature in those blazing black pupils and it was not a human one. He didn't need to question why he no longer felt any pity for the girl as he'd felt from the minute he learnt of her disappearance or why her very presence in his car filled him with dread and aversion, even terror. But for Qwa, but for the poor, deluded and grieving mother, he would abandon his car and its unholy cargo at the accursed coffin-littered village and run for his life without a backward gaze.

Femi executed a U-turn and set the wheels home-bound. A terse silence pervaded the car, broken only by his harsh breathing. He turned on the radio, low, in keeping with the sombre mood in the car. Again, he took a quick look in the rear mirror against his best intentions. He gave an inward sigh of relief. The girl's face had replaced the death-hag's, young and human. Her eyes were shut once again in sleep and Qwa had finally succumbed to tiredness. She was dozing with her head resting against the left shoulder of her daughter. In sleep, she looked so fragile and sweet, his heart melted anew. He dragged his eyes away and focused on the black asphalt of the road   .

The rest of the drive back to Ukari village was uneventful. His two passengers slept right through the two-hour journey till he pulled up just before sunset outside the white-washed bungalow nestled in the mango grove. Qwa's eyes flew open as soon as the car stopped. Fear clouded her pupils till she turned to look at the girl by her side and relief and joy suffused her face.

'Aku!' Her voice was soft, tender. The girl slept on. Femi observed the sleeping girl surreptitiously as he spoke to Qwa.

'Madam Qwa, we're home finally. You were asleep and I didn't want to wake you up.' *Oluwa! God above! He was right! The girl's chest was still, as still as a flat slab of concrete; no*

264

movement, no heaving, no breathing! 'If you want, I can help you take your daughter into the house and maybe we can ask her some questions and find out what happened to her, who kidnapped her...' *Please God, don't let her accept his offer. He didn't want to touch the thing in his car or have any contact with it.* 'Or if you prefer, I can come back tomorrow after you've rested. I know it's been a long day and you must both be very tired.'

The girl began to stir. She whimpered softly, shaking her head, her eyes tightly squeezed. Femi felt the familiar dread wash over him afresh. He braced himself for her awakening, for the terror he would yet again encounter in her black dead eyes.

'Mama...Mama...' Aku jerked into wakefulness, terror darting her pale blue eyes. She looked around, a confused glaze in her eyes, before she sank back into the seat in what appeared to be a faint. Femi dashed behind and tried to help bring her out from the car. A tight knot formed in his throat. Guilt wracked his body. *Stupid, stupid fool of a man that he was!* He had allowed his imagination to flourish unfettered. He was no better than a teenage girl...*worse.* Any fool could see that the young girl he held in his arms was a living traumatised girl who had escaped the worst nightmare imaginable. *So much for being a bloody detective.*

Between him and Qwa, they managed to get Aku into the house and into her bed. Femi had literally carried the girl in. She had returned to the catatonic state again. He suggested they take her to a hospital for a thorough check up but Qwa refused outright. She was quite capable of taking care of her daughter, she said. He helped the sleeping girl into her bed and withdrew from the room.

Femi looked around Qwa's living-room and his eyes widened with incredulity. A feeling of déjà vu overwhelmed him, coupled with bitter nostalgia. Qwa's living room was a replica of his late father's bedroom, the room he had spent so many tortured hours of his early years struggling to learn the ancient arts that was their family's heritage, failing to make himself worthy of his great father and their fearsome deity. His ordeal had only ended when his younger brother, Olu, began to exhibit the occultic powers that had been his natural gift from birth. Their father had quickly turned his attention to his younger son and left Femi to his own devices. It had taken years to overcome the feeling of failure, the knowledge that he had been a disappointment to their father and unworthy of their deity's love. Conversion to Christianity had been of little help and he had eventually given up the church for the force. In the end, the police force had been his saviour. Detective work had been a natural progression. His success as a detective was phenomenal. His instincts were uncannily accurate, coupled with his brother's unsolicited help.

Femi could not count the number of nights Olu had called his mobile phone in the middle of the night to give him a message from the oracle, a name, a location, a motive, a weapon, something that would instantly solve a puzzling case of which his brother had no prior information. He owed his brother not just his success as a detective, but also his career. But for his reputation, his superiors would have since ended his career due to his perceived stubbornness and outspokenness.

Femi's wandering gaze took in the numerous earthen jars in various sizes, containing hidden herbs and potions. The only furniture in the room was a table stacked high with rocks, cowrie shells, dry plants, Kola-nut pods, bottles of fluids and oils in various colours and textures and various beads and feathers from unknown birdlife. There was no television, radio, sofa, or photos hanging on the bare walls. Straw mats in different stages of fraying covered the cement floor. A tight knot formed behind Femi's throat. He had hated and loved his father's room. His banishment from that sacred room had symbolized his failure and the loss of his father's love.

Femi walked out of the living room without a backward look and drove away from the little bungalow that was the first place that had felt like home to him in a very long time.

****

Eze stared at his exposed chest in the smudged glass of his bedroom mirror. He leaned into the upright mirror, peering into his reflection with an intent concentration that furrowed his brows. His right hand reached up to stroke the fading mark on his shoulder, just as he had done an hour before. Observing his naked body in the mirror had become a compulsion with him since his last visit to Dibia Ogam. Each time he pulled off his clothes and stood before the mirror, his heart would pound like thunder, constricting his breath. His mind kept replaying the witch-doctor's words – *the wrong corpse, the wrong corpse, the wrong corpse.* Again, he recalled the *Dibia's* warning on the fateful day The Black Hand touched him - *Nurture it well, for the day it vanishes from your shoulder is the day you will die.*

Eze stared at the slowly fading mark with renewed terror. Thoughts raced through his mind like scattered ants. *He had to do something before it was too late.* Eze didn't need to be told that his life was at stake. Already, he could feel his enemies circling him like vultures to a rotten corpse. The events at the village police station coupled with the witch-woman's stake-out of his house had finally forced the DPO's hand. Invitations to the police station had been handed to Eze and suddenly, the DPO could no longer be reached on his mobile phone. It was as if the man had never accepted a single coin from the numerous bribery packages Eze had given him over the years.

Worse, the wretched priest had survived the assassination attempt and had identified his two henchmen as his attackers. The state governor himself had ordered an immediate investigation and

Eze's chairman had equally ordered his suspension pending the outcome of the investigation. Eze had sent messages to the boys at the police cell through their mothers, ordering them to stay mute about everything. The thugs knew enough to bring him down in the most inglorious manner. His instincts told him it was only a matter of time before they talked and his instincts had never let him down.

Eze slumped on his bed and stared into the overhead fan slowly circling the stale cigarette air inside the air-conditioned room. He allowed his mind to think through his troubles, one at a time, in a bid to find solutions. Foremost were the thugs, Uche and Donatus. He had to find a policeman he could bribe to ensure the boys never left the police cell alive. With their deaths, no one could link him to the attack on the priest or the girl's murder, save the girl's cousin, Enu. He feared no trouble from the woman. She was as compromised as he was. Even without that, he knew Enu would never talk. Save for the fact that she was from the wretched *Nshi* clan, he would have wooed her for his fourth wife. It was rare to find a woman who thought and acted like a man, a woman he could respect like a man. Still, he had his hands full enough with his three quarrelsome wives without bringing in more complications.

His mobile phone rang and Eze checked the caller I.D. It was the elusive DPO. *Finally!* He scrambled up from the bed, his movement rushed and clumsy. He knocked down the small silver clock by the side table and cursed. The bed groaned beneath his weight. Pressing the mobile to his ear, he quickly stooped to pick up the clock before speaking into the phone.

'DPO Egede!' His voice was that of a farmer that finds his crops have escaped a locust plague. '*Enyi,* my friend, I was starting to think I had lost your correct phone number. Either that or you've travelled out of the country. I've been calling you for days now and not heard anything from you.'

'I'm still here doing my job,' the DPO's voice was brisk. It was a tone Eze had never heard in all their years of dubious association. 'I'm here with my commissioner of police and need you to come down to the headquarters immediately. I've assured the commissioner that we don't need to send police officers to your house to bring you in,' the unspoken threat was clear, together with the tacit warning. Eze's heart began to pound. The vultures were truly circling closer. Again, he pushed his shirt aside and dashed over to the mirror to take another look at the mark of The Black Hand. *Was it his imagination or was the hand looking paler than it was a few minutes ago?*

'Chief Eze, do you hear me?' The DPO's voice broke into his musings. 'We shall expect you in an hour. You'll need to bring your passport with you. Bye.' The phone went dead and Eze stumbled back to his bed. He slumped against the headboard and stared into the ceiling, his eyes blood-hued like one that had been without sleep for weeks. His heart raced like a deer and his breath was as harsh as the sound of the air-conditioner. His bedroom suddenly felt like a prison to him.

It was the midget witch-woman. Eze's mind raced in dark circles. He blamed the *Aghali* witch for everything. Ever since the death of the four policemen, the DPO had turned into a woman overnight, weak and quaking with an over-active imagination. Eze cursed aloud. He was no fool. When the police ordered you to bring in your passport, it was their way of telling a person they were no longer free to travel out of the country and escape justice. Worse, an invitation to the force headquarters signified the highest risk of an arrest and exorbitant bribery in the guise of bail, money he could ill afford with everything now happening in his life.

Eze hissed, shaking his head and grinding his teeth. He needed to make another visit to Dibia Ogam without delay. And this time, he would ensure his sacrifice would not be the wrong corpse but the greatest sacrifice a man can offer. The good book, the bible, stated that Abraham offered his only son Isaac to God. Eze would mimic the great man. He had several useless daughters loitering around, making a huge dent in his purse with their greedy mouths and incessant demands. One less daughter wouldn't be a loss to anyone save whichever wife happened to be the mother of the chosen daughter. His eyes lit up with glee as he allowed his mind to think about each of his three wives in detail. From the depths of his memory, he pulled up past insults, injuries to his manhood, acts of disobedience and omissions by each of the women. He had always suspected his second wife of marrying him for his wealth and of all his wives, she was the most arrogant, being the only one with a university degree. She carried herself as if she were a queen doing him the favour of being in her presence. She rarely spoke, even after he'd thrashed her for some unrecalled offence. But then, she had luckily ended up being the only one to give him his son and heir, Caesar. He quickly ruled her out. Even with her arrogance and pride, she was the mother of his only son. Her two daughters would live.

The choice now boiled down to his first and last wives. His first wife had never supported any of his later marriages to her sister-wives. In fact, the woman had turned all her five daughters against him, especially his first daughter, Princess, a girl he had personally named and had loved as much as he'd loved his late mother. These days, the girl could barely speak to him or visit with his grandchildren, all thanks to the indoctrination of his first wife and her bitterness towards his marriages. Yes, the fat, old bitch deserved to feel the pain of losing one of the three daughters still living with her. After all, she had enough grandchildren from her two married daughters to make up the loss of one of the other three girls.

A deep frown settled over Eze's features as his thoughts turned to his third wife, Oge. Twenty-five years younger than him, Oge had made no secret of the fact that she was in the marriage for the money. She flirted with every man within a mile of her vicinity, including his two thugs. But for the fact that he was yet to catch her out with a lover, he would have since sent her packing. Of all his wives, Oge was the one that treated him with the least respect, relying on her youth and looks to keep him chained. Perhaps losing one of her twin girls would wake the slut up to the realities of life. If she wanted money then she should be prepared to make her own sacrifices too for the money. Oge was the most expensive wife to maintain and it was time she paid up with one of her twins. *Yes, the girl - what was her name? Promise? Theresa? Whatever. He could never tell between the two twin clones of their mother, hard-faced skinny runts, who had mastered the art of cosmetic makeup and attitude from their crib. Whatever her name, she'll be sacrificed to the deity of wealth, Aku n'uba.* His mind was made up. This time, there would be no hiccups. This time, he would be offering not just a child, but a virgin child and his own blood as well, all in a single sacrifice. What greater gift can the god of wealth demand from him? Even Dibia Ogam would be impressed.

Eze's heart was pounding as he jumped up from his bed. It was a thud of joy and excitement. There was a sudden light at the mouth of the cold, dark cave that he'd been trapped in ever since

273

his first contact with the witch-woman. The road was now mapped out clear for him. Suddenly, he couldn't wait to get himself to the police headquarters and find out what that scaredy woman that called himself a DPO wanted.

A few minutes later, as Eze walked down the same staircase his late father, Agu of Onori clan, had once trod with pride, he almost got toppled by the twin girls playing on the steps. Shouting a loud curse, he gave the nearest twin a hard cuff on the back of her head. The child howled and ran upstairs towards her mother's bedroom, followed by her clone. Her cries raised his ire and doomed the child. *She would be the chosen one,* he decided. *Promise!* That was her name. Why didn't he ever realise how grating girls' cries were? Caesar, his only son, was the same age as the twins, five years to the day, but already with the heart of a warrior. You would never catch the boy crying like his stupid sisters, except when his mother was around. Then he would bawl at the slightest sneeze. That's what mothers did to sons, turned them into simpering girls if left unchecked. He was watching his son like a hawk, ready to knock out any evidence of woman-weakness from him at the first sign.

From one of the bedrooms upstairs, Eze heard his third wife, Oge, scream at him, her voice shrill, coated with the contempt in which she held him.

'Fat fool! Useless man! Shameless bully who won't fight other men and instead, flexes his muscle on children and women.

274

Thunder will crack your ugly, useless head the next time you hit my children, rubbish man, devil bastard.'

Eze's temper flared. He turned to march upstairs to give the woman a dose of his fists. He paused, glancing at his watch, debating his options. He could swear the crazy woman actually derived a masochistic thrill from inciting violence in him. His other two wives would cower in terror for months after receiving his special brand of chastisement. They would be at their best behaviours, their voices barely raised beyond a whisper, even his second wife who was a university graduate. *But not Oge, the psycho bitch.* Even while he had her pinned to the floor and raining blows on her skinny body, her tongue would continue its vicious assault on his manhood. Neither swollen eyes nor split lips cured the woman's recalcitrance. Acid would continue to spill from her lips, eroding his self-esteem and dignity. He always left Oge after each trashing, feeling like the one battered instead of the one doing the battering.

Eze began walking down the stairs once again. No, he wouldn't give Oge more excuses to dent his confidence, not now that it was at its lowest. The punishment he had in store for her was better. The loss of one of her precious twins would tame her more than his fists. A cold smile creased his scarred features. Suddenly, he wasn't sure which gave him the most pleasure, the fortune he would acquire after the sacrifice or the sight of Oge's grief-stricken face at the loss of her child. As for the *Aghali* witch, he would soon come up with a final solution to his problems with her.

*** *

Femi woke up the next morning more refreshed than he'd felt in a long time. He was surprised at how soundly he had slept considering the terrible events of the previous day. He had expected to be plagued by nightmares of walking corpses and scratching skeletons. Instead, his sleep had been dreamless, deep and long. A warm feeling of satisfaction brought a small smile to his face. *He had fulfilled his promise to Ọwa. Against all odds, he had brought her daughter back to her.* He now had the physical evidence to put away the fat criminal for good, with or without the co-operation of the DPO. All that was needed was the girl's statement to bring that corrupt politician to a well-deserved punishment.

Femi quickly dressed in his civvies and got into his car. There was a sudden rush of adrenalin, a breathless thrill that left him feeling like a teenager. *He was going to see Ọwa again.* He realised the thought had been with him from the time he woke up, a constant silent refrain in his head. In a few minutes, he would once again look into those mesmerising, dancing blue eyes and perhaps, hold her again as he had done at the police station the first time they met. Femi recalled the feel of her body in his arms as she sobbed, wracked with grief at the disappearance of her only child. She had felt so little in his arms, her breasts soft against his stomach, a woman that made him feel like a king and brought out every protective instinct in him. He yearned to keep Qwa safe and happy. He knew she was capable of keeping herself safe... *ha! capable of keeping him safe too.* Still, her small womanly body pulled every nerve in his body as nothing had ever done. Now that her daughter was safely home, maybe she would finally allow herself to be wooed.

On his way to her house, Femi stopped by the roadside mini-market to buy some fried *Akara* beanballs, plantain and *Agidi* corn cake for Qwa. He didn't want her to stress about breakfast after all she'd been through the previous day. At a nearby kiosk, he bought tins of milk powder, *Bonvita* chocolate powder, a packet of sugar cubes, tins of sardines and a loaf of bread. It felt good to shop for Qwa. It gave him an intimate feeling that was strangely arousing. He could imagine them shopping for groceries together, in a different town and a different life, him and Qwa, together, husband and wife, inseparable.

Femi shook his head, shutting down the tantalising thoughts. Despite it being a Sunday morning, he still had police work to do, a victim's statement to collect from Aku, reports to prepare, charge sheets and arrest warrants to sort out for all those involved in the abduction of the girl. He knew he would have a fight on his hands where the corrupt politician was concerned. Taking on an influential man, especially when he wasn't even an Igbo man himself, was a big risk. Femi was from the *Yoruba* tribe, a detective persecuted by his superiors for his refusal to so-called "play ball". His primary suspect, Chief Eze, had both money and power, many allies and the benefit of being an Igbo man living in an Igbo village, surrounded by Igbo friends and family. They would cry foul as soon as Femi started his investigation, pull the tribalism card and turn the case into a debacle of Igbo nationalism. It would soon become a case of a *Yoruba* policeman attempting to frame an Igbo man in his own mother-land. Worse, because his victim was an albino girl, there would be minimal outcry against Eze's crime by a society who consciously and subconsciously viewed people with albinism with disdain, loathing and even fear. A more sympathetic victim might have made his work easier but Femi was determined to see justice done; not just for the girl's sake, but most especially for Qwa. No mother should have to go through what that poor woman had endured at the hands of The Fat-Man and the entire village.

***

Femi parked his car outside Qwa's bungalow and walked towards the front-door. There was a stillness in the compound that gave it an abandoned air despite the few chickens and goats loitering

278

around the sandy grounds. At the door, he paused and ran a hand over his head, patting his bald smoothness as if it nursed a full yield of thick, kinky hair. He adjusted his black polo-shirt, making sure it was well tucked inside his belted jeans. A whiff of his aftershave infused his nostrils with well-being. He was all set to go.

Femi knocked, at first, tentatively, then with more force when no one answered. The door opened and Ọwa stood before him, looking up at him with blue eyes that darted with impatience. Femi's heart plummeted. There was no smile on Ọwa's face. He could have been any stranger for all the welcome she gave him.

'Ọga Femi,' her voice was deeper than he recalled, raspy, as if she'd been coughing or maybe, crying. 'Good morning, sir. I hope the day finds you well.' Her words were as dull as the grey aura that cloaked her body. Her braided hair was hidden behind a bandana-style headscarf, the same black colour as her long-sleeved cotton blouse. The straw-coloured braids hung low and long on her shoulders, making her look even younger than the middle-aged woman he knew her to be.

'Femi, I told you to call me Femi, not *Ọga* Femi,' he tried to infuse an air of lightness to their exchange. 'I doubt if I or anyone can ever be your master, ha, ha! Here, these are for you, breakfast, and some other stuff for you and Aku,' he thrust the bags of shopping into her hands. The stunned look on her face was his reward, a bitter sweet reward that brought an unexpected lump to his throat.

'For me? Me?' She stared at the bags and looked up at him, then back at the bags again. 'You bought all these for me?' She made a quick curtsy. 'Thank you, sir; my heart thanks you. May the good Earth Mother reward your kindness. May your goodness never go unblessed. Thank you, sir,' she curtsied again, a shy smile on her face.

'I told you not to call me "sir",' his voice was gruffed by embarrassment. Her humility hurt him for her. He should be the one bowing to her, he who had witnessed her breath-taking powers not once but twice. 'Maybe we can all share breakfast together, eh?' He smiled down at her. She returned his smile.

'Yes, come in sir… sorry, Femi. Yes; come in, Femi. You are most welcome in my house.' She held the door wide for him. Femi stepped into the living-room and again, the sense of déjà vu was overwhelming. 'Wait for me, please. I'll be back in a second,' she dashed towards the room he remembered as Aku's room. She soon emerged carrying an arm-chair. 'Here, take the chair, rest your legs,' she placed the chair near him and stood aside, waiting for him to sit down. He noticed that she kept wringing her hands and glancing about as if expecting uninvited visitors. He was glad he wasn't the only one suffering from nerves. Femi sat down, making a big fuss about it with loud grunts and exaggerated body adjustments. It calmed his nerves and even brought a smile to Qwa's face as she hovered at his side.

'Won't you sit down too?' He asked. She shook her head.

'I'm fine. I'll get you something to eat,' she stooped to pick up the shopping bags before walking over to shut the front-door. The room was immediately plunged into an unnatural gloom. Qwa dashed over to the wood-panelled windows and pushed them open, letting in the morning sunlight. A fresh breeze followed the sunlight into the stuffy room, cooling Femi's heated skin. 'I'll be back soon,' Qwa said, heading out of the room.

'Where's Aku?' He rushed his question before she could leave. 'Is she still asleep or can I talk to her now?' He gave her a wry smile, making a helpless gesture with his hands. 'Police work, you see. I need to take her statement and file my report and with luck, we'll find the people responsible and bring them to justice. I hope she wasn't badly hurt.' Femi prayed Qwa wasn't a mind-reader amongst her other talents. He didn't want her to catch the vile images flashing through his mind, visions of the fat bastard, his henchmen and gang-rape, thoughts that brought so much rage to his heart he wanted to take his gun and fire and keep firing till no-one in the blasted village remained standing. They were all in it, at least, a lot of them knew what happened and who was responsible, he thought. He'd questioned a lot of people in the village over the course of three days and had experienced their evasive eye-contacts and meandering answers that signified guilty knowledge. Yet, they weren't talking. He couldn't wait for them to see the girl alive and healthy and realise that their vile secret was about to be exposed. Even if the police force had to confiscate the fat devil's house and turn it into a makeshift police cell, he would ensure every single person involved paid for their evil crime.

'*Oga* Femi, please, please, don't tell anyone about my daughter,' Owa's voice startled him out of his dark thoughts. She had fallen on her knees by his chair, clinging to his right leg. 'No one must know she's alive. They'll only come back for her again and I can't survive her murder again.'

'Madam Owa, calm yourself, my dear,' he stood up, helping her to her feet. '*Kai!* How you women worry your little heads for nothing. Your daughter wasn't murdered, thank God and as God is my witness, I shall not let any harm come to her again, I promise you. I shall arrest every person involved in her abduction and bring them to justice regardless of their wealth or power. No one is above the law and I'm not a man that can be bribed.'

'May the Earth Mother grant you a long and healthy life,' Owa said. 'But you don't understand, sir. This thing is bigger than you or I. Aku must never be seen in the village and no one must know of her return, not yet. Please *Oga* Femi, do me this small favour. Let it all rest. Throw away your file about my daughter and let us carry on with our lives. You know how things are. There's already been enough trouble without me making things worse for ourselves in the village.'

'Aahh! Now I understand your worry.' Femi frowned. 'You don't want to antagonise the villagers for fear that their hatred against you will turn violent, is that it?' He folded her into his arms, holding her close, just as he'd dreamt and wished. But this time, his actions were not prompted by lust but pity, deep sympathy for this tiny woman, so cowered by the collective hate of her community that she would forego justice rather than draw further enmity to herself. Her fear increased his rage and his determination to give her justice and security. He pulled her closer, feeling her body tremble against his.

'I don't want you to worry your pretty head about a thing, ok? You forget your friend is a police officer in charge of the village station. I too, can make their lives miserable and I intend to make it clear to them that you're now under police protection, my protection. Any attack on you will be viewed as a personal attack on me and I deal ruthlessly with anyone that attacks me.'

'You don't understand,' Owa pulled herself from his embrace. He let her go, reluctantly. 'Come, sit down, sir. I'll get you something to eat, then I'll tell you the whole truth and it will be up to you to make your choice on what actions you'll take. You say you're my friend and I believe you. Your actions so far have been one of a true friend and I will forever be in your debt. You share the same background as me and understand my trade better than anyone else. So perhaps, you will appreciate my predicament when I tell you the truth. But first, sit down and let me feed you. You will need a full stomach for what I have to tell you.' She pulled him by the arm, down, lower, till he was back in the arm-chair once again. His head whirled with thoughts, apprehension once again prickling his skin as memories of the previous day returned to plague his peace. *What did Owa's cryptic words mean? What terrible secret was she about to spill into his ears? Worse, what choice would he be forced to make? Would he be pushed into betraying the police force he revered in order to live up to her friendship? Whatever it was, he knew he suddenly didn't want to hear it, didn't want to be forced into a compromising situation that would demand something in him he wasn't sure he possessed.*

***

Two hours later, Femi sat stunned on his chair, unable to digest both his breakfast and the story he'd just heard from Owa. Breathing was as hard as the feel of the chair on his bottom. The urge to flee from the room was strong, almost overwhelming. It took everything, every ounce of manly bravery he still possessed to resist the pull of the doorway. *He had been right all along! He had seen death in the girl's face in the rear-mirror yesterday! It hadn't been his imagination after all. Owa had brought back death,*

284

*returned life to a corpse, a decayed body whose putrefaction he
had smelled and failed to recognise till it was too late.* Oluwa! *God
in heaven! What had Ọwa brought back from the grave?*

'You cannot let it... let her live,' Femi's voice was hoarse. He
cleared his throat and gripped Ọwa's hands. 'Surely, even you
must know that this is a grave mistake...forgive me... I mean, a
bad mistake. Believe me, I don't say this lightly. The girl in that
room is not your daughter. I saw its true face yesterday, inside the
car, in my rear mirror. I saw her eyes and they're not human. Your
daughter is gone. You must let her sleep. Return her body to the
grave where it belongs so that whatever is living inside her can
also die.' Femi's eyes burnt with desperation, driven by fear and
love.

Ọwa shook her head, a stubborn glint in her darting eyes. 'I
hoped you of all people would understand, see things from my
angle. You have children of your own, even grandchildren.
Imagine how you would feel if anything happened to them and
then think of how it is for me who has just the one child. Consider
how you would feel if you knew your brother has the powers of
your deity to bring back your child and put yourself in my place.'
Ọwa was now the one gripping his hands, her small hands hot and
hard in his palms. 'All I ask is for four days...three days now...
just three days with my child to say my goodbyes properly. Surely,
you can hold your report for three days. No one would know she's

back with me. I'll keep her indoors and when the four market days given by the Earth Mother are done, I'll let her go and learn to live without my child.' Tears poured freely down her cheeks and Femi's heart melted. He leaned over and folded her into his arms again, holding her close, rocking her, calming her. Her body shook with the force of her tears as emotions, tightly held in check, finally found grateful release.

With another woman, Femi's inbuilt cynicism would have screamed "female manipulation". But with Ọwa, he knew everything was real, without guile. She was as she was, as true as the deity she worshipped. Just then, a loud scream came from one of the bedrooms across the living-room, Aku's bedroom. Ọwa pulled free from his embrace and ran towards the shut brown door. Femi rushed in her trail. There was no time to think or imagine what was happening in the room. His hand was already reaching for his non-existent gun, instinct overshadowing every other emotion. He cursed as he realised he'd left it with his uniform at home. Ọwa pushed the door open and rushed to the low, single bed pushed against the blue-painted walls. On the bed, Aku's body jerked as one pulled by a hundred demons in a hundred different directions. She screamed as if she were being butchered with a blunt knife, her voice shrill, deafening. Ọwa threw herself against her daughter's body, pressing heavy as she fought to hold Aku down, still her struggles and end her pain. But her strength was no match for the girl's. Femi joined her on the bed and together, they fought to control the screaming girl.

'Mama... save me! Please, I don't want to die... stop... oh holy Mary save me... Mama! Tell them to stop... I'm hurting... pain... pain... my heart... Mama please... stop them, save me.'

Femi felt his blood run cold, a sudden chill peppering his skin in goosepimples. If he ever had any doubts about Qwa's story, there was none left. This was horror beyond anything he had ever imagined or experienced. The girl was re-living her death, the gruesome torture inflicted on her by the witch-doctor and The Fat Man. No mother should have to hear this from the lips of her child. It was a miracle Qwa was still sane. Her bawling voice was deeper than he'd ever heard as she struggled to control her grief and soothe her daughter at the same time.

'Shush, my child... cry no more. Mama is here; I'm here. No one will hurt you again. I will kill them all, every single one of them, I promise you. Look, open your eyes now and see. You're in your room, in your bed, in your Mama's arms. You're not dead, you're not dead, Earth Mother forbid such evil. You're alive. It's just a dream, a bad nightmare. All is well, my daughter. All is well.'

As Qwa spoke, the girl's struggles subsided, her limbs went limp and the tension seeped away from her body. Her screams turned into soft sobs, punctuated by hiccups. Femi let go and stepped away from them, watching mother and daughter on the bed, his heart hurting from their pain and the rage burning within against the fat bastard. After what he'd just heard, death was too good for the beast. His eyes met Ọwa's tear-filled own as she looked at him over her daughter's shoulders. *See what they did to my child. Will you deny me this time with her?* Her eyes spoke into his mind. He shook his head, answering her question.

'It will be as you will. I will do as you ask. In three days, I shall return and we'll talk. I'll let myself out. You know where to find me if you need anything, anything at all, ok?' She nodded, silently, thanking him with her eyes, her bloodshot eyes which danced with the fury of hate and the passion of a mother's love.

Femi let himself out of the house and walked to his car. He didn't think about the choice he had made, about the ethics of police work he was betraying. The situation was beyond rational thoughts and actions. Sometimes, a man must let himself to be led by the forces of fate. This was one of those few times in his life when he knew he was powerless against a greater force. What will be, will be. He would wait and see; that was all he could do. Wait and see.

Ω Ω Ω

13

Dead Corpse

She stares at the plate in front of her. Her body is unmoving on the mat, almost like a clay statue, save for the slight tremors that rattle her frame at intervals. The silver metal dish is loaded with her favourite breakfast foods, fried plantain, Akara bean balls and Akamu corn cereal. Her mind recalls the flavour of the food, the taste of it in her mouth. But she cannot raise an appetite for food or drink. Maybe because her nose can no longer savour the delicious smells of the dishes.

Since waking up from that terrible nightmare, she's not felt like herself. For one thing, she's lost all sense of smell. Mama had washed her like a child afterwards, something she hasn't done since she turned into a teenager. She can't recall smelling the soap or coconut body-oil applied to her skin afterwards. She can't smell the familiar scent of their house, the mish-mash of smells hatched from the various ingredients of Mama's craft. And the cold; the bone-chilling cold that freezes her heart till she can feel no life-thuds. It's a cold like no other, a chill that turns her hands to ice and mocks all the wrappers shrouding her shivering body.

'Eat your food, my child,' Mama's voice breaks through her thoughts. The sound hurts her head, just like every sound does. She

290

wants to cradle her head in her hands like a fragile egg, shield it from every sound. She lifts her hands to her head and catches the thin red line on her right wrist. Her hand stops midway. Her heart leaps, then begins to pound. It feels like a pound but she cannot feel the movement in her chest. Her nightmare comes flooding back into her head in full coloured clarity; the rainbows of Enu's chandelier, the brown dustiness of The Fat-Man's car boot, the green lushness of the bush as she's dragged out of the boot, the white colour of the converse trainers that kicks her on the head, the black gleaming coldness of the mirror room and the red warmth of blood... her blood, spurting from her severed hand, her tapping fingers scrambling frantically on the bloodied mirror floor, seeking her wrist, their owner.

'Mama, the dream... it seems very real,' her voice is soft, wobbly. 'I know you say it's just a nightmare and it has to be because I'm here with you, in our house and not... not dead. But, look at my wrist, Mama. You saw my chest. I just don't know how these marks can be there, exactly as I dreamt.'

'I told you it was a demon attack through your dreams,' Mama's voice is firm, without doubt. Mama's certainty calms her own fears. 'I kept telling you to concentrate on your lessons, learn the secrets of the shrine in order to protect yourself. You know about the malevolent spirits. You've seen me fight with them on numerous occasions. They now know that they can't fight me. I'm

too powerful for them. So, they attack you instead, my child, the one thing I love more than life. They know you're not powerful enough and they know they can hurt me through you. Don't worry, child. I'm watching them now. They'll never hurt you again. Eat now, don't think about bad things. I've made your favourite dish for you. Eat it while it's still hot and after, I'll braid your hair for you and make it nice.'

The word, hair, brings another memory-thud to her heart, a fearful thud. Beyoncé hair extensions comes to her mind. From a distant place, she recalls the dark scarred face, the bloated features, the piggy eyes and the smell of cigarettes, sweat and aftershave. Another scent comes to mind, the smell of holy communion wine. Images are like flashcards in her mind, making the pain in her head hotter than burning rods. Enu's house, her angry made-up face, The Fat-Man smiling down at her paralysed body on Enu's leather chair.

'Mama, have you ever been inside cousin Enu's house?' She asks. Mama's neck whips round, her eyes dart with shock.

'Why do you ask such a thing? You know how Enu and I feel about each other. Why would I ever go to her house?'

'In my nightmare, I was in her house. I remember walking home from the market square after my fight with Ego. It was raining and Cousin Enu's car pulled up. She said she will give me a lift. I didn't want to enter her car because I knew you'd be angry with

me. But she ordered me in and people were watching from their houses so I didn't want to make a fuss. She drove me to her house. I've never seen such a house in my life. I think you're right, Mama. It was definitely a nightmare. No one can live in such a lovely glass house.' She goes silent, lets her thoughts roam through the living-room she's seen in her dream, the impossibly massive television set mounted on the wall.

'Don't stop. Tell me everything, everything. Did you say your cousin Enu took you to her house on the day you disapp... I mean, in your nightmare?' Mama's voice is urgent, her eyes dancing frantic darts of agitation. She bites her lips. She doesn't want to talk anymore. She can see her nightmare worries Mama more than she's letting on.

'It's okay, Mama. It's nothing, just a silly dream. Let's forget it.'

'No!' Mama's voice is almost a scream. It startles her, startles Mama too. She stares at Mama, her mouth wide. Mama gives a small shrug, a wry smile. *'Ignore me, my child. I'm a bit frazzled today. But please, tell me everything. I need to know everything so I can protect you from future demon attacks in your dreams. You were telling me Enu took you into her house. Go on, tell me all that happened in your dream, everything you can remember.'*

She shrugs and allows her mind to recall her dream as she begins to speak again. *'Cousin Enu told me to sit on her leather sofa. She said she wanted to wee. Then she gave me a glass of wine. I did not want to drink it because I remembered your warning. But she gave me her own glass and took the one she had given me originally, so I figured there was no poison. I drank it and it was sweet, nice. But she got angry for some reason and I wanted to leave her house but I couldn't move. My entire body was paralysed but my eyes were open and I could see, hear everything. Just that I could not move. Then the doorbell rang. Cousin Enu had a bell in my dream, Mama, a singing bell so people don't have to knock like they do when they come to our house.' She pauses as her mind recalls the beauty of her cousin's house. She marvels again at the clarity of her dream.*

'Go on, keep talking. Forget about the wretched doorbell. What happened? Who was at the door?' The urgency is back in Mama's voice.

'It was The Fat-Man, the one they call chief Eze, the one I told you abducted me and cut off my hand and heart in my nightmare,' her voice turns into a whisper. The trembles in her body worsen. She cannot go on. She does not want to remember anything after her cousin's house. She gets up from the mat, seeing the stunned look on Mama's face, the redness of rage in her skin. Mama is struggling to breathe. Her body is shaking like leaves. She should have kept silent about the dreams, spared Mama the worry about the demon attacks. She leans over Mama and hugs her.

'It's only a nightmare, Mama. Don't let it get you so worked up against cousin Enu or The Fat-Man. It's just the demons being mischievous. I'm tired now and I think I'll go and sleep since the nightmare ruined my sleep.' She laughs; tries to laugh. But the sound that comes out of her mouth is not one she recognises. It's like a creature trying to learn how humans laugh, a hollow sound without emotion. She leaves Mama staring at her own uneaten breakfast and returns to her bedroom. Her legs feel wobbly and she struggles to maintain her balance. She makes it to her room and shuts the door behind her, shutting out the world. She doesn't understand why she suddenly feels a sense of peace in the bedroom she's always hated. All she knows is that she doesn't want to leave their house again, doesn't feel like going to school or visiting her friend, Ego, ever again. In fact, she does not want to see anyone or do anything. She just wants to sleep and never wake up. She prays she doesn't get the nightmares again. No one should ever dream of themselves dying such a gruesome death. She stretches herself on her bed and shuts her eyes. In a wink, she's out, plunged into a dreamless nothingness of total oblivion.

***

Owa sat on the mat long after Aku had retired to her bedroom. Her breakfast dish, the delicacies brought to her by Femi, grew cold and moist in the metal plates, her plate and Aku's. Her body was shaking, her fingers trembling, unable to grip her spoon. Thoughts raged in her mind, dark thoughts of torture, very slow painful torture, Enu's torture. All this while she had thought her enemy was Eze, son of Agu of Onori clan. She had bested the demon, Dibia Ogam, and was gearing for her confrontation with The Fat-Man. For him, nothing less than the *Leloole* curse would do. She was biding her time for another visit to *Mbana-Oyi* to complete the quest she'd started on the night she discovered her daughter in the blood-sludge. It would take time, patience and effort. The best revenge was the bountiful feast served chilled. Let the fat fool wait; let him start to forget, believe that he'd got away with his evil. Let him begin to enjoy his life, his only son and his wealth. That would be the perfect time to strike. But first, she needed to prepare a new shrine-goat to replace poor Ebele. Without a soul-guide, she could not make the dangerous journey to *Mbana-Oyi* to learn the secrets of the *Leloole* curse from her mother, Xikora.

Aku's revelations had blown Owa's plans in all directions, just like her thoughts. She could barely restrain herself from rushing straight to Enu's house to plunge a thousand knife stabs into her filthy, whore body. She knew Enu loathed her but never in her wildest thoughts did she imagine that the woman would betray the bond of blood in such a terrible way.

Owa's heart pounded with fury. *She'll deal with the whore, watch the lying lipstick-coated lips of the vile murderer turn black in agonised death.* Qwa jumped up from the mat and dashed towards the small mud hut that housed the shrine of the Earth Goddess. Even before she reached the dwarf wooden door, she had pulled off the last item of clothing on her body. Her skin was coated in sweat, both from her exertion and the perpetual oven temperature of the shrine. She hurried over to the wicker basket in the dark corner that housed the ingredients of divination and began to assemble her arsenal. One of the white shrine chickens in the cage joined the hoard, its blood soon painting the black statue red. When she was done, Qwa quickly anointed her body with kennel oil and the special herbs of divination before prostrating before the austere statue of the earth deity.

'Earth Mother, great deity, SHE that was before creation, giver of life and keeper of souls; great goddess, I come to you again with my empty plate in hand, just like a fat child whose mouth is eternally open. I am a beggar, a worthless human, unworthy of your attention or largess. I know I come at the wrong time, while the sun still roams the skies. But a great evil has befallen your child and she cannot await the dawn of the moon. Harken to my cries, great deity. Hear my pain, a mother's anguish. See your daughter's injury and grant her justice. I come in the name of *Ofor n'Ogu* as I speak the name of my enemy before your presence. ENU. ENU. ENU. Three times I have called her name and three times will she pray for death and release.'

Ọwa plunged the shrine knife into her skin and watched her blood drip on the foot of the statue. It was an old wound from her previous requests. She moaned softly and bit her lip. 'Great Goddess, I call on Enu's name and ask for the bleeding death. *ENU! May you endure a monthly bleed that never ends. May the blood gush in an endless flow from between your thighs so that everyone will see your shame and smell your stench. Let the flies dog your every step that the world may see your rottenness. May the shame be so great that you beg for death.*' Ọwa inhaled deeply and wiped the pouring sweat from her face. She lifted her face to the black statue, her eyes burning her rage. 'Great Mother, stay your hand. Do not grant Enu her prayers for release. Keep Enu alive that her death may be slow and painful, just as she gave my daughter.'

From the small calabash by her side, Ọwa took out the shrivelled eye of a dead owl and placed it over the congealing blood at the foot of the goddess, her blood. She sprinkled hot pepper powder and salt over the dry owl eyes. She lit a fresh candle and placed it next to the dead bird's eyes. 'Great goddess, I call on Enu's name and ask for the sleepless death. *ENU! Lift your eyelids for eternity so that the peace of sleep be denied your mind. You will watch the night go by in an endless slow stream, while the rest of humanity enjoy the deep bliss of sleep. There will be no distinction between your days and your nights. Your head will split in pain from endless hours of sleepless nights. Your eyes will burn from the glare of the sun as if you were an Aghali that you so detest. Your body will grow weak and your walk will be like a drunken man's stumble. Your thoughts will be the scattered thoughts of sleepless confusion, a forgetful mind that will fill your daily life with frustration and anguish. Yet, sleep will flee your eyes. Enu, you will beg for death, for the final rest to dull the brittle pain in your sleepless eyes.'* Qwa again, lifted her gaze to the black statue. 'Great Goddess, I beg you, stay your hand. Keep Enu alive that she may pay for the evil inflicted on my child.'

Qwa reached into the calabash to extract the grey bulbous substance normally found nestled within the skull of living creatures. It had been inside the head of a pig. The mushy brain seemed to pulse with a secret life-force of its own, a malignant intelligence. Owa smiled. This curse would seal the whore's doom, drive her to screaming insanity by the time she was done with her. 'Great Goddess, I call on Enu's name and ask…' Qwa stopped. The ground shook underneath her. She stared at the statue and smiled. 'You have come,' she whispered. 'You're here. Your servant welcomes you, great deity. I await your will.' She bowed her head low.

The fly landed on her head, swiftly followed by several others. From a gap in the floor, the flies poured into the shrine, their buzz filling the dark room. They headed in the same direction, Qwa's head. Soon, her normally straw-coloured hair was a swirling, buzzing black wig, soft and heavy. A stench of damp soil, decay and lush plant life, filled the shrine. The temperature within rose to near boiling point. Qwa knelt before the statue, her sweltering body quivering, anticipation colouring her sweat-drenched skin a bright red hue. She waited in breathless expectancy for the voice, the soundless communication of the earth deity inside the deepest recesses of her brain. She didn't have long to wait. The Earth Goddess seemed in a hurry to speak to her. The message filled her head with bullet speed and thundering clarity.

'Daughter, hold your rage. Stay your hand. Allow your goddess to fight your battle for you. They will all pay, one by one. Even as we speak, the instrument of their punishment is being wrought. You ask for Enu's death and you will get that death. Her doom is already sealed. But not yet, my daughter; not yet. Enu has a task to perform, a debt to repay. Ask no further questions of your goddess and seek no more vengeance. Your daughter will be avenged, that I promise you. Go, now. Spend the precious hours you have with your child and heal your heart. Remember, guard the Ash of Immortality with your last blood. Guard it as you've never guarded anything in your life.'

The flies fled her head in a swift dive, back into the cracked soil of the shrine. The temperature dropped to the usual warm humidity of the hut. Qwa's head swelled, contracted and expanded in rapid succession. The fog rushed into her eyes and her head. She felt herself falling, crashing into the hard soil of the shrine. Her head connected with the calabash, squashing the pig brain within to mushy pulp. Regret stirred briefly in her mind. *The final curse would have been a befitting end for Enu, the grave curse, a terrifying curse that would repeat itself night after endless night, till the whore was reduced to shrieking lunacy. But the Earth Mother had decreed otherwise and* Aná *always knew best.*

Qwa allowed the darkness of oblivion to claim her mind as she slumped into a deep sleep on the floor of the shrine. By the time she awoke an hour later, Aku was gone.

***

The three policemen guarding the entrance to the state police headquarters stared at the young albino woman making her way to the shut metal gate. It wasn't the woman's pale skin that brought the astonished look on their faces, though. Instead, it was the cool confidence of her walk, a swagger executed on bare, dusty feet. The total lack of fear or hesitation in her demeanour held them in a state of shock. They were used to instilling fear and meekness in people, milking the power they held with ruthless brutality. No one, not even the richest, came through the high metal gates without first debasing themselves or greasing their palms with lots of *Naira* notes. The albino woman had neither a posh four-wheel nor impressive rich garbs. Her yellow floral dress was not sophisticated enough for her to be the mistress of any of the top officers who had plush offices within the police headquarters. As far as they could see, she had no visible cause to approach them with such arrogance, especially as she was clearly too wretched to afford the cheapest flipflops. Worse, she was an albino woman, admittedly, a pretty albino girl, but still an albino all the same. What right did she have to approach them with such irreverence?

The three policemen bristled. It was going to be a pleasure beyond orgasm to bring her down a hundred pegs. It was always a pleasure to bring women down, especially women who thought themselves better than men and behaved as if the world owed them unquestioning adoration. The policemen braced themselves with menace, spreading their legs and reaching for their guns. In the blistering noonday sun, their black pupils shot darts of cold brutality.

'You! Yellow Woman! Stop there!'

***

She watches them as they watch her, the three guardians of the metal gate. Her eyes glitter with gleeful malice. She'll not speak to them, not yet. Her silence is her weapon. It will reveal their leader to her, the one they'll turn to for direction when she refuses to obey orders or speak.

'Albino woman, you not hear us?' Their anger grows, pride burns. Her silence is an affront to their power. 'Stop there or we shoot you!' They cock their long guns, point their nuzzle towards her, their eyes, icy flints.

She continues to walk, holding their gaze, seeing the brief turn of their necks as they seek the final order from their leader. A name flashes in their minds; Sergeant Emeka. She smiles and fixes her gaze at the short man in his black police uniform. She's not surprised he's their leader. Short people are always leaders in the midst of their taller peers. They need to prove their superiority with power, as if to make up for their deficiency in height. She turns to Sergeant Emeka and gives him her full attention, her dazzling smile.

'Sergeant Emeka, I'm happy to meet you at last. Your wife said to introduce myself to you as soon as I get here.' She watches as a frown furrows his forehead, curiosity fighting the suspicion in his eyes. He motions his two subordinates to open the smaller side gate.

'Who are you?' His voice is rough, hard. She maintains her smile. 'I'm the lady who saved your child from getting knocked down by a car on the way to her school.' She's not sure if he has children, if his children are girls or boys. She waits for his thoughts as the names of his children flash through his mind; Obi, I.K and Adamma. There's tenderness in his heart when he thinks of

the last name, his only daughter, Adamma. She smiles again. 'Are you telling me that your wife didn't tell you how I saved your daughter, Adamma, how I looked after your sons, Obi and I.K, while your wife calmed Adamma after the near-miss?' She brings a look of incredulity into her face. She sees the suspicion disappear from his face, replaced by embarrassed friendliness. He doesn't like to be kept in the dark about anything or have himself shown up before his subordinates. He lets out his anger at them.

'You, idiot man! Why you stand dere like a fool? Open de gate for de woman immediately before I count up to one.' He turns to her, a smile on his face. 'Come in, my sister. Come take chair. Chei! You women! You know how to keep secrets, so? My missus never tell me anytin' at all. I tink she be afraid I go break her silly head for not taking better care of de children. So, she not tell me anytin'.' He ushers her into a white plastic chair by the security gate. 'So, what bring you come see us today, my sister?'

'I need to see the DPO that supervises Ukari police station,' her voice drops its friendly tone. 'It's a secret matter of the utmost importance, life and death.'

'Aah! DPO Egede!' He smiles. 'You be in luck, sister. I just see him finish his meeting wit de commissioner just now. I tink he be in his office now. Come, I will take you dere myself.' He turns to the other two policemen. 'Watch de gate while I take my sister to DPO Egede's office,' his voice is back to its hard ruthlessness.

She thanks him as he leads her towards a large story building to the left of the large car-filled compound. She reaches into the pocket of her dress and feels the two kennel nuts nestled within. Their round hardness brings a smile to her face.

'So, my sister, what you want see de DPO for? I swear, de whole of Ukari village have been in de headquarters since dat albino girl disappear dere. Even de deputy local government chairman just leave de station now wit his two boys who he just bailed because of dat missing albino girl. You be de sister of de girl, so?' He seems to notice her skin colour for the first time. He notices other things about her as well. 'Chei! Sister, you not wearing your sunglasses in dis bright sun! Bad enough you be walking about without shoes but you can't joke with your sunglasses. You want blind yourself, so?'

She laughs, a merry tinkle. 'I don't need sunglasses, my brother. I am a special lady who can see as well as a cat without aid. I am lucky, I think.'

She sees the wonder in his eyes as he gives her a long stare. She holds her pupils, returns his stare without the usual eye-darts. It's one of the many things she can do these days, stop her pupils from dancing the albino darts. He shakes his head and smiles at her.

'I swear, you be de first albino I see who not wear sunglasses and keep steady gaze. Dat's why your eyes see well-well to save my daughter from de accident. I thank you again, my sister. God

bless you. Anytime you want police help, just ask for me, you hear?'

She smiles her reply. She'll not be needing him again. He'll be needing her when he discovers that there was never an accident, that his daughter was never in danger, that his wife never sent her to him. He'll want to punish her for her deceit but it'll be too late by then. She thinks her heart beats with excitement but she can't be sure, She feels no movement in her chest. Her body feels nothing, pain or passion, heat or cold, hunger or satiety.

Sergeant Emeka leads her into a room filled with visitors. There's a woman behind a paper-littered desk. The woman's unsmiling face looks up at their entrance. The cold look disappears from her eyes.

'Sergeant Emeka! My eyes see you well. What brings you to my office today?' Her voice is raspy, as if she spends all day screaming at people.

'I bring my sister here to see your Oga. It's important matter. Oga DPO free?'

'He just finished with those Ukari people just now. Just go in. He'll not mind, seeing it's you,' she waves them in. There's a low grumble among the crowd waiting in the room. They're not happy about the preferential treatment. The secretary barks an order at them and they subside to reluctant silence. She's the guardian of the DPO's door and will decide who sees her master or not.

Sergeant Emeka leads her into a large air-conditioned room. She hears the humming of the air-conditioning unit even though she has no idea what it is. She listens to its sound for a few seconds, seeking its secret message, its hidden meaning. She turns away with disinterest. The air-conditioner's hum makes no difference to how her body feels or how her mind thinks. Its noise is without intelligence.

'Oga DPO,' *Sergeant Emeka bows to the big man sitting behind a large desk eating roast groundnuts and banana.* 'Oga, sir, I bring you a visitor who want discuss important matter wit you, sir,' *he urges her towards the front of the desk.* 'She be good friend of my missus and she be de one who save my child's life. I beg sir, give her audience, thank you sir, thank you sir, God bless you, sir.' *Sergeant Emeka bows again, an obsequious smile on his face.*

The DPO looks stunned as he sees her. He looks like one that has seen a bad spirit spraying his bedroom with smelly piss. She fixes her eyes on him to catch his thoughts. It's not as easy as it was with his sergeant. The DPO's thoughts are like ants, scattered ants, restless, running all over the place... God in heaven, this can't be the murdered girl! *His thoughts shout into her mind. She cocks her head to listen, soaking up his deepest fears.* This girl fits every description... no way... Sergeant Emeka says it's his wife's friend, so it can't be the same girl. Oh God! This whole albino business is starting to get to my mind. They all look the same. You see one albino and you see them all... except the witch-woman. You can tell that one by her child size... I wish I'll never lay my two eyes on another albino for the rest of my life... all the trouble they've brought me. Oh God! If not for the money Chief Eze has already spent, I swear I'll tell him to just leave me alone and sort out the dead girl by himself. He's already put me in enough trouble with my commissioner... But, I must finish building my village house and our police salary is rubbish. Without Chief Eze's generous gifts, I'll end up without a village house where my children can bury me when it's my time to join my ancestors. Oh God! Better get rid of this albino girl quickly before someone sees her and tells the commissioner an albino has been to see me and get his interest re-awakened again. I don't want to share any more gifts with the bloody man. But for him, the ₦500,000 Chief Eze just paid to bail his boys would have all gone to my pocket. Instead, the greedy man has left me with a miserly ₦100,000, despite all the money he earns as a commissioner. Bastard man! Life is not fair. Man is working and the Baboon is enjoying. If not for me, Chief Eze wouldn't be a free man today after the business with the albino girl. But see the useless commissioner getting the lion's share of the "thank you" gift, as if he did anything save flash his rubbish badge. *Chei!* These albinos are just popping out everywhere you look, causing trouble. Why God decided to add them to humanity is beyond my understanding. They're nothing but bats, neither mammal nor bird, not black or white, just a strange aberration of nature...

She's heard enough. Her heart rages inside, a murderous rage. She's glad he likes gifts. She will give him a gift he'll never forget. She flashes him her most dazzling smile. 'Oga DPO, I come with special news that will make you very happy and make your commissioner even happier, so that the Baboon will stop enjoying and make way for hardworking men,' she says. She sees the stunned look on his face, as he leaps up from his chair, staring at her with fear-widened eyes. 'It's ok, Oga; I come with a gift you will like,' she says, reaching into her pocket. She sees the spark of interest light up his eyes, quickly replaced by a secretive glint, then suspicion. Sergeant Emeka's ears prick. He can't conceal his curiosity. He turns to her with wide eyes. The DPO orders him out of the office, getting up from his swivel chair to lock the door behind the unhappy sergeant. He turns back to face her, a frown furrowing his brows.

'Who are you? Who sent you here? What message have you brought for me and my commissioner?' His voice is brusque. His eyes reveal his contempt for her, his belief that nothing she has to say will be of any importance to him. She sees his black pupils carry out a quick inspection of her, her cheap yellow dress, her bare feet coated with dust, her untidy yellow braids. He sees neither briefcase nor handbag on her, something that would hold a

handsome haul of money gift for him. His dismissive tone cuts deep into her pride. She is tired of the games. Her eyes harden and halt their dance. They search for his soul and probe his mind. She reaches deep and tussles with his will. It is a brief contest, yet, a tough fight. He is a stubborn man and will not bow his will to a woman. But she's no ordinary woman, she tells his resisting mind with a grim smile. And in little time, he yields to her.

She imprisons his will, twisting his mind, squeezing his thoughts, holding his gaze until his mouth hangs open in mindless stupor. She smiles. She has him now. The hand inside her pocket emerges, holding the two kennel-nuts within.

'Oga DPO, this gift is for your first son, Nnanna. That's his name, isn't it?' The man nods, his eyes vacant, like his hanging features. 'This is our own "thank you" for all your efforts when Qwa lost her daughter.' She smiles as she sees the startled look on his face at the mention of Qwa's name. Despite her hold on his will, his soul still recognises danger and shivers with fear. 'You will take these two nuts home and you will give them to Nnanna, only to Nnanna and no one else, do you hear me?' He nods again, a slow nod, a reluctant one. He's still putting up a fight, a losing battle. She places the nuts inside his hand and guides his hand into his pocket. 'You will leave your office as soon as I go. You will remember nothing until the minute your son chews up the sweet juice of the kennel-nut. Then, will your mind be free and you will

recall my words, remember my face and rue the day you sold your soul to the wrong deity.'

The DPO is still standing by his desk when she leaves his office. Her hollow laughter follows her out of the room, blending with the deeper roil of the air-conditioning unit. Her heart expands and soars. In a few hours, the money-whore of a cop will feel the sharp blades of pain slice his heart into a million tiny pieces. She grinds her teeth. She will not kill him, not yet. He will live to suffer, just like the rest of them in the accursed village. By the time she's done with them, they will pray for the grave-worm. They will once again remember the taste of fear. And they will weep.

Ω Ω Ω

14

These Days of Fear

Ọwa was startled by the loud knocks on her front-door, frantic knocks that had the urgency of desperation. Her heart did a sudden leap into her mouth, racing with breath-stealing speed. She got up from her mat, her movements slow, hesitant. She'd been expecting something like this ever since discovering Aku had left the house that day. Despite her warning, the girl had decided to expose herself to the very people she needed to hide from.

On finding her missing, Ọwa had run off towards the village square, hoping to find her and bring her home, away from prying eyes. Her mind raced with thoughts, what she would find, the answers she would give to astonished questions from stunned villagers, if Aku was safe or been abducted again by the very people that had murdered her the first time. *If only she hadn't gone to the shrine to commune with the Earth Goddess, none of it would have happened.* She should have remembered the effects any close contact with the deity had on her, how it always left her drained each time she was possessed by the Earth Mother.

Her search had yielded nothing. She hadn't asked any questions but then, no one had said anything to her about seeing her daughter. It wasn't something the villagers would have kept silent about had they seen her. The search had left her with a numbing feeling of déjà vu, a re-run of that terrible day Aku had gone missing and never again returned from school. She'd been tempted to go to her cousin Enu's house but she knew she wouldn't be able to reign in her rage against the evil woman. And that would be against everything *Aná* had ordained. For reasons which were still unfathomable to Ọwa, the Earth deity wanted her cousin spared, at least for the time-being. She would have to live with that restriction, survive the burning hate in her heart till the Earth Goddess set her free. *Aná* knew best and had never let her down.

After hours of fruitless wandering, Ọwa, had returned to her house, her body as weary and heavy as her heart. She tried to force some hope into her mind. *She hadn't gone through everything for nothing. No! No!* Her silent shrieks were like drums inside her head. *Aná* hadn't returned her daughter from the grave only for Aku to be murdered again. Her daughter would come back from wherever she was. Aku must come home to spend the remaining three days they had together before her final return to the grave. Three days only, three precious days which were not enough, not by a long mile; three short days for her to tell her child everything in her heart, to love her child as she should have been loved and once more, feel the gentle essence and the vibrant soul of her only child. Ọwa, moaned, a deep groan that squeezed out through constricted windpipes. *Aku...Aku...my sweet, beautiful daughter...*

She walked into her living-room and shouted, a scream of shock and dismay. Aku was slumped on the floor. Ọwa wasn't sure if she was in a deep sleep or a dead faint. She rushed over to her daughter and started to shake her, searching her body frantically for signs of new mutilations, a fresh attack by enemies. There were no bruises or injuries. In fact, Aku looked fresher and healthier than she'd been since her awakening the previous day. Save for the lingering smell of decomposition and the flat immobility of her chest, one would mistake her for any normal young girl in peaceful slumber.

Aku stirred and opened her eyes. She looked like a child pulled from a comatose sleep. Her eyes were hazy, their darting sluggish. She was disoriented, unable to recognise Ọwa or her surroundings.

'Aku! Daughter, where have you been?' Ọwa's voice was shaky with tears. 'I've searched everywhere for you today... everywhere! What made you leave the house? You know how dangerous things are out there. I told you to stay indoors while the demons persecuting your dreams finish their mischief. Tell me, are you ok? You don't look too good to me. Come, get up. Let's get you into bed and get you something to eat. You didn't have your breakfast today and I bet you haven't eaten anything all afternoon either.' Ọwa's words tumbled one after another, relief bringing the drunk-like looseness to her tongue. She helped Aku up to her feet, straining every muscle in her body. The girl was a weight that defied human size. It was as if she had swallowed ten slabs of concrete overnight. Her steps were unsteady as Ọwa led her into her room. She stumbled like one drugged. Even before Ọwa laid her on her bed, Aku's eyes had shut in deep sleep. Ọwa lifted her legs into the bed, wiping the heavy coating of dust on her feet, a sign that her daughter had done a lot of walking during the period of her absence. *But where? Where had she been? What long miles had these two feet covered? What had she done? Who had she seen? Who had seen her? What will they do?*

The questions tormented Ọwa's mind as she stretched herself on the floor, resting her back against the bed. She would let Aku sleep, keep watch over her to ensure no further unpleasant surprises occurred, claw back the precious hours lost, imprint the sleeping image of her daughter in her mind, every tiny feature of that beloved face. It was late afternoon and the brief time allocated by the Earth Goddess was flying with the speed of lightning.

Again, Ọwa's heart constricted and the hot tears which were now her constant companions, poured down her cheeks. *How could she let her daughter go? How could she bury her daughter, put her beautiful body into the grave soil in just over two days?* She saw herself digging the soil at the back garden, preparing the grave that would receive the young body of her only child. The image was too much to bear. She shut her mind against it and reached up to hold Aku's hand, her cold hands that would not get warm no matter how thick her clothes or how hot the earth baked

317

underneath the sun. She watched her chest, the quiet chest that housed Aku's still heart; her chest that would not rise and fall with the breath of life, the heart that would never re-animate her child to full mortality again. And her tears were like an endless river coursing a current of pain down her face.

That was when the knock shattered the silence of the house, the knock she had been expecting since Aku strayed outside the protective walls of their house. Ọwa dragged her slow steps to her door, debating whether to open the door or feign deafness. The screams decided her, the hoarse screams that sounded eerily like her own inside the accursed Grand Room of Mirrors.

She pulled the bolt across, opening her front-door. The dying glows of the sinking sun followed the visitors into her living-room, together with the wave of buzzing flies. And the smell. Ọwa gagged, forcing back the vomit. She dashed across to the windows and flung them wide open, uncaring of the mosquitoes that would fly inside in search of blood to bloat up their death-infested bodies. The open windows were a psychological relief, rather than a physical one. The still evening air remained outside her building, unwilling to defuse the odious stench of her visitors.

'Madam Ọwa, please help me, help my son, please… please, forgive me, my knees are on the floor, I'm begging… begging for your forgiveness and help. My son is innocent. He never hurt a fly, just a small boy with his whole life before him. Please, please,

318

don't take that future away from him. Let him live out the lifeline of his palms. Lift your curse on him, please. Set my son free, I beg you.'

A hot hand grabbed her arm, pulled her with force into the pit of the funk. A body was thrust into her face, a fly-infested body that reeked with the fermented pus of a thousand boils, the body of a little boy at the start of his primary school years. Her stomach heaved. Her eyes darted with terror. A tight band gripped her chest, twisting, choking off her breath. *It was impossible! It was impossible!* Her mind shrieked the denial with silent horror. She had heard about it; all her life she had lived with the tales of the ghastly curse. She had even sought the power for herself, fool that she was! *Merciful Aná, forgive her!*

Qwa shuddered as she stared at the young victim of the dreaded *Leloole* curse. It was the first time she had ever seen a victim of that fearsome hex. *But it was impossible!* Her mind continued to deny the evidence of her eyes. Only Xikora had the power of the *Leloole* curse and Xikora was trapped deep in the blood sludge of The Cold Realm.

But, Aku wasn't.

The thought sneaked into her mind like the slimy touch of a snake. *No! No!* Qwa fought the thought, pushed it away, deep into the dark place of her mind where it wouldn't find its way out.

'You have your daughter; she's alive despite everything that happened. You yourself sent her to my office today with the cursed nuts. You know what it is to love a child. Why would you want to kill my son, a child that has done you no harm? Kill me instead. My life is worthless without my son. You have every reason to hate me, to punish me for what I did to you when your daughter went missing. But, don't punish my son whose hands are clean. Don't make him pay for his father's crime, I beg you.'

No! No! The words shrieked inside her head, the terrible thoughts escaping the confines of her mind to deluge her limbs with ice. Her daughter was not evil. Aku would never inflict a child with such horror, an innocent little boy whose low moans were fast fading into comatose silence. *Unless her soul has been soured by the corruption of the blood sludge… unless she resurrected, tainted with the evil of The Cold Realm.* Owa felt the cold crawl of skeletal claws up her spine. For the first time since she resurrected her daughter, she felt fear. *What had happened to the child? What kind of powers had she returned with? She thought the child had no recollection of her death save as a bad dream. But she was wrong, if she could believe the evidence of her eyes. Earth Mother spare us! How far would Aku go to exact vengeance for what was done to her?*

Owa stared at the broken man at her feet, a face she recalled with hate, the same man that had debased her on the night he raided her home with his policemen, his brutal officers who had lost their lives to the deadly flies of the Earth Mother. She recalled his arrogance, his contempt, his nastiness to both herself and Detective Femi. Only a terrifying power beyond the realm of man could reduce a pride-drenched man like the DPO to such abject humility.

Again, Qwa forced herself to look at the dying child, at the weeping pustules, the buzzing flies that coated his fast-decomposing body, flies that brought her the peace of the Earth Mother but were agony to the boy. Pity overwhelmed her. No child should have to suffer such torture. She reached out and folded the boy in her arms, struggling to hold him firm. His skin was like dead fish left to rot under a hot sky, slippery and wet. She forced herself to inhale the stench of his skin, absorb the pus from his boils into her own flesh. The flies recognised her, her essence, her soul. They abandoned the child for Qwa's body, coating her with their dark mesh, granting the child some relief.

The DPO's eyes widened in wonder as he saw the flies flee his son's body. He grasped Qwa's hand with fevered desperation. *'Chei!* Thank you, Ma! Thank you! Save the child, please. Cure his boils and free him from pain, please. I will do anything you want. I'll arrest Chief Eze this very evening and order my men to kill him inside the cell. Anything you want, Ma, I will do. Just lift your curse on my child, please.'

His words brought a chill to her soul. They were confirmation that so many people were complicit in her child's murder. Burning rage flared in her heart, followed by joy at the man's anguish. *He deserved to suffer, deserved everything he got from Aku. Let him suffer as she had suffered, feel the pain she had felt and the utter helplessness that was worse than any hell imaginable.* The child moaned in her arms and her fury died. Tears of pity pooled in her eyes. The child was dying and there was nothing she could do to save him apart from dulling his pain.

'*Oga* DPO, I swear by everything I hold holy, in the sacred name of *Aná*, that I never sent anyone to hex your son. I would never harm an innocent child no matter how evil the father. You say someone gave you nuts in my name. What did the person look like?'

'It was a young girl, around the same age as your dead daughter...I mean, your missing daughter. She was dressed in a yellow dress the same colour of her braided yellow hair, an albino like yourself. She stole my mind and the minds of my officers too. She arrived in bare feet, no shoes, no handbag, yet she walked through the tight security of the headquarters and entered my office with the ease of grease. If you didn't send her, who did? If you didn't send her, why would she punish my child in your name?'

Because you killed her, you bastard! Qwa's scream was a silent cry of rage. She had caught the man's slip of tongue, the proof that

322

he knew her child was dead, murdered by his vile friend, The Fat-Man. She forced the racing in her heart to halt, her hard breath to soften. There was no need to curse him. What was done was done. He was paying for his evil. Aku was avenging herself on her murderers. What mattered was the boy, the dying child caught in the crossfire of her daughter's vengeful rage.

'I have no answers for you,' Owa said to the DPO, handing him back his son. She walked over to the table that held the tools of her art. From there, she brought a jar of *Okwume,* the thick oily fat drained from the skin of a python. It was infused with special herbs that killed pain and brought relief for a multitude of ailments. She handed the jar to the DPO. 'I cannot save your son. I'm sorry, but this hex is beyond my powers. All I can do is give your child some relief from his pain. The end will not be long. He will not suffer for much longer. Take him home and prepare for his final departure. May the Earth Mother grant his innocent soul a peaceful journey and a glorious rebirth, *Ise!*'

The DPO was sobbing, his body shuddering with violent grief. He would not accept the inevitable. He pleaded and begged for some miracle, anything that would save his son. Owa remained silent, clothed in the buzzing flies that weaved their music over her body. Her silence finally pierced through the man's desperate anguish. He lifted his son and stumbled out of the house. The flies dived after them, abandoning Owa for their original feast. She heard the DPO shout as the flies resettled on his son's rotting body. She waited till the sound of his car engine died out in the distance. Then, with heavy steps, she walked into her daughter's room to take a proper look at the girl lying on the bed, the innocent girl who looked like her daughter but harboured a deadly evil that sent the cold chills of terror down Ọwa's spine. *Earth Mother spare them all! What had she brought back? What had she gone and done!*

***

Ọwa stared at her daughter, trying to gauge the truth behind the words, the lies behind the dry tears. Aku had been crying ever since Ọwa woke her up and confronted her with the DPO's case. Her tears were without moisture, invisible tears that revealed themselves in her trembling voice and choked words.

'I didn't do it, Mama. Please believe me, I didn't.'

'Don't lie to me, child. Don't you know that there's nothing you'll ever do that will kill my love for you?' Ọwa held Aku's hands in hers, her cold hands that would not warm with the flow of red blood, living blood. 'I know it was you at the DPO's office. He described you down to the yellow dress you're wearing now. How did you learn the *Leloole* curse? Why would you use it on an innocent child who never did you any harm? Why, my daughter? Why?' Ọwa's question was a bewildered wail.

'Mama, I've told you again and again that I didn't do it. I haven't been out of the house since yesterday. I don't even want to go anywhere, not even to school or Ego's house,' Aku's voice was dull, as if she lacked the energy to speak. Her eyes darted in agitated rapidity. 'If he said I did it and you say I did it, then it must be true but I swear in your name, Mama, *in your name*, that I didn't do it. You know how hopeless I am with divination. How could I know such a powerful charm as the *Leloole* curse, something even you can't do?'

'That's exactly what I've been asking myself, "how did she learn that terrible charm?" But, have you seen your feet?' Owa nodded at Aku's dusty and blistered feet. 'Look at your feet and tell me you haven't been out walking, a very long walk by the look of things. Look at your feet and tell me that's not the same feet that took the evil walk to deliver death to an innocent child.'

'I see my feet, Mama. I see them and I don't know how they came to be the way they are. You know me. I would never, ever, leave the house without wearing my shoes. The only explanation I can think of is that I must have sleep-walked,'

'No one sleep-walks in broad daylight,' Owa cut in, her patience waned. 'I don't know why you insist on denying what you did. It makes me feel bad, makes me feel I must be such a terrible mother that you would stick to your lies rather than come clean because you fear my wrath. How many times must I tell you that you are everything to me…everything. I haven't told you enough times just how precious you are to me, how my life would be nothing, nothing at all without you.' Ọwa squeezed the hands she held, massaging the cold palms. 'We will let it go. I won't talk about it anymore. It's done and maybe, that's how fate has decreed that things must be. The DPO is an evil and greedy man. What will be, will be. Come, cry no more. I know you haven't eaten all day but I understand you young girls like to diet and watch your weight so I won't force food down your throat, ha!'

Ọwa's laugh was a desperate bark, a hollow sound to cloak her despair, her realisation that her child could never again feel hunger or thirst, that all the delicacies she'd prepared would go uneaten. Worst of all, Aku must never know the truth of her condition. The truth would bring her a worse death than the one she had already died.

'I'm sleepy, Mama,' Aku said, starting to stumble to her feet in the clumsy motion that Ọwa had observed since her return. 'I think there must be something wrong with me. All I want to do is sleep. I swear, Mama, ever since I had that awful nightmare, I just haven't been myself. I feel like someone who's been attacked by the *Amosu*, soul-vampire,'

'Don't worry yourself. It's a bug you've picked up,' Ọwa quickly reassured her. 'It'll pass in no time. Come, let me help you into bed. Sleep is good for you. Nothing heals a sick body like a good sleep.' She took her daughter's arm, feeling the girl lean deep and heavy into her. Tears again burnt behind her pupils. This was what she had wanted, what she had asked the Earth Mother for, her daughter returned to her from the cold grip of death. Except this wasn't the daughter she wanted, a daughter whose spark had died with her soul, a girl who slept away every second of the day and lived in a fog of confused thoughts. *Yet, she had found the strength to walk the long journey to the DPO's office to deliver death to him. How could that be? How was it possible?*

***

Eze watched the clock by his bedside with the intensity of a doctor monitoring the vital signs of a critical patient. The hands seemed to take forever to travel to the next number on the round, shiny surface. He stood up from his bed and lumbered over to his mirror. He stared at his exposed shoulder and groaned, a low moan of anguish. The Black Hand was almost a faded dream now. He could barely distinguish the finger marks from his own dark skin. He was running out of time. He never realised how quickly The Black Hand could vanish, heralding his death. The albino witch had to die without delay.

He walked back to his bed and picked up the dagger lying next to his mobile phone. It was a good weapon for its purpose, long, strong and sharp. Just one plunge would be enough to finish the midget witch. But he intended to leave her with more than a plunge. By the time he was done with her body, no one would recognise it as human. Her house would be a pool of blood that would never dry, save by demolishing the hovel that she called a home.

The clock struck 3am, the hour to kill a witch, neither 12am when witches communed with spirits and were at their most powerful nor 6am when they communed with the ancestors and their deities and were equally dangerous. Even a witch had to sleep and most witches were lost to the world at that critical hour of three o'clock in the morning. It was a secret he'd learned from his late mother, who was deeply steeped in occultic rituals in her life-time. Eze picked up his mobile phone, his car keys and the dagger, the hard metal blade that would remove the obstacle that'd been blocking his progress.

His movements were stealthy as he left his room. Across the corridor, he could hear the loud snores of his third wife, Oge. He smiled, a vicious glint in his eyes. For someone so skinny and beautiful, the wretched woman snored louder than a pregnant pig. *Not for long, though. Before he's done with her and one of her precious twins, she'll struggle to remember the way to her bed or how to spell the word, "sleep".* He stole down the stairs with only the faint light of his mobile phone to guide him. Outside, he made his way to his car with firm steps. He had already given his *Aboki*, gate-man, the day off. The less people knew his movements the better. With one murder hanging over his head, he couldn't afford to be linked to a second murder, all within the same family. This time, even the greedy police commissioner and the wretched DPO would not cover his crime for all the bribery *Naira* notes in the government treasury.

Eze opened his gate wide, lifting the metal door high to ensure it didn't scrap noisily against the cement flooring of his compound. He released the handbrake and rolled the car out, pushing it silently till it was out of the compound. The exertion brought on hot sweat and harsh puffs, together with several silent curses. A safe distance from his home, he jumped into the car and started the ignition. In no time, he was cruising along the silent pot-holed tarmac towards Qwa's house at the village boundary. The sound of his engine in the silent gloom of the village was like a siren at a wake. A new moon grew in the sky, a perfect banana moon, a young sapling yet to mature to full blaze. Beneath it, the village languished in shadows, relieved by the occasional electricity bulbs from the various churches that held night vigils through the week. His headlamps lit up the blackness of the night, casting the road in a bright yellow haze. He eased his foot off the pedal and allowed the car to coast in neutral. His heart pounded, adrenaline in over-drive. It had been a long time since he last did his own killings. His thugs had made him lazy, turned him soft. It felt good to be back in action, dispatching an opponent with ruthless totality, feeling the warmth of spilled blood from severed arteries, knowing he held the life of another completely in his hands.

A few yards from Ọwa's house, Eze killed his engine and got out of his car. The sweat was thick on his body, leaving damp patches on his shirt. He felt light-headed, a small giggle escaping his lips. He wished he had someone with him, his two useless thugs, to witness his feat, see him slay the witch woman. That'd shut them up for good, inspire a healthy fear and deeper respect in them. A pity he couldn't make use of her body parts, what with her type being rejects of the deities, if one believed what Dibia Ogam said. Still, he might yet sell them in the black market to some unwary buyer for a handsome profit. The sale of a set of Albino hands or breasts would easily foot the DPO's next bribery pay-out.

Ọwa's compound was silent, still as a graveyard. Like the rest of the village, the skies hoarded their light here, leaving a state of gloom that only cats, bats and owls would thrive in. Eze walked like a foal, stepping gingerly, wary of arousing the sleeping resident. Dry leaves rustled underneath his shoes while his shoulders brushed roughly against yam poles. He was tempted to switch on his mobile phone torch, fearing snakes and scorpions lurking in the grassy grounds of her small farm. Instead, he rubbed the steel hilt of the dagger and took deep breaths to calm his racing heart. The thought of snakes had suddenly stolen his peace. He hurried his pace to get out of the bushy farm. Within minutes, he found himself in front of Ọwa's bungalow, facing the wooden front-door, flanked by a round earthen pot to the right and a large water drum to the left, positioned underneath the sloped roof to collect rain water. Eze paused, debating whether to go through the windows or the front-door. The wood-panelled windows looked dodgy; he wasn't sure he could squeeze through them. The front-door was his only option. He would have to force his way through if it was locked. The place was so isolated no one, save himself and the witch-woman, could hear a sound for miles. He'd be so quick forcing his entry she'd have little time to prepare for his assault. His strike would be swift and deadly, sweet as red wine.

He reached out and turned the rusty knob. The door opened, drawing itself into the dark room within and releasing the musky odour from the house into his nostrils. He almost sneezed but managed to stifle the urge. He stared at the open door, an uncertain frown on his face. He hadn't expected things to be that easy but then, the woman had no need to lock her door. Most people in the village lived without locks, unless they had offended someone who was an *Amosu,* a secret night-flyer, a soul-vampiring witch, who plagued people's dreams or squatted on their chests, bringing wakeful paralysis and night terrors. The witch midget on the other hand, was the night terror from whom people locked their doors. She would have little need to barricade herself. Fool woman probably felt no one would dare confront her in her own lair. *Unless they went by the name of Eze, son of Agu of Onori clan, that is.* He grinned. He was the unknown entity she had offended, the one person that could strike terror into the heart of the demon. He had already taken her only child, struck her in the core of her soul. She would be joining her dead daughter in a few minutes. He could barely wait to see the fear in her eyes when she woke up to see him by her bedside, killer dagger at the ready.

He stepped into the house and nearly tripped on one of the worn mats covering the hard cement flooring. He steadied himself with a low curse and pulled out his mobile phone. *Fuck it all!* In a second, his torch was on, filling the cramped living room with a dusky yellow glow. He looked around, scanning the room, taking in the various articles cluttering the room. There were three doors leading off the living room. He paused again, uncertain which door to try first. The last thing he wanted was for the witch to hear him trying out the wrong door.

That was when the light came on in the room to his right, seeping out from the high gap underneath the shut door. *Fucking witch had wakened.* Eze cursed and reached for the light switch on the nearest wall, flooding the living room with light from the single dusty bulb overhead. There was no time anymore for caution or delay. He rushed to the door, his movement surprisingly swift, adrenalin fuelled. He turned the knob and pushed the door in with a loud shout, intent on shrieking terror into the heart of his opponent.

His shout caught in his throat. Hot piss gushed out of his bladder, washing his trousers with terror ammonia. A tight band gripped his heart, squeezing the breath out of his lungs. He stumbled back, backwards to the door through which he'd crashed into the room. His eyes, horror-wide, starred at the apparition before him, the albino girl he had last seen inside a secret shrine, drenched in her own blood, her warm heart pulsating inside the witch-doctor's bowl. Eze moaned, his lips quivering like a child deprived of food. Her cackle hit him like a bullet, sending chills right through his veins to every nerve in his body.

'Old friend, don't you want your sweet thing anymore?' Her voice was a gleeful shrill. Her eyes danced a merry beat as she advanced towards him, nursing her breasts in her hands. 'Don't you like my breasts, my poor, sad breasts who have lost their nice, little nipples?' Her face faked a sad droop, her lips curved in a downward pout. Suddenly, her hand shot out, grabbing his shirt before he could escape, pulling him close with a strength that matched a pulley. A foul odour seeped from her skin into his nose, the stench of decay.

Eze screamed and lashed out, plunging the dagger into her neck. Again and again he struck, stabbing and screaming as she continued to hold his shirt, refusing to set him free. The blind haze began to lift from his eyes, bringing worse terror to his brain. There was no blood on his blade. There was no blood on her body. He could see the holes, the cuts, the damage done to her body by his dagger. Yet, he could see neither blood nor fright on her. A black chill covered his body as her hand reached for his head, her cold, numbing hand, her corpse hand. His knees buckled as he fell at her feet, blubbering, shaking, gasping for breath, seeking oblivion from the terror that threatened to steal his sanity.

'*Mmo… Mmo…*ghost' His voice was a trembling croak, a terror-drowned whisper. A door opened. Footsteps dashed across the floor. A scream pierced his drums, a harsh shout that seemed to come from the throat of a man.

'*Aná* save my soul! Aku! What is this? What is going on here?' Shocked pale eyes met his own, surprise rapidly replaced by blistering hatred. Qwa's finger pointed her rage at him. 'You! Demon son of a pig! You!' He could see her tiny body quivering with fury underneath the thin cotton of her short *Bubu*, kaftan. 'Murderer! Vile vomit! You dare to show your face in my house, IN MY OWN HOUSE! Aku, move aside. This battle is mine, child. I can deal with this bloated worm.'

The girl's name on Qwa's lips sent a darker terror to Eze's soul, cementing a reality his mind had desperately resisted. *It was the same girl; the same girl he had watched die, heaven help his soul! Ozu…corpse! How was it possible? How did the witch bring back*

334

her dead daughter from the grave? Jesus! Jesus, save his soul! He was staring at an Ozu, a living corpse! Why did he never realise the power of the witch? A Dibia that could raise the dead was not one that should be made an enemy of. He was a dead man, just like he'd known with the fading of The Black Hand. He didn't like pain, Jesus help him! He didn't want to die a painful death!

Tears streamed down his face, tears that merged with his sweat and snot. He saw Owa stoop and pick his dagger from the floor, the same weapon he had fashioned for her death. Dark rage once more flushed her face a deep red as she looked at the dagger and realised its import. He shut his eyes as she lunged at him, her arm raised, deadly dagger in hand.

'No! Not yet! Let him be!' He heard the girl's voice as if from a dream, a distant dream. Except it wasn't the voice he knew, the gentle frightened voice that had pled for her freedom and her life inside the Grand Room of Mirrors. This was a voice that rang with authority, a cold voice that struck a deeper terror in him. Eze's lids flew open, catching the stunned look on Owa's face, a shock that mirrored his own. She stared at her daughter as if the girl was a stranger she'd met for the first time, a fearsome stranger. The girl rubbed the top of her nose with her finger, a contemplative look in her eyes as she stared down at him. 'Our friend loves blood; in fact, he came here to drink more blood. So, we shall be good hosts. We shall feed him enough blood to last him a lifetime, a river of blood for him to swim in to his heart's content.' The girl steered her mother aside as if she were the adult. She reached out her hands towards his head.

Eze shrank away from her hands, scrambling away on hands and knees. She laughed, a gleeful cackle and barred his escape. This time, when she reached for his head, he knew the futility of resistance. Her hands were hard bars of ice. He gasped, feeling his head contract and expand, a deafening pounding roaring in his ears. His body swooned. He heard himself whimpering like a puppy, a puppy cornered by a Pitbull.

'Swim, little kitten. Swim for your life before you drown in the river of blood.' He heard her voice in the deepest recesses of his mind, heard the wave approach, saw the river grow, the thick red water that rushed towards him with raging force. He scrambled to his feet and began to run, hearing their laughter behind him, the roaring waves rushing closer, *closer*. He daren't look behind. The front-door was wide open, just as he'd left it, waiting for him, calling to him. He dashed through it, into the cool darkness of the night and plunged into a deep river that cut off his escape, trapping him in its thick red mire.

Eze began to drown. He opened his mouth to scream and swallowed coppery blood. He choked, flapping, thrashing wildly in the blood river. He had never learned how to swim; had never ventured near any large body of water save as a car passenger

336

crossing a bridge. The blood forced its way into his nose, leaving a tight and blinding pain that pushed right up to his eyes, his ears, his head. His arms were heavy, struggling to push through the thick warm blood and propel him to safety. He held his head high, kicked his legs against the heavy pull, weeping, shuddering with horror and repulsion as the silky blood covered his head over and over underneath the red waves.

Just when he thought he couldn't stand another second of the torture, the crawling sensation of blood against his skin, the coppery taste in his mouth, Eze saw his car, his white Peugeot, waiting for him just a few yards from the river of blood. Relief sent his heart soaring, adrenaline coursing through his body as survival suddenly became a possibility. He pushed against the waves with renewed force, surged his body forward with greater desperation. All the while, the sound of their cackling, their mockery, followed his trail, stealing his sanity and killing his man-heart.

With a deep groan, Eze clambered out of the river and collapsed on the hard, dusty ground by his car. He leaned forward and retched, spilling his gut, emptying the gallons of vile bloody water he had swallowed. His heart burnt and his stomach cramped up. His body ached all over, shivering, alternating between cold and heat like a malaria victim. He looked across the river and saw them standing by the open doorway of the house, watching him, their faces frozen, unsmiling. The sight chilled his blood afresh, sending him scrambling into his car. He tried to start the engine but his hands shook so much that he began to sob, deep shuddering sobs that rocked the car. The engine started after the third attempt and Eze lurched the car forward, braked violently, changed gears and backed a manic escape from the two, pale, watchful terrors.

A foggy haze cleared from his eyes and mind. He touched himself and felt dry cotton. Save for the damp insides of his trousers, he was as dry as when he first arrived at the bungalow. The smell of dust and his urine almost choked him. He touched his head, his wet head that had been submerged numerous times underneath the blood waves. His hands came out coated with dust and fine sand. The truth began to hit him, the terrible truth of his ordeal, the theft of his mind and his will by the witch-woman. He began to tremble, mumble prayers to his ancestors, his deities and Jesus. He had been hexed. A powerful *Juju* had been placed on him. It was downhill from now, unless he could get to Dibia Ogam quickly enough with a new sacrifice. Just as he re-joined the pot-holed asphalt, he heard a voice inside his head, a cold voice that stamped its total mastery over his will.

'We shall meet again, you and I. The dog that buried its bone must forever dig till it finds its treat. Where the shit goes, the fly must follow. Go for now, Eze son of Agu of Onori clan. Go with your life for now but wait for me, look out for me, because I will return to you, old friend. I will return.'

338

***

They watched the car disappear down the dusty pathway that led to the main road, following the trail of the headlamps till it vanished back into the night.

'Come, we have work to do,' Aku said, looking down at her mother from her superior height. 'You have grown careless, left yourself exposed like a chicken that has wandered away from underneath its mother's belly. The hungry kite will pluck it for its meal with daring impunity. Are you a witch-doctor or a wife? What has happened to you? How could you leave yourself so exposed, allow vermin like that fat fool to hold you with such contempt that he dares confront you in your own house?'

Owa stared with stunned silence at her daughter, at the ferocious tiger that had taken over the gentle kitten that used to be her daughter. Every doubt she ever had about the DPO's hex vanished. She had just witnessed a demonstration of power beyond any feat she had ever performed, seen a man's mind manipulated to the point that reality ceased to exist. As she'd watched The Fat-Man thrash about on the sandy ground of her compound, drowning on dry soil, a part of her had felt pity, a small pity for the human being, not the man. He deserved death for what he had done to her child and what he had planned for her. A painful death, swift and sure with a knife, would have put an end to his miserable life if Aku had let her follow her urge. But the girl had executed her own

339

brand of justice, a terrifying justice that filled Ọwa with disquiet, even fear.

'Don't feel pity for the pig. You have the wrong heart for our art. Come, follow me to the shrine. We have work to do and so little time,' Aku strode towards the little hut that housed the statue of the Earth Mother.

Ọwa's head reeled. *Our art! The girl had said "our art!"*

'Daughter, stop… I said stop,' Ọwa raised her voice when her daughter ignored her call. Aku paused, amused irritation darting her eyes. She stroked one side of her nose with an abstract finger. 'Where did you learn what you just did? It was you at the DPO's office after all, wasn't it? Despite your denials, it was you that hexed his mind the same as you did to The Fat-Man tonight.'

'What difference does it make whether it was me or anyone else?' Her answer was given with an arrogant dismissal that stunned Ọwa. 'The man was evil, together with all the other cohorts of Eze, son of Agu of Onori clan. From the one that calls himself a chief, that dog-whore, Enu and her vile gang, the two bully boys and their parents, all of them have blood on their hands. And I'll make them pay, to the last one, down to their sons and daughters, innocent or guilty, they will all pay. So, don't bother me with your silly talk about poor, innocent children and instead, worry more about your innocent daughter, brutally butchered by The Fat-Man and his vile allies,' Aku's voice dripped with sarcasm, biting and hard. Her eyes glittered with dark malevolence, her black, black, pupils, so different from Aku's soft, blue gaze.

Ọwa's eyes grew wide with shock. Her heart raced so hard that breathing was a struggle. She stared at her daughter, shaking her head over and over, as if shaking off a deadly spider.

'I'm not sure I know who you are anymore, daughter,' Ọwa's voice was a whispered gasp. 'Regardless of the painful truth you speak, the daughter I knew would never have killed an innocent little boy nor speak to her mother the way you've spoken to me tonight.'

'The daughter you knew was as big a fool as her mother and paid for her stupidity with her life. Had she dedicated herself to her art, she would have never fallen for the trap set by that ignorant pretender that goes by the name of blood kin. My sister was an envious bitch with zero talent. Her daughter is no different from what I can see. And you, you, my own flesh and blood, you've allowed those worthless things to turn you into a mouse, render your powers worthless. Have you never learned that power un-exercised is akin to abject slavery?'

Cold shivers ran down Ọwa's spine. She stared up at her daughter...at the pitch-black eyes of... *her mother! Xikora of the Leloole curse! Aná have mercy! Xikora! How could she have been so blind? All the signs were there, yet, she had misread them.* She followed the motion of Xikora's finger stroking an invisible mole

341

on her nose in the characteristic habit she recalled from her childhood.

'M..mama? Mama, is this you?' She reached out a shaking hand to touch Aku. She peered into the aloof face in the slowly fading gloom, searching, wondering. *It was her daughter. It was Aku, her daughter. Yet, it wasn't. What trick was this that the Earth Goddess had played on her? Where was her daughter if this was her mother, Xikora?* 'Mama, answer me please, is this you? Is this really you in the flesh?'

'Yes, daughter, it's me, free, free!' Xikora hooted with joy. She turned and pulled Ọwa into her arms in a tight hug, a cold hug that chilled her to the bones. 'It took you long enough to recognise your own mother. I bet you never thought the day would come when you and I would converse in the flesh, right here in the mortal realm, Ukari village, away from the horrors of *Mbana-Oyi*?' Again, Xikora cackled and twirled them around in a frantic dance that left Ọwa dazed. 'I saw my chance and took it. Had Aku paid more attention to her training, she would have recognised the black Ash of Immortality for what it was when its whirlwind hurtled towards her as she languished in the blood sludge. But I saw it and knew it for the salvation it was. My soul reached for it and I leaned over and hugged the girl close, held her numb body till the sacred whirlwind hit us both and lifted us back into mortality. Oh daughter, that I, Xikora, should once again walk on the very soil I had once ruled!' Xikora's voice broke, the first tender emotion Ọwa had seen in her mother since her stunning revelation. She extricated herself from the cold embrace and shook her head. Her eyes darted in all directions.

'Mama, where is Aku? Where is my daughter?'

'She sleeps,' Xikora's voice was dismissive. 'That's all she does, sleep and think. I'm tired of picking her thoughts because all I get is self-pitying mush and woeful ruminations. I tell you, daughter, I'm disappointed in the grand-daughter you gave me. How could you let her grow so weak, so distant from our art? Yet, each time you visited me at *Mbana-Oyi,* you told me she was growing in our art. But the girl knows nothing, cares nothing for her heritage and worst of all, has yoked her soul to another deity, the foreign deity, Mary, which those Jesus-People used to prattle about in my old life. Did you know about that?' Xikora's glance was accusatory, her eyes scorning Ọwa from the face of her daughter, Aku.

Ọwa bristled, struggling to accept the reality that her dead mother now wore the flesh of her dead daughter.

'You have no right to speak about my daughter like that, no right whatsoever,' Ọwa said. 'Where were you when I was a child? Where were you when I needed a mother to protect me from the abuse and ostracism of your sister and the villagers? At least I was there for my daughter. I did not put my pride and my husband before my daughter's welfare. I did not disrespect the Earth Mother and leave myself a prisoner of the evil duo that rule The Cold Realm. So, please don't preach to me about your disappointment in my parenting or in my daughter. I want my daughter now. Wake her up please. I want to speak with my daughter. Now! Aku! Aku, where are you? Wake up now, daughter; wake up and speak to your mother, please... pl..ease...'

Qwa's voice broke as tears pooled in her eyes. She began to sob, her shoulders heaving with the force of her grief. She had lost both her mother and her daughter and now she had them both with her, a brief reunion that would end in just over a day when the four market days given by the Earth Goddess ended. She'd spent so many years dreaming of the day her mother would be free only for that day to arrive and bring her pain, leave her fighting with her mother, when she should be celebrating. 'I'm sorry, Mama. Please forgive me. I didn't mean anything I said. It was just the shock. I am happy that you are free from that dreadful realm. It's what I've always wanted, dreamt about. *Nno*, Mama. Welcome. Your daughter welcomes you back, great priestess.'

'And your mother is happy to walk the same soil as her daughter again,' Xikora hugged her once more, holding her close for several seconds, stroking her hair, her face, just as she used to do in her childhood. A tight knot formed behind her throat. 'But come, we waste time. I need to protect you. We must create a new shrine-goat that will be your guide for your night diplomacy. It was a good thing you got rid of the other one…what was its name again?'

'Ebele,' Qwa's voice was dull.

'Ebele, that's it. Whatever made you choose a male goat as your shrine-goat? Haven't you realised that the entire male species, animal and human, are useless when it comes to the rituals of the Earth Goddess? All that lazy goat cared about was food and more food. You'll see the difference in the new shrine-goat I'll create for you, the difference between a male and a female, the difference between competence and stupidity, passion and laziness. Come, later you will talk to your daughter for as long as you like. But for now, we have work to do.'

And for the first time since *Nne*, Old Mother, died, Qwa let go of all earthly worries that had dogged her for as long as she could remember. Like the child she suddenly became once again, she allowed the unstoppable force that was Xikora to drag her along in her blistering trail. All she now needed was for her beloved grandmother, *Nne,* to show up and turn back the clock once again, to a beautiful time when innocence and security were things she took for granted and failed to cherish until it was too late.

***

Ego was alone in the house when the knock sounded on the door. Tap-tap-tap (pause), tap-tap-tap (pause), tap-tap-tap-tap-tap. The final set of taps were the loudest and the longest, the final proof of who the visitor was. Ego screamed and rushed to the door. She flung the door open and shouted again, hugging the girl that stood before her with fierce ecstasy.

'Aku! Oh Holy Mother of God! Aku! It's you! You're back! I can't believe my eyes! You're safe! My sister, come inside. Come and sit down! *Chei!* You're freezing! Where have you been? I just can't believe my two eyes, that this is you in the flesh, alive and well!' Ego guided her guest to one of the white plastic chairs in the small living-room, leaving the door open behind her. Aku sat down and smiled at her, her eyes blazing with a light Ego had never seen in her friend. It was as if Aku had exchanged her familiar gentle, pale eyes for a darker, fiercer pair.

'Yes, I'm back,' she repeated Ego's words with slow emphasis. 'I'm back, indeed. And no thanks to you. With friends like you, does anyone need more enemies?'

'Aku!' Ego exclaimed. The smile died out on her face.

'What? Why do you look so shocked as if you don't remember what you did? You knew how much the villagers hated me, yet you abandoned me to my fate because I wasn't like my grandmother, Xikora. In fact, if I remember correctly, you said I deserved everything I got from the villagers, didn't you? Yet, here

346

you are, pretending you're happy to see me. Ha! You little hypocrite.'

Ego's face fell. A stunned look replaced the joy in her eyes. Shame and shock warred in her heart as she stared at Aku, who returned her gaze with cool disdain, a contemptuous smile twisting her lips. Ego was the first to look away. Thoughts raced through her mind like multiple clusters of whirlwinds. *What had happened to her best friend? What in Christ's world had changed her gentle friend into the hard and cruel person before her, who seemed to derive immense pleasure in taunting and belittling her. It was as if Aku had shed her mild and sweet soul and infuse her body with a different person, a mean and spiteful stranger.*

'Aku, why are you saying such horrible things to me when you know you're like my own sister and I would never wish any harm on you for all the money in the world?' Ego's voice was uncharacteristically shaky with tears. Even as she spoke, she felt the guilt overwhelm her again as she recalled the harsh words she'd spoken to Aku on the day she went missing.

When the rumours began circulating in the village that Chief Eze of Onori clan had murdered Aku for ritual purposes, Ego had wanted to kill herself. Going to the market square had been her idea, just as everything they'd done as friends had always been her idea. Leaving Aku all alone at the market that day was a cruel and thoughtless act and Aku was right in her accusations. She had behaved worse than the worst villagers that day. She blamed it on her period, the monthly curse that played devilish havoc with her emotions. Only God knew how badly she wished she could turn the clock back, take back her words, save Aku's life and their friendship. It would appear that her Novenas had been answered and her friend's life had been spared but clearly, not their friendship by the look in Aku's strangely dark eyes. Ego lowered her lids in shame.

'So, you would never wish any harm on me for all the money in the world, eh?' Aku stood up and came close to her, looking her deep in the eyes. Ego forced herself not to cover her nose with her hand. Her friend smelled like meat that had gone off for weeks. It was a big shock to her, knowing how fastidiously clean Aku was. 'Money…hmm…money.' Aku's lips curled in a bitter smile. 'You have no idea what people would do for money, even you, Ego. I mean, that's all you've ever talked about, moving to the big city and making lots of money. That was why we fought, wasn't it? Because I wouldn't ask Ọwa to use her powers to make us rich. Ha!' Once again, Aku laughed, a hollow sound that had no likeness to the gentle laugh Ego recalled from their happier days. 'Money! How do I know what you would or wouldn't do for all the money in the world, eh? Come, tell me, Ego; Would you sell my yellow hair or maybe my albino fingers or even my dancing eyes to some rich demon who wants them for ritual *Juju* magic for five or even ten million *Naira?* Come on, I'm waiting. Why do you stare at me as if I've farted in the priest's face and pooed in front of the church altar? Ten million *Naira* is a lot of money. I bet you wouldn't think twice about selling some parts of my body for such a huge amount. That would set you up for life and you could build your mum a nicer house than this hovel you live in.' Aku's voice dripped with sarcasm. The dark eyes fixed on Ego's shocked face glinted with mockery.

Ego took a step backwards, away from the venom directed at her, the cold hatred she saw in her friend's eyes. A sudden sense of unease grew in her, an unease that rapidly turned to fear. She tried to talk to her fear, remind it that she was the stronger of the two, the one who had always held the power dynamics in their relationship. She was the leader while Aku was the meek follower. There was no way that she could fear any threat from Aku; *no way, no…way…*

Aku grabbed her hand before she realised her intention. Ego winced and tried to wrestle her hand free. It was an exercise in futility. Aku's fingers were like metal bands on her wrist, ice-cold bands, hard and chilling. They hurt, dousing her with sharp pain.

'Aku! Let me go at once,' Ego shouted, her habitual anger overriding her fear. 'What's the matter with you? Who do you think you are, coming here and saying all these nasty things to me just because I left you to walk home by yourself that day?' Ego felt her rage grow with each word she spoke. 'So what if I left you? Are we not the same age? If I can make my way home safely without getting lost, you should be able to do the same for yourself instead of disappearing and causing everyone to panic for your safety for no reason.' Ego tugged harder trying to release her hand but Aku would not let go. 'Let go my hand now, I'm warning you. Let go my hand before I lose my temper with you.'

Aku looked at her and smiled. It was a smile that turned Ego's legs to mushy pap. She gasped as she saw the habitual rapid darts in Aku's eyes still, as if they had never moved from side to side in an unfocused dance. Her pupils were deep black orbs that blazed with malice and something else that sent the chills of terror down her spine. The grip on her hand tightened, bringing a soft moan to Ego's lips. She tried to prise Aku's fingers from her hand but Aku grabbed the other hand and began to twist and bend them till Ego thought she would break her bones.

'Go on then and lose your temper. Show me what you can do when you lose your temper,' Aku's voice was friendly, conversational. Her hand continued to inflict icy torture on Ego's throbbing fingers. 'Or would you like me to show you what I do when I lose my temper, eh? Would you like to see what happens when I lose my temper?' Ego shook her head, pain glazing her eyes.

'Please, just let me go,' she heard her voice pleading, her shaky frightened voice which no one had ever heard from her, not even herself. Tears filled her eyes, tears of pain and humiliation.

'I can't let you go till I show you something,' Aku said, her voice still calm, neutral. 'You say I should have made my way home safely that day, just as you did. And you're right, Ego. I should've got home safely if my skin were black like your own...sorry, I forget. You did say I mustn't moan about my *Aghali,* albinism, and I won't,' Aku barked a loud laugh, her eyes suddenly blazing with dark fury. 'Do you want to know what happened to me that day, eh? Do you want to know what some evil people did to me that day? Come, place your hand on my chest,' Aku placed Ego's resisting hands on her chest. 'Can you feel my heart beating, eh? Go on, look at it. See, I've let go of your hands. Use your eyes instead. Look at my chest and tell me if it's moving, if it's rising and falling with the breath of life,' Aku bared her chest, revealing the pale skin beneath, the dark jagged ring around her chest.

Ego gasped, staring at the exposed flesh with eyes widened by horror. 'Aku! Oh my God! My poor, poor sister, tell me what happened to you. Who did this to you? What did they do to you? Oh Holy Mary, Mother of God. Come, my sister; please sit down, sit down again let's talk like we used to do. Tell me everything. *Chei!* People are evil, wicked. I hate this village, I swear.'

She guided Aku back to her chair, pulling up another chair close to her. Then she dashed into the kitchen to get a bottle of cola drink, Aku's favourite. 'Here, drink your Pepsi first before we talk,' she placed the bottle in Aku's hand. Aku looked at the bottle as if it were cat's piss before placing it on the floor by her side. 'Don't you want to drink it?' Ego asked, surprise raising her voice. 'I've never known you to turn down a drink of Pepsi. But no matter. Talk to me, tell me everything, my sister.'

Aku was silent for a long time, staring at Ego, observing her like one would an unknown insect. Ego soon grew uncomfortable under her silent stare. 'It's ok; you know me. I won't say anything if you want me to keep it a secret. You know you can trust me.' Ego rushed the words, needing to break the silence.

Aku smiled, a wry smile, the type a mother would give a silly child. Again, Ego marvelled at the new maturity in her friend, a hard maturity. 'They tried to use me for rituals,' Aku finally said, her voice low. 'They abducted me on my way home that day and took me to a witch-doctor's shrine and tried to use my body for *Juju* magic. They almost succeeded but I escaped before they could complete the ritual. I haven't even been home yet. I don't want my mother to see me like this.'

Ego shouted and jumped up from her chair. She went over and hugged Aku, tightly, fiercely, not minding the smell and the clammy coldness of her skin. Tears once again pooled in her eyes, tears of pity. *Her poor, poor friend!* Now she understood why Aku smelled the way she did, why she behaved as she did. *Who would go through what she had endured and remain sane?*

'It's ok, I'm fine,' Aku gently extricated herself from Ego's arms. 'Well, truthfully, I'm not fine. That's why I came here first before going home. As I said, I don't want my mother to see me this way. I need your help and you must promise not to tell anyone, not even your mother or my mother till it's over.'

'Of course, I promise. Anything. Tell me what you want me to do and I'll do it.'

Aku reached into her pocket and withdrew a small glass bottle that contained a black, powdery substance. She pressed it into Ego hands. 'I want you to guard this bottle with your life. The ash inside will destroy the evil inflicted on my body and return me to how I used to be. I'm sure, you'll be happy to see me back to my old self again, free of this horrible smell that clings to me. It's the *Juju* potions they rubbed on my body. It can't be washed off with ordinary water, only this magic ash potion which I stole from the witch-doctor. I'm going to sneak back into my room now. I want you to climb in through my window just after midnight tomorrow. Don't go talking fear into your head with your rubbish thoughts of ghosts and walking alone at night. Nothing's going to happen to you, I promise. Just come to my room after midnight, not before. It's important you do not come before midnight, ok?' Ego nodded, her eyes wide. 'I'll be asleep on my bed. You mustn't try to wake me up or make any noise that would attract my mother's attention. My mum will probably still be in my room. If she's awake, wait till she sleeps, ok? If she's sleeping, don't worry; she's a very deep sleeper and only a scream will wake her up. Sprinkle this ash on my chest, my head, my stomach and my hands and my feet. Make sure you empty the entire contents of this bottle on my body. When you're done, you must recite this chant, bring your ears close that I may whisper it into your ears.'

Ego leaned close, her heart thudding. A sense of excitement sent the adrenalin coursing through her veins. *She was going to do real Juju magic! She was learning powerful secrets, words of Juju rituals, reserved only for great witch-doctors like Aku's mother!*

'You must make sure you whisper these words into my ear, directly into my ear so that no one else, not even an ant, can hear. When you're done, you'll forget everything you just learnt. You must never tell anyone else what we just discussed, not even your mother. Promise me by everything you hold precious, promise.' Aku's eyes blazed with urgency. Ego nodded, sweat layering her forehead.

'I promise. In the name of our Holy Virgin and Jesus and all the archangels, I promise not to tell.'

'Good; good girl. Now lean closer let's practice the words till you can recite them without making any error. By the time you come into my room tomorrow, you must be able to chant these words as if they're the alphabet we learnt as children.'

***

Femi parked his car outside Ọwa's house and killed his engine. For several minutes, he sat in the car listening to one of his favourite artist, King Sunny Ade, the undisputed king of Jùjú music. He allowed the distinctive drumming rhythm to calm his heart and marshal his thoughts. He hadn't planned on visiting Ọwa till the next day after her daughter....

Femi pushed the thought away. He didn't want to go there, didn't want to ever lay eyes on the girl, the thing Ọwa had dragged back from the grave. Not after all he'd heard from the police headquarters that day. But it was his duty to warn Ọwa, to tell her that the thing she resurrected had turned itself loose on the community and was now breeding fear and hostility within the police force, especially after what had happened to the four dead officers. There was talk of arrest at the station but no one had the guts to initiate the warrant after the terrible affair concerning the DPO. Still, all it took was for one reckless fool to take it into his head to shoot before arrest and that would be it. Femi wouldn't live with himself if anything happened to Ọwa.

He switched off the CD and stepped out of the car. He walked to the door and knocked. *Please don't let the girl open the door.*

Two chickens wandered towards him, chickens the likes of which he'd never seen. They were white hens, plump with eggs. He could tell they were white because he could see some feathers that still retained their original colour. The rest were covered in a startling red paint, as if they'd been dipped inside a basin of blood. Thin, green palm-fronds were tied around their necks, coupled with a dirty, thick cord. The area around their eyes was painted a deep black circle that made the hard, glittery eyes appear larger, malignant.

Femi shuddered and stepped away from the chickens. They followed his movement, seeking him without fear. He knew them for what they were, shrine-chickens used in divination. Yet, these were no ordinary shrine-chickens, food for the deities. These were chickens with a purpose, a sinister purpose. *Voodoo chickens!* He thought he knew who was responsible for their creation and that person wasn't Qwa. He would stake his life on it. Qwa wouldn't know how to create evil and the two bloodied chickens were evil in its most primitive form. It was a good thing he had paid his unexpected visit. It wasn't a minute too soon.

The door opened and Qwa looked at him with eyes awash with tears.

'*Oga* Femi! *Aná* be praised for bringing you to me today,' her voice was deep with relief. 'Come, let us go and talk in your car. I don't want to be inside the house. It's better in your car.' She took his hand and led him towards his car as she spoke, shouting a curse at the two chickens as they made to follow them. The chickens strutted away, their movements almost as reluctant as a human's. Femi watched them go, a cold sensation prickling the back of his neck. He hurried his steps to his car, letting Qwa into the passenger side before taking the driver's seat. He turned to face her.

'Qwa, what is going on in your house? Why are you crying, my dear? Talk to me, tell me everything and I'm sure we'll sort it out somehow.'

'It's all so terrible...terrible. I don't know where to start. It's Aku...no, my daughter is innocent. She's not involved in all of this...it's my mother, Xikora. She's the one doing everything, hurting everyone. That's why I didn't want us inside the house. You don't know this but in her time, Xikora was a mind-reader, amongst her other powers. She can read and control any mind at will. I don't want her or her chickens to hear what we discuss.' Qwa paused, glancing around her compound fearfully. 'You must believe me, *Oga* Femi, I didn't realise in time who she was...I thought it was my daughter all the time; Aku, my poor child. I thought all the bad stuff happening was her fault, that her soul had come back soured by the evil of *Mbana-Oyi*. But it wasn't just Aku that returned. She brought back my mother with her, Xikora, known in the twelve villages and beyond as Xikora of the *Leloole* curse. Believe me, you don't want to know what she can do. She's gone out now… don't ask me where she is because I don't know. She only tells me what she wants me to know. My head is all over the place, *Oga* Femi. I don't know where to turn, what to do.'

'I knew there was something wrong,' Femi said, taking her hands in his to stop her frenzied twisting of them. 'That's why I came today even though we'd agreed I would visit after she had die…I mean, returned…you know…' Femi shrugged. 'Listen my dear, there are things you may not know about, things she's done that may jeopardise your safety. Initially, when I heard the story, I wasn't too happy with you because you had begged me to keep quiet about her and assured me she would never step out of the house. So, when I heard about what she did, I blamed you. Forgive me, my dear. If I'd known what you were going through, I would've been here earlier. Why didn't you call me?'

'I was planning on visiting the station today after I discovered she's gone out again. You said you heard something. What is it?' Her voice exposed her fear, rushed and husky.

'It's that DPO, my boss. You remember him, the one that arrested you when your daughter went missing. Anyway, they say he was visited by an albino woman who had glamoured the security men and gained entry into his office. The story goes that the girl put a curse on both him and his first son. They say the boy's body festered and rotted within hours and he died just before dawn. The DPO took his own life this morning, shot himself with his gun. The entire station is in a state of shock as you can imagine. The good thing is that the DPO was a very unpopular man, with many bad-wishers who aren't too unhappy to see him dead. But no one is happy about the boy's death and some are suggesting they come and arrest your daughter. Worse, some villagers have been to the station, claiming they've seen your daughter wandering around the village, acting in a manner that has frightened them, telling secrets they had locked inside their heads and threatening them with doom. They say she told them to prepare for days of fear. She told them to gather their basins to collect their tears. From what I can see, the villagers don't need to await any days of fear. It's already here with them. In all my time here, I've never seen such an atmosphere of dread in the people. Tell me she's still going back tomorrow. We can't afford to have her around anymore. It's not safe for you and you know how I feel about you. I can't afford to let anything happen to you, my dear.' He let her see his heart in his eyes. He was done with hiding how he felt about her. His heart demanded answers, something to keep him hopeful. Qwa looked at him, a shy look tinged with wonder. She looked away and lowered her eyes. 'I'm sorry if I've embarrassed you with my words, my dear. But I hoped by now you would've known exactly how I feel about you.'

'I am married to the shrine. *Nshi* women do not marry,' her voice was low. He heard something that sounded like bitterness in her tone.

'I know that and I would never ask you to betray your goddess. But surely, *Aná* will not deny you a bit of happiness, a partner who will be there by your side while you carry out your duties, someone who will love and cherish you the way you deserve to be loved. That is all I ask, just to love you and share whatever part of you that you're willing to share with me. We are not young people seeking to raise a new family. I have my family, siblings, children and grandchildren, who will be happy to welcome a special person like you into their hearts. I'm not asking you to uproot yourself immediately. Maybe later, when all this is over and you are ready to begin a new life away from all the pain. We shall build a better shrine to your goddess, one that she'll be proud of. So, what do you say, my dear?' He waited for her words, his heart thudding hard underneath his shirt.

'Thank you, *Oga* Femi. You're a good man and…'

'Stop calling me *Oga* and don't thank me or tell me I'm a good man,' impatience raised his voice. 'You know what I want to hear. If you don't feel for me as I feel for you, then tell me. I'm not a child. I won't cry and I promise you it won't stop me from being your friend and helping you as much as I can. But, I need to know if my feelings are reciprocated, that's all. Just tell me if I'm

360

wasting my time or not. I know this may not be the best time with everything going on but then, when will it ever be the best time with you? Your life is so full of events that mere mortals like me must squeeze in our wishes at the slightest opening,' he laughed, trying to lighten the heavy air in the car. Ọwa kept her head down, her yellow braided hair glowing in the bright afternoon sunlight. Femi reached out a hand to stroke her hair, feel its silky kinkiness. She looked up, her skin going a bright red.

'I like you too…Femi, very much. I'm not used to men or this kind of thing. I don't talk to people save as part of my work. But my heart thrills each time I see you and it's a strange emotion for me.'

'What was it like for you and your daughter's father?' The question was finally out, the jealous thought that had pricked at his heart for weeks.

'I only met him once, the evening the Earth Goddess sent him to me to give me Aku. *Aná* revealed him to me in a dream, so when he came knocking, I recognised him immediately. He left a few hours later and I never saw him again. I didn't even ask for his name or his town. All I know is that he's a *Fulani* man from the northern part of the country. He was the first and last man to know me. My life is dedicated to the service of my deity as you well know. It's the heritage of my clan.'

Femi felt a lightening of his heart. It was as he'd hoped. Ọwa was as pure as the deity she served. He cupped her face in his hands, holding her shy gaze with his own, stroking her cheeks with his thumbs.

'I promise I'll not rush you, my dear. We will go at whatever pace you like. The important thing is that you feel as I do. The rest will work out in time.' He leaned forward and kissed her forehead, letting his lips linger on the soft pale skin. She giggled, a girlish sound. He laughed, a male chuckle of satisfaction. He held her hands again. 'So, tell me, what's the story behind those chickens?' The seriousness was back to his voice.

'My mother created them for me last night after Eze, son of Agu of Onori clan, came to murder me,'

'What?' Femi's shout echoed in the car. 'Did you say Chief Eze came to your house last night? That he tried to kill you? Tell me everything. What happened? Where is the man now? *Oluwa!* Lord! I can't believe what I'm hearing!'

With halting words, Ọwa told him the events of the previous day, starting with the revelation about her cousin Enu's betrayal, to the visit by the DPO with his cursed son. She recounted the attempted murder by The Fat-Man in its grisly details before finally narrating her discovery of Xikora's identity. All the time she spoke, Femi listened with a growing look of horror on his face. His heart beat with hard thuds as he recalled the eyes he saw in his

362

rear mirror, the blazing death he had seen in the girl's pupils on the day she was resurrected. It was the mother all along, Xikora, the fearsome priestess whose name still struck awe and terror amongst the villagers. Little wonder his station was filling up with people terrified out of their wits. The priestess was back in her old playing grounds and up to her old mischief. Femi knew that save for the Earth Goddess, none could stop Xikora or halt her rampage. All who were complicit in the murder of her granddaughter would feel her deadly wrath, down to the tiniest ant in their houses. The woman was a terror in her previous existence and needed little provocation to inflict pain. Now, she had a reason, several reasons, to seek vengeance. She'd promised the villagers days of fear. Femi shuddered. It was a promise that would be fulfilled unless she died again, quickly.

'What time will she die tomorrow?' He asked.

'At midnight. They'll both die at midnight. Xikora will return to *Mbana-Oyi* while my daughter will return to her own deity, Mary of the *Oyibo,* white, race.' Qwa's voice broke as she fought to hold back her tears. Femi leaned over and held her in his arms, folding her head into his chest. 'My daughter didn't want to return. All she yearns for is the eternal sleep of death. Whenever Xikora is not in possession of her body, she just sleeps her days away, unwilling to face this existence she now finds so frightening. She's plagued by recollections of her death and it frightens her so much she doesn't want to wake up and recall. I did a bad thing bringing her back. I was only thinking of myself. Now, because of my actions, many people will suffer, the innocent and the guilty. Xikora knows no boundaries. At least, everything will end tomorrow night when the four market days given by the earth deity ends. Yes, everything will end and my daughter can finally sleep.' Ọwa hesitated before continuing, her voice muffled against his chest. '*Oga* Femi, please, will you help me dig her grave and lay her to rest?'

'Of course, my dear. You didn't need to ask. Why did you think I said I'll visit after the fourth day? It was for that precise reason. If you like, I can bring one of my officers to help us dig the grave,'

'No…no strangers please,' Ọwa cut in. 'I don't want any strangers seeing my child and my mother return to their grave. I'm sure we can dig it between us. It's the rainy season so the ground is quite moist and soft underneath the dust. If we start by dawn, we'll definitely be done before noon. I'll cook us something to eat and make sure I keep plenty of palm-wine for you.'

'What are you trying to do, woman? Get me drunk so you can have your wicked way with my body?' Femi laughed, lifting her face with a gentle hand. His teasing eyes smiled into hers, hoping to bring her some relief. It worked. She went a bright red, her eyes darting manically everywhere. He laughed again and stroked her hair. 'It's ok, don't sweat it. I won't rush things between us, as I said. But you know it's going to happen sometime, don't you?'

364

She nodded, saying nothing. 'When it does, I promise you it will be beautiful, for both you and I.' He returned his hand to the steering. 'Ok, that's enough for today. I think I'd better leave before she returns. I don't want to get on the wrong side of your mother.' He got out of his car and led Qwa back to her front-door. 'Will you be ok, my dear?' He asked. She nodded, smiling, a shy smile, yet a happy one. He pulled her into his arms and held her tight, pressing himself into her. Her body quivered in his arms. She wrapped her arms around him, pushing into his hardness. The heat rushed to his groins, quickening his breath. He released her and walked briskly back to his car without a backward glance. *Their time will come, very soon.*

As he started the engine, a movement caught his eyes. He looked out to see the two bloodied chickens, standing with unnatural stillness at Qwa's front-door, watching him with an intensity that sent the cold chills to his spine. He drove out of the compound without a backward glance.

***

Eze lay shivering in his bed. The clock on his bedside table chimed the time at regular intervals. The last time he heard the chime, it was six o'clock in the evening. He had been trapped in his room since his encounter with the two demons the previous night. His body felt as if he'd been run over by a lorry, throbbing with aches and pains, trembling with cold and sweating with heat. He hadn't slept in over twenty-four hours and his eyes were gritty from lack of sleep and the dust that had coated them the night before. He refused to sleep. He dared not sleep. Her voice had promised a visitation. He knew the visitation would occur the second he surrendered his mind to sleep. That was when the witch would possess his dreams and send madness to his mind.

His wives had knocked several times to ask if he was hungry. He'd chased them all away with a screamed curse. They had sent his son, Caesar, to him. He'd played with the child and held him close, seeking the protection of his innocence against the evil that stalked him. The child looked up at him with the special adoration that filled his heart with pride and love. Caesar was worth more than all his nine sisters, more than all the money in the world. Once he felt better, stronger, he would take the twin girl, Promise, to Dibia Ogam's place. Her sacrifice would guarantee his son a strong future. Money and power were the currencies of a worthy existence, the tickets into the paradise of earth. Caesar would inherit more than he himself had inherited from his late father.

His mobile rang and Eze looked at the caller-id. His heart lifted. It was his clansman, Chief Igwe, their village chief and one of the handful of people he could still count as true allies. He'd been avoiding calls all day, unwilling to feed the rumour mills spreading stories of his arrest and suspension from the local government.

They'll all see; it was just a matter of weeks before his fortune turned. They'll all come crawling back to him once again, seeking his goodwill, fawning over him as they used to do. Then, he'll show them all, show them what it means to kick a strong man when he's down. He has a long memory and he'll never forget all those who turned on him, from the chairman of the local government to that stupid DPO, whom he'd paid so much bribe money in the past.

'*Nwanna,* clansman, how are you? It's good to hear from you,' Eze's voice was hoarse, like one fighting a cold.

'My brother, how are you? I know the vultures are gathering, hoping to circle round a corpse but yours is a living body that will rise to send them all scattering back to the bushes they came from,' Chief Igwe paused as if choosing his words. 'Brother, tell me, have you heard any of the news circulating today?'

Eze's heart lurched. *Not again. Which of his hidden deeds were about to be exposed this time? What latest secrets had those two worthless, blabbermouth thugs revealed?* The only reason Eze had bailed the thugs, was to buy their silence. The current pressure he was undergoing made it hard to arrange their deaths. He would sort them out later, after things reverted to normal. They were on his long list of people on his revenge plot.

'I've had my mobile switched off all day. I think I'm coming down with malaria. I've heard no news, good or bad. Feed my ears, my good clansman.'

'Unfortunately, I have no good news. It's all bad. Let me start with the first. Your friend, DPO Egede, shot himself today after his son died from a curse which people are saying was put on him by your friend, the *Aghali* witch.'

'She's not my friend,' Eze's voice was vehement. 'Don't even joke about it. What kind of curse did she put on the child?'

'That's the strange thing. From what everyone's saying, it sounds like the *Leloole* curse. Now, that is one curse I haven't seen nor heard of since the witch, Xikora, died. I never knew Owa could use that hex. Had I known, I would have advised we treat her differently. Believe me, it's one curse you do not want to mess with,' Eze heard the fear in the chief's shaky voice and his own heart mirrored the quake. *If the chief knew about his encounter with the witch last night, then, he would really have something to fear.*

'You say the DPO is dead? DPO Egede? Are you sure?' Eze asked.

'Of course I'm sure. I spoke to the commissioner of police myself. He's dead, alright. But that's not all. The commissioner also mentioned that they were investigating a link between the deaths of the DPO's four police sergeants and a similar death in Oghe village. Gear yourself, my brother, for this bad news. It appears that Dibia Ogam is dead.'

368

Eze gasped, jumping up from his bed. 'What did you say? Repeat what you just said,'

'I said that the great Dibia Ogam is dead. But worse, it would appear that he was killed by somebody we both know, guess who?'

'Qwa?' Eze's voice was stunned.

'Right first time,' the chief's voice was grim. 'There were villagers who witnessed the fight between the two *Dibias*. They say that Qwa killed Dibia Ogam before rescuing a young albino girl held hostage by the witch-doctor. People saw them leaving together, Qwa and her daughter. I thought you told me that the girl was dead, that her body parts were used for the *Juju* ritual to the deity, *Aku n'uba*? How come the witnesses swear they saw her alive? And not just in Oghe village, but here in Ukari village too. Villagers have been trooping to my house all day, saying they've encountered the girl in the village and she's been hexing them and threatening them with doom. If this is true, then at least, that's one good news for you. No one can accuse you of murder anymore and we'll just work towards raising enough bribe money to buy off the commissioner and "disappear" the file regarding the priest's case.'

Eze was no longer listening to Chief Igwe's voice. The mobile phone slipped from his hand and fell to the tiled flooring of his room with a loud crash. His heart pounded so loud he thought he would suffer a stroke. *He had thought the girl was a mirage, just like the blood river. He had believed the witch had hexed his mind*

369

and made him see her daughter, just to torture him for what he had done. But it was all real! Jesus, save his soul! The girl was real, the girl he had watched die in a pool of her own blood. It was no mirage, no hex. Hadn't he stabbed her flesh over and over with the dagger, wounds that would have guaranteed instant death to any living being. But how can you kill what is already dead, something that neither bleeds nor breathes? The witch-woman had brought her dead daughter back from the grave and the girl was out to get him; she and her witch mother. They were coming for his blood, together with everyone involved in her death. Dibia Ogam was dead and now the DPO. He was next, he knew it. It was her voice he had heard inside his head last night, promising a visitation. If the witch could fell such a powerful Dibia as Ogam, plus the DPO and his son, then who was he to escape her wrath?

Eze returned to the mirror, barring his shoulders for a final look. He knew what he would see, the dark plump flesh of his left shoulder, devoid of marks. The Black Hand had completely vanished, leaving no trace to show it'd ever inhabited his body, promising him the world. The last grey middle finger had disappeared that morning. That was when he knew his time was up, that any sacrifice to Dibia Ogam would be a waste. And now, Dibia Ogam was dead and he was doomed. The child, Promise, would live. Her *chi*, fate, was a lucky one. His own *chi* wasn't so lucky after all.

He returned to his bed and lay down. The room was now in a deepening gloom. Night was fast approaching. He got up from his bed and switched on the light, flooding the room with florescent brightness. *Thank you, NEPA!* At least, there'll be light on the day he died. He opened his door and screamed for his wives. He heard their footsteps rush up the stairs, his first and second wives. Oge was the last to arrive, her steps slow and leisurely as she sauntered up the stairs in the high-heeled sandals she would insist on wearing even inside the house. *If only she would topple down the stairs one day and break her scrawny neck, the skinny bitch.*

'I'm hungry. I want a special meal tonight. You!' Eze pointed at his first wife. 'Prepare a dish of pepper-soup for me, using the best cow meat you can find. And you!' He turned to his second wife, the university graduate who fancied herself a gourmet chef. 'Make me chicken salad and fried rice immediately.' He turned his gaze to his third wife and frowned. *Lucky bitch had escaped his vengeance. Might as well make her pay for it.* 'You, go make me a hot bowl of pounded yam and Egusi soup immediately and make the soup with assorted meats. I'll give you all two hours at the very most to present the food to me.'

'Ha! This man! You will kill me one day with your craziness!' Oge's amused voice dripped with mockery. 'If you think I'm going to sit around in the kitchen pounding yam for you at this time of the night, then you must be mad. I cooked rice and beans and that's all I will serve you. If you want pounded yam and assorted meats, then you'd better go to a hotel and eat,' she hissed and turned away.

Eze saw red. With a scream, he lunged at her, grabbing her by the neck. He began to choke her, squeeze the life from her lungs. She fought and scratched his face, his arms, kicking his knees, seeking his groin. The other wives screamed and tried to separate them. Eze smacked and punched them, sending them toppling to the ground. Oge escaped his strangle-hold, coughing, gasping for air. He reached for her again, determined to put an end to her life once and for all, restore his dignity in his own home before he died. She might as well make the journey to the grave with him. With her gone, there would be peace in his house since the other two wives knew how to get along.

He looked up to see the twin girls crying, asking him to leave their Mammy alone. He shouted at them and threatened them with violence. But this time, they would not go, unlike other times. It was as if they sensed that this could be the last time they'd see their mother alive. The other wives joined the children in begging him, their faces bruised from his punches. He ignored them and pressed down tighter. Oge was tiring, her kicks growing feeble, her eyes starting to pop.

That was when he heard the gasps, the excited voices of his children, the terrified screams of his wives. A faint smell wafted into his nostrils, a scent that sent a prickling to the back of his neck. He turned to see the women staring at a point behind him, towards the staircase. He followed their gaze and looked. The strength drained out of his bones. His grip on Oge's neck loosened. He heard her gasping coughs as if from a great distance. His body began to tremble, hot sweat breaking out of his pores, drenching his face in seconds.

Aku walked up his stairs, her eyes glittering with unholy glee. Except she wasn't alone. By her side was Eze's only son, Caesar, his right hand clutched in hers, his left hand holding a bloodied chicken with black circled eyes. Around them were three of his youngest daughters, chattering excitedly, crowding close to view the voodoo chicken.

'Papa, look at the present the auntie gave me,' the child squealed, breaking free to dash up to the landing, the chicken clasped close to his chest. Eze screamed, his shout echoed by his wives.

'Drop that chicken immediately, son. Now! Drop it now and run. Run son, run away from her,' Eze's shout was almost drowned out by his wives' screams as the boy's mother pushed through everyone to grab her son. Caesar looked confused by all the screams and began to cry. His mother tried to grab the chicken from him but the child wouldn't let go.

'It's mine,' he wailed. 'The auntie gave it to me, not them,' he cast a baleful look at his sisters gathered around him. Their hands reached for the chicken, their eyes aglow with excitement at the wondrous sight of the strange bird. Caesar held on tight to his prize, turning his back to his sisters to keep their hands from the chicken. 'I'm not giving it to them, it's mine. Auntie, tell them you gave it to me,' he turned beseeching eyes to Aku, who remained at the bottom of the stairs watching the commotion with a cold smile.

'She's not your auntie,' screamed the mother, finally wrestling the chicken from the boy and flinging it at Aku. The chicken flew, a pathetic flight that wasn't the typical soar of the bird family. It landed clumsily on Aku's chest. She caught it, rubbing it fondly against her face, while her eyes remained fixed on Eze. The women gathered the children in frantic flights to their various rooms along the corridor, turning their keys and drawing the bolts to reinforce their safety. Oge struggled to her hands and knees, coughing, trying to swear at him, her voice raspy. She was assisted to her feet by her twin daughters, whose eyes were wide with fear, frightened by the terror of the adults and the look on their father's face. Eze was babbling, his eyes wide, weaving the sign of the cross over and over in manic repetition.

'Jesus! Jesus! Jesus!' He gasped, backing towards his room, his steps clumsy on legs jellied by terror. He saw Aku whisper words into the chicken's invisible ears before stooping low to release it.

374

The chicken flew up the stairs and Eze screamed. He turned and started to run. He glanced behind to see Oge and her twins scramble away from the chicken, which ignored them and continued its purposeful strut-flight in pursuit of Eze.

He made it to his room and banged the door against the chicken, turning the lock with trembling fingers. He heard another door bang along the corridor, Oge's door. An eerie silence descended on the house. He backed away from his door, listening, heart thudding, staring at his locked door, waiting for the crash that would signify his death. He had expected her, knew she was coming for him, thought he would be ready when she came. Reality was different. He did not want to die. *Jesus, help him;* he did not want to die at the hands of a vengeful corpse, a corpse he had created.

Seconds turned to minutes as the bedside clock in his room ticked away the time. His door remained locked and the house remained still. He pulled out his mobile to call for help. DPO Egede might still do him one extra favour. He was about to speed-dial the number when his thumb paused. DPO Egede was dead, killed by the thing beyond his door. Terror washed over him afresh, sending chills across his body in waves. He dashed over to his window and flung it open, angry thoughts fighting his fear. *His stupid gate-man; the wretched fool that had let the corpse into his house. By the time he was done with the wretch, he would wish he'd never stepped foot on Igbo soil, the bastard. That's the problem with hired help. Feed them too well and what do you get?*

'Aboki! Aboki!' Eze's shout resounded around the empty compound like a knell. His gate-man came running out of his little security hut. He switched on the outside security bulbs, lighting up the compound in seconds.

'*Oga*, chief,' the man ran towards the main house, stopping underneath the window, looking up at his master, an expectant look on his face. He never knew what new orders would issue from his master's lips. If he were lucky, it would be a shopping errand that would enable him to pocket some loose change.

'Idiot man! How dare you let that woman into my house?'

'Woman?' The gate-man looked baffled. '*Oga*, no woman come here, *walahi*, I swear in the name of Allah. I never see any woman at all.'

'Because you didn't switch on the outside lights, you fool. You were asleep yet again inside your hut instead of guarding my house. Pack your things and get out now. You're fired; d'you hear me? Fired. Get out of my compound now.' Eze slammed the window shut before he could hear the man's wheedles. This time wouldn't be like all the other times he'd sacked the fool only to relent after his cries and promises and apologies.

He turned back to stare at his door, feeling a sense of relief after his fractious interaction with the gate-man, another human being.

He padded quietly across the room and pressed his ear to the door. He heard nothing, not a sound from the wives or the children. Maybe the corpse had gone. He didn't dare open the door to check. He dashed to the window and opened it again. As he expected, his gate-man was still standing where he last saw him, mumbling unintelligible words in his *Hausa* language, his arms weaving in manic gesticulations. He looked up with a gloomy face when Eze's face appeared at the open window.

'Sorry master; sorry chief; *Insha Allah*, I will watch this gate with my life from today. I'll never sleep again, day or night, I swear. Even food, I'll not eat. Just will stand for the gate and watch it till forever. *Kai!* If *Oga* send me home, what will happen to my poor children and my sick mother who have no one to care for her, only myself, just myself carrying all the troubles of the world on my shoulders. *Oga* knows that I suffer from...'

'Shut up you fool and listen,' Eze cut him off. He'd heard the same mantra from the man multiple times in the ten years he'd worked for him. 'Get yourself inside the house now and search every room till you find the woman. Also find the chicken she brought with her and remove it from the compound, you hear? Go, now!' He shut the window again and slumped on his bed, a sigh of relief escaping his lips. *His gate-man would find the corpse and lead it away from his house, together with her chicken. If the thing killed him, then let the Aboki be the human sacrifice that might appease the angry ghost.* He shuddered as he recalled the terrible appearance of the chicken and the silent mockery of the corpse girl. An uneasy feeling descended on him, a niggling thought that teased the edges of his mind, refusing to be grasped. *The chicken... the chicken... something about the chicken that wasn't right.* A deep frown creased his forehead.

'You like mirrors, don't you, old friend? You like to know what the future holds for you, yes? Why don't you look in your mirror and see your future? Go on, fat fool, look in your mirror, look in your mirror, look in your mirror!' The voice shrilled inside his head as if the speaker's lips were pressed against his ear, shouting the words.

'Jesus!' Eze shouted and jumped from his bed. The pounding returned to his heart, growing, rising till it hit his head. He knew that voice. He had heard that voice only last night, as he drove away from the witch's house. *The corpse.* She was still in his house, lurking somewhere, waiting… *watching.* He began to look at his mirror and quickly turned away. The chills quaked his large frame again. *Why did she want him to look in the mirror? What other future would he see except his death? Was she taunting him, showing him how she planned to kill him, maybe remove his chest, his wrist and his nipples just as he'd done to her...or worse, perhaps, castrate him as well?* Eze backed away from the mirror, pressing his back against his wall. He would not look, did not want to see. Ignorance was peace. He would know his death when it came calling.

A gentle knock on his door startled him. His eyes widened as his heart dropped to his feet, then raced back up to his chest, thudding painfully against his ribs. It was a woman's knock, gentle, insidious, deadly.

'*Oga,* I have finished search. I not find any woman anywhere and no chicken in the house,' his gate-man's voice was like ice water to a dying man lost in a desert. Eze ran across his room and flung open his door. He almost hugged the small, skinny man smiling up at him but managed to stop himself just in time. But the man had seen his face and grasped his opportunity. 'So, *Oga* will let his poor Aboki stay now, yes? Aboki will watch chief's gate very, very well now,'

'You can stay, you fool. But, let this be the last warning. Next time, I won't even bother to look at your face, you hear me?' The gate-man nodded, several times, smiling and wringing his hands as he bowed himself away from Eze.

'Allah bless you, *Oga.* Thank you, sir, thank you, sir, thank you, sir...' His voice trailed away as he exited the house still voicing his gratitude. Eze looked at the shut doors of his wives' bedrooms and debated whether to leave them to their terror or alert them that all was ok. He didn't really care about their feelings but he had to maintain his status, show them that he wasn't afraid of any voodoo chicken like they were, prove to them that he was still the man of the house, able to protect them against everything.

He called out to the women to come out of their rooms, deepening his voice and adding menace to his tone. Two doors opened, just as he'd expected. Oge's door remained locked. He felt a slight remorse for his attack on her. He wanted to go into her room and apologise but didn't want to do so in front of the other wives. It would diminish him in their eyes and breed further hostilities in the home. He never apologised to any of the wives after disciplining them, only Oge, and always in secret, in the dead of night when no ears would hear him begging her to do things to his body no other woman had ever done, things that kept him enslaved to her.

'Papa Caesar, where is the albino girl?' His second wife asked. He caught the ugly look in his first wife's eyes. He used to be "Papa Princess" before the birth of his only son. Princess was his first child, his daughter by his first wife. But Caesar's birth had changed his title. A man must always be known as the father of his heir. To be called a daughter's father was a slur to his virility.

'The girl is gone. I want you all to keep a watch out for her and avoid her like the plague. She's a witch and we have to make sure that she has no contact with the children.'

'A witch? Did you say a witch?' His first wife screamed. 'What does a witch want with us, Jesus save me? The only witch in the village is the albino woman, Qwa of the Nshi clan. Who is this other one?'

'It's the woman's daughter, our first,' replied his second wife before Eze could respond. All the wives addressed his first wife with the respectful title of "our first". 'It's the girl that's been missing, the one the people are saying our husband killed. You remember how her mother camped outside our house for two nights asking for her daughter. It would seem our husband didn't kill her after all. But he must have done something to upset her otherwise, why would she come seeking him with that horrible chicken?' She gave Eze a dark look weighted with suspicion before turning to her son. 'And talking of chicken, Caesar, if I ever see you accepting anything from anyone again, I'll flog you seriously, you hear me?' The child's renewed cries distracted the mother and deflected further questions about his guilt. Eze left the women and children to their squabbles and returned to his bedroom, locking the door once again. *That was the problem with marrying educated women,* he thought, a frown furrowing his brows. *They think things over, analyse issues they had no business doing as women, add one and one and come up with two hundred.* He knew he wasn't done with his second wife yet. Others might keep themselves busy worrying about hexes and enemies but not his second wife. She'd mull over every tiny detail and come up with an answer very close to the truth. Eze hissed. *He'll deal with her if it ever came to that.* In the meantime, he now had to think about better security to keep the corpse away from his house. He didn't want to think about how she gained entry despite the locked gate and high walls; he didn't want to instil more fear in his heart.

Something flashed across the room, a movement in the mirror. Instinctively, he looked, his action swift, fuelled by adrenaline. By the time he remembered the voice in his head, recalled that he had sworn never to look in the mirror, it was too late. The image reflected in the shiny rectangular surface held him gripped in its thrall. He stared with mounting terror at the image of his son, Caesar, plastered on the mirror like a scene in a silent movie. The child lay on his back on a straw mat, his eyes shut as if in sleep. He was completely naked, save for the copper bangle around his tiny wrist, a gift from his godfather, Chief Igwe, to ward off evil.

Except the gift wasn't doing its job and evil was having its merry way with the child. The bloodied chicken the corpse girl had given Caesar was perched on the boy's chest, doing a manic dance on its skinny legs. Its claws scratched the child's chest, leaving blood trails on his skin. After a few seconds of dancing, the chicken bent its head to peck on Caesar's body, peck, peck, peck; then another crazy dance before another bout of pecks.

As Eze watched with horror-glazed eyes, each peck began to hatch. Like seeds on fertile soil, they grew into boils, massive, festering pus-filled pustules the size of kennel nuts. In seconds, the boy's naked body was covered in weeping abscesses that popped and bled, releasing a thick sludge of poison goo all over the child's body. The chicken did a final manic dance and returned to Caesar's chest and squatted, starring directly into Eze's eyes in the mirror, its dark little eyes holding a secret smile that seemed to say, "See what I've done! Aren't I the clever one?"

But it wasn't the chicken's malice-filled eyes that held Eze's attention and brought the awful howl to his mouth. It was his son's eyes, Caesar's small eyes that dripped with blood, eyes that stared at him with terror and pain, accusing eyes that screamed its message into his brain – *See what you've done to me, Papa. I thought you loved me, Papa. Why did you do this to me? Why, Papa, why?*

Eze began to howl, loud wails that woke the entire house and sent numerous footsteps to his door. His cries drowned out their shouts, their knocks, their own cries. Over and over, he heard the question in his head – *why, Papa, why?* He had no answer for his son, no antidote to the curse delivered to the boy by the corpse girl. All night, he lay huddled in his bed, the lights blazing in his bedroom, both the overhead florescent and the reading lamp. He waited for the sun to rise with the desperation of a man lost in vampire land. And when the sun eventually rose, it brought with it the horror he'd been expecting through the terrible, long hours of the night.

His second wife's scream was the first alert he had, followed by the wails by the other women. Even Oge's voice joined the screams. They banged on his door, called to him to come out and see his son, his only son who had gone to bed healthy and never opened his eyes again; his son whose skin used to smell of innocence and food but now stank up the house with the foulness of corruption; his son who would never run up to him again with the joyful scream of "papa!"; his son whom he had loved beyond life and killed as surely as if he'd pumped Caesar's blood with the poison that stole his young life. Curled up in his bed, Eze's body trembled and burnt with a sudden fever that bred the first seeds of insanity in his brain.

Ω Ω Ω

15

Ash of Immortality

●

She sits crossed-legged on the hard red-mud flooring of the shrine, mixing powder potions inside a metal basin that contains the drained blood of a goat. Her naked body glistens with scented oils, lithe and strong. By her side, the dead animal stares with unseeing glassy eyes at the black statue of the Earth Goddess, its long tongue sticking out at the side of its mouth. She doesn't waste a glance on the carcass. She has no further use for it now she has its blood in her basin.

As she mixes secret potions and chants ancient incantations to invoke the Leloole imps, her eyes blaze with joy. It's been so long since she practiced the true art, so long since she enjoyed the practical application of witch-doctoring inside a proper shrine. These couple of days have been the best since the last time she walked the earth. There's so much to do and so little time. She's not sure she can trust the air-head girl, Ego, to carry out the resurrection in a few hours without a hitch. But she's her only hope. She'll not return to Mbana-Oyi again, not if she has any say in the matter. She's already collected enough ash to last five resurrections, powered them with a spoonful of the original Ash of Immortality she's retrieved from its hiding place. She'd asked Aná to bless the ash but the goddess had remained silent to her pleas. She guesses she's still in Aná's bad book but there's no cause for alarm. Aná can only dictate the number of days a corpse can return, not the efficacy of the Ash of Immortality. The ash will always return life to a corpse, every dead thing that has previously walked the earth. Even if she walks for one day each return, it will be enough to complete her mission. She knows Owa will wail when she finds out what she's done but she has herself to blame for leaving her thoughts open to be heard. And anyway, everything she's doing is for their good, all for them and the Earth Goddess.

She grimaces. Left to Owa, wrongs will never be righted and vengeance will remain a meal that will never be eaten. It kills her soul to realise that the poor girl has the powers but not the right spirit for their art, otherwise, what happened to the child would have never occurred in the first place. She'll bring back fear and respect for the goddess, restore their name and status once again in the community. Even if the girl messes up the resurrection (Aná forbid), her feat this night will be enough to cement their legacy again in the twelve villages and beyond.

She gathers the six white chickens to her, all hens. Vengeance is best suited to females, humans and animals. She allows her thoughts to wander as she strokes the chickens. She had walked the village by noonday, basked in the terror reflected on the faces of all who saw her, people that had heard about the sudden hex-death of the only son of Eze, son of Agu of Onori clan. The villagers had avoided her, scuttling into their houses and locking their doors behind them.

From the market square, she had made her way to the whore-bitch's house, Enu of Nshi clan. She'd left that visit as her last because it was the one that would give her the greatest pleasure. The sight of the whore's house had filled her with bitter fury. The house she had grown up in, the ancestral home of her mother, had been razed to the ground and replaced with a glass monstrosity that reeked of dirty sex. Even the small hut that was her shrine, the very room where she had breathed her last giving birth to her poor dead son, had been demolished by the whore and turned into a flower garden. If for nothing else, she would ensure the bitch-whore felt the full blast of her wrath.

She had knocked on the door, banged as if she still owned the place. She kept banging until the woman screamed her irritation through the locked door, threatening to break her head for knocking with disrespect. The threat increased her rage and the volume of her knocks. She banged with the fury of a tornado until finally, the door flung open and she faced the Mbarama, the great whore.

She smiles again as she recalls the look on Enu's face when she saw her standing at her doorstep that afternoon. It was terror beyond anything she's witnessed since her return, save perhaps the look on the fat fool's face in her bedroom when he came to assassinate Owa. Enu had shrieked and started to run, right back into her glass house. She followed her in, through each room she entered, right back to her plush living room, where she finally trapped her. The woman had collapsed on the floor, her body trembling like a wet cat, howling for forgiveness, pleading for her life, calling on Jesus and Mary to save her from doom.

She had helped the Mbarama up from the floor, guided her back to the same sofa she had sat the child on the day she sold her to The Fat-Man. Enu had sat there blubbering, accusing The Fat-Man, blaming everyone but herself, all the while pleading for forgiveness. Her silence had been her weapon, as she watched the whore talk herself into blind terror and when she finally spoke to her, she'd called her "auntie Enu", just as the child had done on that fateful day of evil betrayal. She requested a glass of red wine, the same wine she had given the child. Enu had stared in open-mouth consternation before scrambling to her feet and dashing in to get the drink.

She followed the Mbarama into her kitchen, watching as she poured the drink with trembling hands. As she took the glass, she dropped a black kennel nut into the drink, watching it settle to the bottom of the glass. The drink began to bubble, foaming like angry waves. She waited till its rage abated. Then she passed back the drink to Enu.

'Drink first, auntie Enu,' she smiled as she returned the glass to the quivering woman. Enu shook her head, staring at the nut through the glass. 'Drink, now!' She shouted the command, watching the whore jump in shock. Enu took the glass and began to plead once again. She fell on her knees, begging for mercy, for the glass to be taken away. She stared down at the whore's creased face, at the black paint running down her eyelashes and staining her cheeks, the smudged lipstick and the patchy powder.

And her loathing was complete.

'Drink it up now!' Her shout this time was a brutal order without mercy and Enu drank; gulped the drink till the glass was empty, save for the kennel nut. 'Chew the nut, all of it. Chew it and swallow it,' she commanded. Enu gulped, deep, starting to shake all over. She tipped the glass till the nut rolled into her mouth. Then she began to chew, slowly, reluctantly, her face squeezed like one chewing the bitter leaf, Onugbu. When she was done, she looked up, her eyes terror-wide, awaiting death.

'Good auntie, you did well' she smiled at her, walking away from the kitchen. 'Bye-bye, auntie. Don't worry; your death can wait for the time-being. We're not done yet, you and I.' She walked out of the house, the weeping voice of the whore following her all the way to the front-door. Her job was done. Her vile niece feared the Leloole curse, little realising that hex was too good for her.

She laughs again, a sound of wild exultation and leans forward to grab her first white chicken. She gently soaks it in the charmed blood, taking her time to wash each silky feather with the thick blood, chanting Juju spells into its ear. When she's done, she paints in the black circle around its eyes with Uli, black dye, and wraps the palm frond around its neck. With careful deliberation, she carries out the same process on the remaining five chickens. When she's done, she raises her voice and gives them the message of doom.

'Go, chickens of death. Save for the two names, Eze, son of Agu of Onori clan and Enu of Nshi clan, go and seek out everyone who saw and did not help, who heard and did not tell, who knew and did not share. Find all that celebrated instead of mourning, those that cloaked the evil within their veils of mockery and glee. And to each of them, give to them as they deserve, as their actions have earned. Go, my chickens of death; roam the village, every compound, every farm, every path and every stream. Seek them out and inflict the guilty with the Leloole curse! Your mistress, Xikora, sends you. Do not fail me.'

She blows her breath into their faces, their shiny cold eyes and sharp beaks and sets them free. They march out in a silent, orderly formation, as if orchestrated by an invisible conductor. She knows the death chickens will find them all, from the chief to the thugs, Enu's gang of vicious women and all who have knowledge of the

391

evil done to her daughter and grandchild. By morning, the village will be in a state of mourning. Precious sons will die and parents will go insane. Fear will rule once again and the name of Aná and her priestesses will be names to be respected once more.

As the shrine empties, she heaves a deep sigh. It is done. She gets up and bows to the black statue. Aná returns her look with a cold, remote stare. She shrugs and leaves the shrine. She feels the girl's spirit growing stronger within, pulling her towards the dark void, the total blackness of eternal sleep. She tries to fight it but knows it's a futile battle. Their four market days are up and it is time for their final goodbyes, daughter to mother and mother to daughter, Ọwa to herself and Ọwa to the girl. She prays the other girl, Ego, comes through for her. She's not ready for forever goodbyes.

***

'Wake up; come child, wake up now. It's not time for you to sleep yet,' Ọwa shook her daughter for the third time in the hour. Aku opened her eyes, a confused glaze in her pupils.

'I'm tired, Mama. So sleepy. Let me sleep and we can talk tomorrow,'

Ọwa shook her head, determination fighting the pain in her heart. Again, she glanced at the small round clock on the wall. It was just over 11.30pm, less than thirty minutes to her child's

392

death. Thanks to her mother, she'd barely had the chance to spend time with her daughter, to say all the things she never said in her first life. It had been less than two hours since Xikora stumbled into the room, naked and oiled, evidence that she'd been spending time, yet again, in the shrine, up to her usual mischief. Qwa had left her to her devices, knowing anything she said would be disregarded with the same arrogant scorn that was Xikora's response to her pleas. It still unnerved her how by a simple flash of eyes, a tone in voice, a swagger in walk, Xikora managed to obliterate her daughter entirely from Aku's own body.

All day, Qwa had received visitors, more visitors than she had had in a thirty-day period, people coming to offer their belated commiseration for the loss of her daughter and their congratulations on Aku's return; people bearing gifts for her, offerings for her daughter, voicing solicitous concern for their welfare. She had marvelled at the unusual outpouring of kindness from the villagers till Mama Ten visited and informed her about the sudden hex-death of the only son of Eze, son of Agu of Onori clan. Then night suddenly became day, bringing clarity to her - *Xikora had struck again with her terrible curse, once again, upon an innocent child.*

Mama Ten also revealed that her cousin Enu had been seen running around the village square, shouting dark secrets that sent several people in the village cowering in shame while others were righteous with outrage. Enu claimed to have been hexed by Aku, cursed with *Ile-Nkata*, the leaking basket tongue, a seeping mouth that would eternally expose every bad deed, hers and those committed by everyone in her circle and beyond. Already, marriages were being wrecked, friendships broken, relationships ruined and blood enemies made. Enu had confessed her dastardly plot with Eze, son of Agu of Onori clan and people were casting the demon over their shoulders, covering their ears against the evils spewing from her lips. Mama Ten said Enu was wailing even as she ruined herself with her own words. She said Enu tried to cover her mouth with her hands but her teeth bit off the very skin from her palms and freed her tongue to spew damnation. *Ile-Nkata* tongue was a self-destructive curse that would neither be reigned nor killed till its owner was ruined. Enu was now a pariah in the village. She that had once boasted the friendship of three dozen women, now had no one she could whisper her troubles to anymore. Mama Ten said the villagers were now walking in fear. No one knew who would be next on Aku's hit-list. Thanks to Enu's very public confessions, everyone now knew something evil had happened to the girl, something that had turned her to the death-machine she had become.

The elders said it was as if the dreaded Xikora of the *Leloole* curse walked the earth again, such was the terror gripping the entire village. Mama Ten said there was talk of sending a delegation to Qwa's house to seek appeasement but everyone was awaiting directives from someone. That someone used to be Chief Igwe, the village leader. But after Enu's confessions, people were spitting on the name of the chief and the entire Onori clan. No one had attended the hasty funeral in Eze's compound, the sad burial of his little son, Caesar, not after hearing what Enu revealed in the market square. No one wanted to fall foul of the raging albino girl, armed with a deadly curse.

But it would appear Xikora's quest hadn't been all for vengeance. One villager, Mama Ten, had escaped her wrath and instead, been blessed. According to Mama Ten, Aku had walked into her small bar just after midday, sending her few clients scattering in different directions. Even Mama Ten's daughters took to their heels, terrified of the *Leloole* curse despite their innocence. Mama Ten said Aku had thanked her without telling her what she was being thanked for. Then she had gone outside the bar and dropped a couple of kennel nuts, chanting words in an unknown tongue. Before she left, she told Mama Ten to prepare for abundance.

Qwa could still see the stunned look on Mama Ten's face as she recounted what happened next. According to her, within minutes of Aku leaving her bar, a bus carrying several passengers broke down right in front of her bar, forcing the passengers to troop to her shop for cold drinks and food. Under an hour, she had sold out everything in the bar, earning more than she would normally make in a whole day of trading. Less than an hour after the bus had departed, another bus, loaded with more passengers, had a punctured tyre next to her shop. Mama Ten had come to personally ask Ọwa to thank her daughter, Aku, for the miraculous gift which meant she never need worry about providing for her ten children ever again. Ọwa wanted to tell her that her benefactor was none other than Xikora, but did not want to frighten the simple woman.

After Mama Ten left, Ọwa retired to her room to avoid the influx of villagers. Xikora returned at sun-down, her voice loud and merry in an off-key song. Soon, Ọwa heard her pottering noisily inside the shrine. When she followed her into the shrine, Xikora waved her away, demanding total privacy, taking over the shrine as if she were the high priestess in-sitting and not Ọwa. She felt no resentment or envy. Xikora was ten times the priestess she was or would ever be. She was welcome to her shrine. All she wanted was her daughter, Aku, to see those gentle eyes of her daughter, hear the sweet, hesitant voice and share the loving soul that was her child. *If only Xikora would give the child's body some rest.*

When Xikora stumbled out of the shrine several hours later, naked and dazed, Ọwa knew her daughter was back again in her own body. Except all Aku wanted to do was sleep, just as she'd been sleeping whenever Xikora let her be. But Ọwa was determined to drain as much time as she could from their final minutes together. She shook Aku again, her hands rough, hard.

'Daughter, please try and stay awake,' she urged, adjusting herself where she was perched on the edge of the single bed. 'I want to ask you a few questions, just a couple of questions and then you can sleep, ok?' Aku nodded, yawning, smiling sheepishly.

'Sorry Mama, I'm trying, honest. I'm really trying to stay awake but my eyes are so tired. Is it alright if I just shut my eyes and listen to you? I promise I won't sleep. I'll just rest my eyes while I listen.'

'Ok, but I'm warning you, I won't let you sleep till I'm done,' Ọwa said. Aku hhmmed with a lazy smile, shutting her eyes.

'Daughter, I want you to tell me the truth. Have you been happy? Have I given you a happy life? Is there something I could have done to make you happier which I never did? Tell me the truth, daughter. Don't spare my feeling, please.' She waited for Aku's response but again, the girl had slipped back into sleep. Ọwa shook her, harder, longer. 'Please, Aku, stay with me. Don't leave me, not yet, please,' she was crying, tears hot on her cheeks. The long hand on the clock seemed to run on antelope heels. Just five minutes left, five short minutes. 'Daughter, open your eyes. Look at me. I need to tell you something.' Aku dragged her lids open, as if she were lifting concrete slabs. 'I love you, daughter. I love you more than I can ever express. I named you Aku, meaning, wealth, because you are the greatest wealth I ever had. You are my heaven and my earth, my pride and my glory, the reason for my existence, my beginning and my end. There will never be another you. I want you to know that your mother has loved you more than the world, more than her life and more than her goddess,' she saw the brilliant smile on her daughter's face, a smile that was reminiscent of her former life.

'Thank… you, Mama. I love you too… and wish…wish you could share this sleep with me. It's the best sleep ever…the best slee…'

Aku died.

And Ọwa began to howl, wail, mourn her daughter anew with a bitter keening that broke her heart into a million scattered, fragments of pain.

***

He had gone to kill her and had ended up making love to her. As he lay on her king-size bed, sweating in the aftermath of their coupling, Eze wondered what other surprises life held for him, how much longer he could hang on to an existence that was no longer worth living. By his side, Enu sobbed, her voice muffled against the pillow. He let her cry, too drained to offer her any comfort. They were both damned, both in need of comfort which neither could offer the other. Whoever claimed there was honour among thieves never came across these two thieves, he thought with unamused despair.

Eze's thoughts drifted to the events that took place in his house that morning, the chaos that had resulted in his visit to Enu's house. He recalled the incessant banging on his bedroom door by his wives, freed from fear of his wrath by their own terror and pain. When he wouldn't let them in, they brought in the male members of his clan and broke down his door. They brought into his room the sight he had dreaded seeing, confronted him with the stinking, putrid decay that was once his happy little son. No one would touch the boy save his mother, his raging mother, whose grief had turned her sanity. She had called him a murderer. In front of all his clansmen and household, his second wife had accused him of ritual murders and occultic evils. She blamed the unnatural death of her son on him, called him out to confess to his crime, the evil he had buried that had returned to claim the life of her son.

Eze pushed the thought away, his heart thudding painfully against his chest as he recalled the sight he would forever remember, his little son as he last saw him before he was put into the soil, his little body covered in black, weeping pustules that destroyed his features, shrouding his face beneath a pebbled towel of fermented boils. His thoughts raced to the sermon delivered by the priest they had quickly assembled to consecrate the child's body, the open accusation by the priest who said that his presence there was solely for the innocent child and not the father, a man who had to examine his soul and ask himself deep questions about his eternal life and the consequences of his actions on earth. The priest had spoken without fear, looking Eze directly in the eyes, his message clear and loud. Everyone heard and reached their own conclusions. And when halfway into the sermon, some villagers invaded the funeral to say that Enu had gone crazy at the market square and was spilling terrible, dark secrets, including her collusion with Eze in the *Aghali* girl's murder, chaos ensued.

Everyone abandoned the funeral, leaving Eze to bury his son alone, together with the boy's mother, who began packing her things as soon as the last soil covered Caesar's grave. She wasn't alone. Oge and her twin daughters had already driven out of the house in the small Passat car he'd given her as a wedding present. He had watched her go, too tired to make a fuss and exercise his male authority. By the time stories began reaching his ears about Enu's revelations, his house had turned into an abandoned school, inhabited by its insane principal, together with his loyal *Aboki* gate-man and his weeping "our first", whose three daughters were begging to leave the house for the safety of their big sister's matrimonial home.

The final straw was the arrival of the *Akwa-Igwe,* shame-singers, outside his house, chanting his crimes for the whole village to hear. Their words sent the rage to his heart, driving him out of his room and into his car, headed to Enu's house. *He would kill the blabber-mouth whore; throttle her throat till her eyes popped.* To think he had thought her trustworthy, someone he could do business with in total confidence. Instead she had opened her big ass and defecated all the filth inside her filthy bottom all over the village, revealing things nobody else had any business knowing.

Except the woman he met at the glass front-door wasn't the one he'd expected when he arrived at Enu's house. Gone was the haughty, strong woman he knew, replaced by a quivering bundle of terror. Even before Enu gasped out the name of her visitor, he already knew that he was looking at the one person in the entire world who understood his story and shared every scene in the dark narrative.

'Eze, do you realise that we're both walking corpses, that she won't rest till we're destroyed?' Enu's voice quivered with ill-suppressed terror. 'Can't you do something, maybe send your thugs to sort her out?'

'What do you mean by "sort her out", you stupid woman? Don't you realise she's dead, that she's a living corpse? You can't kill a dead corpse.'

'But I don't want to die,' Enu wailed, sitting up in the bed, her naked breasts flappy against her chest. 'It's your fault I'm in this mess. If you hadn't decided to use her for your *Juju*, none of this would have happened.'

'And who forced you to sacrifice your own cousin for money, eh? Did I hold a gun to your head?'

'You didn't need to. Seeing your thugs was enough pressure. Everyone knows what you and your thugs get up to. I'm a single woman with no one to protect me. Do you think I'll take the chance of not going along with your demand and risk being killed by your thugs? I don't think so.'

'You talk too much, woman. That's your problem. That's why it was easy for the witch to hex you with the *Ile-Nkata* curse. You're lucky I didn't kill you as I'd planned.' He rolled off her bed and began to get dressed. 'From here on, it's each man for himself. Look after your back and I'll do the same. She's not done with us yet but I have nothing to lose anymore. She's taken my only son, the one thing I loved more than life. Maybe she might be satisfied with that. I don't know. But, as I am right now, nothing matters anymore.' He began to walk out of the room.

'What about me? What's going to happen to me? I don't want to die; Help me, please. Stay here with me or let me come to your house. I don't want to be alone here.'

'Go to your cousin and seek her forgiveness. She's your family after all. Maybe, she might reign in her daughter, return her to the grave. I don't know and I truly don't care anymore. Take care now and if we meet again, I pray it'll be under better circumstances than this.'

He walked out of the house and got into his car, Enu's wails following him. For several minutes, he thought about his options. His house held no attraction for him anymore, especially since the *Akwa-Igwe*, shame-singers, started gathering outside his house following Enu's revelations. The group of raggedy women were from a long line of shame-singers, whose grandmothers and great-grandmothers had been shame-singers before them. They were the moral police of the village, visiting homes of wrong-doers to sing out their crimes to the hearing of the entire village and shame them within the community. People shamed by the *Akwa-Igwe* were banned from participating in village activities like the *Odo* masquerade festival, the New Yam harvest festival and the Ancestors' Day festival. They were ostracised for a twelve-month period before being allowed back into the community after making the *Salaka,* sacrifice of penance and cleansing, to the ancestors.

Eze thought about leaving the village and moving into a hotel in the big city but his finances were now tight. He had to watch every coin after all the steep bribery money he'd paid the commissioner of police to escape prosecution for the attempted murder of the priest. With a deep sigh, he started his car engine and drove back towards his house. *There's only so long a man can run before he decides to stand firm and face his foe.*

***

Ọwa added an extra teaspoon of spice into the bowl of oil next to where she sat on the living-room mat. It was the burial oil she would use in preparing her daughter's body for its final journey to the ancestors' realm before joining her chosen deity, Mary, of the pale skin. Just as she stirred in the spices, the night's peace was shattered by screams. Voices were coming from her dead daughter's room, voices that screamed in three distinctive voices. Two of the voices she instantly recognised, two voices that sent the sudden chill down her spine. *Xikora and Aku, her mother and her daughter!* The third voice was also a female voice but she did not recognise the voice. Shock and terror paralysed her on the mat, only for a second, before she was up on her feet, running towards Aku's bedroom.

She pushed open the door and her scream joined the others. Ego, her daughter's best friend, was standing by the bed, her wrist gripped tight by Aku's convulsing corpse. The girl was shrieking, trying to extricate her hand from the metal grip of the writhing girl. When she saw Ọwa, her eyes opened wider with terror.

'Help me, auntie Ọwa; please help me,' she begged, tears coursing down her face. 'I'm sorry... she asked me to do it. I forgot the words. I swear I practiced them and practiced them but I just forgot them and I'm sorry, auntie. Help me, please.'

'You stupid, stupid girl!' Qwa screamed at her, pushing her aside and prising her arm free. 'Get out from here and don't you dare repeat anything that happened here tonight or I'll deal with you.' She barely noticed the girl scramble out of the open window as she threw her entire weight against the thrashing body of her ash-coated daughter.

'Let go of me, you vile creatures! You're not keeping me down with you, despicable, useless deities!' Xikora's voice shrieked out from her daughter's lips.

'Mama... Mama! Help me... the pain... I'm dying Mama... Oh Mary Mother of God, save me... please, Mama, stop the pain... stop the pain...'

Her daughter's voice was a sharp blade in her heart, twisting, killing her soul. Tears filled her eyes as she struggled to still the shuddering body, tears of anguish and rage, pain for her daughter's suffering and fury at her mother, whose selfish greed for life was responsible Aku's torture.

Qwa began to recite the words of resurrection, the ancient words of life which the stupid girl, Ego, had botched. How Xikora could be so reckless as to entrust such a monumental task to a total novice was beyond her comprehension. Now, they were stuck in-between realms, neither with the living nor the dead, both going through the agonies of a half-born resurrection. She pressed tight against the thrashing body, gasping the secret words into her ears.

The more Ọwa chanted the words, the less the struggles grew and their screams subsided. Finally, after what seemed like hours, Aku's body stilled, the screams died out and sudden silence descended in the room, broken only by Ọwa's harsh breathing and the steady ticking of the wall clock. Sweat poured down her face, drenching her top. Her hands were covered in dirty ash. She stood up and stared down at the sleeping form of her daughter as thoughts raced through her mind like restless ants. *How could Xikora do this? How could she, Ọwa, have been so careless about her thoughts, about the secret location of the Ash of Immortality, knowing that her mother was a stealer of thoughts?* The Earth Mother had warned her to guard the sacred ash with her life and instead, she had allowed it to fall into the most ruthless hands ever created.

Ọwa dashed out of the room and through the front-door. She ran without stopping, to the bushy area by the shrine where she'd buried the sacred ash. Even in the clear light of the full moon, she could see that the soil had been disturbed. She started digging, frantically, knowing that her search would be futile, yet seeking for a different reality. The little earthen pot that contained the Ash of Immortality was gone. Again, fury raged in her heart as she ran back into the house. *Mother or no mother, she was done playing second fiddle to Xikora. She would tell her exactly what she thought about her thoughtless, selfish and heartless act.*

A soft sob stopped her race, a hushed cry that came from her daughter's room. She dashed in and found Aku sitting up in the bed, her arms wrapped around herself, crying, sobbing as if the world had ended, swallowing everything she held dear. Ọwa wrapped her arms around her, holding her close, forcing her body to absorb the chilling skin of her child's body without flinching. The smell of decayed flesh was stronger than it had ever been.

'Mama, what is wrong with me?' Aku sobbed, her eyes wide with confusion. 'Why do I keep getting these awful ghastly nightmares, dreams of being killed, my heart gorged out of my chest, my nipples and wrists severed and dying a slow, painful death? Why, Mama? Why?' The last question was a wail. Ọwa held Aku tighter, rocking her, stroking her cheeks, her hair, her cold, cold arm.

'Sshh... it's alright my daughter; it's ok. The nightmares will be gone for good, very soon. I promise you. I will deal with those demons that torment your dream. Your mother will not let anyone harm her beautiful daughter. Come, let's go into my room. Come and share your mother's mat with her and everything will be just fine. No demons will dare come into your dreams or your life while I'm around.'

She dressed her daughter's naked body and guided her out of her bedroom. Aku stumbled, walking her now familiar clumsy walk. Ọwa sat her down on her sleeping mat, switching on all the lights in the house. Then she sat herself next to Aku and began talking, telling her stories about their family, each ancestor, good, bad and crazy. She narrated funny stories about the various festivals held in the village, folktales, playground tales from the few years she had spent in formal education before her calling, anything to keep Aku from falling asleep and letting Xikora in. As long as Aku remained awake, Xikora couldn't take over her body and Ọwa was determined to find a way to send her mother back for good before she did more harm. Each time Aku yawned, Ọwa would raise the volume of her voice, urge her to her feet in a frenzied dance to silent music, her small body bearing the shambling weight of her drowsy daughter in a disorganised rhythm. Her voice grew hoarse and her limbs weak; still she talked and sang, laughed and cheered, till she heard a sound she had been waiting for all night, the sound of a car engine breaking the silence of dawn. Her heart soared.

Femi had arrived.

'Aku, don't sleep now, ok? Stay awake while I let in a friend,' she said scrambling from the mat and dashing to the front-door. Femi's hand was raised to knock when she opened the door. His face was sombre, his eyes grave as he searched her face.

'*Oga* Femi! Praise be to *Aná* for you, come in, come in.' She pulled him into the living room, shutting the door behind her. 'I don't know what to do. I've ruined everything… everything. I'm

408

not worthy to be called a priestess. I'm not good for anything. I couldn't protect my daughter, either in life or death. Come and see what my mother has done to my child,' she pulled him by the arm towards the open door of her bedroom. As they entered the room, Ọwa screamed and ran over to her mat where Aku was slumped in a deep sleep.

'Wake up, daughter; wake up, come on, wake up,' she shook Aku, dragging her arm, forcing her to a sitting position on the mat. She heard Femi's soft gasp behind her.

'I thought she was gone, that it was the last night?' His voice mirrored the shock she saw on his face when she looked up.

'That's what I was trying to tell you,' she said, still shaking Aku, forcing her lids apart with her fingers, shouting her name. 'My mother stole the Ash of Immortality and brought them back again. I can't let Xikora return. As long as Aku remains awake, my mother can't take over her body. Come, please help me get her to her feet and walk her around till she wakes up.'

Aku stirred, shuddered and opened her eyes. Ọwa gasped, dropping the arms she held, stumbling back.

'Daughter, we meet again,' glittering black eyes blazed with triumph as Xikora stood up and stretched, releasing the sour odour of decay inside the room. Femi gagged and stumbled out of the room. Xikora laughed, her voice a merry tinkle. 'So, this is the one that brings the glow to my daughter's heart,' she said, following

409

Femi into the living-room. 'As you can see, you've had a wasted journey. There'll be no graves dug in this compound today. The only graves will be in the village and I'm afraid I must leave you two lovebirds to your merry ways while I go and inspect the yields of my hard labour. And don't worry, I'll not touch you since that's all your mind seems capable of thinking. And a grown man like you too!' With another squeal of glee, Xikora ran through the open door and disappeared into the early morning light.

Femi slumped on the chair, the sole chair in the house. His face was an ashy shade, his eyes wide with horror.

'She read my mind,' Femi gasped, his voice trembling like his hands. 'She read everything I was thinking! What are you going to do?' He raised stunned eyes to Ọwa. 'How can anyone contain such a fearsome ghoul?'

'I have to go and consult the oracle, hold my divination with the Earth Goddess. That's my only hope, the only way I can give my child eternal sleep. I've let down my goddess and my daughter. I know you're disappointed in me even though you do not say so, but…'

'How can you ever think that I'm disappointed in you?' Femi cut her off, getting up to fold her in his arms. She was so small that he lifted her up and sat her on his laps as he returned to the chair. 'Don't you know how much I admire your strength, your humility, your goodness?' He drew her closer to his chest. 'Rest, my

410

priestess,' he murmured against her hair, rocking her, soothing her frenzied thoughts. 'Shut your eyes and rest, just for a few minutes. The world will not collapse and your goddess can wait. I bet you haven't slept a wink all night. Shut your eyes, my dear. Let me hold you, for a little while.' His voice was a soothing balm over her frayed nerves, his arms, a sanctuary from the horrors that threatened to steal her mind. She had never been held by a man like that, been so intimately close to a man. Yet, it felt right, good, peaceful. Her long night seemed a distant dream, the restless thoughts giving way to drowsiness. Her limbs went boneless, her eyes weighted with blocks. She curled deeper into Femi's arms, inhaled the clean scent of his man's body and gave in to the silent dark of sleep.

***

Everywhere she visits is shrouded in fear. She hears endless wails, mothers keening the loss of their sons and sons, the loss of their mothers. A mourning dirge is howled in almost every compound in the village, amongst the highest and lowest in the community. People are dropping like flies, each marked by the distinctive seal of her curse. The sound of their pain fills her with exhilaration. She hears their thoughts. It fills her with pride. No one knows who will be next, whose compound will feel the terror of her curse. The old ones amongst them recall the days of Xikora of the Leloole curse;

her name. They quake and worry. The evil hatched in the deepest night is now exposed in the brightest day. The blood chickens of death have marked all whose hands are red with blood. And the air is black with their fear.

She giggles as she listens to the elders speak. They summon an emergency meeting at the village church hall. They tell the villagers that they are all tainted with the blood of the murdered girl. Their cruelty to the Aghali witch-doctor and her daughter is solely responsible for everything that's happening. But for their guilt, the Earth Goddess would not permit the evil that has befallen them. The elders select a deputation to visit Ọwa to seek her forgiveness and halt her rage. Some church-goers amongst them advise against the pagan solution. They suggest that a Catholic mass be prayed inside the various village churches. They point to the large wooden cross with the crucified plastic body of Jesus Christ, crying blood tears for them by the pulpit. Surely, the blood of Jesus will overcome every evil, they plead.

The elders shout them down. To fight the devil, you must use the devil. Even the bible says to give unto God what is God's and to Rome, what is Rome's. These are days of fear and desperate times demand desperate remedies. They will approach the high priestess of the Earth Goddess in the old way, the ways of the old ancestors, with total humility and reverence for the deity she serves. The elders instruct the villagers to contribute to the purchase of

412

chickens, kola-nut, palm-wine, palm oil, Nzu chalk, yam tubers, sea-salt and a few more ingredients needed as appeasement offerings to the Earth Goddess.

She laughs at their blindness, even as she bristles at their ignorance. The fools think her daughter is responsible for their woes, that Owa has the power to inflict such terrors on them. She'll soon open their eyes to the truth. She gate-crashes the gathering inside the village church hall, shutting the heavy oak door behind her, trapping them inside the holy hall with their terror. She listens to their shrieks, smiles at their quakes until some able-bodied youths rush at her. Their mothers call them back while the villagers cheer them on. They come at her with their fists, wooden chairs, a pen-knife, a heavy bible from the pulpit, everything they can lay their hands on. Some of them have lost family in the twilight of her purge. Their blood boils with vengeance. They fall on her like a swamp of gym-muscled locusts.

She feels herself topple to the ground. She knows they must be inflicting damage on the body she wears but she feels no pain. She tries to rise but the weight on her holds her down. She allows herself to pick their thoughts and shout out their secrets. She tells the one called Ike, that his fiancé is pregnant by his best friend; tells the one called Afam, that his little sister with the blind eyes has been bitten by Echieteka, the deadly viper, whose victims never live to see the rise of a new dawn. She shrills the shameful secret in the heart of the one they call Obi, who yearns to have sex with a fellow man rather than a woman.

She feels the weight lift off her as her voice creates havoc, turning her attackers on themselves. The elders shout at the warring families, trying to regain the order she has destroyed with her words. She lifts herself from the floor and hears their gasps, reads the terror in their eyes. She has been stabbed and butchered, yet she walks, free of blood; she has been battered and murdered, yet she smiles, her eyes ablaze with life.

She looks at the elders, the ones who lived in her days, who shared the same sun and the same history with her. There is no recognition in their eyes. All they see is the girl, Aku, the ruined body of the witch-doctor's murdered daughter. She shouts out their names and their deeds; "Nnadi, I see that the finger you broke on the day you fell off the Alusi tree in our childhood days, has never mended." She smiles at another elder, "And you, Ibu-Dike, I see you married your Agbomma that you hankered after through our youth. Did she still give you the five sons you wanted?" She hears their gasps, hears the name, "Xikora", whispered, the whispers growing in volume till pandemonium breaks out in the hall.

As the hall empties in screaming panic, she walks back into the bright noon day. The village square is deserted, the village shrouded in silent fear, save for the occasional wail from an enclave where a new death has occurred. She passes the large house of the one that calls himself a leader, Chief Igwe. The keening is loud in the compound. They have two deaths to mourn, two putrid corpses to bury, the chief and his first son. Every gate and every door is shut against her but still she walks, her dress torn, her skin withered by the scorching sun that burns overhead. She knows this body cannot carry her for much longer but she has one more home to visit, one final score to settle before she can let the girl back into her ruined body.

Eze's gate is shut to the world. She pauses beyond the gate and marshals her powers. Her mind seeks out the mind of the one they call, Aboki. He's saying a prayer to his deity, the one he calls Allah. It endears him to her. A man that honours his deity is a man with a blessed life. She will not harm him. She calls to him in the voice of his wife, his wife who waits for him with their children in the far-away Hausa lands that he calls home.

Aboki hears her voice and opens the gate. The shock on his face changes to smiles when he holds her gaze and sees a friend in her mask. Happily glamoured, he leads her into the main house and withdraws to continue his prayers, his wife's voice still ringing in his head. She walks through the empty house, following the trail of the other one's thoughts, the one she has come to visit. He's thinking about his son, Caesar, about his late father, Agu, about his heir-less status, about his chairman who has betrayed him with his wife, Oge. He's thinking about how he'll drive to the chairman's house and shoot both him and his whoring wife. His thoughts turn to his second wife, the educated bitch-mother of his dead son, who has turned her diary over to the press. She has documented enough crimes to bring him down. His phone has not stopped ringing all day with calls from the media, seeking clarification. He's thinking he should have killed the woman before letting her leave his house, that he should never have married a university graduate with enough brains to bring down a kingdom. He's thinking about everyone he's lost, the sudden deaths of his clansman Chief Igwe and his first son, the deaths of his two thugs, Uche and Donatus, together with their parents, all struck down by the same deadly hex that stole his child, Caesar's life. Miraculously, the fat fool is thinking of everyone and everything, except the girl, Aku, her grand-daughter that he murdered in cold blood. And for the first time since she resurrected for the second time, she rages with a fury that sends a blistering inferno into the thoughts of her foe.

From the staircase, she hears him scream as he feels his body burning up in the raging fire that engulfs him right inside his bedroom. He's beating himself, rolling on the floor, howling, as his body is rapidly consumed by an invisible fire that burns only in his mind. He looks up to see her standing by his doorway, watching him writhe in agony. Through his howls, she sees the look of resigned terror in his dark eyes. It infuriates her. She'll not let him die that easily or quickly. Her thoughts shift gear, weaving new hallucinations. She creates a pool of cool water for him, laughing as he crawls towards it, towards the en-suite bathroom that houses a large white bath-tub and walls made of black tiles. She watches as he stumbles into the tub, hears his sighs of relief as the pool quenches the fire eating up his skin. Then, she sends him his greatest nightmare, the one he has kept hidden from the world, his terror of the creature that stole his half-brother at noon-day, a slithering, black creature with the fatal poisoned fangs.

In seconds, the water pool turns into a swamp of wriggling, black vipers, a black cauldron of slimy, biting death. He shrieks as he's covered by the vipers, bitten by a hundred poisoned fangs. The poison travels through his veins in minutes, freezing his blood. The snakes wrap themselves around his throat, strangling, squeezing, choking his breath. He's foaming at the mouth, watching her smiling face at the open doorway of his bathroom. Inside the empty white bath-tub, his body is a writhing, thrashing bulk of pure agony.

'I'd have thought that a snake like you will be happy in the company of your kind,' she says, her voice chatty, like a friend in conversation. 'I never really introduced myself to you, did I? Did anyone ever mention the name of Xikora to you when you were growing up? Did they never tell you that Xikora is not one to ever let a slight go unpunished, certainly not when you trifle with her

daughter or grand-daughter?' She sees the truth dawn in his eyes, eyes already fading in approaching death. 'Oh well; I'm afraid I have to leave you and you, sadly, now have to leave the world. Goodbye, old friend. May our paths never cross again.' She watches the snakes swim into his mouth, stuff his cheeks and puff them out. They bite his tongue and clog up his throat, choking out his screech. He jerks, once, twice, thrice and slumps against the white ceramic of his bathtub his eyes wide with a terror only his mind can see. She walks away from his room, his house, his death.

Her job is over. She knows that in the years to come, the villagers will remember the day that Xikora walked again with awe and terror. Her legacy with remain for generations to come. Once again, the people will learn to fear the name of Aná and her priestesses. She has done well by her goddess and surely, this time, even Aná, herself, must finally set her free from Mbana-Oyi.

Ω Ω Ω

16

To Kill a Medicine-Woman

It had been hours since Ọwa woke up on one of the living-room mats, where Femi had left her covered with her cotton wrappers. In that time, she had washed herself, tidied the house and prepared fresh burial oils.

She had also visited *Aná*.

It had been a visit that destroyed the last shreds of her battered heart; a visit that still left her trembling each time she recalled what she must do. The next few hours would test everything she knew about *Juju*, every lesson she had learnt from the first time Xikora found her in her dreams. All she had was her trust in *Aná*'s wisdom and her love for her daughter to bring her through the pits of hell.

Ọwa began preparing the shrine. She cleared the space where her daughter's body would lie and die. Using *Nzu* chalk, she drew in the circle of entrapment and fortified it with the mystic salt from the white lakes of *Agulu* and the fine corn flour from the Earth Mother's blessed cobs. When she was done, she went outside to check over the high pile of dry wood she had been gathering all day. She added a few more twigs to it, weighed up the jerry-can of kerosene again, before returning to the shrine.

Inside, she brought the new shrine-goat to the altar of the Earth Goddess and presented her to *Aná*. She plucked a white chicken from the cage and sliced its throat with cold efficiency. Holding it high, she drained its blood over the shrine-goat and the statue of the Earth Goddess, chanting loud invocations. She hadn't named the new goat that replaced Ebele. There was no bond between her and the goat, not yet...*perhaps not ever*. Several names came to mind but none of them seemed right. And when the right name finally came, she wanted to slap herself for her slow wits. *Xikora-Two*! Of course! That was the only fitting name for an animal whose strength would eclipse that of any before it, being the creation of none other than the greatest of medicine-women.

Qwa left the goat tied up by the statue and began to light the black candles that circled the statue and build the fire of soul-cleansing, which would burn away unwanted entities that would otherwise cling to a wandering soul during night diplomacy. When she was done, she sat down inside the circle of entrapment and began to prepare her body with sacred oils. She tried to fix her mind on the job, stop it from straying to Femi, wondering if she should make the long walk to the village police station to see his beloved face once more... *just in case*. Thinking about Femi brought a bitter-sweet pang to her heart. How tragic that when she finally found the one man she could love with a passion she hadn't realised she possessed, it all had to end this way. But perhaps, it was for the best. He would have become a distraction, one that would bring *Aná*'s ire on her. For the first time, she realised how it must have been for Xikora and her father, the burning passion that drove her mother to yield everything to the man she had lost her heart to, against the wishes of her goddess.

Ọwa walked over to the shrine door and shut it tight, shutting away her thoughts with it. Her mother would seek her out when she was done with her mischief. Already, a couple of the death chickens had returned to the compound, coated in dust, dazed and weak from a long night of terror. One had collapsed and died, right in front of their entrance door. Ọwa had left it where it lay. *Its mistress will find it and do with it as she wills. She'll not taint her hands with evil.* Still, the presence of the chickens in her compound allowed her to carry out her work without distraction. Several times during the day, she'd heard voices, many voices, as villagers trooped to her house, only to disperse in terror at the sight of the voodoo chickens. She did not need to wonder about their visit. Where Xikora walked, death trailed.

Just as the sun began its early slide to the west of the sky, Ọwa heard the sounds she'd been expecting and dreading, Aku's stumbling walk. *Xikora was done with her daughter at last*, she thought, starting to get up to guide Aku into the hut. Aku wouldn't know to look for her inside the shrine. But the steps drew closer to the shrine instead of the house, until the door burst open and Aku

422

stumbled into the room, sending the door crashing against the mud wall of the hut.

Ọwa gasped.

Her daughter's body was a battered wreck, as if it had been mauled and savaged by wild dogs before getting mowed down by a truck. She peered into her daughter's eyes and was met by a pair of blazing black pupils. *Xikora was still in residence.* Instantly, Ọwa killed the pain in her heart, the anguish brought by the sight of her daughter's ruined body and cloaked her thoughts with the image of Xikora-Two. Henceforth, she must only hold the image of Xikora-Two in her mind. No matter what she saw, how she felt, her mind must never stray from the white shrine-goat.

'Mama, what have you gone and done to my child's body?' Ọwa's voice was as cold as her eyes.

Xikora laughed, a contemptuous cackle. 'I see you've been busy, daughter. Perhaps, instead of seeking ways to destroy me, you might find it in your heart to thank me,'

'Thank you for what, Mama?' She asked, arms akimbo. 'Thank you for putting your selfish desires before the welfare of your own grand-daughter? Thank you for subjecting my daughter to re-live the agonies of her death each time you decide to resurrect instead of lying still? Thank you for all the young, innocent souls you've massacred in the village in a blind quest for revenge better left to *Aná*, our Earth Mother? Thank you for now making my life untenable in the village because people blame me for all your mischief and will now shun me worse than a leper, all because of your insatiable appetite for vengeance? So, Mama, tell me again, why should I thank you?' Qwa's voice rose with rage as she spoke, her body trembling, eyes flashing as hard as her mother's.

'Foolish girl, blind and misguided child,' Xikora turned at her with a fury that eclipsed her own. 'You stand there in judgement of me; you, whom I left with everything, gave you land, money, powers to ensure you would live like the queen you were born to be, a high priestess of the Earth Goddess. Instead, you squandered away my gifts with your stupid humility and your pathetic scruples. You allowed the vultures to graze where once the eagles had ruled. Had you been half the high priestess that I was, that I trained you to be, none of this would have happened. No one would have dared lay a finger on your daughter and the people would have held your name in awe and respect. Instead, they mock you. The whore that is your cousin, Enu, lives like a queen in the homestead that should have been yours. Your powers are held in contempt and the ungrateful villagers run ropes around you, using you for their needs and scorning you to your face. And you dare stand there and judge me!' Xikora barked a laugh, a sound that rang inside the shrine with ruthless satisfaction. 'Go today into the village. Take a walk through the market square and see if you'll be shunned like a leper or treated with contempt. In your grief, you allowed murderers to roam free and evil to flourish. I have made right of wrongs and restored the name of the *Nshi* clan to its former glory. True strength is without emotions, without softness. An iron rod will not remain strong if it's melted by the fires of conscience. The children died to bring home the lesson of revenge to all who harboured the secret of your cousin and the fat one's evil,' Xikora paused, rubbing the side of her noise with a distracted finger, an icy look in her eyes. 'You have no idea how many people shared in the knowledge, how many people sealed their lips whilst you wandered the breadth of Ukari in search of your daughter. Now, they're all gone, each with a child in tow, a beloved child put in the grave before them, so that they'll know the pain of losing a precious life. Graves are being dug in almost every enclave in Ukari and the air stinks with the rotten foulness of countless *Leloole* corpses. And all because of me. Me!' Xikora pounded her chest with a clenched fist. 'So, daughter, I expect you to thank me and if you can't, then at least, let me live instead of trying to destroy me. Remember, that just like you, I am a servant of the Earth Goddess and everything I do, I do in her name.'

As she listened, Qwa's heart broke into sharp, little pieces of pain. Regret and shame warred with love and pride. One part of her wanted to throw herself at her mother's feet and seek forgiveness. The other half wanted to throw herself into Xikora's arms and shower her with love and praise. She did neither. She kept the image of the shrine-goat in her mind, fixing her thoughts on its glittering, cold eyes.

'Where is the Ash of Immortality, Mama?'

'Somewhere you'll never find it till you give me your word that you'll use it to bring me back for as many times as it'll last,'

'You know I can't do that, Mama. The Ash of Immortality is not meant to be used with selfishness and greed. You've done what you returned to do, dispatched all our enemies to their ancestors' hell. Now you have to go back; you have to allow my daughter to sleep.'

'Go back to where? To that unbearable dark realm, *Mbana-Oyi*, a plaything of the vile duo, Walking-Grave and Corpse-Maker?' Xikora's eyes flashed. 'You've been there several times, daughter. Is that where you wish your mother to reside forever, when you hold the power to keep me here under the sweet warmth of sunshine, with you, my own flesh and blood?'

'Of course, I don't want to see you trapped in *Mbana-Oyi* for eternity, Mama. You know how hard I've been praying to our Earth Mother to forgive. We must trust in *Aná*, in her wisdom and her mercy. You've seen *Aná*. Like me, you've been possessed by her in the past. You know her powers and you know her infinite love. Let us accept her wisdom and wait for her time. SHE is everywhere, in the trees, in the soil, in the air, in fire, water and wood. SHE has seen the feats you've performed and *Aná* will not forget. Your freedom might be sooner than you expect but you have to let it happen the right way. You must give me back the Ash of Immortality that I may continue to be its guardian till *Aná* sends us a new priestess.'

'No!' Xikora's voice was an explosion. 'And stop thinking about that stupid goat while you speak to me about *Aná*'s wisdom. I make my own destiny. Haven't you heard a word I said? Those who wait instead of taking action achieve nothing in life, like yourself, who've let your powers go to the dogs. I will not wait, not when I can choose to remain on earth.'

'Then, you must do so by yourself, Mama. I can't help you.'

'Fine! Let it be on your head that your daughter will suffer the same fate with me in *Mbana-Oyi,*'

Owa's heart quacked. 'She won't. *Aná* has promised that Aku will return to her own deity, Mary,'

'You little fool,' Xikora laughed, a gleeful cackle. 'That was *before* she came back with me. Do you think her deity will want me to join her or accept the two of us into her realm? Sorry to disappoint you, daughter, but Aku will return with me to *Mbana-Oyi* and stay there with me for as long as you, YOU, decide we shall remain. At least, I'll have company with me there.'

'Surely, even you, Mama, can't be so cruel as to condemn your own grandchild to such a fate!' Owa's eyes showed her consternation even as she forced herself to think only on Xikora-

427

Two. 'Separate yourself from her please, Mama. Return alone to *Mbana-Oyi* and let Aku soar free.'

'If I agree, will you bring me back?'

'How can I bring you back when there's no body for you to possess?'

'If I arrange for a body, will you bring me back?'

Despite her resolution, Xikora's words chilled her to the bone.

'What body are you talking about, Mama? Whose body do you want to use?'

'Who else? Your vile cousin, of course. She's from our bloodline, an *Nshi* woman despite everything. Better Enu than anyone else. That's why I've let her live. I knew you'd come up with this question.'

'I loathe Enu as much as you do, Mama; even more. But I can't let you harm her. *Aná* has decreed that I must let her live. I do not question *Aná*'s will.'

'Excuses, excuses. That's all I get from you. Right. The ball is in your compound now. You know what you have to do. I'm done with you.'

'And I'm done with you too, Mama,' Qwa said, flinging the binding salt she'd been clutching all the while they spoke, trapping Xikora on the spot she stood. She saw the shock on Xikora's face, the fury blazing in her dark pupils as she realised she'd been outwitted by her own daughter. Before she could speak, Qwa

428

pushed her into the ring of salt and locked her in with the charms of entrapment.

'I'm sorry, Mama but you've given me no choice in the matter,' Qwa's face showed the anguish she was going through, the sense of betrayal that threatened to derail her purpose. She could not look at her daughter's face without feeling hard, painful knots at the back of her throat. She spoke to her mother, yet, beheld Aku's beloved face. She loved them both with a passion that hurt. She forced back the stark image of Xikora-Two into the fore, knowing it was the only way to stop her mother from manipulating her mind. She was going head to head against her own teacher, her mother, the greatest medicine-woman that ever walked the twelve villages and beyond. To kill a medicine-woman, you must first die to yourself, hold no value to your life, because a medicine-woman will come at you like the viper that she is. There would be no second chances if she erred or allowed herself to be weakened by love. As Xikora said, an iron rod will not remain strong if it is melted by the fires of conscience.

Inside the ring of entrapment, Xikora cursed at her, shrieked her fury as she tried to break through the salt bars that held her trapped within its circle.

'Tell me where the Ash of Immortality is hidden, Mama, and I'll let you go,'

'What do you take me for, a fool like yourself?'

'I'll never take you for a fool, Mama. Only an imbecile or a person with a death-wish would dare take you for a fool. I will honour my word and I'll let you go. But first, you must reveal where the ash is hidden.'

Xikora stopped her screaming, a calculating look in her still, dark eyes as she studied Ọwa. The movement of her finger on the side of her nose was frantic, leaving the skin there an angry red. Ọwa felt a sudden searing pain in her temple as Xikora pushed, probed Ọwa's mind, seeking to read her thoughts. She averted her gaze and pressed her head, squeezing in the pain. Xikora struck again and met the blank wall of the shrine-goat. She turned and screeched at the goat, hurling curses at it, shooing it away, hoping to distract Ọwa and penetrate her mind. Ọwa held firm, looking at everything but into Xikora's eyes. The effort brought sharper pains to her head till her eyes flooded with tears. Finally, Xikora gave a deep sigh, a sigh of defeat.

'It's hidden inside the carcass of the first shrine-goat you buried, the one you named Ebele. Whoever heard of a shrine-goat getting named?' She hissed.

Ọwa stared at her mother, a reluctant smile of respect darting her eyes. Xikora's deviousness was without parallel. But then, everything about her mother was without parallel. Nothing would have drawn her mind to the hiding place of the Ash of Immortality. She had buried Ebele herself, placed the sweet goat inside the wet

430

soil, little realising she was also burying the sacred ash with its carcass.

'I'll go and retrieve the ash first before releasing you,' she said, walking towards the exit. 'It's not that I doubt you, Mama, but I need to have that ash in my hands before I set you free.'

Xikora ignored her, lapsing into a brooding silence that was always the catalyst for a new war. Ọwa shrugged. She would deal with her mother's troubles as they came, one trouble at a time. She left to retrieve the Ash of Immortality from its rotten, hiding place.

She returned several minutes later clutching the smelly earthen pot in her hands.

'So, now you have it. Set me free from this stupid ring,' Xikora's voice was sullen.'

'I will, as soon as I repair the damage you did to my child's body,' Ọwa replied, placing the jar by the feet of the Earth Goddess, bowing deeply before picking up the bowl containing the burial oils. 'By the way, what happened to you?' She asked.

'Your stupid villagers attacked me, but as you can see, they couldn't kill me,' Xikora giggled, regaining her good humour as she recalled her recent exploits. 'Eze, son of Agu of Onori clan is dead,' she announced, waiting for Ọwa's reaction, dark eyes blazing with hawk-like intensity. Ọwa's heart lurched, blind fury rose in her heart. Her body began to tremble. The hand holding the bowl of burial oils shook so much she replaced it on the floor.

431

'He was mine to destroy, not yours,' Ọwa shouted, her skin turning a bright red with rage. 'He owed me a life and I was the one that should have taken his life. You've denied me what is rightfully mine, Mama.'

'What does it matter who kills the useless lout, you or I? The fact is that he's dead and that he died a very painful death. I watched him burn and watched the pool of vipers devour him inside his own bath. Never has a man met such a horrible death, believe me. And stop thinking about *Aná*'s death-flies. While that particular death was suitable for the others you've destroyed, the fat one deserved something worse, a bad meal that I gave him in full measure.'

Ọwa was silent, trying not to dwell on Xikora's revelations, forcing her rage to subside and her mind to shield her thoughts till she had executed *Aná*'s instructions.

'Lie still, Mama, while I clean my daughter's body,' she murmured, gently removing the tattered shreds of the cotton dress. Xikora eyed her with weary resignation and covert observation, like a child that knows that the only way she'll get a sweet is by holding her tantrum.

With a wobbly voice, Ọwa began to chant the invocation of the dead. In the dim confine of the shrine, her voice reverberated with mournful anguish. She rubbed the spiced burial oil into the badly bruised body of her child, forcing her mind away from the pain, the agony of seeing the damage done to her daughter's body by the villagers. Fury again, rose in her heart against them, an intense hatred for the people that would still inflict such cruelty on another being, her poor daughter they'd already murdered once. She pushed back the anger, saved it for a future time. *Aku can't feel the pain; remember, Aku can't feel any pain anymore.*

'But you're wrong, daughter. Aku feels every single cut, every blow, every bruise on her poor body. If only you could hear her cries within, you'll know what the poor girl is going through and let me live to take vengeance for her,' Xikora's voice was a soft blow in Owa's head, dragging back her wandering attention. She squeezed her mind shut, tight, fighting the sharp probes digging burrows in her brain. *She'll not respond or pay any attention to anything her mother says.*

She raised the guard of Xikora-Two and began kneading limbs, soothing frowns, singing peace into frenzied hearts, hers and Xikora's. From the look in Xikora's eyes, she could see that Aku was starting to reach out, seeking to reclaim her body for her third death, her final death. Owa was determined never to let her daughter go through the excruciating agony of another resurrection. She intensified the dirge, allowing her voice to rise and fall in the liturgy of the dead.

Before long, Xikora started yawning, long, deep yawns that came in quick succession.

'Daughter, please don't let me die,' Xikora's voice was soft, cracking with tears that could not fall. 'Please, let me live. I can't die again, not now that I've lived, walked the earth and practiced our art once more. Let your mother live, my daughter... please...'

The flash in her eyes faded into a hazy glaze. The darkness left the pupils as Aku's pale blue eyes returned. The tenseness left her features, replaced by a gentleness that heralded the awakening of the true owner of the body trapped within the ring of salt.

'Mama...' the voice was faint, weary. Owa leaned down, pressing her ear close to the bruised, swollen lips.

'Yes, daughter, your Mama is here. What does my child want?' Owa's voice was as soft as Aku's own, cracking with the tears she had so far restrained while Xikora spoke. Her hand rubbed Aku's cold hand with tender strokes.

'I want to sleep, Mama...please, stop... waking me... up. Let me sleep... Mama...please...'

Owa was crying, her body shuddering with the force of her sobs. She gathered her daughter's body into her arms, held Aku tight, not wanting to let go despite the chill frosting the smelly body she held. All she wanted was to keep hearing Aku's sweet voice, keep believing she still lived, for as long as the illusion would last.

'You will sleep soon, daughter; I promise. It's almost time for you to sleep for as long as you want,' she murmured into Aku's

434

ears. With sudden resolve, she released Aku and dashed over to Xikora-Two. She untied its long rope and led it into the salt ring of entrapment. Once inside, she wound the rope around Aku's body, tight, till both girl and goat were merged as one body, one atop the other, goat upon girl. The goat wrestled, kicking frantic legs as it tried to free itself but the rope held it tight to Aku's body. Its loud bleats were deafening inside the gloomy hut. Owa gulped deep breaths as she rose from the floor, exhausted by the struggle with Xikora-Two. *It was almost time, the time for her daughter's final death.*

Owa began to chant the words of soul-separation, her voice a deep lament in the silent night.

'I call upon a lost soul in the name of *Aná*, great Goddess of Earth and all that walks on land, wife to the great lord of the skies, *Amadioha* of the eyes of lightning and the voice of thunder; SHE that was before the creation of life and will be after the end of life. I call upon Xikora of the *Nshi* clan, high priestess of *Aná*, prisoner of the rogue deities, Walking-Grave and Corpse-Maker, poor lost soul in a body that does not belong to her. In the name of *Aná* and *Amadioha*; in the name of *Ndi-Ichie*, our old ancestors; in the name of *Mmuo*, every good spirits, known and unknown, benevolent entities watching over the air; in the name of *Obala*, every pure blood that's been sacrificed for the protection of mankind, I call on you, Xikora, high priestess of *Aná*; I order you to vacate this body that does not belong to you; Xikora, high priestess of *Aná*, I order you to vacate this body that does not belong to you; Xikora, high priestess of *Aná*, I command you to vacate this body that does not belong to you.'

Before she could complete the third and final command, Owa heard the piercing shriek that burst from Aku's mouth, a howl of fury as Xikora fought to cling on, resist the pull of the dirge of soul-separation. Aku's body began to jerk, bucking wildly underneath the weight of Xikora-Two. The goat bleated, its eyes wild with fear. The lighted candles flickered, some winking out, plunging the shrine into a deeper gloom. Owa increased the volume of her voice, calling on Xikora to vacate the body of her child. Her mother must not be allowed to remain inside Aku's body at the time of her final demise.

Suddenly, with a terrifying howl, Aku slumped against the ground, still as a corpse. The ropes holding the shrine goat to her body snapped into several pieces, sending the goat shooting high into the roof before slamming against *Aná*'s statue. The goat jumped up and began running around the tight confines of the shrine in a mad frenzy, driven by the fury of the powerful spirit it now hosted. Owa knew she had to act without delay. There was only so long the shrine-goat could contain Xikora's spirit before she rode it to death and escaped. Thankfully, Xikora had created the goat herself, fortified it with powers that would ensure its

436

survival till Qwa was done. Any other animal would have been useless for the rite, even her beloved Ebele.

She took Aku's arms and began dragging her corpse out of the shrine. She shut the door behind her, ensuring Xikora One and Two would stay trapped within. With gritty resolve, she pulled the dead weight of her daughter's body to the pile of firewood she had built earlier in the day. Her body poured with sweat and her breath came in loud gasps as she picked up the jerry-can and emptied the kerosene on the wood. Then, she picked up the box of matches and struck a match, and another, watching the flames burst. She looked at the naked body of her daughter and began to howl, her eyes darting wildly with a pain that formed a tight knot in her heart. Images flashed through her mind, images of Aku as a baby, as a laughing little girl, chasing butterflies, a moody teenager, reading endless books, a caring daughter, massaging away the tension from her neck after her night diplomacy.

She caught a sob and dragged the corpse to the pyre, lifting it with an impossible strength born from desperation and anguish. She smelt the first odour of burnt flesh before she heard the sizzling sound of her daughter's burning body. She watched as the skin-oil dripped from Aku's flesh, feeding the fire. The smoke filled the air above her, seeming to rise into the very skies. Her nostrils choked with the smell of her daughter's burnt flesh. She watched the black smoke as she sobbed, forced her eyes to follow the total obliteration of her daughter's body to ensure Xikora would never inhabit it again. The Earth Goddess had decreed it so and she had obeyed.

'*Kachifo*…goodbye d…daughter,' she hiccupped, her arms wrapped tight around her waist as she rocked forward and backwards in a haze of pain. 'May your deity receive you with loving arms. You will be reborn, someday, into a better life, a happier life, a safer life in a better place. In your next life, you will live to a ripe old age, free from harm, disease and hate. The children that you did not have in this life cycle will come to you in numbers that will ensure the perpetuity of your name. And when you sleep, it will be the good sleep of the peaceful and contented, free of ghosts, demons, evil and harm. Soar free, my sweet child. Fly like the eagle and conquer the skies. We shall meet again, my child. In this life-time or the next, our paths shall cross again; for the bonds that hold us together shall never be broken. *Kachifo*, may morning come for you, sweet child, bringing to you eternal years of eternal bright days.'

Owa trudged back to the shrine, locking the door behind her. Every bone in her body ached, like cooked cocoyam that had been pummelled to mushy paste with a wooden pestle. She welcomed the pain. It was proof that she still lived, that she had a body that could still feel pain when her heart was dead. Inside the shrine, Xikora-Two was lying by the edge of the ring of entrapment, panting, her eyes wide with terror and approaching death. It had fought a brave battle, withstood the assault of the powerful spirit it harboured for longer than the strongest human could have done. Qwa bowed her gratitude and respect to the goat, before gently dragging it into the ring of entrapment. She stroked its head tenderly, soothing it with soft words, calming it in its final moments of life.

Qwa cast eyes filled with despair at *Aná*'s black statue, seeking reassurance, any sign from the goddess that she was on the right path, that everything would turn out fine in the end. She knelt, picked up the knife and shut her eyes, squeezing them tight. The hand holding the knife trembled, like her body. She took a deep breath and plunged the blade deep into her heart.

Her shriek pierced the silent night. Warm blood gushed into her palm, draining from her body in a thick, slow sludge. Her hand fell to her side as she toppled to the ground, gasping for breath, twitching, jerking. She felt something wet between her thighs, as she pissed on herself. Intense shame filled her heart, briefly, even as she heard the death-rattle of her own breath, mimicked by Xikora-Two. She wanted to stroke the goat in their shared bond but her limbs were like lead, her thoughts fogged up.

Suddenly, something slammed into her, hard, bringing a searing pain that obliterated all thoughts. Her body was on fire, burning fiercer than the inferno that devoured her child. Yet, she shivered from a chill that burnt like live coals, felt her head swell up to bursting. She was screaming, right inside the core of her brain, trying to shout down the other shrieking voice that was all fury and madness. She could not think, could only feel. Terror, pain, confusion, anger and panic were sensations drowning her in a black sea of approaching death. Xikora was like a swarm of piranhas, devouring every inch of her body. Their minds clashed, separated, clashed again, duelling for mastery of her body. She felt herself weaken, her will cower, a gradual yielding to the superior mind fighting her own.

She knew when they arrived, sensed their presence in the deeper chill that was reminiscent of their realm. The scrambling within her increased its intensity, like a trapped roach seeking a hiding place. Xikora shrieked and cursed, no longer seeking dominion over the dying body she now inhabited. She pushed and pulled, seeking an opening to escape from Ọwa's body and her deadly pursuers. Her struggles dragged Ọwa's body in all directions, flung her against walls, bumped her head on hard surfaces and twisted her limbs to unnatural angles. Her sense of kinship with Xikora-Two heightened. They were both reluctant hosts of a reluctant guest, a raging spirit that would ride them to death in her quest for escape.

Ọwa dragged her lids apart and stared at the familiar terrors that had plagued her dreams from the day she first saw them devouring her mother's branded body inside the birthing-hut. *Walking-Grave and his fearsome sister, Corpse-Maker.* They filled every space of the shrine with their mammoth blackness. Terror sent the chills over her body, freezing her thoughts. She shut her eyes, squeezed her lids tight, shutting away their ghastly visages. She heard their heavy breathing, the gurgling rattles of their blood-gorged lungs. Cold claws reached for her legs, her head, her heart. She was crying, just like the other one within, who was cursing with thwarted rage. *I'm sorry, Mama... so sorry. This is the only way... I can't let you possess my body... I can't. I'm no match for you and we both know what you'll do with my body and our combined powers once you take over my mind. My death is the only way to draw out the guardians of Mbana-Oyi. I'm sorry Mama... please forgive me and trust in our Earth Mother. Aná knows best and will yet do right by all of us.*

Her body was a mass of agony. The pain was like fire, like ice. She felt the pull, the sensation of being disembowelled, as Xikora was captured and dragged out, shrieking and scratching. The death deities cackled, pleased with their catch. They turned their attention to Qwa, leaning close for her final breath, her immortal soul.

Suddenly, the earth began to shake, tremble as if the soil was made of feathers. A familiar scent filled the shrine, a dank smell that brought a feeling of intense joy to her heart. Even before she

441

heard the buzz of the million grave flies drowning the rattles of the death deities, Qwa knew that *Aná* had awakened. A weary smile creased the tortured planes of her face. Then, everything went numb, as a deep blackness descended over her brain.

Ω Ω Ω

17

New Beginnings

Ukari Village, 2016

The woman on the king-size bed let out a piercing shriek, her eyes wet with tears. She stared at the bent head of her birth-aider, Ọwa, who was gently massaging the aging mother's bulging stomach, pressing down, willing the baby within to exit.

'*Ndo…* sorry,' Ọwa consoled, her eyes focused on the blood gushing out of the woman like red piss. 'Your baby will be here in seconds. Just a little more push now…that's it, we're almost there,' Ọwa's voice was almost as desperate as the woman's labour screams. She cast furtive glances at both the blood-drenched bed and the sweat-drenched woman giving birth on it. Her own sweat covered her face, leaving damp patches on her lacy, blue top. Her pale skin glowed from the purification oils she applied for each birth-aiding assignment, oils symbolic of *Aná's* blessings, ensuring a safe delivery for both mother and child.

Except this time, the sacred oils appeared to be losing their powers for some unfathomable reason. Ọwa's eyes glazed with subdued panic. No birthing mother had ever died in childbirth whilst in her care, not even when premature twins were in the

444

deadly breach position. It was her special gift from the Earth Mother, that she would preserve the lives of every mother and infant she ministered to in the birthing ritual. But this time, something was different, something wasn't right with the birth. She was facing the possibility of her very first death and this was ironically, the one life she wished to preserve the most, if for nothing else, to stop tongues of suspicion accusing her of deliberately killing the mother out of bitter vengeance.

She'd sensed trouble from the time Mama Ten came for her in the middle of the night to request she attend to her cousin, Enu's labour bed. Her first instinct had been to refuse, flat out. Thanks to *Anā*'s edict, the woman had escaped punishment when all the others in her conspiracy of evil had paid with their lives. She would not lift a little finger to assist Enu in giving birth to her child, not when it was thanks to the whore that she had buried her own child.

But Mama Ten had begged, reminded Owa of her calling and threw in a few Christian parables of forgiveness and rejecting the doctrine of "an eye for an eye". It was all hogwash to Owa, who had nothing but contempt for Christianity and its hypocritical tenets. It was only when Mama Ten quoted the powerful phrase, "vengeance is mine, says the lord", that Owa recalled *Anā*'s directive that she must never harm Enu. In her rage, she had forgotten the Earth Mother's commandment.

Qwa had returned to the bedroom she shared with Femi to explain her visitor's mission and seek his thoughts.

'Can you live with yourself if anything happens to your cousin and you didn't help?' Femi had asked, his eyes soft with interrupted sleep.

'Yes,' Qwa didn't hesitate. 'She owes me a life and until she's rotting under the soil, my heart will know no peace.'

'Then don't go,' Femi said with his characteristic directness, reaching out an arm to pull her down to their bed. Qwa resisted, giving him a playful shove.

'*Oga* Femi, behave yourself,' she said with a mock frown, belied by the tender look in her eyes as she reached out a hand to stroke his face, his beloved face she would never tire of seeing from the minute she awoke inside the shrine on that fateful night, drowning in a pool of her own blood, to see him leaning over her, tears streaming down his face, shouting her name and dragging her back from the depths of hell.

The trip to the hospital had been a blur to her, as were the days she hovered between life and death, tortured by visitations from the evil due whose chilly presence she felt with every laboured breath she took. Once, she had seen Xikora in her dream, wearing a face she had never seen in all the years she'd known her. She looked beaten, weary, with an apathetic glaze in her eyes that brought the wails to Qwa's lips when she returned to wakefulness.

That look of hopeless resignation in Xikora's face had spurred her recovery. This time, she would get *Aná* to relent, even if it meant sacrificing her own life. There was no greater tragedy than the sight of a fallen elephant or a dying lion. Hopelessness and weariness must be given no room in Xikora's indomitable heart.

Femi had been by her side through the long weeks of her recovery from the stab wound that miraculously missed her heart. Had he not arrived when he did that night, she would have surely bled to death and dragged into *Mbana-Oyi* by the greedy death deities. She knew *Aná*'s intervention had stopped Walking-Grave and Corpse-Maker from speeding up her death that fateful night of Xikora's capture.

On her release from hospital, Femi had insisted she return to his flat but she had declined. She was still the high priestess of the Earth Goddess and had her duties to perform for the deity. Most importantly, even though she didn't mention it to him, she had several sacrifices to perform to *Aná* and plead for Xikora's release. In the end, they had reached a compromise. He would spend the nights at her house on weekdays when he wasn't on night duty at the police station, while she spent the weekends at his flat. It was an arrangement that had worked for them in the eight months since her recovery. Femi's car was now a permanent fixture outside her compound and the villagers had since stilled their excited gossip.

The first thing Femi did on moving in was to purchase a double bed for her room and a couple of soft sofas for her living room. He covered her floors with carpets and repainted the entire house, save for Aku's room. That room was still left as it was the last time her daughter slept there. It was to Aku's room that Ọwa returned to vent her grief when the pain got too much to handle, when the loss hit her at the most unexpected times. Like on the day the village delegation of elders arrived at her house with gifts for the Earth Goddess, to beg *Aná*'s intervention with the wronged and vengeful ghost of the murdered young girl, Aku.

'My daughter is not vengeful,' Ọwa had screamed at them, her deep voice startling the few amongst them that had never heard her speak. 'My daughter was wronged, very wronged. She was a gentle girl, who never did any of you any harm. All she wanted was to be allowed to live her life without being judged by the colour of her skin. She didn't make herself an *Aghali*. She was as *Aná* made her, just like the rest of you. And she was beautiful the way she was, absolute perfection,' Ọwa paused, overcome by intense grief. She turned away from the men, fighting her tears. She caught their shame and guilt in their averted eyes. 'You all deemed my daughter unworthy of your attention, undeserving of your respect. All of you gathered here today may not have personally harmed her, otherwise, you wouldn't be here now. But you knew how we were both treated in the village and by your

448

silence, you sanctioned it. You are the elders who should lead by example but you all harbour the same dangerous prejudices that eventually led to my daughter's heinous death. Now she lies in that grave beside my house, an early grave created for her by your collective scorn,' she pointed at the fresh mound Femi had dug to shield the truth of Aku's fiery burial. 'But, my daughter did not harm you. Know it now. Aku was too good and gentle to harm a fly, even her vile murderers. But her grandmother raged for her and you all know that truth in your deepest hearts. Xikora was never one to let any slight go unrevenged, even in death,' she saw the startled look in their eyes and heard their soft gasps and nervous coughs. When they next spoke, there was guilt in their words of penitence.

'Good priestess, you speak well and true,' their leader, Ibu-Dike, a man who had been a playmate of Xikora's in their childhood, spoke for the group. 'Our faces are covered with shame and our hearts quake with fear. When you grew up and took over from Xikora as *Aná*'s high priestess, many heaved a sigh of relief in the village. Having lived under the tyranny of your mother's custodianship, we were mostly fed up with everything to do with the cult of *Aná*, including her new priestess, your good self. And you are right. We're all tainted with the evil brought about by our prejudices and ignorance. But, I can say with all sincerity, that we have seen the errors of our old ways. That it took so many deaths to open our eyes to our wrong-doings is something we shall forever regret to the day we lay down our heads in the final sleep,' Ibu-Dike paused and the elders nodded their heads in silent assent. 'There is none amongst us sat here today, who did not witness the terrifying return of the great Xikora of *the Leloole* curse. She spoke to us, addressed us by our true names and told us things only Xikora would know. Today, the village is still shrouded in the dark cloud of terror she left behind. Once upon a time, Xikora's infamous death was the legend that was shared across the twelve villages and beyond. Today, it's her terrifying return and the curse of her voodoo chickens that is on every lip, young and old. Little children and grown men are still reduced to quivering leaves at the sight of a chicken. No one is sure that Xikora's vengeance has run its deadly course and that families can sleep with both eyes shut, in the knowledge that the rise of dawn won't reveal a new boil-infested corpse in their homes. The *Akwa-Igwe,* shame-singers, have been busier than they've ever been in the last few weeks. It will take them over twelve moon-cycles to compose and sing enough shame songs for all the people involved in your daughter's murder. Thanks to the *Ile-Nkata,* diarrhoea tongue, with which your cousin was hexed, the evil that was hatched in twilight has now been exposed under the brilliant sun. We all know the guilty and the dead. The last of the conspirators that still lives, your cousin, Enu of *Nshi* clan, is now ostracised from the village and

450

can no longer consider herself a part of our community. Is that not true, brothers?' Ibu-Dike turned to the other elders for confirmation which they gave with loud yeses and vigorous nods. 'It will be a long time before Ukari recovers from this evil. But we want you to know that things have changed. It's not the old Ukari you knew that exists today. Our visit today with this little offering to the great Earth Goddess, *Aná,* is only the first of many more to come. We want *Aná* to know that we're grateful for her goodness and her protection, and most especially, for her kind priestess with whom she's blessed us, your good self, sister Qwa.'

As one, the men got up to shake hands with her and pledge their loyalty to *Aná.* They all called her "Sister Qwa", a first in all her years of existence in Ukari village. Their words brought more tears to her eyes, coupled with a sense of relief and a lightness of the soul, as a long-borne burden was finally lifted from her shoulders. She knew she would never again experience rejection and hate in the village. Where the elders led, the others followed. *If only Aku had lived to see this day.*

When the elders were gone, Qwa had locked herself in Aku's room and wailed till her voice was hoarse. When she was done, she had a quick shower and dressed herself in fresh talcum powder and clean clothes to receive Femi. And when she told him what the elders had said about Enu, he'd asked her the same question that was to leave his lips several times in the course of their eight months together, each time another snippet of bad news concerning her cousin reached her ears.

'Are you happy now, my priestess? Is your heart now at peace?'

And each time, her reply was always the same. Until Enu was a rotting corpse deep in *Aná*'s soil, her heart would have no true peace. She didn't realise she could harbour such vengeful thoughts about another being. But every time she thought about the gruesome manner of her daughter's death, knowing that her cousin was the catalyst for everything, she wanted to plunge a knife into Enu's heart and gouge it out the way Aku's heart was defiled.

Which was why when Mama Ten came again with more bad news about Enu, she had refused to help. Mama Ten was the only person in the village that made visits to Enu's house, secret visits, made in the dead of night, in the terrifying knowledge that she faced dire sanctions from the elders if they discovered she was fraternising with an outcast. It was from her that Qwa first heard about Enu's pregnancy, a fact that both shocked and infuriated her. It was as if the woman was mocking her by her actions, rubbing painful salt into her open sore. She could almost hear Enu's contemptuous sneer in her ears, *"Look, Nwa-Ntu, Ash-child, see how I'm having a child for myself now that I've killed your own. Aren't I the clever one?"*

For several days after hearing the news, Qwa had howled inside the shrine, begging *Aná* for answers, for the freedom to take her

452

revenge on Enu. But the Earth Goddess had remained silent, deaf to her cries. Femi had comforted her, held her in his loving embrace through countless nights of tears and rage, till gradually, her heart learnt to live with that bitter reality and she re-trained herself to live in unquestioning obedience to the unfathomable will of the Earth Goddess.

And it was in obedience to *Aná* that she had finally followed Mama Ten back to Enu's glass house to do what she had been born to do, bring babies and mothers safely through the birthing ritual, even when her heart wished nothing but death for the mother. Mama Ten said that Enu was in a bad way and had begged for a car to drive her to the big hospital. But nobody in the village would accept Enu's phone call or assist her. An outcast was invisible, unseen and unheard. Mama Ten said that Owa was her only option at that time of the night and begged Owa to do her duty by both her deity and her conscience.

When they arrived at the house, she had instructed Mama Ten to start boiling water with the electric coil. She could hear Enu's moans from her bedroom across the living room. On entering the room, she couldn't tell who was more shocked, Enu or herself, as they both stared at each other for several stunned seconds before Owa recovered herself and walked briskly to the bedside.

'I'm just going to feel your stomach to see how far the baby's head has dropped,' she said to Enu, trying not to look at the ravaged face of the woman in the bed. Her cousin was never a fat woman but in her tall stateliness, Enu had been an impressive specimen of womanhood at her peak. Ọwa had never seen her without heavy make-up, gaudy gold jewellery and a healthy dose of attitude, mostly bad. The woman groaning on the bed was a stranger she would have walked past in a busy street, a filthy beggar she would have given some coins for sustenance, a mad woman she would have avoided like Typhoid fever, for fear of the evil entities that had taken possession of her senses. If she ever doubted *Aná*'s justice, the ruined husk on the bed restored her faith in the Earth Mother's great wisdom.

'*Nwa-Ntu*, I see you've finally come to kill me, eh?' Enu's pain-wracked voice held a tinge of the familiar mockery.

'My business here is with the baby, not you,' Ọwa forced herself to remain calm in the face of provocation. Enu knew how much she loathed her childhood nick-name and was trying to goad her.

'How noble of you,' Enu sneered, before another spasm hit her, bringing a scream to her lips. Ọwa pulled aside the thin blanket covering Enu and gasped. The bed was soaked with blood. *Aná have mercy!* Ọwa shuddered, a cold chill coating her skin in a blanket of goose-pimples. Never in her history of delivering babies had she seen that much blood. It was as if Enu's life was flowing away from her in a steady stream of thick, red water.

'How long have you been like this?' She asked, trying to get herself to overcome her repulsion and hold Enu's clammy hand, offer her some comfort as was her duty as both a birth-aider and a human being.

'I've been like this for nine months now, ever since this baby attached itself to my womb,' Enu gasped, coughing and groaning. Her hand in Qwa's own was cold and wet, her grip, weak. 'D'you know how many times I've tried to abort this evil baby I carry, how many times I've wished I could reach into my womb and tear out the little bastard and feed it to the vultures?' Qwa gasped, her eyes darting in consternation. Enu saw her shock and laughed, a weak, wicked snigger. 'I bet you think I'm evil, don't you? That no normal mother should talk like this about their own baby, eh? Well, let me tell you a secret. This baby hates me as much as I hate it. It has given me no rest, kicks and pulls my insides as if it wants to kill me. When it allows me to sleep and I dream of it, I hear its hate and its curses ringing in my ears when I awake. If this baby could, it would've killed me long before now. And do you know why? Because I hated its father for what he did to me, how he ruined my life. But for what he made me do, I wouldn't be in this situation today.' Enu saw the dawning horror in Qwa's eyes and smiled, a cruel smile. 'Yes, Eze, son of Agu of Onori clan is the father of my baby. Isn't it strange, that you end up assisting my baby's birth, the child of the two people responsible for your daughter's death. Ha! *Uwa Nkaa,* this strange world of ours!'

Ọwa's body trembled, her breathing racing, hard and painful. She pulled her hand away from Enu's, wiping it against her cloth as if wiping out poison. Her pupils did a manic dance, darting everywhere, mirroring the confused state of her mind. *She couldn't do it... she just couldn't assist this birth. She didn't care if Aná consigned her to eternal servitude to the rogue deities. There was only so much a person could cope with before breaking. This was the feather that tipped the pile of bricks.*

Ọwa began to walk out of the room just as Mama Ten entered with the bucket of boiling water and towels.

'I'm sorry, you'll have to do it by yourself,' she said, seeing the consternation on Mama Ten's face. Enu screamed again from the bed, a howl of pain.

'Please, you can't leave me alone,' Mama Ten begged, dropping the bucket and grabbing Ọwa's arm. 'I'm not trained in this. I know I've had ten births but you aided every single one of them. What do I know about birth-aiding? Please, help me out here. What happened? Is it something she said? Don't take it to heart. You know how we women say terrible things when we're in labour pains. Come, stay your anger, my sister, please; I'm begging you. It's me that will bear this burden if anything happens to her, which might well be the case if I'm left by myself. My life will be over in the village. What will I do if I'm made an outcast too? What will become of my children? Please, help me. Not for Enu's sake but for my sake and the sake of the poor baby, the innocent life in her womb.'

Qwa looked at Mama Ten's homely face, saw the goodness in her heart and the genuine terror coating her eyes. Realising the huge risk the woman was taking for her old friend touched a nerve. If this poor woman could risk everything for human decency, what right did she have, a high priestess of the Earth Goddess, to betray her calling and abandon her duty?

With a deep sigh, Qwa turned back and returned to the bedside of the screaming woman. Another quick glance at her cousin showed her that Enu was fast failing. *Not on her watch*, Qwa thought, removing her headscarf and pulling the bucket of hot water close. As she watched, another gush of thick blood pumped out from Enu's open thighs. She moaned, softly, her eyes starting to roll back.

'*Ndo*...sorry,' Qwa murmured the comforting words, an instinctive habit that came with a lifetime of working with the greatest pain mother nature had ever given mankind. Just then, she saw the tiny blood-streaked head pushing through the flood of blood. Qwa gasped and began to manoeuvre the baby out, her movements gentle, yet rushed. The last thing she wanted was for the child to choke in a flood of blood. With a loud pop, the baby exited the womb, save for the umbilical cord attaching it to its dying mother.

Ọwa gasped. Her hands holding the infant began to tremble. Cold shivers wracked her body. She snipped the umbilical cord with hurried distraction, wiping off the slimy and bloody gore coating the baby's skin, revealing skin the colour of the sun and thick kinky hair of golden straw. She looked down. It was a girl. *Of course*! Her eyes followed an upward trail to the baby's face and another hushed gasp escaped her lips. A thick mole, the size of a tiny nut sprouted by the infant's little nose.

Ọwa's heart soared. Joy beyond bliss flooded her eyes with hot tears as she stared into the baby's pale face. Even before the infant opened its eyes and gazed directly into her face with blazing blue eyes, Ọwa already knew the identity of the baby she held. The baby's eyes flashed briefly with recognition before gentling into innocent blankness. Ọwa's shoulders shuddered with the force of her sobs as she held the tiny bundle closer, tighter, wrapping it into her chest. *Thank you, Earth mother, thank you, thank you.* Over and over, the words repeated themselves in her head.

'Mama... *Nno*, welcome,' she whispered into the baby's tiny ear, her voice soft, her smile tender. The baby cried, an angry wail, as if it had been made to wait for its milk. Ọwa laughed, a merry chuckle. Patience was never Xikora's strong point. Mama Ten crowded close, staring with awe at the pale, albino skin of the baby.

A sound came from the blood-soaked bed, a whimper. Ọwa looked at Enu's sweaty face. She quickly handed the baby to Mama Ten and returned to ministering to the mother, birthing the placenta with swift efficiency, hoping to stem the flow of blood. Suddenly, nothing mattered more than saving the life of her cousin.

'It's no need... I told you that the baby will kill me,' Enu gasped, pushing her away. 'Let me see the little bastard before I go...' Enu's breathless whisper broke through her long-held hostility. Ọwa looked at her cousin and pity flooded her heart. For the first time since her daughter's death, she was free of the hate that had eaten up her peace. She motioned to Mama Ten, who brought the baby over to Enu. She stooped and handed the infant to its mother.

Enu stared at the baby in consternation. Her eyes widened into saucers as she let out a piercing shriek, thrusting the child away from her. Ọwa's swift action saved the baby from falling to the floor. Enu trembled, babbled, insanity fighting the wild terror in her eyes. Over and over, the word, "*Mmuo*, ghost" came from her lips. Even as she spoke, Ọwa felt a sudden chill descend in the bedroom, a chill she knew like the palms of her hands.

They were not alone in the room anymore.

She grabbed the baby from Mama Ten, hearing Enu gasp her last with a loud inhalation that was never exhaled. She didn't want to spend a second in their vile presence, the death-deities of The Cold Realm. Mama Ten howled as she realised Enu was dead. She started pulling her hair and stamping her feet in the age-old display of raw grief. Ọwa grabbed her arm and urged her away from the corpse and the death-room, into the plush warmth of Enu's living room.

'Go home now,' she said to the kindly woman whose puffy face looked drained. Despite everything, Mama Ten had loved her wayward friend and the harrowing events of the night had taken their toll on her. 'There's nothing we can do for her now. I will do the rites of burial for her body and tomorrow, I'll let the elders know, so they can arrange for her corpse to be buried in *Ajo-ofia*, the bad forest.'

'Dibia Ọwa, can't you plead with them not to discard her corpse in the bad forest?' Mama Ten begged, her red-rimmed eyes frantic. 'Surely, she's paid for everything she did with her life. Is it fair to keep punishing her even in death? I know you have no reason to help her after all she did to you but since God in His infinite wisdom has punished her already, won't you find it in your heart to forgive her now?'

'I have forgiven her, believe me,' Ọwa said, meaning every word. 'But I do not make the laws of the land and I alone can't

460

change a tradition that has existed beyond the memories of our forefathers. All we can wish her is a better reincarnation and pray that one day, her soul will find its way from *Ajo-ofia* to our ancestors' realm.'

'The baby, what will become of it now that…'

'Don't worry about the baby. She will be just fine with me. She's an *Nshi* child after all. I will raise her as it's my duty to do, as if she were my own.'

'She's beautiful,' Mama Ten leaned in to stroke the baby's head with gentle hands. Qwa knew what she was thinking, the same mistake Enu had made before her death. *They thought it was her murdered daughter, Aku, re-incarnated. She'll not correct them. Aná's miracle was for her alone to know.*

'Yes, she is beautiful,' Qwa agreed, placing a tender kiss on the sleeping baby's golden head. 'She's perfect in every way, just beautiful.'

***

The next night, for the very first time since she cremated her child, *Aná* visited her dreams and spoke to her. She was asleep on the bed that was once her daughter's, inside the room she had converted to the baby's nursery. Femi had spent all day painting the room, purchasing things for the baby. She'd been prepared to do battle with him about the baby but to her surprise, Femi had taken to the tiny bundle with excitement, just like a new father. Even when the baby screeched with bad tempered persistence through the day, Femi had laughed at its feistiness and proclaimed she would have a great future as an *Akwa-Igwe* shame singer. By the time night fell and the bawling baby finally fell asleep, Ọwa had crashed out by her side on Aku's old bed. For the first time, she slept in Aku's old bedroom without tears drying on her face, without the familiar ache in her heart which a visit to her daughter's room wrought.

That was when *Aná*'s voice filled her dream. The Earth Mother's voice was like silk, honey and pap. Ọwa had never heard such warmth in all the years she had served the Earth Goddess.

'Your mother was one of my greatest priestesses and she will yet become my greatest. This time, she will be taught by my best, you, Ọwa, my humble child. In her time, Xikora brought great honour to my name. But for her pride, she would have done greater things in my name. This time, her arrogance will be tempered by the humility you will teach her. Your days of service to the shrine are almost done. Your cousin is the first of future birth-deaths at your hands. I think you will be happy with your life now. You'll do your goddess greater service by raising for her the greatest priestess the world will ever know, Xikora reborn.' *Aná*'s voice rang with pride, the pride of a loving parent. 'Show her how to use her powers only in service to her goddess and not for her own end. Teach her well that she may know the difference between pride

462

and arrogance, confidence and ego.' In her dream, Owa wept as the Earth Goddess spoke. She did not know why she wept, except that the tears would not stop and her heart's pain choked her breath. *Aná*'s voice in her dream was tender, soothing. They healed the open sores festering in her heart.

'The other was never meant for my work. You know it in your deepest heart. You cannot force a tree to walk or a cat to roar. The body you burnt, no longer hosts your daughter. Weep not for her anymore, for she is finally still, free from dreams and wanderings, reunited with her own deity, Mary of the pale skin. She is truly at peace. I have seen her and she flies in light and laughter, sings with joy and peace. This is the truth from your goddess who has never lied to you. Your daughter is finally happy. Let her be and look to the one that I've returned to you, one already filled with dormant knowledge and eager to learn and grow. Guard this my wayward child well, teach her and love her well and you will remain as ever, the truly blessed of your goddess.'

End

Igbo Terminology

Aboki – A common name for a gate-man, security-man.
Afa – Divination ritual
Agbalaka – Thunder
Aghali – Albino
Akakpo – Midget, Dwarf
Akala-aka – Destiny or palm-lines
Akara – Fried savoury buns made from bean flour
Aku – Wealth, Riches
Akwa-Igwe – Clothes of Steel, Chastity covering, Beyond corruption.
Ala-Mmuo – Land of the Dead or ghost realm
Amadioha – God of thunder and lightning
Amosu – A female soul-vampire or witch
Ana – Earth Goddess, Earth Mother, Earth deity

Biko – Please

Chei! – A common exclamation, an expression of shock, surprise, horror.
Chi – One's personal god, or guardian angel
Chukwu – big god, top god, god of gods.

Dibia – Witchdoctor, Medicine-man or woman, Root-healer, diviner or psychic
Duwe Anyi – Lead us, guide us or protect us.

Ebele – Have mercy, pity
Ekwensu – Devil, Satan
Enyi – Friend

Igu – Palm frond
Ise – So be it, So it shall be
Ile-Nkata – Literally, Basket mouth, leaking mouth, loose tongue

Kachifo – May morning come, goodnight

Mbarama – Prostitute
Mmuo - Ghost

Naira – Nigerian Currency
Ndewo – Greetings, Hello, Goodbye.
Ndi-Ichie – The Old Ones, The great ancestors
Nku – Feather
Nne-Ochie – Old Mother, Grand mother
Nno - Welcome
Ntu – Ash
Nzu – White chalk which has a salty taste

Obala - Blood
O ga-adi mma – All will be well
Oga – Master
Ofor n'ogu – Clean hands, blamelessness, Karma-like state of innocence and retribution
Oji – Kola-nut, a soft nut which can be white or red, used for important ceremonies and rituals
Onukwu – Dimwit, retard
Onwu-atu-egwu – Fearless Death
Owa – Moon
Owu – Death
Oyibo – White person, Caucasian
Ozo – peer group of wise and respected men
Ozu – Corpse

Tufia – Heaven forbid!

Xikora – Let the world see. Show the world this glory!

About the author

Nuzo Cambridge Onoh is a British writer of African heritage. Born in Enugu, in the Eastern part of Nigeria (formerly known as The Republic of Biafra), she lived through the civil war between Biafra and Nigeria (1967 – 1970), an experience that has influenced some of her writing.

Nuzo attended Queen's School, Enugu, (Nigeria), before proceeding to the Quaker boarding school, The Mount School, York, (England) and St Andrew's Tutorial College, Cambridge, (England) where she obtained her A' levels. Nuzo holds both a Law Degree and a Masters Degree in Writing from Warwick University, (England).

Her book, *The Reluctant Dead* (2014), introduced modern African Horror into the mainstream Horror genre. Nuzo has two daughters, Candice and Jija and lives in the West Midlands, England, with her cat, Tinkerbell.

Website: www.nuzoonoh.co.uk
Twitter: @nuzoonoh